DICK TRACY

THE OFFICIAL BIOGRAPHY

JAY MAEDER

A PLUME BOOK

PLUME
Published by the Penguin Group
Penguin Books USA Inc., 375 Hudson Street,
New York, New York 10014, U.S.A.
Penguin Books Ltd, 27 Wrights Lane,
London W8 5TZ, England
Penguin Books Australia Ltd, Ringwood,
Victoria, Australia
Penguin Books Canada Ltd, 2801 John Street,
Markham, Ontario, Canada L3R 1B4
Penguin Books (N.Z.) Ltd, 182-190 Wairau Road,
Auckland 10, New Zealand

Penguin Books Ltd, Registered Offices:
Harmondsworth, Middlesex, England

First published by Plume, an imprint of Penguin Books USA Inc.

First Printing, June, 1990
10 9 8 7 6 5 4 3 2 1

 REGISTERED TRADEMARK—MARCA REGISTRADA

LIBRARY OF CONGRESS CATALOGING IN PUBLICATION DATA:
Maeder, Jay.
    Dick Tracy : the official biography / by Jay Maeder.
        p.   cm.
    ISBN 0-452-26544-4
    1. Gould. Chester.   2. Dick Tracy (Comic strip)   3. Comic books,
strips, etc.—United States—History nd criticism.   I. Title.
PN6728.D53M34   1990
    741.5"0973—dc20   90-7402
                                                         CIP

Printed in the United States of America
Set in Melior
Designed by Julian Hamer
Art and color restoration by Pure Imagination, NYC.
Chief technician: Steve Scanlon.

CONTENTS

PREFACE

IT WAS ENTIRELY AN ACCIDENT. THE AMERIcan funny papers had been just brightly colored circulation draws when the newspaper barons Joseph Pulitzer and William Randolph Hearst invented them at the turn of the century, and no one of the pioneer cartoonists ever imagined that he was creating something vital in the culture. Thirty years later, Mutt, Jeff, Jiggs, Maggie, Barney Google and Spark Plug, Andy Gump and Min, Tillie the Toiler, Jerry on the Job, and all the rest of them were everybody's dearest friends, and citizens in every hamlet and valley of the land took it for granted that they had at least as much God-given right to their funnies as to their snorting motorcars, their scratchy Victrolas, and their crackling radio sets.

By now the Cartoonist was a celebrated Type, a famous and well-to-do gent who went clubbing with cuties, sat ringside with Lardner and Runyon, drove a sleek roadster, and wintered in Palm Beach, and newspaper bullpens were full of ambitious youngsters who wanted to be just like him. Some of them made it. A lot more of them didn't. Any one of them would have happily drawn almost anything if it meant a syndicate sale and the promise of a daily run in the comics. In the advertising-art shop at the *Chicago Daily News*, for example, there was a young illustrator named Chester Gould who had been trying to click for years, and who so far had managed to land several very minor and very short-lived gag strips, but who otherwise had been no more or less successful than dozens of diligent fellow strivers, who, like himself, worked like dogs every day of their lives dreaming up notion after notion, firing them off to some editor, hopefully introduc-

ing themselves again and again with their hats in their hands, trying to strike upon the single inspired idea that would make their fortune.

And but for extreme pluck and not inconsiderable luck, Chester Gould might easily have ended his days at least as everlastingly obscure as anybody else in this life.

It happened, however, that in the late spring of 1931 he ground out another set of tryout strips, and this time the idea happened to concern an honest policeman in this astonishingly lawless time when every pol was plainly scum and every judge was bought and sold like a can of tomatoes and ganglords ran the cities and had a good hoot about it as meanwhile an ordinary hardworking stiff like yourself was only trying to make a decent living, and this time the submission was finally noticed and mulled over by one of the day's single most important editors.

And thereafter Chester Gould would go on to be hailed as one of the great storytellers of the twentieth century, a man equal in his own time and place to Dickens in his.

This book is about the workman Chester Gould and the great and enduring American icon named Dick Tracy that he wrought, and it is about the successes the two of them attained over nearly fifty years together, over the course of an incandescent period when the times cried out for exactly such figures as themselves, and it is about the twilight they together suffered when the times turned away from them, and it is about the inexorable process of cultural retrieval that assures both of them their immortality.

This book is about the American policeman named Dick Tracy. This is the story of his life.

CHAPTER 1

SHOT HIM DOWN LIKE A DOG

The Testament of Plainclothes Tracy

"**G**OOD EVENING, MR. TRUEHEART,**"** said the pleasant young fellow with the black suit and strikingly square jaw. "How's the delicatessen business this evening!"

The nice old man was taking off his apron. "Well! Hello, Dick," he said. The blondie daughter was on the stair. "Gee, you look pretty," the visitor said, taking off his hat. "Well, why not, for my very bestest boyfriend," she purred.

Up to dinner they went. "Mamma, the bread-eaters are all here," the old man beamed. "Oh,

and am I glad you've come!" said the nice old lady, gratefully throwing down the lurid evening news. "It'll get me away from this paper and these tales about gangsters."

Many years later, the robust, prosperous, and much-celebrated Chester Gould, by now a man read every day by sixty million people worldwide, sat with another of his respectful interviewers and recalled once again the beginnings of his famous cartoon strip DICK TRACY. Well, there had been a girl, he said, Tess Trueheart she was called, and one night at dinner her old shopkeeper father Jeremiah had been stuck up by thugs and he'd been shot and killed on the spot, and that was what had moved this fellow Tracy to join the plainclothes squad, you see.

Chester Gould gleamed and licked his chops. "Yep," he cackled, "I let poor Jeremiah have it right through the heart. Shot him down like a dog."

He had not technically invented violence in the comic strip medium, but he had pretty well cornered the market early on. His startlingly brutal strip had stood out at once in that era of gentle family funnies and had become an instant sensation. Gould had long since come to prize his stature as the king of the bloodcurdlers, and the fact that his memory was in this instance misserving him—old man Trueheart's Christian name had been Emil, not Jeremiah—diminished it not at all.

Millions of readers loved Dick Tracy with all their hearts. The great detective ran in hundreds of newspapers, he enjoyed a successful crossover to radio, movies, and television, and for much of the century he was never less than a fundamental component of the American popular consciousness.

The respectful interviewers came and went, and Chester Gould repeated his tales many times, and he would nod in pride and satisfaction and he would look back.

IT WAS 1931, AND THUGS ROAMED THE STREETS

unchecked, and one night they invaded Emil Trueheart's deli and plugged the old man before Dick Tracy's eyes, and Tracy signed on with the law on the spot. Chester Gould posited a cop ineluctably dedicated to the eradication

The law: Plainclothesman Dick Tracy, sidekick Pat Patton, Chief of Police Brandon; a promotional illustration appearing on the cover of the trade magazine *Editor and Publisher*, July 23, 1932. The sensational new feature had fast become a runaway hit. "More favorable comment on this strip than on anything we have ever used," the flagship New York *Daily News'* circulation manager was quoted. "One of the most popular comic strips the *Chicago Tribune* has ever printed," added his counterpart to the west. "It's new . . . it's sure-fire," the Chicago Tribune Syndicate's ad copy boasted. "It's bound to be popular."

of the period's crime gangs—brave, incorruptible, a figure much in the mode of the day's real-life Eliot Ness, pledged to rub out crime wherever it rattled, sworn to make the world clean again. And from virtually the first minute, Tracy charged into a clamorous collection of goons, torpedoes, and sleek gang bosses, bringing them to their knees, destroying their nests, wiping out their designs against decency. In a world fed up with their foul depredations, he overnight became the nation's foremost emblem of swift and unforgiving punishment. Indeed, wrath was the whole point. More recently our culture has been reduced to wibberings over what has come to be regarded as Dirty Harryesque vigilantism. In 1931, it was something you liked in a cop.

The cop had a hat and a trenchcoat and a chin so resolute you could clean your fingernails on it. As per the cadre requirements of the period, he had a dependable if not very bright comic partner named Pat Patton, a devoted if frequently querulous girl named Tess Trueheart, and a scrappy little kid sidekick named Junior, who followed him everywhere and never once let him down. He lived in a never-named but usually midwestern city suggestive of Chicago and he had all the day's scalding headlines working on his side. His strip was defined by fast-action story lines that could kick the breath out of you, arrestingly stylized artwork that was both super-realistic

As comic-relief sidekicks went, roly-poly Pat Patton at first was exactly the sort of dope who would peer through a keyhole for a glimpse of known machine gunners (top, December 2, 1931). The early running gag posited Patton as a onetime welder who had somehow blundered into a career as a thoroughly inept policeman; indeed, he once smashed a concert violinist's priceless old instrument because he thought there might be a gun inside it, and he was endlessly reading how-to-become-a-plumber books and moaning that he was in the wrong line of work. "I'm a washout," he kept blubbering. "You don't use your noodle," Dick Tracy was always saying, shaking his head. The dunderhead soon learned to become a reliable backup man (middle, with Chief Brandon, January 25, 1935), and eventually he would even save his critically wounded buddy's life with a blood transfusion (bottom, February 17, 1936).

The essential Tess Trueheart, February 4, 1934.

and weirdly cartoonish, a famous rogues' gallery of villains, an unrelievedly grim Calvinist conscience that informed every move every one of its characters ever made—and always, always, the pathological mayhem. The strip was a dark and perverse and vicious thing, sensationally full of blood-splashed cruelty from its first week, the single most spectacularly gruesome feature the comics have ever known; there has never been another newspaper strip so full of the batterings, shootings, knifings, drownings, torchings, crushings, gurglings, gaspings, shriekings, pleadings, and bleatings that Chester Gould gleefully served up as often as he possibly could.

Ultimately the feature was to become dominated by Gould's legendary Grotesques, deformed and disfigured misfits possessed of visages and tics as repulsive as their rotten criminal souls, and ultimately everything became so unremittingly and unbearably horrible that Gould had to devise a standard riff to soothe the scoutmasters and the civic clubmen and the ladies from the PTA who were forever mewling at the unwholesomeness: The criminal impulse, he explained, was an ugly thing, and to soften the ugliness was to be fatuous and sappy and nothing less than dishonest with one's children. That always made them scratch their heads and appoint committees to discuss

matters further. The argument usually bought him friends. Sometimes the civic clubs even changed their minds and presented him with awards.

Elsewhere in the funny papers, over at LI'L ABNER, the parodist Al Capp's Mammy Yokum often made pretty much the same point—good is better than bad, Mammy declared, because good is nicer—but really, Gould was never kidding about any of this, and whatever his occasional opportunistic panderings, his strip was always firmly and evangelically in the service of those bedrock moral standards to which the reasonable citizen would surely choose to subscribe. It probably isn't more than a small stretch to suggest that the classic DICK TRACY ranks near the least cynical literature of all time.

For indeed, TRACY was also always full of warmth and humor and high spirits and simple heartland Christian fellowship. The players gathered for toasts on holidays, they bore witness to the births of new babes, they reaffirmed the verities at festive wedding anniversaries, they solemnly attended funerals, they regularly fell into worship when one of their number was somewhere imperiled. Bullets and prayer: such were the devotionals of a great and enduring American fiction obsessed with the preservation and protection of the God-fearing commu-

The essential Junior Tracy, September 10, 1933.

nity and the absolute destruction of the marauding evils.

DICK TRACY WAS FORMALLY APPOINTED A detective, attached to the City's police plainclothes unit, on October 22, 1931, nine days after old Emil Trueheart died on the floor of the little flat above his deli. On November 26, Tracy made his first kill, in a midtown-traffic shoot-out with a carful of machine-gunning assassins. The dead meat was a goon named Crutch. He was the same stickupman who had pulled the trigger on old Emil a few weeks earlier. In the forty-six years Chester Gould and Dick Tracy had together on this earth, very few circles were to be left unbroken.

"Not a bad Thanksgiving at that," the detective smiled as the gunsmoke cleared.

Police Chief Brandon hires a plainclothesman, October 22, 1931.

Redemptive gunsmoke, November 26, 1931.

CHAPTER 2

YOUR PLAINCLOTHES TRACY HAS POSSIBILITIES

The Captain and the Cartoonist

AT THE BEGINNING, THERE HAD BEEN
Captain Patterson.

Joseph Medill Patterson, an heir to the dynasty that had published the *Chicago Tribune* since 1855, was a rich and idealistic socialist, a privileged patrician who emphatically believed with some of his heart in the glory of the post–Great War workingman and who in June 1919 created a great, brawling New York City newspaper specifically to minister to what he decreed were to be that workingman's tastes. The rowdy little sheet, America's first tabloid, first called the *New York Illustrated News* and subsequently the *New York Daily News*, rapidly went on to become the largest-circulation daily in the world. Patterson would remain until his death in 1946 a powerful man in a powerful chair and a dominant figure of the day, revered by millions, loathed and detested by millions more. Many citizens regarded him as a leading Third Reich apologist before the Second World War; President Roosevelt once personally sent him a German Iron Cross, observing that no man in America deserved it more than he. Brooklyn housewives, meanwhile, sent him freshly baked cookies. Whatever else he was or wasn't, Joseph Medill Patterson was one of the patriarchs of the burgeoning pictorial entertainments that were the nation's funny papers, and he had a great deal to do with determining their contents.

Patterson's Chicago Tribune Syndicate and William Randolph Hearst's King Features Syndicate were the two colossi of newspaper feature syndication for several generations, powerful news organizations that inculcated the American people with many of the day's popular values. They dispensed, among other things, the nation's most widely circulated comic strips. King's offerings included THIMBLE THEATRE and BRINGING UP FATHER and THE KATZENJAMMER KIDS and BLONDIE and an endless parade of other features. The Tribune shop fielded Sidney Smith's sentimental THE GUMPS and Harold Gray's endearing LITTLE ORPHAN ANNIE, the both of them firmly installed in the hearts of every funnies-loving American, along with Frank King's sweet family saga GASOLINE ALLEY, Frank Willard's uproariously lowlife social document MOON MULLINS, Walter Berndt's office-boy laugh riot SMITTY, Martin Branner's pretty-girl confection WINNIE WINKLE, and Carl Ed's flaming-youth merriment HAROLD TEEN. As America moved into the 1930s, Captain Patterson was regarded as an uncannily prescient and virtually irrefutable arbiter of the public temperament. If the people wanted comic strips, so then did The Captain; if The Captain gave the people comics, why then, so were these some of the comics the people most wanted to read.

And so then was The Captain's comics stable where much talent desired to be. The aspirants

Captain Joseph Medill Patterson, circa early 1930s.

included the world-famous foreign correspondent Floyd Gibbons, who in 1930 was trying to market an early adventure strip based on his own thrilling life and times. The aspirants included the entertainer Rudy Vallee, who in 1931 was associated with a proposed Hollywood-comedy feature calculated to ride the coattails of his sensational personal popularity.

The aspirants always included somebody in Chicago named Chester Gould, who week after week kept sending The Captain bundles of new tryout drawings for one proposed new strip after another, along with cordial handwritten notes that never failed to conclude with the confident young man's warmest personal regards to one of the most singularly feared publishers in America.

CHESTER GOULD HAD BEEN BORN A NEWS-
paper editor's son in Pawnee, Oklahoma, on November 20, 1900, and his first published work had been the cartoons he had done as a lad for his father's small paper, the *Pawnee Courier Dispatch*, in the days when Oklahoma

Chester Gould, circa early 1930s.

worked variously at the *Tulsa Democrat* and the *Daily Oklahoman*, doing sports cartoons and a few politicals; that was where he had come from. He was not a particularly promising illustrator so far as that went, and all his days, by nature a humble and unblustering man, Gould would cheerfully admit that he knew this about himself. He also knew that he aspired to a lot regardless. Many years later, quite late in his life, he would tell an interviewer that he hoped "the Good Lord would take me while I'm trying to do something that's too big for me."

He would arrive in the mecca Chicago in September 1921, he would work as a staff artist for nearly every paper in the city at one point or another, he would meanwhile attend Northwestern at night and earn degrees in commerce and marketing, for he also recognized in himself the instincts of the canny businessman. Through many of the Chicago days he was a Hearstman, laboring for the *American*, and accordingly for a time he produced a gag strip called FILLUM FABLES, because Mr. Hearst had not been in a position to land Ed Wheelan's MINUTE MOVIES and desired a similar feature. The *American* also ran Gould's THE RADIO CATTS, a broadcasting comedy. The *Chicago Daily News* ran his pretty-girl strip THE GIRL FRIENDS. There are tales that Mr. Hearst's LITTLE ANNIE ROONEY was offered to him at one point and that he declined this not inconsiderable property, preferring to work up a running series of proposals for his own feature.

None of them took the world by storm. The Chicago Tribune Syndicate paid no attention to Chester Gould, and usually he would have to

was still Territory. On many occasions over his lifetime he was called upon to recount his origins, and the never-wavering story was that he had been a cartoon-minded little boy who doggedly copied out the drawings from the Sunday comics that were always in his home; he had particularly loved MUTT AND JEFF; at age sixteen he had won a national magazine's contest for Best Patriotic Drawing; he had taken business courses at Oklahoma A&M; he had

THE RADIO CATTS, by Chester Gould. *Chicago American*, April 1924.

THE GIRL FRIENDS, by Chester Gould. *Chicago Daily News*, July 1931. "Dot" apparently had a twin sister named Tess Trueheart, who subsequently showed up in DICK TRACY.

write several times just to get the submissions returned. As Gould was always better fixed than many of his cartoonist buddies, who regarded him as having married well—Mrs. Chester Gould was, indeed, a banker's daughter, and the couple lived not so badly in the nice Chicago suburb of Wilmette—he sat things out in relative creature comfort and continued to bang away. And it became nothing less than his mission in life to bombard Captain Joseph Medill Patterson of the *New York Daily News* with feature after feature after feature. It is known that he tried out comedies called TICKER STREET, ROCKEY (sic) MOUNTAIN RED, and BRAINY BOTTS; multitudes of others are unrecorded. For a time in 1930, he was putting a copy of his regular Chicago editorial cartoon aboard the night train to New York, attention The Captain, every single day. Under separate cover, he dropped The Captain personal notes. On February 4, 1930: "You'll hear from me till I connect. I'm absolutely raring to get going." On March 25: "I CAN do a moneymaking feature for you. I'm capable and determined—give me a chance. Won't you believe me when I say I know my stuff and can deliver the goods?" The long silences from New York didn't seem to trouble him in the least. He kept at it.

On January 2, 1931, The Captain wrote him a small letter. "I suppose I am discouraging," Patterson told his energetic correspondent. "I hope you will keep on trying."

The endless rejections, Gould would always say later, "were building blocks for me." The Captain's note, he said, was "a sacred thing."

And he kept on trying.

The luck of the draw for the sunny young gag man was a gritty realistic-action strip featuring a tough, trenchcoated detective at war against the underworld. Gould's Chicago, a frontier railroad town grown monumental, had been openly under the thumb of Al Capone for years. Street massacres were commonplace. Cops and ward bosses were openly on the take. A citizen could get indignant sometimes. Gould did a week's worth of samples. The detective was raiding gangland dives, kicking down doors. Gould called him Plainclothes Tracy. It was early June 1931 when Gould cooked this up, and maybe it was no longer at the front of his mind a couple of months later, when the telegram showed up. Laboring at his newspaper job, Gould one hot day had a telephone call from his wife, who read him the wire from New York:

```
230-17 ST WILMETTE ILL-        1931 AUG 13 PM 2 30
C43 29 DL- NDN NEWYORK NY    13 25 8P
CHESTER GOULD-
YOUR PLAINCLOTHES TRACY HAS POSSIBILITIES STOP
WOULD LIKE TO SEE YOU WHEN I GO TO CHICAGO
NEXT STOP PLEASE CALL TRIBUNE OFFICE MONDAY
ABOUT NOON FOR AN APPOINTMENT =
J M PATTERSON..
```

They met in The Captain's office at the Tribune Tower. The story goes that Gould was wearing a sharp new suit for the occasion, but The Captain had only a few minutes for him and didn't appear to be impressed. The Captain was busy thinking.

PLAINCLOTHES TRACY, by Chester Gould. Unpublished submission to Captain Joseph Medill Patterson of the New York *Daily News*, June 1931. These are three of the tough tryout dailies that won Gould his famous, long-running detective strip. The cop's black suit was the same, but this early cutie Tracy sported a boater and he was never seen without a cigarette. Al-Caponesque mob boss "Cleaver" subsequently reappeared in DICK TRACY as "Big Boy"; the Texas Guinan-derived "Texie Garcia" was carried over into the modified strip, though she became a brunette; and Gould appears to have always intended a sidekick named "Pat," though this one bore no resemblance to the later Patton character. Gould reused the tinkling-piano passage in DICK TRACY in December 1931.

Chester Gould was standing before a publisher who fancied himself a dramatist and who had seen a number of his plays produced. He took an abiding interest in his strips' story lines, and beyond his demanding other activities —hobnobbing with royals and cabinets, devising foreign policy, flying with Colonel Lindbergh —he devoted much of his energy to dealing with his cartoonists, firing off wires to them, regularly suggesting new characters and situations, fine-tuning dialogue. It was The Captain who had created THE GUMPS and who was still often supplying Sidney Smith with detailed story treatments. It was The Captain who had instructed Frank King to bring a foundling baby boy into GASOLINE ALLEY. It was The Captain who had called in Frank Willard and ordered him to come up with a strip about a vulgar pool-playing sort of character named Moon Mullins who was to have banjo eyes and a cigar and a small brother named Kayo. Little Orphan Annie had in her submission stage been a boy orphan named Little Orphan Otto until The Captain de-Ottoed things. "I hope The Captain never learns how to draw," said Frank Willard in a 1938 interview, "or I know about five or six comic artists who'll be looking for jobs."

Now, on this day in August 1931, The Captain was examining PLAINCLOTHES TRACY, and he was fiddling already.

Well, he didn't like the name. Too long. Something punchier was needed. George Tracy . . . Jim Tracy . . . Dicks, they called policemen dicks, didn't they? Dick Tracy. And he didn't care much for the opener. Have the fellow not be a policeman just yet. Have the fellow, oh, have him visiting his girl one evening. And stickup-men would burst in and shoot down her shopkeeper father, and then this Tracy fellow would join the police department to avenge the killing. That was it. That was the ticket.

Chester Gould blinked and picked up his hat and went home. Publicly, all the rest of his life, he professed nothing but admiration for The Captain's great sagacity. Privately, there are suggestions he felt mildly violated; but for an instant's whim, he might have spent forty-six years doing a strip called GEORGE TRACY.

On August 27, he wired New York that he had mailed the first two weeks of redrawn dailies and was starting on his Sundays.

The first DICK TRACY Sunday page appeared in print on Saturday, October 3, 1931, solely in The Detroit (Week-End) Mirror, a minor tabloid The Captain had recently acquired from the publisher Bernarr MacFadden in the same deal that gave over The Captain's flourishing Liberty magazine to the MacFadden empire. Folded in August 1932, the Mirror remains the odd footnote entirely by reason of its having given DICK TRACY its historic first publication.

The early Sunday page was a self-contained weekly episode at first, unrelated to the main daily story line to follow. The New York Daily News, for one, didn't bother with it for another couple of months.

The daily strip, meanwhile—the primary, canonical DICK TRACY—was launched in the News on Monday October 12. There was a bit of fanfare for the new strip and it replaced Bud Fisher's MUTT AND JEFF, which happened to be running in the News at the time, and it was immediately and distinctly, with LITTLE ORPHAN ANNIE, an Unfunny in a small sea of comedies. The opening strip got a nice positioning, far to the front of a paper whose practice it was to strew its strips throughout rather than station them all on one page. On Tuesday, it was flung well back, left to fend for itself in the rough-and-tumble New York market.

In all of comics in 1931, the true Unfunnies could be counted on fingers. ANNIE. TARZAN. TAILSPIN TOMMY. BUCK ROGERS. WASH TUBBS. A few others. Several of them were quite full of thrills, but they weren't particularly morbid thrills. People didn't die much. A character who had won some affection in THE GUMPS had once passed away of natural causes, and the nation had been stunned, and comics readers were still chattering about it and shaking their heads, and that had been two years earlier.

Now, in another few days, they were going to watch a nice old man get murdered in cold blood before their eyes.

The first DICK TRACY daily, Monday, October 12, 1931, seen only in the New York *Daily News* and the *Detroit Mirror* (the Detroit sheet had previously carried two trial Sunday pages, October 4 and October 11).

ALL RIGHT, MILLIGAN, I'LL LEAVE YOU BOYS HERE — FROM NOW ON I'M WORKING ALONE — YOU DON'T KNOW ME — NEVER HEARD OF ME AND DON'T KNOW ANYTHING — SEE? THAT'S THE UNDERSTANDING I HAD WITH THE CHIEF.

CHAPTER 3

THINGS AIN'T GONNA BE DE SAME FROM NOW ON

Plainclothes Tracy and the Rats

THEY'D BEEN SENT BY THE BOSS. "HE KEEPS this savings on the second floor," one furtive mug whispered to another as they knelt murderously in the dark outside Emil Trueheart's delicatessen on the strip's second day, Tuesday, October 13, 1931. "De Big Boy says it's a cinch."

That's what bigshot crime bosses did in Plainclothes Tracy's town. They sent mugs to knock over delis. Big Boy (first appearance, October 24) was the first official TRACY villain, the Chicago ganglord Capone pointedly deglamorized into a contemptible fat slug with a cigar and a sneer and mouthful of gold teeth. "The King Cobra of Gangland," he was called. "The coldest-blooded criminal of modern times." Big Boy was plainly used to running the town his way and he didn't quite get the gag with this new guy Tracy who was shooting things up. "Just a poor sap like all the rest of his kind," he chortled to his gorillas. "Probably read a wild west somewhere and decided to chase robbers."

Yeah? That's what Big Boy thought. "You birds can't get away with this!" Tracy had cried over Emil Trueheart's poor dead body, and that was a blood oath, and anyway the mugs had also snatched his girlfriend and he had to square that, too, and now this new guy Tracy, on the plainclothes squad for only days, was already undercover in the City, calling himself Joe Smith, hanging out in the meanest joints, introducing himself around. Unshaven, sitting on his cheap flophouse bed, Plainclothes Tracy made a speech to his gun the first time he ever held it in his hand (October 27). "Old horse," he said, "you and I are going to have to stick together pretty close, I'm afraid."

The just-arrived drifter Joe Smith dealt himself into the action, and soon enough Big Boy's torpedo Ribs Mocco was explaining how things worked. "Ain't you ever heard of Big Boy?" Mocco grunted. "He comes in on everything, then if anything goes wrong, his mouthpiece fixes it up. Dat baby's got everything greased from th' big shots down!" The newcomer Joe marveled. It sure was a great racket.

Presently the undercover man smashed a payroll job, busted Ribs Mocco, gallantly recovered Tess Trueheart, and sent Big Boy into convulsions of rage.

"Git a line on this dick that upset the works," Big Boy ordered. "It's curtains for Sherlock."

Plainclothes Tracy undercover, with Ribs Mocco, October 30, 1931.

Back at headquarters, Police Chief Brandon, a gruff old-timer who had evidently never had a man like Tracy on the force before, was wondering about that himself. "Your life isn't worth two cents after the way you smashed into Big Boy's baddies," Brandon reflected.

"What am I supposed to do?" Dick Tracy shrugged. "Buy a one-way ticket to Brazil?"

Well, readers ate this stuff right up. New York wasn't quite so flagrantly corrupt as Chicago, but it had its moments, and here at last was a hero for the age, a man who was going to stand up against the rats of the land, jaw thrust forward, guns blazing. In his cell, one of Big Boy's rats spoke prophetically for all as he stared at the wall and dolefully divined the writing on it. "Dat guy Tracy is dynamite," the rat realized. "Things ain't gonna be de same from now on."

AND NO, DEY WASN'T. PLAINCLOTHES TRACY

handily survived the ensuing assassination attempt, although Emil Trueheart's slayer did not.

Neither did a luckless cabdriver, the first of countless such innocents who were forever blundering into the Tracyscape at the worst possible time (see Chapter 13), though the fast-moving, bullet-sprayed new police astonisher didn't have much time for condolences ("Done for," Brandon noted). Then Tracy was on Big Boy's heels again, and things never stopped moving after that, and as the time passed, Tracy's famous jawline got only sharper and sharper.

Complicating matters were the lawyers, lifeforms that the TRACY strip, to its readers' delight, openly viewed as among the lesser dirtballs of the earth. Much later in his life, Chester Gould would become famously crusty on the subject of constitutional protections of mollycoddled criminals and in that more socially liberal time he would come to be widely regarded as a crank, but his contempt for smarmy lawyers

Ribs Mocco reports to Big Boy, November 17, 1931. Gangland's King Cobra, none too pleased that the new cop in town appeared to be taking his job seriously, summarily detailed Mocco to kill him. The assignment left Mocco severely shot up.

Raiding Big Boy's apartment, December 1, 1931. The sequence notably reprised the action of the earlier PLAINCLOTHES TRACY tryout strips, and this strip marked the first appearance of sidekick Pat Patton as well. The uniformed "Milligan" was also a cadre player in the beginning, though as time went by, he became increasingly generic, his name regularly invoked whenever the action demanded a harness cop. The strip was full of Milligans for decades, and they were almost never the same guy. Indeed, Milligan was shot to death on several occasions.

who were in league with crooks and pols was just as profound in 1931 as in 1975. Ribs Mocco, for instance, was out on bail in the payroll job in less than an hour. "What've I been paying ten grand a month to a couple of big shots for?" Big Boy boasted in his hideaway.

Meanwhile, the slinky gun moll Texie Garcia, jailed after a raid on Big Boy's quarters, was shortly visited by a lawyer named Habeas, recognized by Tracy to be a well-connected figure and a man worth trailing. Hy Habeas, the first of TRACY's lifelong series of despicable shysters, mouthpieces, and silver-tongued scoundrels (first appearance, December 14), proved to be tight with an influential ex-pol named Dubbs, who wanted Texie dead. He'd done a few deals with Big Boy, and Texie was blackmailing him. Dubbs and Habeas were, in fact, on the verge of strangling the girl with wire when Tracy arrived to bust it up. On December

Plainclothes Tracy learns the facts of life, November 19, 1931. Evidently rats could swiftly get out of jail if they desired. This strip marked the first appearance of the great detective's famous trademark trenchcoat.

28, Dubbs—"I've been tortured enough! I've lived a life of fear and h--- for years and I'm sick of it"—shot himself like the slimy coward he was, the strip's first suicide.

So there was never a real history of attentiveness to the civil niceties here, and Dick Tracy and his partner Pat Patton reasonably felt themselves to be under relatively few constraints as they war-whooped their way through the 1930s. "Button up, hood, or this rod's liable to go off, and it might not be accidental!" "A murdering rat like you has no constitutional rights!" "Stand up like a man, you mug, or I'll drill you on the spot and claim you were trying to escape!" The rats and their mouthpieces just hated this, but nobody else minded much, circumstances being what they were, and it certainly got the job done. Indeed, when the great final histories of everything are compiled, it is likely to be contended that, generally speaking, the Rubber Hose was a more useful crime-fighting tool than, for example, the Miranda Reading.

By the flowering spring of 1932, Dick Tracy was on his way to becoming a remarkable national phenomenon, and public schoolchildren were proudly wearing pin-back buttons with his picture on them. There was something fresh in the wind in general. Out there in the real world, in the flowering spring of 1932, the federals finally even managed to put away Al Capone.

Craftily disguised Tracy gets a line on the crooked mouthpiece Habeas and the ex-pol Dubbs, December 19, 1931.

CHAPTER 4

WE'RE GOING TO LET 'EM HAVE IT
Building the Better Plainclothesman

SHORTLY BEFORE THE SPRING OF 1932, Chester Gould had looked at his drawing board and realized he didn't have a story. Big Boy was on the lam. Ribs Mocco and Texie Garcia were more or less done with. "I had run out of ideas," he admitted later. He hadn't yet been at it long enough to fully grasp that, as he liked to say, "Cartoonists run out of ideas every Monday morning." He would have forty-six years' worth of Monday mornings to come to terms with the natural order of things. At the moment, what he grasped was that DICK TRACY was being widely advertised as the hottest new strip in the country and that its creator didn't have the slightest idea what he was going to do next.

Gould's compositional habits were not formal. He made up his stories as he went along, sometimes even panel by panel, and he seldom had a clue where any of them were going before they got there. On hard deadline, this right-on-the-edge manner of doing business sometimes skated the strip straight into the rocks—whole passages were known to hang on dubious coincidence or a preposterous deus ex machina—but on the other hand, most of the time the total absence of outline lent it a crazed urgency as Gould sped along in units of action that existed pretty much for their own sake. It was obvious that the cartoonist wanted to find out what was going to happen next just as much as the reader did. And Gould was sufficiently a politician to understand that he and his readers were thus in solidarity.

Thus neither he nor they discerned that he was now, in 1932, suddenly and entirely intuitively establishing a series of devices that would come to be long-standing conventions in his strip.

FOREMOST AMONG THESE WAS PHYSICAL TOR-ture. If the guardians of public morals thought suicide or cold-blooded murder amounted to

Broadway Bates softens up Tracy, March 25, 1932.

rough stuff, they hadn't seen anything yet. Forevermore a strip signature, Physical Torture was first applied when the dapper, monocled confidence man Broadway Bates captured Dick Tracy, bound him into a chair, stripped off his shoes, and, on March 25, 1932, ordered a blowtorch turned on the detective's bare feet.

Bates was attempting to force Tracy to write a letter demanding $10,000 from Mother Trueheart, who had reopened her late husband's deli and was bravely going forward on the highway of life. In league with his confederate, a bob-haired blonde named Belle, Bates had already been doing his best to swindle Mother Trueheart out of old Emil's insurance money, but she hadn't fallen for his investment schemes, and he was irritated, and now he had to cope with the meddlesome Tracy, who was always snooping around. Bates settled the detective's hash by dropping a suitcaseful of bricks on his head from a second-story window. Now, with Tracy his prisoner, laying hands on the $10,000 looked like a piece of cake. "I said you're going to write a couple of letters," Bates said. "I've got a sprained finger," Tracy growled. What followed for Tracy could have been worse yet had not Patton and Brandon and a good Samaritan named Heinie Steuben raided Bates's flat and put a stop to things. The actual flamethrower of record, a hood named Spike, historically significant as Dick Tracy's First Torturer, was shot to death.

Simultaneously with Torture was established, indeed with Heinie Steuben, the durable strip tradition of the Samaritan, the loyal, law-abiding citizen who saw his public duty and was determined to do it. Heinie was the lovable old Dutchman Mother Trueheart had brought in to run the deli for her ("Dill pickles mitt der garlic!") and who, greatly suspicious of Bates and Belle, had kept an eye on them, and who, after Tracy disappeared, tipped off Patton and Brandon to the swindlers' address. "The hero of the hour!" Tracy applauded him. "Ach," Heinie shrugged. There would follow a long line of Samaritans who elected to get involved in things, and Tracy would owe his life to many of them, and the strip was often an inspirational study in participatory good citizenship. On the other hand, quite a lot of the Samaritans got themselves tragically killed for their butting in, so the moral was ambivalent at best.

Beyond Torture and Samaritans, several other strip identifiers that Gould the storyteller would come to lean on through the years to come were firmly established in 1932. These did not include the famous Grotesques, whose time was yet to come (see Chapter 10), but they did include:

THE NEAR-DEATHTRAP. Not to be confused with Physical Torture. Broadway Bates, for example, was not necessarily trying to kill Dick Tracy, who otherwise distinguished himself throughout his career by somehow managing to live through and extricate himself from patently unsurvivable situations. Bullets were nothing. Dick Tracy ate bullets for breakfast. But there were dozens of other ways to eliminate a nosy cop. In May 1932, the reemerged Big Boy (see below) threw Tracy over the rail of a passenger liner into the Atlantic Ocean; in June, Tracy came this close to an auto crash after the counterfeiter Alec Penn jimmied with his brakes; Penn also nearly gassed him to death that same month, and in July Penn came close to burning him to cinders in a torch job. "Slickest customer I ever ran across," mused Tracy of the constant Alec Penn.

This was only the beginning for Tracy, who thereafter often found himself getting starved, speared, poisoned, frozen, blown up, buried alive, thrown to bulls, abandoned in wells, entombed in wax, suffocated, boiled, bludgeoned, blinded, electrocuted, dragged behind cars, hung out to dry in general. Fortunately for Dick Tracy, however, he had been born indestructible. He

Near-Deathtraps in general:

(1) Sabotaged roadster, June 9, 1932.
(2) Shrinking room (electrified),
    April 22, 1934.
(3) Compression chamber,
    December 22, 1937.
(4) Pit of Doom, November 1, 1938.
(5) Collapsing subway,
    September 4, 1940.

1

4   5

1

2

3

Scientific Detection:

(1) Adventures in chemistry, August 28, 1935.
(2) Professor Groff's all-purpose ray machine, July 24, 1932.
(3) The miracle of modern fingerprinting, December 3, 1937.

could get out of Near-Deathtraps when even Chester Gould himself had no idea how he was going to do it, as was the famous case some years later when the cartoonist dropped him into a deep hole and then suddenly realized there was no way out of it. Didn't matter. Piece of cake.

SCIENTIFIC CRIME DETECTION. Tracy was, by Gould's design, a close relative of Sherlock Holmes, a man who routinely used his powers of keen observation and shrewd deduction to spot telltale metal particles on the soles of dead men's shoes and to realize that the tire tracks in the snow over here had something to do with the bloodstains in the closet over there. The classic proceduralist sleuth, Dick Tracy cleverly disguised himself quite regularly. Dick Tracy was

a man who kept an encyclopedic file of fingerprints in his own apartment, for God's sake. Meanwhile, this being the twentieth century, he packed a machine gun as well.

And forward-looking Chester Gould made it his business as well to keep up with all the leading-edge developments available to a law officer in the war against crime. In 1932, these were quite wondrous things. In June, Tracy made his first telephone tap. That same month, he used a sophisticated "electrical phonograph recording machine" to record the voice of a suspect in whose office he'd concealed a microphone. In November, he employed the science of ballistics to pin a shooting on the gunman Dan Mucelli, who was quite surprised ("It's the trick of discovering which gun a bullet came from by comparing the markings made on the piece of lead by the inside of the gun barrel. That bullet came from your gun." "You lie!"). In December, the chop-shop queen Larceny Lu became the first to go before the awesome lie detector.

On the other hand, some of the Scientific Crime Detection began to owe a lot to *Weird Tales*. In July, the strip introduced a Professor Groff, "famous scientist," a white-bearded wizard who kept a contraption called an "ultra-ray projector" in a secret laboratory full of mysterious coils and tanks and switches and beakers and leaping electrical arcs. Not only was the room-sized ray machine able to spectroscopically distinguish one brand of ink from another by their "electrical vibrations," it was also "silver-sensitive" and accordingly it was called upon to unmask the counterfeiter Alec Penn, who had a silver plate in his skull, as the European swindler Count Gordon.

The ray machine might have had other capabilities as well, but it abruptly disappeared. The reason was probably Captain Patterson's deputy Mollie Slott, a tough and ambitious lady who had worked her way up from steno to assistant syndicate manager, who had a lot of say in the syndicate's editorial calls, and who made a point of riding hard shotgun on Gould. Mollie Slott didn't much care for what she called "blood and thunder" strips to begin with, and she was no big fan of DICK TRACY, and Gould got away with as much as he did purely because The Captain always had a soft spot for the fine young fellow who had written him such courteous letters. Mollie Slott particularly didn't like DICK TRACY's Scientific Crime Detection sensibilities. "Please keep science out of your strip," she would wire Gould. "No one here is either a chemist or an engineer." She blew up in September 1933, when Dick Tracy blithely used a "secret truth serum" to wring a few facts out of a thug he was interrogating, and she demanded that Gould redraw a week's worth of dailies; he refused, and as the sequence survived intact, it appears that The Captain upheld him. Surviving syndicate correspondence shows that she blew up numerous other times, and that on a couple of occasions Gould was forced to back down. It is known that he detested the woman, and it's possible to view many of his excesses over the years as nothing more than Molliebaiting.

Mollie Slott notwithstanding, Scientific Crime Detection went on to become one of the strip's best-loved staples, and toymakers produced many official Dick Tracy scientific crime-fighting kits, and through the '30s the nation brimmed over with cleverly disguised little boys who were sending one another secret invisible messages written in lemon juice. As for Gould, years later he was still happily inventing 2-way wrist radios, atomic cameras, and magnetic space coupes.

THE CRIMINAL PET. A striking number of the villains Dick Tracy went up against over the years kept pets of one species or another to watchdog their turfs, eat their rivals, run useful errands, and so on. The first of these, in July 1932, was the private zookeeper B. Bellas, a.k.a. Alec Penn, a.k.a. Count Gordon, who concealed his operation behind a cageful of vicious lions that would have devoured Dick Tracy and Pat Patton save for the timely appearance of a Samaritan with a rifle (an outstanding example of strip-device cross-pollination, in this instance a Samaritan rescuing Tracy from a Near-Deathtrap that was filled with Criminal Pets).

The Criminal Pet would come into significant usage. In 1933, one Maxine Viller was seen to keep a fanged beast of a dog named Satan to run crosstown messages for her. The mad hunchbacked Doc Hump (1934) maintained a stable of rabies-foamed hounds the better to

Doc Hump and faithful pet, November 4, 1934.

21

menace his prisoners. The Ozark gunman Cutie Diamond (1935) maintained his hideout behind a cageful of clawing cats even as B. Bellas had done. The midget Jerome Trohs (1940) galloped around on the back of a huge, blank-eyed St. Bernard named Tip. Mrs. Pruneface (1943) had a rat. The fur bandit Mousey (1949) had lots of rats, and she used them to spook fur sales-ladies in the commission of her capers. The gang overlord Mr. Crime (1952) fed his foes to his pet barracuda. A character named 3-D Magee (1953) had a pocketful of killer ants. Uno Hardly's slot-machine mob (1959) kept a lion around to enforce mob will. The animals were some-times known to turn on their masters, as when Trusty Hubbub's leopards playfully tore Trusty to shreds (1961).

It was not only the criminals who kept pets, to be sure. Dick Tracy himself had a faithful boxer dog for a while in the late '40s (See Chapter 24). And animals figured directly in many story lines. Jerome Trohs was brought to justice specifically because he made a national newsreel spectacle of himself aboard a rodeo horse (1940). A stray cat led police to the hid-ing place of the fugitive Empty Williams (1951). A nightclub singer died in 1956 because her flapping parakeet spooked the man who was holding a gun on her. An informer who had the goods on a racketeer named Rhodent (1959) got himself tossed into a piranha tank. Indeed, so many creatures routinely abounded in the strip that after several decades, infinite configura-tions with the other standing conventions be-came possible. In 1963, for example, Gould cooked up a talking raven named Stoolie, who randomly issued legal opinions and who thus achieved the fascinating confluence of Crimi-nal Pet and Lawyer.

THE BOY SIDEKICK. In September 1932, Gould in-vented the comic tradition of the Boy Sidekick by introducing a waif called Dick Tracy Jr. (see Chapter 7). A decade later, BATMAN creator Bob Kane codified it with Bruce Wayne's ward Dick Grayson. Kane usually acknowledged that he had lifted the premise straight from DICK TRACY.

THE FEMALE VILLAIN. The Crime Queen went on to become a particular and often uncommonly vi-cious subset of TRACY villain, particularly through the '40s. The first fem heavy was Lar-ceny Lu (first appearance, December 7, 1932), hag mistress of the city's hot-car racket, a stout, fur-muffed, and behatted matron who talked like a longshoreman. She had just a brief ap-pearance as Dick Tracy dismantled her chop-shop operation and then gave her a high-speed, cross-country car chase, but she would be back in a couple of years with her wickednesses honed further.

THESE WERE THE KEY COROLLARY FUNDA-ments—pain, inescapable conundra, the more or less scientific approach, zoology, Junior Tracy, witches— as Gould's young strip was borne through its baptismals to turn its face toward the greater body of work stretching before it, and they were in place and on line and in service before DICK TRACY had seen out its first year.

But at the center were always still the crimi-nal rats.

Gould had been making it clear that he hated the rats and that he for one wanted them exter-minated, and he had launched his strip on the popular wave of revulsion against rat rule to begin with. But he had really only been talking about scum who whacked old men in their delis and fat fixers who bought aldermen. Sud-denly, things got much awfuler.

One cold March night in 1932, the real world dealt Chester Gould and Plainclothes Tracy a major break. Someone stole into the New Jer-sey home of the hero aviator Charles Lindbergh and carried away his infant son. The laughing little boy was the living symbol of everything that was good and golden and bountiful about America, and a citizenry far from inured to what would someday become just normal numb-ing everyday horror was plunged into the black-est of gloom at the thought that the world could really come to something like this.

Luck was running with Chester Gould, pro-duction-wise. He was already wrapping up the Broadway Bates yarn, and he could get a new story into print in just weeks. On Tuesday, April 12, 1932—two days after the Baby Lind-bergh story took a sensational ransom-pickup

Rat Smashing:

(1) February 5, 1932.
(2) July 22, 1932.
(3) January 14, 1934.
(4) June 28, 1936.
(5) February 27, 1937.

turn in the real world's headlines—Dick Tracy read a bulletin from the headquarters ticker: "John H. Waldorf's two-year-old son kidnapped from the Waldorf home in Elton today at noon. Watch for blue sedan with no license plates."

Tracy goggled. "THE John H. Waldorf, the international financier? Who'd dare?"

Chief Brandon cried out in despair. "Tracy, this country is in the grip of a plague worse than war!" He shook his head. "Gangsters are striking at the foundation of America—the home."

Indeed, the Lindbergh kidnap was a staggeringly brazen thing. Never mind payroll jobs. Never mind judges and juries in somebody's pocket. Now the rats were snatching children. Now it was time to really do something.

This year Tracy was out to get them.

GOULD MILKED THE BABY WALDORF SNATCH

for everything it was obviously worth. Some of this was certainly opportunism: the marketing student could hardly have failed to see the possibilities. But of course this decent and law-abiding man was as traumatized by the shocking Lindbergh case as every one of his fellow Americans. It happened that he was in a position to whip up some serious hanging frenzy.

"Listen, you birds," Tracy barked at Patton and the boys, "we're combing this man's town like it's never been combed before! Get me? Gangland's called for a showdown and we're going to let 'em have it."

Indeed, Tracy's crimebusters tore the City apart, rounding up and third-degreeing every Known Criminal in the book. In the real world, Al Capone himself pledged from his cell that the Lindy snatch could not have been a gangland job and that he would personally do what he could to help recover the baby. In DICK TRACY, meanwhile, certainly it was a gang job. Presently all clues were pointing to a mysterious gold-toothed man.

At this point, Pat Patton, the comic-relief partner heretofore known for mucking up practically everything, brought everlasting credit upon himself by doping something out and, by stating his divination aloud, formally inaugurating still another of the strip's eternal traditions—the backward-spelled name.

On April 19, 1932, Patton excitedly presented Tracy with a telegram he'd laid hands on. "Mr. Yobgib, Hotel King, Phila.," it read. "*Alonia sails from Boston Tuesday.*"

Tracy scratched his jaw. "I don't get it," he said.

"Gee whiz, don't you see?" Patton cried. "The

The Buddy Waldorf kidnapping: Marching orders, April 14, 1932.

At sea with Big Boy, his luckless accomplice, and Baby Waldorf, May 16, 1932.

name 'Yobgib' spelled backwards is BIG BOY!''

Darned if it wasn't. Why, the rats would stoop to anything. Tracy headed for the Boston docks, where, cleverly disguised as a newspaper peddler (''Now with a little spirit gum and greasepaint—''), he immediately spotted a woman with a familiar-looking child board the France-bound *Alonia*. A few minutes after that, Big Boy himself bought a paper from him. The Lindbergh baby hunt should only have been so simple. Hot on the case, Tracy leaped aboard the ship as it put to sea, cleverly disguised himself as a hook-nosed, square-jawed old lady (''Now for a few shadows and wrinkles from this burnt cork—''), and was immediately made by Big Boy, who threw the flatfoot over the rail into the cold mid-Atlantic in the middle of the night.

There was a brief thrilling aside as Tracy clung for days to a handily passing plank, perhaps on loan from one of the Saturday-morning bijou cliffhangers, and then was picked up by a Norwegian fishing boat, transferred to a British aircraft carrier, and delivered back to the *Alonia* by a military amphibian. All this took less than a week, strip time—nothing ever moved faster than a TRACY story when Chester Gould was rolling—but Big Boy had already decided that the jig was up and he was busy eliminating the evidence. He had just shoved his never-named woman companion out a porthole. Tracy and

the ship's officers burst into his stateroom just as little Buddy Waldorf was about to go into the drink, too.

''The vilest murderer and child snatcher that ever walked on two feet,'' Tracy growled, throwing down his gun and rolling up his sleeves. ''I've got a date with a big piece of human scum.''

Big Boy blanched. Big Boy gulped.

''You could use a coupla dozen of those gun-toting bodyguards of yours right now, couldn't you?'' Tracy grinned, moving in.

Big Boy feebly put up his dukes.

Dick Tracy beat him to a pulp. Then Dick Tracy beat him to a pulp again. Then Dick Tracy literally threw him through a locked door. America's Greatest Detective had triumphed over the King Cobra of the Underworld at last.

BUDDY WALDORF IS SAFE! the strip jubilantly trumpeted, headline fashion, on May 21, 1932. TEARS OF JOY AND HAPPINESS DIM THE EYES OF A WAITING WORLD.

The cheer was probably muted in some households. Nine days earlier, in real life, the New Jersey woods had given up the battered little corpse of what the law identified as Baby Lindy.

Little Buddy was restored to the breast of his mother. Big Boy was brought home in chains. ''That guy Tracy, BAH,'' he grumbled.

CHAPTER 5

NOT A PARTICULARLY NICE BEDTIME STORY

Rough Stuff

THE RAT AT HAND IN LATE 1932 WAS A dope racketeer named Dan (The Squealer) Mucelli, and he seemed to be another bad customer. "One of the shrewdest and most vicious individuals on record," said Chief Brandon, reading from the rap sheet.

"Ha!" said Dick Tracy. "They're all alike to me, Chief."

This was so. They *were* pretty much all alike. "One of the shrewdest and most vicious characters on record" was approximately what the rap sheets had said about Big Boy and Ribs Mocco and Broadway Bates and Alec Penn. A

year into his strip, Chester Gould was beginning to learn how to write it, and he was finding that what he had here was a slate of very similar characters who existed more or less one-dimensionally on the Rat Plane, pulling jobs and growling and sneering and laying traps for Plainclothes Tracy, and who beyond that had little in the way of distinctive personalities. Gould began to do something about this with the chop-shop queen Larceny Lu; otherwise still quite the standard desperado, Lu was at least a woman. As 1932 became 1933, Gould turned his attentions to even greater character development, laying the foundations of the immortal rogues' gallery of great villains that would be the strip's hallmark for decades to come.

The other thing he did was have a careful look at the mayhem level. By the end of 1932, DICK TRACY was already known far and wide as the most violent comic strip anybody had ever seen. It was already old hat. Merely violent. That would never do. As 1932 became 1933, Chester Gould cranked up the voltage.

THE DEPTH AND BREADTH OF STOOGE VILLER'S
character was not inconsiderably established by the fact that Viller physically resembled the actor Edward G. Robinson and therefore arrived in the strip bearing the familiar baggage of Robinson's popular gangster roles. Viller was a well-spoken, well-dressed dandy when he first showed up on January 3, 1933, an out-of-town operator who had been imported by gang underboss Ribs Mocco, and while his Ultra-Violence level was such that he didn't think twice about shooting women (see Chapter 6), his primary function was to set up Dick Tracy on phony charges and ruin his good name.

Stooge Viller schemes to ruin Tracy, January 16, 1933.

Ribs Mocco was running the show these days in Big Boy's absence, and he had concluded that Tracy was essentially unkillable. "We've got to get rid of him, not by violence but by getting him disgraced," Mocco told his boys. "We're going to queer him with the higher-ups."

They came close. Viller, an incredibly smooth pickpocket, slyly planted counterfeit currency in the detective's pockets on a crowded streetcar one day and then sat back beaming as Tracy passed the stuff all over town. Tracy was even found with piles of bogus bills stashed all over his home. Evidence was evidence. On January 22, Tracy was fired from the police department. "What else could I do?" Chief Brandon anguished. "We caught him red-handed!"

"Framed—that's what they did—FRAMED ME!" moaned Tracy, buckling into miserable self-pity for one of the few times in his life.

"Only our past years of friendship and association keep me from arresting you and prosecuting you to the fullest extent of the law," Brandon sniffed. "Good day!"

Former Plainclothes Tracy decided to go west. He had a cattle rancher uncle in Kansas. Circumstances contrived to put him at the train station precisely as Stooge Viller arrived to board the eastbound, and they met, intuitively rubbed one another the wrong way, and had a trackside duke-out that Viller attempted to resolve by pushing Tracy in front of a train. In the wake of this disorderly conduct, it was found that Viller was the man responsible for Tracy's troubles, and Chief Brandon was white about it, publicly making a statement to "beg apologies and admit my shame in falsely judging one of the squarest, finest individuals I ever came in contact with." Brandon bowed his head. The moment certified Tracy's Mr. Clean credentials for some time to come, though he would still have moments.

AFTER STOOGE VILLER CAME STEVE THE TRAMP,
a broadly but colorfully drawn hobo who was already figuring in a parallel story (see Chapter 7). Steve—variously surnamed Maddis and Brogan—became a well-known figure in the strip in the spring of 1933 and he would dominate the proceedings for some time, a seasoned bum

who rode cowcatchers for kicks and who could break his way out of refrigerator cars he was trapped inside, a dim thug who would hijack a rural mail truck and strangle the elderly letter carrier merely to intercept a stray postcard ("Humph! It don't take Steve long to take de starch outta guys like you!"), a beast who would in a minute abandon a drowning pal or a farmer helplessly burning alive in a crashed auto and who would send an innocent woman to her death to buy himself five minutes of time. Steve was a guy who would snarl like a trapped rat on the brink of a cliff as two-fisted Dick Tracy closed in on him and take only an instant to choose the swan dive over prison, and then survive the 150-foot fall by landing in a tree. This was Steve the Tramp.

Steve's trial in May 1933 introduced another of the strip's great loathsome Lawyers, a stentorian criminal defense man named J. Peter Twillbrain, who planned to plead Steve as a mental deficient. "As in all nature," Twillbrain would declaim, "so in the creation of men each and every one is not endowed alike!" Steve didn't much appreciate being called a feeb. "Purely showmanship," Twillbrain assured him. "Purely bunk to fool the court! Those imbeciles love it! They eat it up!" Twillbrain at

Steve the Tramp, April 6, 1933.

Steve the Tramp and Stooge Viller crunch out, June 7, 1933.

work was really pretty wonderful, weeping, blowing his nose. "Look at that face, your honor," he implored. "There is nothing vicious there . . . It is the face of a brother who calls to you in his wilderness of lost hope—" Twillbrain was in the wrong courtroom, though. "PIFFLE! ROT! CLAPTRAP!" cried the presiding Judge Dunne as the entire room burst into claps and cheers.

And off went Steve the Tramp to spend the rest of his natural life at hard labor inside the Big House.

Where, on May 29, he joined forces with a fellow inmate named Viller, doing ten for passing counterfeit dough.

THE TEAM-UP OF THE STRIP'S TWO STRONGEST
characters to date was an inspired doubling of the Rat Quotient, and Stooge Viller and Steve the Tramp stayed side by side through the summer. They had in common a devout hatred of Dick Tracy, the personal standard bearer of every decent instinct, and they were both the worst people alive and deserved to be smashed. Gould couldn't lose on this one.

The two of them touched off a naphtha fire and blew their way out of prison on June 9. "THE MOST SPECTACULAR PENITENTIARY ESCAPE IN THE HISTORY OF THIS COUNTRY!" Chief Brandon gasped. At large for weeks across the nation, the prison-breaking rats stole cars, burst into homes, tortured citizens as it occurred to them ("Shove dat pen knife under his toenails, Stooge!"), and finally worked their way back to the City, where they threw in with Viller's sister Maxine. She was a jewel thief and she kept a demonic dog as big as she was ("Don't go near him! He could bite your hand off with one snap!"), and it was in the course of dusting off Maxine's operation that Tracy finally nailed Steve the Tramp again, although not before he had to endure several more Near-Deathtraps, one by gasoline fire and one by poison gas.

Stooge, solo now, fled to Halifax, where after briefly brushing against another story (see Chapter 7), he threw in with a coastal smuggling operation for a time. Tracy had him back in jail by early September. "You're a dirty double-crossing rat," Stooge announced to the detective, coolly blowing cigarette smoke into his face. "I'm going to spend my every living moment in that pen figuring out how I can get free and kill you!" Dick Tracy smiled, rolled up his sleeves, and beat him into marmalade, and that was the last of Stooge Viller.

INCREASINGLY CONFIDENT OF HIS STORY-marshaling capabilities, Chester Gould now decided to make a last pass at Big Boy, the King Cobra. Before the story was over, it had become Gould's most definitively scalding indictment of pols and fixers and the stinking cesspool of city politics.

There was now in Tracy's City an extraordinarily brazen protection racket at work, apparently operating quite freely, so little concerned with appearances that somebody even fired a taunting bullet through the window into the very offices of the Mayor of the town himself as His Honor met with Dick Tracy and Mr. District Attorney. The mayor, one Freddy (Glad Hand) Turner, pronounced himself shocked. "How does an illegitimate industry like this continue to exist?" Turner demanded. "Why aren't they behind bars?" "I'll tell you why," Dick Tracy spelled it out. "POLITICAL FIX AND CORRUPTION." Instantly, the detective declared the most sweeping war on rackets the City had

ever seen. "I'm going to bust every crooked fixer and politician in this town!" Even Chief Brandon quailed at such a revolutionary notion. "If you go through with this," Brandon offered, "it'll be your end!"

With a small army behind him, Tracy started smashing the rackets wherever they slithered, taking back the festering planet street by street. Goons flew through the air. Underworld dives were demolished. Whole blocks started disgorging their vile criminal populations like so many scrambling cockroaches. "We're going to bust you racketeers if it takes all winter!" Tracy pledged, incorruptible fists at the ready.

Somewhere, it followed, there was a Mr. Big pulling the strings, and soon the trail led to the mansion of the beloved retired politician "Boss" Jim Herrod. Pat Patton, on the case, couldn't believe his eyes. "Great scott!" Patton murmured. "There must be some mistake. Boss Herrod is one of the grandest old fixtures this town ever had. He wouldn't be messed up with racketeers." Indeed, Boss Herrod (first appearance, October 2, 1933) was known to be Mayor "Glad Hand" Turner's closest friend.

But these were eye-opening times. Even as Tracy and Patton surveilled, grand old Boss Herrod dispatched a courier to the state penitentiary, where, on October 5, he met with the inmate known as Big Boy, currently doing twenty.

"The heat's on plenty!" the courier trembled.

"Why come crying to me?" Big Boy yawned. "I'm paying Boss Herrod to handle things for me while I'm doing time—and if he ain't big enough to handle the rackets, let him take the rap with me!"

"There'll have to be a shake-up of the police force in this town," Boss Herrod decided. "I'll have to get the mayor to fire Chief Brandon and his staff—including this rat, Tracy!" (Gould, policing himself, possibly for immediate political considerations, made it plain that Mayor Turner was not a party to the racketeering. "I've kept him fooled!" Boss Herrod gloated.) But it was already too late for a shake-up. Tracy, breaking and entering, had slipped into Herrod's home and laid hands on all his incriminating papers. The Boss flew into a rage ("I'LL BUY OFF THE STATE'S ATTORNEY—I'LL FIX THE

The City Hall shootout with big fix Boss Jim Herrod, October 8, 1933.

COURTS—I'LL—") and headed for City Hall.

Where, on October 10, having come in just eight days to be the very emblem of municipal filth, he shot it out with Dick Tracy and lost.

"To think this thing could have happened during my term in office!" mourned Mayor Turner. "I must have been blind!"

And then Big Boy broke out of prison.

BY JANUARY 1934, WHEN THE ASPIRING CRIME

writer Jean Penfield appeared on the scene with a blistering exposé of the City's machinations, Big Boy was beginning to reestablish himself as a power to be reckoned with under the solicitous eye of his mouthpiece, the strip's greatest Shyster Lawyer of them all, Ben ("Anything is fair if you can get away with it") Spaldoni. Indeed, the greasy little Spaldoni was flagrantly ripping off Big Boy for ten grand when he was first seen on November 10, 1933, but by now he seemed to be looking after his client's larger interests and he didn't like the sound of Jean Penfield's book at all. Jean Penfield was a flossy little skirt who was fairly racy by the day's funny-papers standards—Gould often had her in lingerie—and while she appeared at first to be quite out of her depth, she had in fact managed to write a bombshell, as Spaldoni discovered after he purloined the first two chapters and started reading them aloud. "Big Boy, king of the underworld, has on his payroll two aldermen, one state representative, one of the world's crookedest lawyers, and two judges. Their names—HOLY MACKEREL!" Straightaway he was on the phone to Big Boy. ". . . Gambling rights are bought through Aldermen Kernel . . . stolen car racket is conducted under the protecting eyes of State Representative Oscar Milrey . . . Why, boss, if this girl's book is allowed to get into print . . ."

Flimsily clad crimebuster Jean Penfield tangles with the mob, January 28, 1934. Several tries later, they rubbed her out.

Tracy figured the same thing. "Your life won't be worth a plugged penny," he grunted at Jean. And so it wasn't, particularly after she discovered where Big Boy was hiding and tipped off Tracy, the resultant raid sending the King Cobra back to prison forever. A furious gangland took her for a one-way ride. In late February, the girl author went up in flames when her car was sent slamming into a gasoline storage tank.

Or so it seemed. Shortly after that, a shocking series of articles started running daily in one of the City's newspapers under the byline of "The Phantom." Gangland wasn't pleased. Gangland hit the paper's press room early one morning and threw the foreman into the speeding press.

Gangland came back that night to bomb the paper and execute its crusading editor, but this time Tracy was waiting, and gangland went down. Meanwhile, of course, it was revealed that "The Phantom" was none but Jean Penfield, who had somehow survived the gas-tank inferno and gone undercover.

All by herself, tough little Jean Penfield had done at least as much to dismantle the criminal-political combine in the City as frankly even Dick Tracy. She might have mopped things up a lot more save for Spaldoni, who at this point went after her with a gun and, on April 11, 1934, finished the doll off for real.

Spaldoni—by now, unaccountably, his name was Giorgio Spaldoni—didn't run much longer. His operation broken, the mouthpiece and his mob holed up in an abandoned steel mill and made an explosive last stand against Dick Tracy and did not prevail. The crooked lawyer, full of bullets, confessing to everything, spilling every underworld secret he ever knew, died shivering and terrified in his hospital bed on May 6.

ENTIRE CITIES WERE IN FURIES AT THE MOUNT-

ing carnage. "This is not a particularly nice bedtime story," the editor of the *Tulsa Tribune* had written the syndicate on November 27, 1933, citing an avalanche of reader protests: "One father told us on the phone that he did not want the *Tulsa Tribune* in his house any longer because our comics too frequently caused his children to cry in sympathy for tortured

Spaldoni buys it, May 4, 1934.

victims." On February 6, 1934, the *Salt Lake Telegram* reported that a massive public hue and cry was forcing the paper to cancel DICK TRACY outright—"the most concerted bitterness we have ever had to deal with," publisher J. F. Fitzpatrick wrote syndicate manager Arthur Crawford. "The whole thing has stirred up such a mess that there is absolutely nothing left for us to do but give up the strip."

On the other hand, TRACY sales were now double those of 1933. On April 30, 1934, a remarkable lead editorial appeared on the opinion page of the *New York Daily News:*

There have been many complaints about Dick Tracy. In fact, Dick was thrown out of one paper after an organization of mothers had "persuaded" the paper to cancel.

Well, we'll stand by Dick. . . . We don't think comic strips influence children much, anyway, one way or another. They are for the entertainment of children, just as ball games, movies, theatres are for the entertainment of adults. If Dick Tracy influences children at all, he influences them to follow his noble example and hate and fight crime and crooks. No child that we can imagine, with the possible exception of some little moron who ought to be kept under observation for society's safety, would prefer such an infamous character as Spaldoni to the great detective himself.

How long should children be kept ignorant of the facts of life? We think the people who hope to keep them in ignorance of such facts very long are hoping 1) for the impossible and 2) the undesirable. This is a tough enough world at best. The sooner a child finds out what kind of world it is, the better he or she is equipped to get along in it.

Chester Gould couldn't have said it better himself. Thus, just a few months later, ever mindful of the great detective's noble example and his own responsibility to the children of America, he whipped up a villain who kept a kennelful of snarling killer rabies-foaming dogs that tore people to shreds.

Generic 1933 unpleasantness.

CHAPTER 6

ENOUGH CHARACTER TO BE A REAL SCOUT

The Girlfriend

THE DELI SHOOTING NOT ONLY LEFT OLD Emil Trueheart dead as a doornail, it left old Emil's daughter a spinster for years and years. Wouldn't you just know it? A girl finally gets a proposal and right away her father's shot, her boyfriend's run off to be a policeman, and she herself is tied to a chair, prisoner of the mob. Honestly. It was the sort of thing Tess Trueheart was going to have to get used to, what with one thing after another.

She looked pretty good in ropes right from the beginning. There was regularly something of Imperiled Pauline to Dick Tracy's fiancée; this was a lass who understood that it was her place in life to sigh and shrug and stick out her wrists. "Kinda pretty, aintcha, sister?" Big Boy nodded approvingly, leering at her virtuous, willowy, trussed-up form. Tess wasn't going to have any part of Big Boy for all his pretty talk. "So you ain't swingin'?" he grunted. Certainly she wasn't. She was engaged, for God's sake. Big Boy could only shake his head. Bestirred, for a time he attempted the customary subtle-

ties. "Here's a dozen dresses from the hottest shops on the avenue, sister," he offered. "Take off that rag you got on and git dolled." "Boo hoo!" she wept modestly.

Texie Garcia, the moll, took a pretty dim view of all this. "I ain't standin' for it," she snarled. Well, Big Boy was fed up with Tess anyway. So he decided instead that she was going to drive a getaway car and she shouldn't try any funny stuff or it would be curtains for her. And that's where Tess was, trembling behind the wheel outside a bank, when Tracy leaped into the car and the two of them sped away in a hail of bullets.

At the end of the long night, the knight returned the damsel to the safety of her home, and she gazed softly upon him. It was a moment for affirmation, for poetry, for an eternal seal.

Dick Tracy looked his beloved in her fluttering eyes.

"Well, toodle-oo," he said. "See you in the morning."

One of those darned important moments,
October 13, 1931.

Houseguest of the mob, October 24, 1931.
First appearance of Big Boy.

THIS PRETTY MUCH SET THE TONE OF THINGS

for the rest of time. Tess Trueheart is popularly remembered as having been naught but steadfast and faithful as she waited and waited and waited for her cop to make an honest woman out of her as meanwhile whole battalions of crooks kept trying to poison her or drown her or set her afire, but in fact the romance with the bestest boyfriend was quite on again and off again in those early days. Generally Tess was a pretty good sport, but on the other hand she was only a puppy, not yet twenty years old, and she did begin to grow impatient as straight-arrow Tracy became increasingly proficient at seeing her to her door, solemnly shaking hands, and then vanishing for weeks.

If there was sometimes a certain petulance to Tess Trueheart—considering that, after all, Dick Tracy had become a grim and unforgivingly relentless policeman in the first place to avenge the murder of her own father—it is also true that Plainclothes Tracy was not all that good with the small romantic detail. "Suppose we take in a movie," he would suggest. "Wonderful!" she would squeal. And then suddenly he would be off shooting somebody and kicking down doors and getting bricks dropped on his head, and here was Tess cooling her heels, scowling at the clock. "I don't see why you couldn't have called me, at least," she would crab. "You go away for days at a time! You don't tell me where you're going! I wish you'd give up this detective game." Particularly nettling to her was Tracy's unwillingness to confide secret police information. "You mean you don't trust me?" she would pout. He would sputter and try to explain. "A detective never tells his plans, not even to his fiancée," he would say. "It isn't done, that's all."

The engagement was in trouble by Christmas. "Come on, honey," Tess said, showing up at headquarters one festive day with a bundle of packages. "We're going to have a real old-fashioned Christmas Eve." "Gee, that's great," Tracy said, "but I've got an important job. I'll have to join you later."

She started to sniffle. "Dick, I believe you're more interested in crooks than you are in me."

"Now. darling, it isn't that," he consoled her absently.

"Sob, sob," she wept in the taxi home, surrounded by Christmas presents.

Actually, Tracy did feel sort of bad about Christmas. "Pretty raw of me," he admitted, silencing the bitter plaints by whipping out a sparkler and proving once again why God invented jewelry stores. But even the rock failed to cement things for long. Within a few weeks Tess was kvetching again at Tracy's close-mouthed attitude, this time about an enormously important and extremely secret police raid that was coming up. "Okay then, smarty, then you don't trust me," she wailed.

"Oh, well," Tracy sighed. He proceeded to matter-of-factly disclose every one of the shockingly confidential details of an operation calculated to nail Big Boy, round up all his torpedoes, and demolish the City's entire criminal infrastructure.

The raid collapsed. All the rats were long gone when the cops got there. Big Boy had left a jeering note, and Tracy and the police department were immediately the laughingstocks of the town. Tracy was mortified. "Rottenest break I ever got in my life!" he growled. "Somebody

Plainclothes Tracy and damsel, one jump ahead of the underworld, November 10, 1931.

Plainclothes Tracy strives to maintain professional ethics, January 2, 1932.

Plainclothes Tracy reflects, January 11, 1932.

talked!" Chief Brandon roared. Tracy blinked. Out he rushed to confront his sweetie.

Oh, all right, she admitted, maybe she had mentioned just the teensiest thing to a notoriously gossipy friend at tea the other day, but that was no reason to—"Aw, nuts," Tracy barked. "You women are all alike. Talk talk. Can't keep your mouths shut. Gab gab gab." Into the snowstorm he trudged. "Tess! Of all people! The most important job I've tackled yet! Talked about it to her friends!" Tess was galloping after him in the howling night, and now they were clinched on a lonely winter's bridge as all the choirs of period romantic melodrama raised a joyful noise.

"But you've got to listen to me," she pleaded.

"I trusted you!" Dick Tracy snarled. "Thought you had enough character to be a real scout! And like any woman you blabbed to the world."

"Is that so?" The girlfriend bristled. She had a couple things she was going to tell mister. "Did it ever occur to you," she snapped, "that YOU'RE the one who talked?"

"What?" he said.

"You say I can't keep a secret," Tess Trueheart hissed, a portrait in self-righteousness. "Well, weren't you guilty of the same thing?"

Tracy thought this one over. "You're mad," he concluded.

Well. The ring came off the finger, and into the river it went. "THAT'S what I think of your little old ring," she sniffed. "It was only a half karat anyway," she added, nose high in the air as she stomped away.

Even that wasn't the last of it. In a deep mope, Dick Tracy came down with what was seen as an attitude problem and Chief Brandon straightaway busted him from plainclothes ace to uniformed beat cop in a remote precinct out in the sticks. Here in the freezing 1932 night he had ample opportunity to ponder the heart of the matter. The girl was adorable, no argument there, but obviously she was not only petty and screwball and dim, she was also meddlesome, career-threatening, and probably lethal sooner or later, and besides that she had single-handedly permitted the entire nefarious underworld to continue going about its business for who knows how long. Dick Tracy, hero of the funny papers for less than three months yet and suddenly nothing but a harness bull swinging a nightstick, thought about all this as he trudged his beat, and then he actually kicked a homeless dog.

"Woman trouble," Patton and Brandon agreed sympathetically.

STILL, LEAVE IT TO PERIOD ROMANTIC MELO-

drama to get a fella and his honey back together again. Tess Trueheart was presently run down by an automobile, landing reader sympathy squarely on her side, and anyway she'd been able to slip Tracy some very important information—anonymously, as the two of them were not speaking—that enabled him to make a collar big enough to get back his old job at the plainclothes squad.

That patched things up, and by summer they were vacationing together at a North Woods lodge. Tess didn't even seem to mind that Tracy briefly interrupted the pastoral holiday to go chase a murderer and fight a grizzly bear. By January 1933, things were sufficiently gooey that Tracy put Tess on the lie box to confirm her love ("She's guilty—just as I suspected!") and then proposed again ("Can't you see, dear? We were meant for each other—I'll get us a little place uptown—Name the day!"). Wedding plans were made again. They started shopping for dining-room sets.

And at this point the sleek Stooge Viller set up Tracy good by planting funny money on him, and things fell apart again.

Not only did the detective lose his job and his good name, Tess didn't believe his protestations either. "Oh, Dick, I never thought you'd—" she wept. "Oh, I want to believe you, but . . ." she'd say, and then she'd hang up on him.

And almost right away she was dating Stooge Viller himself, who'd got a load of her and had decided to make some moves.

Stooge Viller was actually kind of slick, all things considered. It's possible to take a lady to worse places and hand her worse lines. "Now that I've known you for an hour, I feel I can propose," Stooge murmured suavely, dancing the night away to the sweetest saxophones of some society orchestra in the sort of ballroom that was certainly beyond Dick Tracy's means. "Why, I wouldn't think of answering that question till I'd known you for at least an hour and a half," giggled Tess.

She was preparing to leave town with him when she all at once learned that Stooge Viller was the man behind Dick Tracy's ruination. So, on February 12, 1933, he had to shoot her.

"We've all been fools . . ." Tess gasped in her hospital bed. "Dick is innocent. . . ."

"What I can't understand," Tracy anguished in the semidark after Viller had been mopped up, "is how you could have taken up with this fellow."

She held her head. "He came along—he completely swept me off my feet with a kind of romance I had never known before—" Tess Trueheart wept. "He offered me a relief from my conscience—I fell in love with him and at the same time hated him and hated myself—"

The girlfriend looked up imploringly. "Oh, I can't expect you to understand," she blubbered. "Do you?"

Tracy stood up and thought about it. "I'm not absolutely sure that I do," he said.

Shot by Stooge Viller, Valentine's Day 1933.

Tess Trueheart in peril:

(1) August 31, 1933.
(2) October 29, 1933.
(3) July 4, 1935.

Tess Trueheart in a snit, March 27, 1937.

The wedding was off. She would call sometimes, and he would be busy. Tess Trueheart fell to her knees in prayer. "I failed him when he needed me—" she sobbed. "Make me worthy of him—nothing else in my whole life will ever matter—"

A FEW MONTHS LATER THEY BECAME CLOSER

again when they together survived a couple of appalling Near-Deathtraps, and it would all go on for years yet, the girl inexplicably going into snits ("I just realize I'm in the way! Get out! Get out! Sob sob sob sob sob.") and the detective spending his whole life pulling her out of flaming basements ("Tess, dear! Are you all right?") and then once again tipping his hat and disappearing. All of it would be one of the strip's trademark leitmotifs, continuing even beyond the memorable moment in 1939 when Tess actually married another gent, from whom she had to be saved yet again (see Chapter 11).

Any rational observer might have noted that there was absolutely no good reason for either one of them to have kept such a nuisance as the other around for more than five minutes. But the funny papers had their rules and regs in these matters of the heart. Like Flash Gordon, chained forever to the ceaselessly whining Dale Arden; like Prince Valiant, pledged for the rest of time to his snotty princess who lay awake nights thinking of all the bone-crushing quests she could send her swain off on to prove his worth; like even Donald Duck, enduring the shovelsful of indignity endlessly flung at him by the impossible Daisy, it happened to be Dick Tracy's lot to be Designated Beau. In those days, when you were somebody's bestest boyfriend, you were pretty well stuck with it.

Bonus portrait:
Tess Trueheart
gratuitously unclad,
January 27, 1932.

DICK TRACY

by CHESTER GOULD

CHAPTER 7

Hands That Would Guard and Protect and Lead
The Kid

HE WAS NINE YEARS OLD, A RAGGED little street urchin with a mop of carrot-colored hair, and when he was first seen on September 8, 1932, he was hooking Pat Patton's wristwatch and galloping off into the rail yards. The kid lived in a boxcar with his guardian, the rod-riding brute called Steve the Tramp, who forced him into thievery and cuffed him up daily, since the boy owned something akin to a personal code of honor ("But, Steve, it—it—it ain't right to steal nuthin' from a dame! I'll swipe from fruit stands and t'ings but I ain't gonna take nothin' off a dame!"). Finally fed up with all the bother ("You lazy little gutter rat!"), Steve the Tramp was flinging his charge beneath the wheels of a train one day when Dick Tracy showed up and put a stop to that. And then, keenly perceiving in the young wretch the qualities of the Algeresque Fine Little Chap, Tracy took him home, gave him a hot meal and a bad haircut, registered him in the second grade at the neighborhood public school, named him his ward, and began the work of imbuing him with a stout sense of self-worth. "I ain't got no name," the kid

mourned. "I never had no folks. Never came from no place." "I know an honest pair of eyes when I see 'em!" Tracy boomed heartily. On September 25, the born-again youngster gratefully named himself Dick Tracy Jr.

Junior Tracy has been a major player in the TRACY cast for decades since, in various successive personae—Resourceful Boy Sidekick, Police Artist, Son-in-Law of the Governor of the Moon, etc.—serving through them all as Devoted Squire, in the Round Table sense, one who has selected his ideal after careful consideration and then attends him and studies him and doggedly emulates him and thereby preserves the leonine heart of the line more faithfully than mere blood ever could. For years he was Dick Tracy's indispensable companion, always coming through in pinches, helping solve crime after crime, frequently saving the detective's life. It was a noble mantle for such shoulders as belonged to one of the more ungainly creatures the funny papers ever saw, a young human of truly weird skull construction and an inconceivable head of hair, no improvement ever having been made on Tracy's initial barberings. In various interviews, Gould affectionately referred to Junior as "that repulsive little kid."

Boy sidekicks were not yet a standard convention in the comics. Little Orphan Annie might have been Oliver Warbucks's boy sidekick had she only remained Little Orphan Otto, but otherwise the likes of Batman's Robin hadn't come along yet and Dick Tracy Jr. was really a pioneer in this particular brand of symbiotic relationship. Dick Tracy and Dick Tracy Jr. were mentor and protégé, trainer and pupil, sleuth and dependable legman, pal and pal forever, bound together in both endearing sentiment and the implicit agreement to stamp out rats. "I'll always stick close to you!" the kid swore. "I'm going to show all de kids at school how to be a detective. Someday I'm going to be a detective like you and stay up all night hunting crooks."

There was one bad moment early on; honest pair of eyes notwithstanding, Junior was, after all, a thief, and momentarily he could not resist swiping Tess Trueheart's jewelry and scramming down the fire escape. He spent the night

Locked and loaded, August 13, 1933.

In the life with Steve the Tramp,
September 15, 1932.

weeping in a filthy alley ("De only guy dat was ever nice to me . . . I stole . . . Honest, Lord, I ain't a human bein'.") and then he trudged home, head bowed in shame. Dick Tracy nodded and said nothing and resumed the schooling in Modern Police Work ("Yeah, Junior, that's a real pair of handcuffs." "Oboy! Let me see 'em!")

Being Dick Tracy Jr. was no imperilous business, particularly in the early '30s, when Chester Gould was gleefully churning out ghastlinesses as fast as he could think of them, and Gould quickly arranged for the kid to get first shot in the chest and then menaced with a white-hot poker. Thereafter, Torturing Junior Tracy became one of the strip's favorite and most revered entertainments as Gould warmed to the task of terrorizing the little boy in more and more ingeniously horrible ways. Fine little chap that he was, Junior mostly kept up his grit and his gumption throughout these bleak ordeals. In November 1932, though, he caved in hard when his pal was shot and critically wounded and everybody at headquarters decided he was the one who'd done the job. Bad customer after all, the lug Chief Brandon decided, ordering him sent to the House of Detention. From which—having, of course, been reared by Steve the Tramp to be a crafty little sneak—Junior in short order accomplished a crunch-out. Tracy, recovered from his coma and horrified by Brandon's show of dim-wittedness—this was nei-

Torturing Junior Tracy: (1) October 31, 1932. (2) November 25, 1933. (3) December 29, 1933.

ther the first nor the last time the chief gave up a previously trusted friend on the flimsiest of evidence—immediately cleared the boy. But by now Junior was forlornly adrift in the City's underbelly, believing himself hunted, resigned to the great dead end. "I wasn't born to be anything but jist a gutter rat, I guess," he sniffled in the cold winter night, sunk to his knees in a reverie that could have failed to moisten the eye of only the most stonehearted reader. "If I only did have a mother . . . I could tell her the truth . . . Mother . . . Dat's a kind woman dat teaches kids not to steal . . . and keeps 'em clean and believes 'em when dey tell the truth . . . Mother . . . Mother . . ."

Junior Tracy's mother was a subject that would have to wait. For now, Gould had to find the kid somewhere to sleep, and the abandoned house that shortly presented itself proved to be the chop shop of the hot-car–racket queen Larceny Lu. The ferocious hag Lu was the first of the strip's female villains (see Chapter 16), and a mean one she was, and Junior—an unjustly accused fugitive detective maybe, but still, by God, a detective—knew he had to get word to Tracy. The missing student and the frantic tutor were touchingly reunited shortly before Christmas, and then both of them moved in on Lu's operation and smashed it. It was the fearless little boy who single-handedly effected Lu's capture, leaping to the spare tire of her getaway car as she fled with her gang ("Hully gee! Dis is me chance to be a real detective! I'll trip dese babies up if it's de last ting I do!") and wild

miles later successfully disabling the vehicle, permitting the pursuing law to catch up.

With this incident, Junior Tracy made his bones. On February 28, 1933, Chief Brandon issued him a genuine department badge and designated him "Operative Number Two."

AND AT THIS POINT THE STRIP'S ACTION MOVED from the City to a ranch in Silver Mountain, Colorado, for the first installment of what was

On the trail of Larceny Lu, Christmas Eve 1932.

to become a multichapter investigation into Junior Tracy's natural parentage. The full story, at once profoundly sentimental and bone-rattlingly murderous, would cover much of the next two years—an ambitious enterprise for the day, particularly for Gould, who generally staged his work in brief and breathless bites—and would measurably affect the lives of all players as the TRACY strip attained its mid-'30s maturity.

As the first chapter opened on March 3, 1933, an elderly gold miner called Blind Hank Steele was recounting the story of his life to his hired hand: The old prospector had been left sightless in a dynamite blast years earlier, and then his wife, a flighty and worthless woman much younger than himself, had thrown in with a traveling man and run off, taking Blind Hank's infant boy with her. Two weeks later Blind Hank had struck it rich. Now, old and lonely, he ached for his lost son, who would be about ten years old. "What a comfort he'd be to me," Blind Hank sorrowed. "I've named the boy in my will. I'll leave him my entire fortune."

The hired man's eyes went alight with inspired schemery. It was Steve the Tramp himself, returned to the strip after an absence of five months, and now it dawned on Steve that he knew exactly where to find a boy about ten years old. He would go snatch Junior Tracy and then pass him off to Blind Hank Steele as his missing heir and collect a reward. How would Blind Hank know any better? Blind Hank was *blind*.

Steve went east. Dick Tracy happened to be out of town, gone to Quebec to bring back a pair of swindlers, and Junior was easy pickings. Together the captive lad and his old tormentor rode the trains west, but Tracy, shrewdly following various clues, got to Blind Hank Steele's ranch before they did. A fracas or two later, Steve was headed for the big house, from which he would shortly embark upon another set of adventures (see Chapter 5).

Meanwhile, back at Silver Mountain, a new drama was being played out, suddenly, poignantly, and wildly improbably: By reason of an identifying scar, Junior Tracy proved to be, in fact, Blind Hank Steele's lost son. His real name was Jackie Steele. The traveling man of ten years earlier had been Steve the Tramp.

Silver Mountain, Colorado, May 5–6, 1933.

Here was Bad Coincidence of the highest order, but the boy who had been Dick Tracy Jr. was obviously required to stay in Colorado with his natural father all the same. Dick Tracy and Junior made their awkward farewells, and then Tracy was gone. The kid, torn between worlds, waved good-bye on May 7, and then he was gone, too.

HE WAS BACK JUST A MONTH LATER. IT SEEMED

that Steve the Tramp and Stooge Viller had busted prison, and Tracy, correctly supposing that the two of them would head straight for Colorado to proceed with Steve's original nefarious get-the-inheritance plan, ordered Blind Hank Steele and his son shipped east for their safety. The two of them, with Plainclothesman Pat Patton bodyguarding, boarded the transatlantic steamer S.S. *Mystic* for a voyage of such duration that surely the prison-breakers would be run to justice by the time the boat made port anywhere.

But there was just one spellbindingly impossible coincidence after another. Beyond the fact that his seat-of-the-pants working habits often

Halifax, July 30, 1933.

forced him to resort to it, Gould always loved coincidence anyway, almost on some kind of spiritual level, and the S.S. *Mystic* straightaway hit a storm and foundered, and its survivors, who included Pat Patton, Blind Hank Steele, and young Jackie, were rescue-boated to the nearest port, which was Halifax. Which, as luck would have it, was exactly the same city that the fugitive Stooge Viller had fled to. In fact, Viller was preparing to board a liner, and he was dockside even as the shipwreck victims came in. Everyone, jaws dropping, suddenly recognized everyone else. On July 29, 1933, in a dark waterfront warehouse, Stooge Viller shot Blind Hank Steele to death before the eyes of his young son.

Viller missed his ship, remained in Nova Scotia for a time, and had another turn or two before Dick Tracy finally brought him in (see Chapter 5). As for Blind Hank Steele, his body was returned to Silver Mountain with approximately the same stately fanfare that had been accorded Lincoln's funeral train, and Blind Hank was committed to the earth and, on August 6, eulogized in a hanky-soaking theatrical aside:

Hank Steele loved his son with all his heart . . . and, while the boy's natural ties of affection were with Dick Tracy, who had first befriended him, he realized his duty was to his father . . . The old man was aware of this quality of devotion and sacrifice in the boy and it made him double proud . . . And as he learned more of Dick Tracy, the detective, he could see a reflection of the detective's character in Junior . . . He breathed his last with the realization that the boy would be in good hands. Better hands than his own . . . Hands that would guard and protect and lead . . . Tracy has a real responsibility on his hands now . . . and to him it's a happy one. He must rear this boy . . . He must teach him . . . He must build him into a fine strong man. . . .

Thus did young Jackie Steele resume his incarnation as Dick Tracy Jr. The will named Dick Tracy the boy's legal guardian and executor of Blind Hank's estate, which was set at about $200,000. There were a few mentions of a trust fund, but Gould was never particularly good about firmly accounting for every dime of the windfall, and neither Tracy nor Junior ever got observably richer.

In Blind Hank's papers, Tracy found a locket containing a faded photograph of a thin, dark-haired woman. "His mother?" the detective reflected on the long train ride home. "I wonder if she's still alive and where she is . . . I wonder . . . ?"

Junior Tracy's mother was a subject that would have to wait. Back home in the City, there were rats to stamp out. "Chee, it sure is like old times!" Junior whooped.

As a matter of fact, it was exactly like old times. In the fall and winter of 1933, Junior was severely burned while rescuing Tracy and Tess from a flaming Near-Deathtrap, and then he was kidnapped from his hospital bed by the Confidence Dolan mob, and then he was tortured for a while by Dolan and a mug named Sandy Maguire, and finally he was welded inside a steel tank and left to suffocate. Junior Tracy is easily the first small boy in all of comics to have been welded inside a steel tank.

After he resourcefully got out of the thing, he found a gun and he shot Maguire. He was not the first small boy in comics to shoot a man, but he's close to the top of that list, too.

These were digressions. The inquiry into his parentage was not yet concluded. There was still the matter of the woman in the locket.

CHAPTER 8

ALWAYS BY YOUR SIDE
Mary Steele

IT WAS HARD TO BELIEVE, BUT IN MAY 1934 Steve the Tramp broke out of prison once again. On the outside, looking for shelter, he threw in with the racketrix Larceny Lu, herself just recently paroled and now back in the chop-shop business. They were a team for a time, but the partnership abruptly dissolved when a third party possessed of a grievance opened fire on them both. Critically wounded, believing himself near death, Steve the Tramp now shared with the somewhat less bullet-struck Lu his last great secret.

"That letter I've been carrying in the lining of my clothes ..." he gasped. "It'll mean a fortune to you ... I'm done for. ..."

Lu bolted with the letter just seconds ahead of the law. Steve, for his part, regained consciousness in the prison hospital. He was alive, he discovered, but he had lost his left leg. He found this pretty funny. "A PEG LEG!" he screeched. "A PEG LEG! HAH-HAW! HAW! Haw haw haw ... haw haw haw ..." Then he grabbed surgical scissors and tried to plunge them into his heart.

Dick Tracy stopped the suicide attempt. And so did the animal Steve the Tramp pass from the strip, doomed to stare at four stone walls.

Holed up in a waterfront hideout, meanwhile, Larceny Lu was opening Steve's letter:

"To Whom It May Concern," she read. "The boy Junior, living with Dick Tracy, is not an orphan but has a mother living at Julep, California. Her name is Mary Steele. She runs a hot dog stand called the Coffee Pot. Mary Steele ran away from her husband, Hank Steele, when the boy was three months old. The man she ran away with was me. She doesn't know where the boy is because I deserted her and took the boy with me when he was two years old. Signed, Steve Brogan."

Larceny Lu's jaw dropped. "What a gold mine!" she whooped. "Steve told me the boy's father left him a two hundred grand legacy. Lu, you're going to be a wealthy woman!"

THE COFFEE POT WAS A WONDERFUL, CLASSIC specimen of '30s roadside American architecture, a five-stool lunch counter that looked exactly like a coffeepot, situated near a filling station on a highway in the California mountains, and when it was first seen on August 17, 1934, its proprietress was gratefully thanking the fates that she had begun to do modestly well with her life.

Larceny Lu and Mortimer case The Coffee Pot,
August 19, 1934.

Mary Steele among vipers, August 26, 1934.

Rebuffed in her attempt to strike up a conversation
with the long-lost little lad, September 16, 1934.
(Kids! Dick Tracy Says: Don't walk through the park
with strangers!)

Mary Steele was now a plain and hardworking woman, humbled and remorseful,
deeply shamed by her errant past, good of heart,
golden of soul. She was no match at all for
Larceny Lu and Lu's confederate Mortimer, who
had motored west to proposition her.

"I just can't believe that you really know
where my boy is," wept Mary Steele, holding
her head.

"And my dear," said oily Lu, "half of the
boy's legacy is a cheap price to pay for getting
him back, isn't it?"

"Any price is cheap for having my boy again!"
Mary cried. Straightaway she sold the Coffee
Pot for $700 and climbed into her new friends'
car for the long ride back east. And soon enough
she found out what was what. By the time they
were back in the City, Lu had relieved her of
the $700 and Mortimer was shoving her around.
Shortly after that, he was at her with a black-
snake whip, demanding she put in her custody
claim immediately.

But the subjugated Mary, despite the beat-
ings, was thinking only of her son. She had
reservations from the beginning. "Perhaps I
shouldn't make myself known," she considered, standing in the bushes across the street
from Dick Tracy's home. "If his foster father is
as fine a man as they say, perhaps the boy is
happier and has better advantages . . . What
could I offer in the way of education, training,
culture . . . ?"

She came back for days, watching and fret-
ting, and both Tracy and Junior had long since
spotted her. Tracy finally treed her and demanded an explanation. She made a clean breast
of things. "WHAT?" Tracy snorted. "Don't pull

that stuff. I want to know who you are and what your game is!" She pleaded. She wept. She produced hard evidence.

"I—apologize," said Dick Tracy, on October 1, 1934.

Tracy set out on the trail of the villainous Lu and Mortimer. "Don't breathe a word to him about me," Mary Steele begged him. "He must not know that I exist."

A day later, she vanished.

"Just one more glimpse of him before I go!" she sobbed, on her way out of town, standing in the dark alley outside Junior Tracy's window. "My boy! I forfeited my right to you years ago. But I shall always love you—I shall always be by your side—forever—"

With her last thirty dollars, she bought a Scottie pup, then walked miles through the rainy night to deliver him to the Tracy doorstep. And then she was gone.

"But who could have sent him?" Junior Tracy scratched his head in the morning. He named the dog Oscar, and Oscar was his pet for years.

MARY STEELE HAD ANOTHER ADVENTURE FOR

a time (see Chapter 9), and when Junior Tracy finally saw her again in late January 1935, something dawned on him. "She reminds me of . . . a locket," the little boy reflected.

He looked again at the faded old photograph. The young Mary Steele had been a lovely woman.

"There's no question about it, Oscar," the lad said. And then he set out to find her.

An occasional visit to Mother, March 6, 1936.

Dick Tracy had sworn never to give Mary's secret away to anyone, and he had honored the vow in full. He was released on February 4, when Junior Tracy and Mary Steele walked arm in arm into headquarters. "I want you to meet my mother," the boy introduced her.

THEY BUILT HER ANOTHER COFFEE POT, AN

exact replica of the California lunchroom, and she stayed on, and through the middle '30s she was an oft-seen figure in the strip, serving up burgers, wiping down the counter. Junior always respectfully addressed her as "Mother," and just as respectfully she recognized that he was Dick Tracy's son, not really her own, and she made no intrusions into his life. As the time wore on, she increasingly retreated from the story line. At some point, it was quietly understood that she had no further purpose. After mid-1938 she was not seen again.

Her absence was not remarked upon. It didn't seem she had gone anyplace in particular. Mary Steele was just no longer there.

Junior Tracy understands, January 31, 1935.

CHAPTER 9

GANGBUSTERS
Across State Lines with G-Man Tracy

THERE WAS, SUDDENLY AND MEASURABLY in the popular history of the American War on Crime, a shift in attention from the Al Capones who had ruled the cities. All at once there were maverick interstate bandit gangs, sticking up every bank between St. Paul and Wichita. Repeal had largely put the old Prohibition racketeers out of business, the emperor Capone had been packed off to the big house, and meanwhile the John Dillingers and the Alvin Karpises and the Baby Face Nelsons were getting out. Thereafter, while Organized Crime went about most of its affairs unobtrusively, it was the cowboys who got all the folk-hero press. Even some of the cops got in on the ride. Through 1934 and 1935, federal agent Melvin Purvis—he had nailed Pretty Boy Floyd and Ma Barker and he took most of the credit

for the Dillinger kill—was getting more headlines than bulldog crimebuster John Edgar Hoover himself, and he finally got bounced from the Federal Bureau of Investigation after the seething Hoover decided he couldn't stand his publicity-happy little subordinate for another minute. From Chester Gould's point of view, meanwhile, Melvin Purvis was getting at least as much attention as Dick Tracy was, and that certainly wasn't acceptable either.

The FBI should only have the 1930s happen to it again. Whatever the dubiousness of some of their latter-day activities, the federals were card-carrying good guys in those days, rapidly notching their gun barrels over the bullet-riddled bodies of public enemies. "Don't shoot, G-Man, don't shoot!" Machine Gun Kelly had supposedly cried in 1933, instantly fixing the word in

DAN DUNN by Norman Marsh, June 30, 1934. Dan's strip, launched in October 1933 by the small Toledo-based Publishers Syndicate, was just one of a number of lesser-circulated policeman comics that began to sprout up in the wake of DICK TRACY's success, but this one was a blatant swipe, and Chester Gould was known to be personally incensed by it. Still, the fact remained that Dan Dunn, also known as Secret Operative 48, was a fed before Dick Tracy was. In 1943 the strip was rechristened KERRY DRAKE.

the language. All at once in America, the G-Man personally represented every standard of ambition, conscience, and might.

Chester Gould looked at the headlines and he looked at Melvin Purvis and he looked at schoolboys noisily playing FBI across the land, and probably he even looked at his most hated rival in the funny papers, Norman Marsh's DAN DUNN, a shamelessly look-alike DICK TRACY knock-off whose hero was a G-Man. It appeared to be time for TRACY to get federal. Through the mid-'30s, America's Greatest Detective spent much of his time facing down the Serious National Crime Wave.

BORIS ARSON (first appearance, November 14, 1934) was exactly the sort of bearded, scowling, foreign-looking person who obviously had to be some kind of Bolshevik archfiend—he addressed his comrades as "brethren," for example, and he kept huge U.S. maps on his walls—and he looked very suspicious to Mary Steele, who, having fled from the life she couldn't face, had recently taken a servant's position in Boris Arson's household. At great peril to herself, brave Mary snatched up a roll of Vital Plans and hied them to Washington, where Chief Morton of the Justice Department took one look and then

telephoned Dick Tracy and pressed him into secret service with the Secret Service. "Your life hangs by a hair," Chief Morton told Mary Steele, sticking her into a witness protection program. "My life isn't really very valuable," said humble Mary.

Actually, Boris Arson was only a safecracker, but he had nationwide designs, and to clinch things, he had an inside man at Della-X, a strategically important nitro-glycerin-manufacturing

Public enemy Boris Arson and his interstate offenders, December 2, 1934.

A jailed Boris Arson scientifically arms himself for a crunch-out, March 14, 1935. Don't try this at home, you kids.

complex located somewhere east of Cleveland. "A limitless source of supply of blasting soup!" gasped G-Man Tracy. "Gosh!" gasped G-Man Pat Patton in stunned agreement. Staking the place out, the two feds instantly got themselves captured by Arson's confederates, but they soon enough turned the tables; Pat Patton in particular showed what he was made of when he took over the gang's transport plane at gunpoint and forced it down at Chicago Municipal. Arson and his mob were behind bars by Christmas Day. "Bah!" Arson said.

A few days later, though, he crunched out and—in a showdown greatly resembling Baby Face Nelson's Thanksgiving 1934 last stand, which occurred at just about the time Chester Gould was drawing these January 1935 strips—shot his way out of a highway dragnet and escaped in a police car. Unlike Nelson, who took a shotgun blast to the belly and who presently turned up in a ditch, Arson suffered mere flesh wounds and remained at large for several weeks, during which time he seized Mary Steele and then Near-Deathtrapped Dick Tracy in a chloroform-filled closet. Justice prevailed, though, and soon enough Arson was jailed again. "Boris Arson," cried righteous Mary, "at last I'm seeing you where you belong—in the toils of the law—YOU KNAVE!"

Bah, steamed Boris Arson, pacing his cell.

This time he might even have stayed there, had he not had a sister.

ZORA ARSON, the strip's second Female Villain and a bad customer on her own merits, tried for a time to whack Mary Steele, the woman responsible for the gang's recent woes, but everything failed, even the grenade, and finally she decided to settle for just springing Boris and beating it out of town. It was Zora who thought of the famous iodine-painted potato.

A year earlier, the bank robber Johnny Dillinger had squirreled out of a hick Indiana jail by brandishing a gun that—at least according to the popular folklore of the day's headlines—he had carved out of wood and painted black. Now, in March 1935, Boris Arson, upon receiving coded instructions from his sister, announced that he was allergic to jail food and asked if might have a hot plate and a few potatoes. "I'm partial to potatoes," he explained hungrily. "Well," Chief Brandon inexplicably decided, "it's against the rules, but . . ."

"You're pulling a dumb stunt," Tracy warned him.

"What damage can a prisoner do with a couple of potatoes?" Brandon snorted. "I'm still boss here, and if you don't like the way I'm running things . . ."

That night Arson burned his hand on his hot

plate and called for iodine. And then he carved a fat potato down into a gun and poured the iodine all over it, whereupon the thing turned metallic blue black and the prisoner used it to bluff his way free.

Gould took a lot of heat over this gag. Science-shy Mollie Slott had wanted the potato angle dropped completely, and Gould had refused to hear of it, and after the strips were in print there was a substantial brouhaha as chemists everywhere wrote in to complain that iodine wouldn't even begin to make a potato look like a real gun. Gould implacably held to his contention that certainly it would. "Please be careful in the future," syndicate chief Arthur Crawford fretfully wrote him.

In any case, Arson was loose and dopey Chief Brandon was on the spot. "OUST THE CHIEF!" cried the furious crowds in the street outside headquarters. "TAR AND FEATHER THE PO-LICE DEPARTMENT!" The mayor was demanding a probe and it looked like Brandon was through. Dick Tracy selflessly saved his chief's job. "The city needs you!" he assured Brandon. "Somebody else is going to take responsibility." He meant himself. Shortly after that—for the second time in his career—Tracy was a harness bull again, walking a lonely beat on Route 66 south of the City. He had a plan, naturally. "I WANT ARSON TO THINK I'VE BEEN KICKED OFF THE POLICE FORCE," he confided, winking. And sure enough, when the Arsons motored past him, Tracy was there to spot them, and right away he and Pat Patton gave furious pursuit in a commandeered car.

It might have occurred to Tracy to phone ahead and arrange for a roadblock, but it didn't, and accordingly the chase went on for hundreds of miles, both law and quarry periodically stopping for fuel and cursing the lost minutes, and Tracy and Patton were really just a jump behind when the Arsons finally found harbor in the Oklahoma hills with a Famous Southwestern Bandit.

CUTIE DIAMOND (first appearance, April 27, 1935) was a take on the period Okie Badman type, Pretty Boy Floyd, Clyde Barrow, that bunch, although Cutie was brighter than those dumb country boys and he'd had the foresight to in-

Cutie Diamond and the Arsons,
April 29, 1935.

stall his fortress in a mountainside behind a cageful of wildcats. He was also the kind of sharpshooter who kept a cop's bullet-plugged skull on a fence post. "And every morning I come out here and shoot through the same bullet hole just for practice! I've only knocked it off that post once in four years!" Cutie thought it was pretty cute that Dick Tracy was on his pals' trail. "Let the big shot Tracy come!" he snickered. Actually, the cats were a bit pesky, as Near-Deathtraps went, but it wasn't long before Tracy and Patton and their Pawnee Indian hill guide Yellowpony smoked out the fugitives with carbon monoxide.

In the blistering shoot-out that followed (May 14–16), Zora Arson was dropped on the spot, Cutie Diamond was mortally wounded, and Boris Arson was taken in. Yellowpony stayed behind to wait for local authorities as Tracy and Patton flew Arson back to the City. On May 22, the Pawnee looked down at the corpses of Cutie and Zora, grunted thoughtfully ("Ugh!"), and issued a classic little speech:

"Big bad gunmen end up helpless bunch of bones. Crime bad medicine! Always lead to same place, long dark night underground!"

Dick Tracy formally codified it on May 26. "They can't win!" he declared as Arson went back behind bars, forever.

"CUT" FAMON (read: "Scarface" Capone) got out of the Pacific rock called Alcoretz Federal Prison on October 2, 1935, after doing a three-

The shootout at Cutie Diamond's Oklahoma hills redoubt, and the end of Zora Arson, May 16, 1935.

year tax stretch, whereupon the famous ex-gangster went straight to the little midwestern town of Homeville (read: Cicero, Illinois) to settle down as a quiet, law-abiding citizen.

It happened that Tracy had been recently called to Homeville. Mayor Waite Wright, an old friend of Tracy's father, had pleaded with the great detective to take a leave and come shape up the little burg's corrupt police force.

And so for a few months, Tracy, with deputy Pat Patton in tow, was a bear-kicking small-town police chief, firing half his worthless department, throwing juice-bearing pols out of his office, cracking down on speeders, delivering himself of many ringing utterances on the nature of public responsibility. ("What do people want? Their children crippled and maimed? OR DO THEY WANT LAW AND ORDER?")

Chief Tracy inevitably ran into "Cut" Famon, who, already organizing a Homeville protection racket with his brother "Muscle" Famon, had imported the gunman "Bail" Gordon (first appearance, November 2) to fix Chief Tracy's trolley. Gordon, however, fast proved to be a G-Man named Jim Trailer, who thereafter joined Tracy and Patton in a climactic shoot-out (December 9–15) with "Cut" and "Muscle" and their shrieking, tommy-gun-happy old mother,

The Famon family makes a stand, December 13, 1935.

On temporary duty as Chief of Police in crooked little Homeville, big-city detective Dick Tracy made himself none too popular with the locals with all his housecleaning October 18, 1935.

Taking out "Cut" Famon, February 11, 1936. Jim Trailer handled this job; Tracy, having been wounded in a previous scrap, was near death in a hospital bed at the time.

"Maw" Famon ("Cops! How I hate cops! Feed 'em the heat!"). In a withering all-in-the-family firestorm reminiscent of the Ma Barker blow-away less than a year earlier, "Maw" and "Muscle" were mowed into pieces. "Cut" Famon escaped and continued to present problems for another few months, though when he finally fell in a terrific highway gunfight on February 11, 1936, he died very hard, eating about ninety bullets. Crime bad medicine. Always lead to same place.

Dick Tracy, meanwhile, his earlier appointment having apparently expired, was formally renamed a G-Man on December 21, 1935. His friend Trailer remained a familiar figure in the strip until 1940.

THE PURPLE CROSS GANG wore uniforms and black hoods and they had Maltese crosses tattooed into their tongues in purple ink, and when this paramilitary band of brigands showed up in October 1936, popping hick banks across the midwest and roaring out of town in fast sedans, they seemed to be some kind of secret ancient order, like the Rosicrucians or somebody, and what a laugh it was to think that some shovel-chin cop like Dick Tracy was going to get anywhere close to them.

They hit-ran Junior Tracy. They left menacing notes for sweet old Mary Steele. They tortured Jim Trailer. They locked Pat Patton in a refrigerator truck and then they sent an execution squad to storm his hospital room. The

Purple Cross Gang was seriously homicidal. Tracy, in fact, was up against the gang of his life.

Running through the greater story was a sentimental thread of subplot. There was one Purple Crosser who had had enough. His name was Florio (Baldy) Stark, and he had a tiny daughter named Angeline, for the all-overpowering love of whom all he wanted to do was go straight. "Why do we have to meet you like this?" the little girl would whimper as Baldy fleetingly rendezvoused with her in some filthy city alley whenever he could. "Why can't you come home with us like other daddies do? Will we have a Christmas tree all alone like we did last year?" This only got harder on Baldy every minute. "I want you to be proud of me when you're grown up," he would cry, and Angeline would go "Daddy! Daddy!" and they would

Purple Crossers disagree (soft version), February 3, 1937.

Captain Bronzen, February 23, 1938.

clutch each other tight and the tears would flow in rivers.

Tracy had been surveilling all this from afar and he decided against moving in as Baldy Stark left town. "You mean you're going to let that hoodlum get away?" Pat Patton puzzled. "I know when a man is talking from his heart," Tracy said. Meanwhile, the Purple Cross Gang fell apart on its own when the boss argued with his boys over the division of spoils and found it necessary to rub them all out in a St. Valentine's Day–style garage massacre (February 2–4, 1937) so horrific that syndicate editors threw out one set of strips and forced Gould to draw a considerably softer second version. And finally, in one of those Gouldesque twists of fate, the fugitive boss and the fleeing Baldy Stark bumped into one another in a distant city and Baldy found it necessary to shoot him dead. So it was that weeping Baldy Stark, mumbling his little girl's name as he was led away, was the sole member of the Purple Cross Gang to go to trial on charges.

It could have been the chair easy, but Dick Tracy, his heart touched, spoke up as a character witness for the prisoner—"in the interest of justice," he told the court—and Stark bought a mere twenty years and he collapsed to his knees in gratitude. "Daddy!" the little girl kept bleating happily, warmed by the knowledge that someday when she was about thirty she would see him again.

STUD BRONZEN (first appearance, December 11, 1937), a brutal hulk of a seafaring man, kept a salvage boat anchored at the mouth of the river, but the operation looked pretty suspicious to Dick Tracy, particularly the leg irons and chains belowdeck. "Smuggling human cargo!" Tracy accused. So began a depraved and misery-stricken white slavery yarn that put Tracy in league with the U.S. Coast Guard on the grimy riverfront, the high seas, and the lurid streets of the City's Chinatown.

Things were unpleasant from the beginning. The Mayor of Chinatown, one Mr. Chiang, civic-mindedly pledged to give Tracy every cooperation and introduced him to a Samaritan named Tau Ming, who volunteered to lead Tracy to Bronzen and who quickly ended up floating in the river instead. "We'll be wading in blood before we lick this outfit," Tracy prophesied darkly. Meanwhile, the smugglers had a fast phantom of a Mystery Ship like the Coast Guard had never seen ("Great Caesar! Disappeared into thin air! Ran away from us as if we were tied to the Brooklyn Bridge"), and CG-619 had its work cut out for it as it put to sea to run the phantom down. On February 11, 1938, those pesky Constitutional protections and freedoms mucked things up again when the pursuing Coast Guard finally caught up with Bronzen's ship and Tracy discovered he was not at liberty to blast the thing out of the water on sight. "We can't do that," his friend Chief Shellbury explained. "WHAT?" Tracy roared. "He's outside the twelve-mile limit," Shellbury sighed. "That rat," Tracy groused. Bronzen and his boys were still having a good howl over that as they took off like a flash and vanished again.

In the exceedingly grim sequence that followed, Bronzen hooked up with a tramp freighter, took aboard a stomach-turning collection of Oriental wretches, bullwhipped them and sprayed them down with disinfectant, dumped them into a hold full of fish ("Lay down there, chop sticks, that sea food ain't gonna hurt you"), and then, as the CG-619 closed in once again off the Florida coast, cold-bloodedly slaughtered them and threw them over the side. The rottenest single human Chester Gould had devised so far finally had his career cut short on March 20, 1938, when CG-619's big guns cowed the phantom into submission and Dick Tracy personally put a slug into Stud Bronzen's forehead. Gould lovingly focused in on a hard close-up as the avenging bullet proceeded to blow out the back of Bronzen's skull and spray the rear ground with gore.

Landside again, Tracy returned to sinister Chinatown to bring in the slavers' top man. To his horror, the trail led straight to the good Mr. Chiang. This Mayor of Chinatown, though, proved to be an impostor, a racketeer named May Lin who had apparently disposed of the real Mr. Chiang and taken over his life and office. The betrayed people of Chinatown, muttering in the streets, took matters into their own hands by storming police headquarters and blowgunning a poison dart into May Lin's throat.

On May 8, the late Mayor Chiang's bones were found in a secret room behind his offices. He had been chained, walled up, and left to starve to death.

JOJO NIDLE (first appearance, July 24, 1938) ran a gang of interstate freight-car thieves that was terrorizing the B&H Railroad, and he came to Dick Tracy's attention after a comic-relief amateur sleuth named Brighton Spotts found his severed finger—Jojo had lost it in a coupling mishap—and brought it into headquarters. The story was a very short one, set largely in midwestern rail yards and aboard speeding trains, but it was among Gould's most exciting period exercises, a mean, hard-driving yarn that concluded when Jojo commandeered a locomotive and fled as Tracy commandeered the big silver passenger streamliner and gave chase on the adjacent track. On September 11, Tracy overtook the bandit and drilled him.

THE '30S GANGS WERE FINISHED. SO FAR AS

that went, the '30s were finished, and criminal sociologies were changing with the times. The "crime gang" would occasionally recur, though as a somewhat higher life-form: In late 1940, Dick Tracy tangled with a professional assassin named Krome who ran an outfit called Crime Inc., which was modeled after Albert Anastasia's very efficient Murder Inc. and was no bunch of outlaw hillbillies. And in the wake of the Kefauver hearings of the early 1950s, Tracy would encounter a series of national-crime kingpins, but they would be businessmen, conducting their affairs on the principles of bookkeeping and accounting and managerial dynamics. There weren't a lot of two-gun train robbers left.

Melvin Purvis, after he left the FBI, briefly aspired to a career in the movies—indeed, it was reported at one point that he was being considered for the role of Dick Tracy in the string of Republic serials that started showing up in 1937—but it didn't work out for him, and he ended up in the late '30s as the crime-fighting spokesman for a breakfast-cereal company. In 1960, long forgotten by the world, he committed suicide.

Dick Tracy was on cereal boxes himself in the late '30s.

But then he was still a G-Man.

The B&H Railroad firefight, July 27, 1938. Badlands train bandit Jojo Nidle is at the wheel of the truck.

CHAPTER 10

POUND OF FLESH
The Grotesques

ON THE NIGHT OF OCTOBER 21, 1937, Junior Tracy found himself bound and gagged underneath a car in a closed garage, exhaust fumes spilling into his face, and it seemed that gangland was gassing him to death.

The mysterious Samaritan who was about to save his life was watching through the window, biding his time. At the proper moment, the Samaritan pulled a rod on the boy's assailants, had them take his place beneath the car, left them there to die, and sped Junior away into the dark. Junior, ordinarily the politest of boys, was having trouble finding words. The Samaritan wore his hat pulled low and his overcoat turned up high, and between the hat and the coat there were no physical features at all, only a smooth, entirely unsculptured expanse of skin. The Samaritan literally had no face.

"You haven't any eyes," Junior gulped. "Or mouth . . . or n-nose!"

"The Blank, that's me," said the Blank.

Junior turned away, horrified. The man was, well, grotesque.

THE BLANK WAS NOT THE CLASSIC SAMARITAN, so far as that went; he was a killer named Ankle Redrum who was engaged in the business of whacking former associates one by one, and his rescue of Junior Tracy had been only a random offhand kindness, and it did not long temper the shock value of his impossible and quite disturbing facelessness. After a time, the eerie, empty visage would prove to be just a sheet of flesh-colored cheesecloth, fixed in place over the remnants of a human face ruined by a shotgun blast years earlier, and the psychological implications of ruined man and deliberately uninformed mask were more than a little creepy, and the freakish Blank firmly assumed his place as a seminal figure in the evolution of a logic wherein physical wholeness and handsomeness were forever doomed to seek equation with moral goodness on Chester Gould's earth.

They were known as the Grotesques, the spellbindingly awful creatures who came to define DICK TRACY over the years, and they can readily be traced to ancient citations throughout world literature, wherein to be beauteous was to be morally good and to be ugly was to be morally dubious. To be Rumpelstiltskin, after all, was to be a child stealer, and the strip had always seen to it that such rats as Big Boy were unattractive. But ugliness in and of itself was not altogether the point, for God was a stern and wrathful God. And if ugliness were not a burden and a curse, then what indeed was ugliness? If deformity and disfigurement were not to be worn as stains, then what indeed was punishment?

Extreme physical caricature is a standard device in the cartoon arts. Major Hoople was fat, Wash Tubbs was a runt, Little Orphan Annie didn't have eyeballs, and Dick Tracy had a chin like a cinderblock. The good burgher Andy Gump appeared to be missing his entire lower jaw, and save for one unfortunately jawless reader who in the 1920s kept going to court to complain that THE GUMPS was deliberately humiliating him, Andy's condition wasn't much remarked upon, but that was Andy's strip. In

In his own nocturnal vigilante way, The Blank regards himself as an agent of justice not fundamentally dissimilar to Dick Tracy himself, November 2, 1937.

Dick Tracy's strip, Andy Gump would have been a monstrous, gurgling thing, struggling toward the formations of simple speech. That was one of the differences between DICK TRACY and most everything else in the funny papers. DICK TRACY was cruel.

But the cruelty was that of a stern and wrathful God. Chester Gould was merely His duty-sworn agent. There were aberrations in this life. Some people didn't have jaws. Some people didn't have ears. Some people rolled around on skateboards. These things happened.

THERE WAS USUALLY A GREAT DEAL OF TEE-
tering ambivalence to Gould's whole notion of the Grotesques. For the most part, they came to be identified with his celebrated rogues' gallery of villains, that great parade of twitching, jittering, limping, squinch-faced, bug-eyed, wrinkle-browed, flat-headed, rat-eared, large-shouldered moral bankrupts still to come (see Chapter 15), but then many other villains were not physically grotesque at all and many non-villains were. And always strewn through the strip, meanwhile, were decent, honest, good-souled people who happened to be maimed or misshapen. The stern and wrathful God was a tough guy to figure.

From the first, DICK TRACY associated the physically deviant and incomplete with the fundamentally foul of heart, though the earlier specimens were tentative. Three Finger Haffy, for example, a minor character from March 1932, was a common thief whose three-fingeredness had little or nothing to do with anything. While the later Gould's more fully developed black humor would certainly have seen to it that anyone named Three Finger Haffy would be either a pickpocket or a concert pianist, in this instance Three Finger was three-fingered purely for the support of his monicker. Considerably more to the point, in late 1934, was the hunch-backed scientist called Doc Hump, a mad little professor who stole neighborhood dogs and spirited them to a secret laboratory where he injected them with rabies and added them to his kennel of crazed, drooling hounds, all of them on line to someday square things with their master's enemies ("Revenge! Sweet revenge on

Doc Hump, November 1, 1934.

that whole rotten bunch! Germs! A whole test tube full of cultures!''). Doc Hump happened to be a pathetic insect rather than a professional criminal, but the point remains that his name wasn't Doc Smith.

Unlike Doc Hump's hump, The Blank's terrible faceless face was only invention, though it happened that the genuine face beneath the cheesecloth wasn't all that pretty. Whichever was the true face of The Blank, its bearer understood that he was a Grotesque, and he understood why. ''I've been an outcast from the world!'' Ankle Redrum cried after Dick Tracy ripped away the cheesecloth on January 6, 1938. ''Society wouldn't have me because of my looks! I had to beg for crusts!'' The early psychodrama was illuminating in light of the fact that as all the Grotesques came and went for years to come, it was evident that most of them had no idea of their own Grotesqueness.

THE COP-KILLER FILLING-STATION BANDIT CALLED

Scardol didn't seem to notice, and Scardol (first appearance, March 10, 1939) was as ugly as they got. Scardol was an uncommonly nasty little rat, a character who might easily have

gone on to more enduring things had he not been so unsightly that nobody could stand to look at him anymore; after just a few weeks, Gould made a point of burying him alive beneath two hundred tons of wet concrete. The strip gave Scardol one of the nicer-ringing obituaries as he disappeared beneath the onslaught: ''FATE DEALS TO ANOTHER DISCIPLE OF VIOLENCE A DOSE OF HIS OWN MEDICINE! TRULY, CRIME EXACTS ITS POUND OF FLESH!'' Later in 1939, the slobbering half-wit cousin of the baseball player Edward Nuremoh (see Chapter 11) didn't grasp that he was a Grotesque either, although that was largely because he was a half-wit. Later still in 1939, neither did the nauseating Professor M. Emirc (see Chapter 12) think to contemplate his revolting countenance. And by the spring of 1940, when the strip introduced the backward-spelled killer midget Jerome Trohs, definitively adopting the practice of giving the Grotesques names that were associated with their grotesqueries, the Grotesques were suddenly already part of the DICK TRACY collective unconscious. Chester

Ankle Redrum in the flesh, January 6, 1938.

Pat Patton and the bread thief, September 11, 1932. Initially the DICK TRACY Sundays were self-contained gag pages unrelated to the grim action of the daily strip, but even after the separate features merged into one continuing serial (on Sunday, June 5, 1932), Chester Gould still did the occasional gag-relief segment. The yaks were usually at the expense of Patton, a hopeless dumbbell in TRACY's early years.

CIGARETTE SADIE, March 12, 1933. The gag companion strip running at the bottom of the early TRACY Sunday page was a standard period dizzy-girl feature, full of hoary old vaudeville licks ("I keep racing greyhounds!" boasts the playboy; "Dear me," goes Sadie, "don't you ever get out of breath?") and quite similar to Gould's pre-TRACY Chicago material. Sadie's strip accompanied Tracy's through June 4, 1933.

At home with Dick Tracy and Junior, October 21, 1934. Junior's pup, Oscar, here joined the strip cast, having been left on the Tracy doorstep by the ever selfless Mary Steele.

Through thick and thin with Junior Tracy:

1. As gangland strikes, June 30, 1935.

2. Undercover as a bellhop, April 12, 1936. Dick Tracy seldom thought twice about sending his nine-year-old pal into lethal situations.

3. Captured by Jojo Nidle's mob, August 28, 1938.

4. Bravely cheering up blind Dick Tracy, November 13, 1938.

5. As gangland strikes again, November 24, 1940. Few nine-year-olds were ever run down by more vehicles than Junior.

The hole in Addie Gothorn's head, March 29, 1936. The sorts of newspaper editors who were inclined to complain to the Chicago Tribune-New York News Syndicate about DICK TRACY gruesomeness were particularly apoplectic over this sequence, and syndicate manager Arthur W. Crawford was constantly pleading with Chester Gould to tone the strip down. "You are sitting on top of the world now, why spoil it?" Crawford wrote on June 23. "After all, we know what our clients prefer. These things are being watched." On June 29 he wrote again: "We've got to combat the torture argument every time we offer the TRACY strip.... The objections are serious.... We have been promoting TRACY and want to send out more, but I can't use strips that haven't anything in them but torture." Gould almost never paid the slightest attention to the front-office bleatings.

Other sidekicks: (1) Chief Yellowpony, April 28, 1935. Of course derived from Gould's own Oklahoma Territory background, the colorful Pawnee was something of a fixture in the strip for a time. (2) Memphis Smith, July 12, 1936. The outrageous Period Negro was Tracy's valet; Tracy was prone to addressing him as "Snowball." (3) Bob Honor, August 9, 1936. Formerly a hood, Bob was several times useful to Tracy in the smashing of various rat gangs. (4) G-Man Jim Trailer, October 23, 1938. Tracy's federal pal showed up often in the late '30s. (5) Dennis O'Copper of the Highway Police, October 25, 1942. Dennis seemed positioned to replace an increasingly absent Pat Patton in the partner job at one point, but Pat eventually returned.

ABOVE: Newspaper advertisement for the Dick Tracy Secret Detecto Kit, May 1938. Two cereal boxtops and one thin dime bought enough amazing Secret Formula Q-11 to print 144 swell pictures. Two more boxtops bought membership in the Dick Tracy Secret Service Patrol; more bowls yet of trigger-fast food energy could win a kid sergeant, lieutenant, captain, and inspector general badges. Ask Mother now.

BELOW: Newspaper advertisement for Dick Tracy Aviation Equipment, August 1938. Via his long-running radio show and popular bijou serials, Tracy acquired parallel identities that had nothing much to do with his canonical strip persona; in the films (*Dick Tracy*, 1937; *Dick Tracy Returns*, 1938; *Dick Tracy's G-Men*, 1939; and *Dick Tracy vs. Crime Inc.*, 1941, all starring Ralph Byrd as Tracy), he was often airborne, and he spun off a fine array of keen Air Detective premiums through shot-from-guns Quaker breakfast food.

Theater poster for *Dick Tracy vs. Crime Inc.*, the last of the famous Republic cliffhangers (1941).

On the high seas with the Coast Guard, February 13, 1938. Chester Gould often joked about his drawing abilities—and indeed he was known to be inattentive to, for example, basic anatomy—but he was also capable of majesty, particularly during snowstorm scenes. This page, from the Stud Bronzen story, is one of his great beauties.

Crime and punishment. By the late '30s, Gould had perfected the celebrated bullet-through-the-forehead closeup scene that came to be an identifying signature of subsequent TRACY sendups (notably the Fearless Fosdick sequences of Al Capp's LI'L ABNER). ABOVE: Hot lead for slave trader Stud Bronzen, March 20, 1938. BELOW: Hot lead for Great Plains railroad bandit Jojo Nidle, September 11, 1938. Note caps flying surprisedly from heads in both instances.

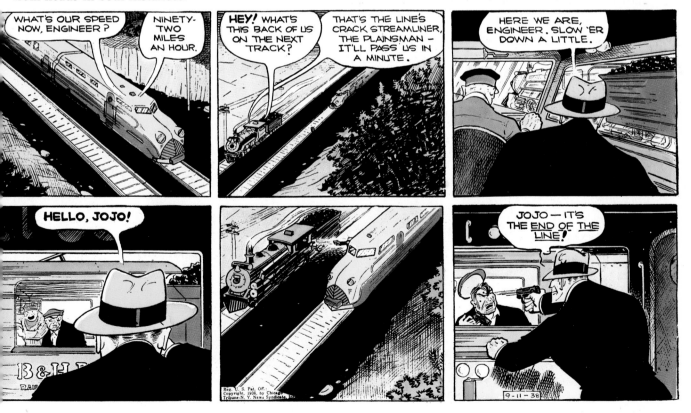

The terrible swift sword of Dramatic Irony, July 2, 1939. This famous Sunday marked the demise of Whip Chute, an ex-aviator who had been working a society con by passing himself off as a European prince.

Scardol, March 16, 1939.

Gould had started doing something akin to another comic strip altogether.

After a point, as the strip became notorious for its Grotesques and they got to be expected, increasingly there was Grotesqueness just for its own sake. Suddenly everyone had one physical defect or another, with a name to prove it—Deafy (1940) couldn't hear a thing, Little Face (1941) had a microscopic physiognomy minutely engraved into the front of a huge head, B-B Eyes (1942) had eyes the size of BBs, Laffy (1943) was forever howling like a hyena, unto the point that his jaws locked and his face froze into position, just as your mother always warned you—and the grotesquery was sometimes a little gratuitous. Chester Gould, though, held fast to True Grotesqueness throughout. For one thing, he was always fond of amputations.

STEVE THE TRAMP HAD LOST HIS LEG LONG

ago. In July 1936, a witch named Mimi had crushed her hand in an auto wreck and gangrene had set in and Mimi had gone to an underworld doc for an operating-room sequence so stomach-turning that the syndicate refused to have any part of it and ordered most of a week's worth of continuity redrawn. And after an early 1941 shoot-out, the gangland assassin

Krome also came down with a gangrenous hand and, desperately lost in a snowstorm miles out in the country, finally found himself at the mercies of a rural doctor named Codd.

"You'll be all right if you can get along without one arm," Doc Codd said matter-of-factly. "I'll call the nurse. She lives just two doors down the street."

By now it was often the case that Gould would bring in some memorable figure for nothing more than a walk-on. The horrible goofy nurse was named Mina and she was in the strip just three days (February 4–6, 1941), but she arguably ranks with the greatest Grotesques of them all, an immense, slovenly, cross-eyed boob who handled anesthetics for Doc Codd for twenty-five cents per operation. Krome thought he was having his worst nightmare, and he wasn't wrong. "Ha! Ha! He won't know nothin' in about a minute!" whooped Mina, popping the beaker.

Krome went under and Mina went about her chores. "Shall I stop pouring this stuff on the cotton now, doc?" she tittered. "Yes, we're about through," Doc Codd muttered, sawing away. "Guess I helped you out pretty good, eh?" the big oaf chortled. "Any time you get any more 'portant operations, let me know!"

That was all there was of Mina. Krome woke

Professor M. Emirc, November 21, 1939.

Krome, Doc Codd, and Mina, February 4–5, 1941. Essential grotesquery.

up with a paw gone, just another city slicker who made a bad turn somewhere, and he fled into the blizzard and before long he was frozen stiff, still staring incredulously at his stump, and this was what DICK TRACY really meant by Grotesque.

Six months later, the sparklers racketeer Little Face came down with a severe August frostbite after he got himself trapped in a cold-storage locker and he was black all over by the time he got medical attention. "Worst case I ever saw," the doc mused, digging out his knives. "I think I can save the hands. In the case of the ears, that's impossible." Worse yet, by the time Lit-

tle Face woke up inside miles of bandages, Dick Tracy was already busting him. "Bless my soul, no ears," the detective said, peeking under the wraps, clucking sympathetically.

So it went for years, one crook after another leaving some piece of himself hither and thither.

By the same token, a lovely lady named Frizzletop, a Samaritan who figured in several '40s yarns, also happened to be an amputee despite her clear and present moral rectitude, and there was nothing faintly grotesque about Frizzletop unless it happened to be the case that one-armed women gave you the willies. Nice people like Frizzletop often had it at least as rough as guys like Krome. Over the years, Gould was particularly partial to blinding them. Sometimes nice things happen to nice people in this life and sometimes they don't. DICK TRACY characters would have to learn that their creator, even as the stern and wrathful God Himself, was not necessarily the pleasantest guy to work for.

A COUPLE OF DECADES LATER, IN THE FALL OF

1959, Gould would do one of his last real Grotesques, a repulsive, ratlike creature called Rhodent who was absolutely inhuman of appearance by anyone's standard—beady little eyes, trembling little snout, twitching little whiskers—and after the Blank, he was the sole Grotesque on record who perceived this. On the lam one day, he stopped off at the home of his kindly old mother and father, the both of them entirely normal of appearance, and he studied himself for a time in a mirror. "Hey,

Mom, I want to ask you something," he said. "Do you think I look different from other people?"

"Different?" the old lady puzzled. "I should say not. You're handsome like the rest of us Rhodents. What makes you ask such a silly question?"

"Oh, I don't know," Rhodent said. "A pal once told me I looked like a rat."

"A rat? A RAT?" Mom chortled. "How ridiculous can you get? Ah ha ha ha ha." Mom and Dad both had a good laugh over the suggestion. "A rat! That's a scream! You young people!"

The reader was covering his face by now. Mom and Dad were both blind as bats, and even now Rhodent was picking Dad's pocket and beating it out the door as the old folks continued to chat gaily with him, tapping their canes around the room, bonking into the walls. "Son? Where did he go, Mom?" "Oh, son! Where are you?"

The spectacularly awful Rhodent (left, June 3, 1959). Disguising himself as a woman (right, August 7, 1959) didn't help things appreciably.

CHAPTER 11

MAD CRAWLING THING THAT LOOKED LIKE A MAN

The Bride of Nuremoh

ALL THESE YEARS LATER, MEANWHILE, THE lovely Tess Trueheart remained unbetrothed, and Dick Tracy in fact was seeing her not a great deal in the later '30s, what with one thing after another. In the summer of 1939, Tess suddenly began to keep company with another gentleman.

Tracy called at her home and sat in her parlor. "I gather that I have waited too long," he offered.

"Your CAREER is your first love," she snapped. "You haven't time to think of anything else! And after all, I'm not getting any younger. Why should I wait?"

Tracy studied a photo of his debonair, obviously very rich, and obviously much older rival. "Nice looking fellow," he said politely.

"If you came here to say MEAN THINGS—" Tess bristled.

Well, that was that. Off Tess whirled with her new beau, who really was just the sort of gent any lass would swoon for ("My car and chauffeur are outside! I want to take you shop-

ping, dearest!"). First seen on July 5, 1939, Edward Nuremoh—readers accustomed to TRACY surnamespell noted at once that this was "home-run" backward—was a sporting goods czar who lived in an opulent clifftop manse called Sandstone Heights. Years earlier he had been a sensational big league ballplayer, a man who had batted .346 for the New York Blue Sox back in '12. "And he's batting 1.000 today!" Tracy cried. "And about to get a new contract!"

Fortunately, that was about the extent of the ballpark metaphors. Tracy really was pretty desolate. "I don't blame her!" he mourned at headquarters. "He has everything—I have nothing. I'm just a detective! As unromantic as a glass of ice water. Ha! Ha! TOO BUSY! That's a good one! Too busy to nourish the most precious thing that ever entered my life." Fortunately, there wasn't much of that either; Tracy subsequently got a grip on himself and got down to the business of doing what any cop does when somebody walks with his chick: Start shadowing the guy right away and find some reason to arrest him. Shoot him even, with any kind of luck.

Tracy barely got started on the case before things started to pop. Not that the bedazzled Tess noticed much of anything, but Sandstone was a very strange place. Nuremoh shared the Gothic old pile with a scheming mother, a crabby old bedridden aunt who controlled the family fortune, and an idiot cousin the ladies kept locked in his room. And Nuremoh, moreover, was quite plainly, as they called his kind in those days, a heel. His impending marriage was a scam to establish himself as a decent family man in the eyes of old Aunt Margot, who would then leave him her millions, and who would then presently die, following which Edward would lose his new bride in some manner and then clear out with the tootsie he kept on the side, a voluptuous lass named Lola. Aunt Margot, too bad for her, made the mistake of changing her will in Edward's favor before the marriage occurred.

On July 30, 1939, Tess Trueheart married Edward Nuremoh in Aunt Margot's room at Sandstone.

"Well, Auntie Margot, aren't you going to congratulate us?" beamed Mrs. Nuremoh, bending over to kiss the figure in the bed, who was at this point stiff as a board. "EEK!" Mrs. Nuremoh jumped.

"Ye gods!" gaped Margot's attending physician. "Must have been dead for hours!"

"No WONDER she didn't congratulate you," someone offered.

Well, it was no heart attack. Aunt Margot had a bullet in her, actually. Arriving officers quickly found the death gun in the imbecile cousin's room. "I heard him threaten Margot myself!" Edward shook his head. "But I never dreamed he'd—" The little softbrain was led away in cuffs, wibbering happily. Back in the City, Dick Tracy was ordered up to Sandstone to take over the case.

Having just been married in front of a corpse, Mrs. Nuremoh was already going to pieces. "Oh, Di—" she blubbered as Tracy showed up.

"Detective Tracy is the name," Tracy introduced himself to the woman he had known once upon a time. "I'm from headquarters. Will you have the butler show me the death room, please?"

EVEN IN HER DAZE, TESS TRUEHEART NUREMOH

had spent too much time around Scientific Crime Detection not to spot the clues that unmistakably pointed the finger of guilt at her husband. Enlightenment came to her through the fog. Why, the balls of mercury in Edward's shoe could only have come from the fever thermometer in Margot's room that of course had been shattered when—

"Yes—I SHOT HER," he sneered. He began to laugh like a maniac. And then he turned on Tess, murder in his eyes.

"This is all a NIGHTMARE!" she screamed. "A HORRIBLE GHASTLY DREAM." She turned and fled—to the Sandstone cliffs, high above the lake, her demented husband on her heels, flinging rocks at her head. Fallen into a ravine,

The wedding of Tess Trueheart, July 30, 1939.

The widowing of Tess Trueheart Nuremoh, August 23–24, 1939.

crawling wretchedly through the mud, dodging the hail of stones, gallant Tess tried one last time to save her marriage. "Edward," she cried, "my death won't solve our troubles."

What solved everything was the paramour Lola, an innocent lass who had never been part of the death plot against Aunt Margot and who, having read about Margot in the papers, had rushed to Sandstone to interfere with destiny. "I must STOP HIM before it's too late," she wept, climbing the rocks, tearing through the brambles, just minutes from the killing field above. Edward Nuremoh had given up on stones. He had a gun leveled at his sobbing, beaten bride. His finger squeezed the trigger. At that precise instant, Lola crashed into mid-frame, and took the bullet squarely between the shoulder blades.

"What have you done?" Tess gasped.

Edward Nuremoh blinked and straightened.

Unexpectedly, for a moment, the loony melodrama achieved a kind of stately grandeur.

"I've run a madman's course," Nuremoh said quietly. "I've reaped the harvest."

He paused to consider things.

"You can never forgive me," he offered Tess. "But you can forget me," he pleaded. "Forget a mad crawling thing that looked like a man! Forget, like a poisonous dream, the cruel wretch that tortured you."

Edward Nuremoh adjusted his tie and looked toward the lake a hundred and thirty feet below him.

Then he lifted his dead beloved and turned toward the cliff.

"Tell them," he cried over his shoulder, "Lola and Edward were united—forever!"

Back at Sandstone, the gabbling Tess was comforted by solid old Pat Patton. "We'll get you out of here just as soon as Tracy comes back," Patton comforted her.

"Tracy?" The ruined girl held her head. "Tracy?" Her eyes glazed over. "That name sounds familiar, like—sun—stars—sky—"

WHEN SHE CAME OUT OF THE SOUP A FEW weeks later, she threw herself at Dick Tracy's feet.

"I'm not worthy of your touch, nor even a word from your lips," she bawled into a hanky. "Just to kneel here is all I ask."

In some other comic strip, this would have been the old clinch scene. Dick Tracy, however, gave Tess a motorcycle escort home, saw her to her door, and tipped his hat.

"Words can't express my thoughts," Tess managed.

"It's all right," Tracy said. "Goodbye, now."

Then he was off on the trail of a gang of fur thieves, scientifically taking plaster casts of tire prints.

The Nuremoh marriage was annulled, all records expunged. Dick Tracy and Tess Trueheart continued to see one another sporadically as the time went by, and the girlfriend was never known to gripe much about anything ever again. At Christmas 1942, the two of them found occasion to have dinner together. "Gosh, Tess," it struck Tracy, "I haven't seen you since last summer!" "I know, darling," she said fondly.

CHAPTER 12

THEY THOUGHT THEY COULD KEEP ME A HOODLUM

The Atonement of Stooge Viller and Steve the Tramp

"**P**ARDON ME FOR MENTIONING IT,**"** Tracy leered at the bagged Nat the Fur King on October 23, 1939, "but I guess you've noticed—YOU CAN'T GET AWAY WITH IT."

It was the old story. Crime doesn't pay, you can't win. The newspaper account of Nat the Fur King's arrest didn't much impress Inmate 2603 up at the State Penitentiary. "Fine," he shrugged. "I go out—he comes in! I'll will my nice clean cell to him. I won't need it after today."

"Hm!" Chester Gould penciled in at the bottom of that panel. "Who IS this 2603? His face looks strangely familiar."

Certainly it did. It looked a lot like Edward G. Robinson's face is what it looked like. The evil Stooge Viller had done his time. "I don't want to see you come through that door again," said the prison warden, shaking Viller's hand.

"Free!" gloated Stooge Viller, looking around

him at 1939. "Everything seems about the same," he mused.

Tracy spotted him in a barbershop. "STOOGE VILLER!" the detective exclaimed, rubbing his jaw. "The only hoodlum I ever sent up the river who's come back."

That wasn't precisely correct—Stooge Viller himself had already come back once already, after his '33 prison bust-out, and so had Steve the Tramp—but this was the first Great Return, after a passage of some few years. The strip was to get more seriously interested in character resurrections later down the road, most notably in the case of Mumbles, who returned from the dead in 1955, eight years after Gould had drowned him (see Chapter 31). In the fall of 1939, though, Stooge Viller's reappearance was quite unexpected.

At headquarters, his comeback was the subject of some discussion.

"That mug's washed up, Tracy," said Pat

Stooge Viller out of stir, October 26, 1939. State law had evidently regarded Blind Hank Steele's murder as a six-year felony.

Patton. "The day of the big hoodlum is over."

"There's one thing you should never become in this business," Tracy said. "That's soft in the head." He gave Pat a friendly tap. "Once a hood," he said, "always a hood."

EVEN GIVEN HIS STARKLY BLACK-AND-WHITE

worldview, Chester Gould was fascinated by the Criminal Type and he regularly pondered its motives. As behavioral theorism goes, many of the meditations were melodramatic twaddle—DICK TRACY, after all, was a funny-papers thriller, not a journal of medicine—but Gould did have things to say about the Criminal Psyche in America, and his strip was often a useful primer on the nature of dysfunction and rage and sometimes even of redemption. Most TRACY villains were merely flat-out bad guys, to the core and forever irredeemably, and others were not necessarily. Tracy had never had any use for the contemptible Stooge Viller, for example ("Steeped in his own egotism and fired by his own cleverness!" it had been observed of Stooge in 1933), but he appeared to regard crazed old Doc Hump as something pitiable, even though Hump was loosing savage rabid dogs on him ("Driven to madness by imagined wrongs!"). Toby Townley's single misstep off the high road in 1935 cost her a period of blindness, and she was the stronger for it. In those days, you were grateful for these character-building lessons. A wastrel rich boy named Johnny Mintworth got mixed up with gangsters in 1937, and they shot him to death, and it was explained that Johnny had

"paid the price for living a loose, careless life. He realized he had paid his debt to society before he died—and he died happily!" A hood called Danny Supeena (1937) saw the whole sorry story as he lay on his deathbed and wheezed out his final words: "I—had—a—great—future when I . . . was young . . . But—I . . . thought I was smart . . . I . . ." The tormented madman Edward Nuremoh, as seen in Chapter 11, suicided his way to moral radiance.

So the once-a-hood stance was perhaps Tracy at his more ungenerous. Indeed, he had been known to hold other views: In the summer of 1936, he had personally insisted on attempting to rehab a thoroughly unlikely subject named Lips Manlis, who had tried to blow him up in an elevator. Letting bygones be bygones, Tracy put him to work as a useful and productive citizen and renamed him Bob Honor, and the onetime powerful gang boss, overwhelmed by such a show of kindness, proceeded to find dignity in his humble nightwatchman's position and resolved to be the best humble nightwatchman he could possibly be. ("Water! Soap! They wash away old dirt!" Bob Honor would cry happily, furiously scrubbing his hands. "They thought they could keep me a hoodlum!") The program had, of course, already been observably successful in the case of thieving little Junior Tracy, whom Tracy could just as easily have jugged.

But it was hard to argue about a guy like Stooge Viller.

OUT OF STIR MERE HOURS, STOOGE VILLER

went into the underworld hardware-supply racket in partnership with an ugly little gnome scientist named Professor M. Emirc—that was "crime" spelled backward—who had come up with such criminal-friendly products as a pocket-size acetylene torch, an automotive attachment that would spray tear gas at pursuing motorcycle policemen, and most ingeniously of all, a gun that would fire unmarked bullets, the better to outwit the science of ballistics. "I can market your products!" Viller assured the professor. And business was brisk, and life was good.

Viller, though, like many another rat before

him, was obsessed with paying off Dick Tracy, and before long he had the detective in a Near-Deathtrap, swinging from a rope deep down in an abandoned well miles out in the country. "Flatfoot, you and I locked horns six years ago and you won!" Viller chortled. "Today it's different!" He was going to let Tracy think things over. "After he hangs a few days," he explained to his boys, "I'll come back and cut the rope."

And he was also obsessed—Stooge Viller's sole claim to humanity—with winning the love of the small daughter who had long been a stranger to him.

He could have taken a lesson from Baldy Stark. Nothing like a brat to wreck a sweet racket.

SHE HATED HIM. SHE WANTED NOTHING TO DO

with him or his dirty gangster money. "You promised Grandma and me you'd go straight," she wagged her finger at him. Her name was Binnie (first appearance, December 2, 1939) and she actually carried strychnine so she could kill herself in the event he ever darkened her doorstep.

Out in the country, desperate Dick Tracy had freed himself from the well by smashing his wristwatch, using the mainspring to saw loose his bound hands, and then climbing the rope topside. Now, exhausted, lost, stumbling through the woods, the detective collapsed unconscious in a creekbed, and that's where one of Girl Scout Troopmaster Tess Trueheart's little charges found him while on a field trip one day.

In the hospital, Tracy blinked at the woman he hadn't seen since the Nuremoh interlude of the past summer, and the two of them had their first intimate words.

"What's that uniform you're wearing?" he inquired.

"It's my scout uniform," she said.

As luck would have it, it was a scout named Binnie Viller who had saved his life. Tracy made the name and pressed the point. The little girl backed away, shaking her head. "I have no family—" She burst into tears of bitter mortification. "Stooge Viller is my—"

He embraced her. "It's going to be our secret," he whispered. "You're my sweetheart from now on," he said. And then they went for ice cream.

Stooge Viller read about it in the paper. "DETECTIVE FOUND DAZED IN COUNTRY RAVINE. DISCOVERY MADE BY GIRL SCOUT." He gasped. "Ye gods! My—my—own—DAUGHTER!"

The former Lips Manlis (left, May 20, 1936) gets another shot at good citizenship (center, May 25, 1936) and law-abidingly proceeds to round up his ex-buddies for benefactor Tracy (right, July 4, 1936).

Father's Day, January 2, 1940.

"YES, THE FINGER OF FATE WRITES STRANGELY," Gould noted in a dramatic aside to the reader.

MADDENED BY THE LITTLE GIRL'S REFUSAL TO

love him, flummoxed by the strange writing of the finger of fate, Viller went slowly to pieces. One morning the stewbum has-been woke up and found his entire mob pointing rods at him. "You WERE the boss," they announced.

Out of gangland he trudged, straight to the house of his daughter, and kidnapped her.

The late Stooge Viller,
January 7, 1940.

"I don't want to BE WITH YOU," she shrieked.

"I'm turning over a new leaf, honey," he pledged.

That lasted just until wrathful Dick Tracy stormed Viller's apartment to reclaim his little sweetie. Viller tried a gun first, but Binnie batted it from his hand. Then the detective and the rat went scuffling, across the room, out to the fire escape, where suddenly Tracy lost his footing and went over the rail, and Stooge Viller savagely closed in for the kill.

Trembling, tears pouring down her face, the little girl picked up the gun and pointed it.

"You can't shoot your own father!" he bellowed as Tracy hung sixteen floors over the street.

And she didn't, really. The gun went off accidentally, when he threw her a swift kick.

Stooge seemed a little puzzled, a little amused. "I had it coming, I guess," he reflected, clutching his side. Down to the street he stumbled, across the busy way, to the river's edge. "It's plenty deep. . . ." he considered. Halfway across, things went black on him. "Much better . . ." he murmured, but Tracy was already pulling him out by the scruff of his neck.

Little Binnie Viller made the last trip to the hospital, sobbing her eyes out as she sat in the backseat with Dick Tracy. "Oh, Mr. Tracy, why does any man have to be like my father? Why? Why? Why?"

He held her close. "I wish I knew," he said.

At the bedside, father and daughter said goodbye. "It's all right, kid," he assured her. He held her close, too. "I'll go back to the big house now and stay out of your life forever," he said. "There's just one thing I want to tell you, Binnie—as you grow older, STAY STRAIGHT no matter what happens. . . ."

Stooge Viller coughed. "You'll be a grown woman—maybe married and with a family when I see you again . . . Whoever you pick, be sure he's on the level . . . You'll . . . you . . ."

The little girl was taken from the room.

"Well, flatfoot, are you satisfied?" Viller snapped.

"Yeah," Tracy said. "Are you?"

Viller closed his eyes. "I will be," he nodded, "if you'll keep an eye on her. She'll . . . need . . . your kind . . . of watching. . . ."

"Do you mean that, Stooge?" Tracy said softly.

"You're okay, flatfoot," whispered the dying man.

They shook hands, the rat and the plainclothesman, at the end of things.

"Always tell her . . ." Stooge gurgled, "I'm in the . . . big house. . . ."

And then, on Sunday, January 7, 1940, Stooge Viller fell dead.

Dick Tracy took off his hat.

"He's right," Tracy decided. "I'll stand by Stooge's last request. I won't tell Binnie the truth."

"Mr. Tracy," the little girl pondered when she was last seen on January 8, "are all penitentiaries horrible places where nobody can escape?"

He kept his hat on. "Not for everyone," he said.

THE CIRCLE CLOSED ON SEPTEMBER 17, 1941,

when shambling, peg-legged old Inmate 2704 was handed his walking papers. "You've been a model prisoner," the warden said. "I've seen a great change come over you since you came here. Good luck and goodbye!"

"I'm just beginning to live," Steve the Tramp replied. He hobbled out into free air clutching a Bible, and he went straight to the nearest church, and he fell to his knees in prayer.

Steve went on national radio to tell his story to the young folks. "To all the boys and girls in America," he said, "I want to repeat, YOU CAN'T WIN AT CRIME."

Dick Tracy dug into his own pocket to set the old man up in business, a streetcorner fruit stand where he labored honestly from dawn to dusk. Junior Tracy often came around to lend him a hand. That was the way Steve left the strip for good, in the autumn of 1941, the tramp and the kid cheerfully working alongside one another amidst the pears and the plums and all the bounty and grace of the earth.

Steve the Tramp starts over again, September 25, 1941.

CHAPTER 13

KID'S BEEN THROUGH SOME KIND OF AN ORDEAL, ALL RIGHT

Mary X and the Innocent and the Damned

IT IS ONE OF THE MOST MEMORABLE OF ALL the classic DICK TRACY passages, a fleeting, dreamlike moment from late March 1940: The girl is an amnesiac. Someone has hit her on the head. She has an unfocused memory of something terrible. She furrows her brow. She leaps from the car. She lurches uncertainly into the swamp and she plunges her hand into the water and momentarily she comes up with a coat sleeve. There is a man's hand. There is a man's body. Her eyes roll. She sags. "I—I don't remember," she wails. "It's no use—it's no use—"

This was Mary X. No name, no history, no clear memory of the events she began to imagine she might have witnessed. The scenario has been a staple of crime literature before and since, but almost never has the claustrophobic desperation of struggling to regain something lost been more powerfully depicted than in this brief lagoon sequence from a mysterious

story where nothing much ever connected and nothing much was ever explained. Dick Tracy had found her sprawled in the backseat of his car. She had no idea how she got there. "My name?" she murmured, rubbing her head. Tracy took her to dinner, and suddenly someone was shooting at her. Who? What? When? Where? Why? Who knew? Mary X wept.

IN DICK TRACY'S BLEAK WORLD, DREADFUL things regularly happened to people who deserved better, people who had committed no offense against anyone, people who just got in the way, and that was the point. This was a very mean comic strip, and when the bullets started spraying, you really couldn't expect that everybody who got whacked was really going to have it coming. From the beginning, Chester Gould's strip had been full of Innocents whose misfortune it was to be in the wrong place at the wrong time. That's the way it went for old Emil Trueheart, who was only eating his dinner. That's the way it went for the cabdriver who got caught in the cross fire in November 1931 during Dick Tracy's first shoot-out. He never had a name and he never had an obituary. Suddenly he was just a corpse in the street.

As Gould honed his Innocents as standard strip Types, they began to acquire names and faces and warm-blooded human lives, and a reader could care about them by the time he gleefully snuffed them or maimed them or merely started tormenting them. The first of the true Innocents was probably Della, who had been Blind Hank Steele's faithful Negress cook in 1933 and who Dick Tracy himself fatally shot in a mistaken encounter during the manhunt for Steve the Tramp. Della died in her bed, poignantly, beneath a portrait of Abraham Lincoln. "Accidental victim of gunfire during the attempted capture of a criminal," the

Toby Townley; blind but redeemed, September 18, 1935.

coroner reported matter-of-factly, and that was that. Under the circumstances, the shooting had not been entirely unjustifiable—Della had shot at Tracy first—and Tracy was not seen to lament the incident overmuch. Still, it was kind of unfortunate.

Another Innocent, after a fashion, was the writer Jean Penfield. Another was Mary Steele, the simple soul who wanted only happiness for her son and had nothing but misery rained upon her for it. Another was Toby Townley, although Toby (1935), like Della, was not wholly blameless in the overall scheme of things. Hapless Toby was a fragile little blonde who was dumb enough to be dating a crooked bank teller and playing the horses with cashbox greenbacks she had borrowed from her employer, Coffee Pot proprietress Mary Steele. She was no more criminal than that, but she went to prison on a trumped-up charge of killing a policeman. The reader knew she had nothing to do with it and Tracy knew she had nothing to do with it, but all efforts to prove her guiltless became immaterial when Toby got herself caught

Random Victim: The louse Steve the Tramp persuades Blind Hank Steele's guileless cook, Della, to bushwhack Dick Tracy, April 20, 1933. Della—a fairly typical specimen of the day's funny-papers blacks—was shot to death by Tracy when she opened fire on him.

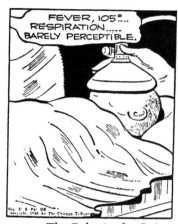

The Baby in the Suitcase, February 29–March 1, 1940. Tracy, seen here praying to the Stern and Wrathful God, had treated the desperately ill child with an illicit serum and now faced a manslaughter indictment if the kid died.

up in a riot at the women's prison and was left blinded by tear gas. Shortly after that, Tracy successfully cleared her of the charges, and she was free, but she was still blind.

Johnny Mintworth (1937) also brought much of his misfortune upon himself. Johnny was a foolish young playboy who liked fast women, and suddenly he found himself in the middle of a scheme to spring one of them from jail, and before he knew it, he was a fugitive. Hungry, broke, on the lam, Johnny fell into the clutches of an insurance-fraud gang that kept beating him up and breaking his arms and put-

ting through medical claims on him. The weak and irresolute Johnny rallied at the last, resolved to help Tracy bring his torturers to justice, and they straightaway shot him to death. Johnny had finally made a man of himself, but on the other hand he was still dead.

Increasingly Gould demonstrated a taste for sticking it to kids. Little Angeline Stark and little Binnie Viller had been luckless enough to have drawn rats for fathers, and plainly they were going to pay for that all their lives. In early 1940, Tracy found an infant boy abandoned in the luggage section of a large department store; the Baby in the Suitcase, as he came to be called, quickly proved to be the grandson of a quack medical experimenter who stole the tyke back and used him as a guinea pig in an alarming germ-injection program and nearly killed him. Indeed, the Abandoned Baby in general would go on to become a distinctive subspecies of Innocent.

So it went in the great morality play of life as DICK TRACY noodled increasingly with the stern notions of punishment and accounts payable and the distribution of destiny's freight. Crime, by God, couldn't win, but beyond that almost nothing was ever fair. Della was buried sweetly. Johnny Mintworth was eulogized. Binnie Viller was packed off for maybe a chance at some kind of future. The Baby in the Suitcase was restored to his mother, who was found to be

Mary X in the marsh, March 28–29, 1940.

none but Toby Townley herself, reprised after an absence of a few years, her sight at this point regained. You try to make things bright where you can.

MARY X (FIRST APPEARANCE, MARCH 10, 1940)

had literally done nothing at all. She merely knew too much about something and she couldn't imagine why. "Kid's been through some kind of an ordeal, all right," Tracy shook his head as Mary X fell into troubled sleep. It was a terrifying story, meandering into dead ends with the logic of black dreams, until suddenly it crystallized in the lagoon, when Mary, blinking, groping, assailed by frightening images, put her hand into the waters and all at once came up with the horrible dead human arm.

She had, of course, witnessed a murder. The dead man was a manufacturer named Freez, and in his machine shop there was plenty of evidence to pin the killing on his business partner Mason. Confronted, Mason made another swipe at Mary X's life and succeeded only in undeleting her memory. Her name was Leota Sunny, she had once been Mason's secretary, and that wrapped the story. The girl who had suffered as Mary X was ultimately rewarded with a job as a big-band singer and perhaps she went on to become a star.

Late in 1947, an Innocent named Kiss Andtel, held in cruel captivity by the murderous Mumbles (see Chapter 15), also ended up as a big-band thrush. Generally, though, the Innocents were less fortunate. A thrill-seeking girl named Ginger Ferret (1941) happened to be riding with the thug Trigger Doom when he cracked up his car, and she burned to death. A waitress named Clara Orlin (1941) made the mistake of spotting a fugitive killer, and he drowned her. The Summer Sisters, May and June (1944), who were pickpockets and really only Semi-Innocents, accidentally crossed the Brow (see Chapter 15), and they were drowned, too. The actress Snowflake Falls (1944) was the drugged prisoner of the confidence man Shaky (see Chapters 15 and 17), and she never recovered from it. In 1946, a sickly old widow made a simple trip to the drugstore and was shot down by the rotten Gargles (see Chapter 15). In 1953, a rich girl

named Cynthia Smithly accidentally stumbled into a murder plot and was stabbed to death. There were many of these people. Their shriekings got to be pretty unpleasant things to have to listen to.

And the point was still the same as it had been years earlier, when old Emil Trueheart picked up his dinner fork and was suddenly dead on the floor, and when a passing cabdriver drove into a hail of bullets and was suddenly dead in the street. It's just a crummy world. These things happen.

Mary X and Benny-Goodmanesque band leader Rudy Seton, March 14, 1940. Seton gave Mary a job when all her trials were over.

CHAPTER 14

I'M GOING TO TAKE YOUR NUMBER, BRIGHT EYES

Dick Tracy at War

THE HEROES OF THE FUNNY PAPERS WERE just as surprised as everyone else when it was announced on Sunday, December 7, 1941, that the Japanese had just attacked the U.S. Navy at Pearl Harbor, and many of them were obliged to drop whatever they'd been doing and go sign up with Uncle Sugar's band. From the early weeks of 1942 forward, many established strips began to transform themselves into military features. Prizefighter Joe Palooka joined the armed services right away. So did the flyboy Smilin' Jack. So did Skeezix Wallet, who did serious grunt time in Italy while his girl Nina Clock hit the production lines and became the comics' foremost Rosie the Riveter. Even Barney Google's little pal Snuffy Smith went off to boot camp. Even Tarzan, swinging from trees in the jungles of Africa, started rounding up Nazi butchers. Prince Valiant was one of the few not called, but he lived in another century.

Dick Tracy wasn't called either, but only mutts were staying out of the fracas altogether, and while the war was never a major presence in the strip, Chester Gould saw to it that Tracy held up his end of things over the next four years. From Tracy's point of view, that meant taking on racketeers, profiteers, and the occasional fifth columnist. First, though, he had to get out of the caisson.

AS NEAR-DEATHTRAPS WENT, THE CAISSON, IN which Gould at his drawing board had stuck Dick Tracy at about the time Pearl Harbor was getting hit, was one of the great imponderables. Tracy, of course, regularly fell into terrifically inescapable situations, and as Gould boasted to *Life* magazine in 1944, "we never know how we're going to get him out. If we worried about that, we'd never get him in." Now, staring at his developing strips of mid-January 1942, Gould suddenly realized he'd put Tracy into a dilly and that he had absolutely no idea how Tracy was possibly going to get out of it this time.

A rat named Jacques had dumped Tracy down a deep caisson tube near a new suspension bridge, and then he had dumped a ten-ton boulder in after him. The rock, slightly larger than the hole, was now slorching its way inexorably downward through the soft clay, inches and feet at a time, and now it was practically atop Dick Tracy and surely the detective was going to be crushed like a bug. Even if rescuers arrived at once, how were they going to dig around the boulder without sending it crashing straight down? What to do? Chester Gould, having thoroughly sucker punched himself, didn't have the slightest idea.

The story goes that Gould's personal solution was the ultimate deus ex machina: the Hand of the Cartoonist. Even as with the dream so excruciatingly baffling that the dreamer simply stops it in its tracks and starts over, Gould actually proposed to interrupt the no-exit story with an announcement on the order of "Okay Gould, you've really done it this time!" and simply lift Tracy out of the caisson with his own fingers and then resume the action. The story also goes that Captain Patterson himself flatly refused to let Gould get away with this—a laudable call, considering that this was, to be sure, as bad as ideas ever get—and ordered his errant cartoonist to think of something, anything, fast. As it turned out, what had been a caisson was now suddenly a ventilator shaft for a high-

way tunnel, and Tracy found that he was crouching on boards and he heard workmen below him, and he pounded and pounded, and the workmen sawed him free from beneath seconds before the big rock slammed down. Actually, it wasn't all that unconvincing. Plot-wise, Gould had done worse than this.

Freed from the perplexities of the caisson, Dick Tracy shot Jacques to death for all the trouble and then, on February 15, 1942, met his first wartime rat. This was a derby-hatted little fellow who had tiny little eyeballs, and he entered the story line by reason of the fact that he was Jacques's revenge-bent brother, and his name was B-B Eyes.

INTERNATIONAL AFFAIRS WERE NOT REALLY
among Dick Tracy's larger concerns. In the fall of 1938, he and his G-Man pal Jim Trailer had tangled with a character named Karpse, who manufactured poison iso-cyanide gas in a South Dakota installation disguised as a dairy-feed factory and secretly sold it to an apparently hostile nation called Bovania. (The precise nature of diplomatic relations was less than clear; in the summer of 1939 the Bovanian princes Jerg and Nestor visited U.S. shores and were feted as vaguely Balkan royals who didn't seem to have anything to do with global conditions.) And in the fall of 1940, Tracy and Trailer had gone up against the unspecific European na-

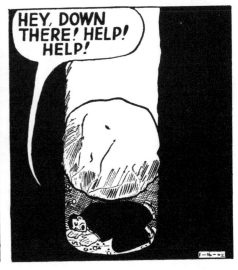

The caisson, January 13–16, 1942.

Karpse, poison-gas dealer to hostile nations, October 8, 1938.

tionalist witch Black Pearl, who was developing and testing a remarkable flying submarine that had drawn the attention of the U.S. government. Beyond those two personalities, the gathering clouds of war hadn't particularly gathered over DICK TRACY at all, and it was B-B Eyes who officially brought the strip into the Big One.

What was hitting home on the home front, so far as the average Joe was concerned in the war's early days, was that suddenly it was tough to get simple gasoline and rubber tires for the family heap. All at once the nation's daily habits were regulated by ration cards, and huge black markets sprouted up overnight. B-B Eyes, it developed, was a tire bootlegger. "We need more men to grind off serial numbers!" B-B Eyes would cry as his busy garage operation whirred efficiently away. It was, in fact, B-B Eyes' car that tipped off Tracy to the racket. "Doesn't it seem strange to you that in times like these, B-B's car should have brand new tires?" Tracy puzzled. "They're HOT TIRES, all right, Tracy!" Pat Patton nodded. Thus did Tracy and Patton plunge into the bootleg-tire underworld in the dark spring of 1942.

"Say, bud," Tracy whispered to a filling-station attendant. "Confidentially, where can a fellow pick up—er—a couple of tires without a priorities order?"

"Listen, brother," bristled the gas jockey on March 11. "You say that again and I'll call a cop. You're talking about BREAKING THE LAW!"

"Well, now, wait a minute," Tracy tried, but the gas guy, a one-day walk-on who obviously stood for everything decent and vigilant about the United States of America, was already whipping out his notepad.

"I'm going to take your number, bright eyes!" he snapped. "There's a WAR on and it's fellows like you we've got to keep our eyes on!"

"Hm!" said Dick Tracy, throwing a knowing grin at the reader as everyone burst into applause.

The trail shortly led to B-B Eyes' garage, where the tire gangster captured both Tracy and Patton by tipping over hundreds of hot tires on them and then inflicted upon the partners one of the most bizarre Near-Deathtraps on record. He encased them in wax cylinders. The plan was to slide them down a chute into the path of a train, but it was such a pointlessly complicated Near-Deathtrap that they freed themselves within minutes and presently had the whole gang on ice.

Gould had lately begun to find wonderful new ways besides bullets to kill off his rats. In July 1940, Jerome Trohs had been scalded to death in a hot shower he couldn't get out of. That September, the mystic swami Yogee Yamma had been incinerated in a hotel-room fire. The gangland executioner Krome had frozen stiff in a snowstorm. Now, on April 12, 1942, B-B Eyes staged a breakaway, flung himself over the side of a river bridge, and landed in a garbage scow full of wet black sludge. "Blub! Help!" were

At Black Pearl's proving grounds, October 17, 1940.

Buying tires in difficult times, March 12, 1942.

his last words as he was swallowed up by the muck in a spectacular finish. Oblivious to its passenger, the scow dumped its load in the harbor. And B-B Eyes was last seen on the bottom, his body stuck fast inside a rubber tire.

BY THE SUMMER OF 1942, IT WAS EVIDENT

that there were worse things to the war than tire rationing. This was somberly brought home when, in July, the wild-haired, one-armed Frizzletop arrived in the strip. Frizzletop had been an army nurse and she'd caught it in the Philippines bombing raids. Now she was home, medicaled out. "I can take it!" the game girl snapped at Tracy when he sympathized. "Just as thousands of others can take it!" It was with Frizzletop, a regular companion of the period, that Tracy met his next wartime rat, the famous, wrinkle-ravaged, profoundly classic villain called Prune Face.

Prune Face (first appearance, October 23, 1942, and initially addressed as "Boche") was a saboteur infiltrator, a trafficker in poison gas, a human so loathsome that at one point he strangled a friendly small dog just so he could cop the animal's winter sweater and cover up his telltale visage with it. He had a fifth-column network in place, he had a Japanese accomplice named Togo, he had a small helicopter in which he bounced from rooftop to rooftop, and he was the most physically repellent creature the strip had seen yet, a landmark Grotesque, miles beyond such relative cover boys as Little Face and B-B Eyes. Hardly likely though it was

that such a striking figure would be much of a secret agent, Prune Face gave Dick Tracy a good run for several months, even despite the fact that he was rooming at Mother Trueheart's boardinghouse. Mother Trueheart had been figuring in the strip from time to time since Big Boy's rats had left her a widow woman years earlier, and she had crossed paths with several villains. In December 1938, for example, she had given a job to war profiteer Karpse. The woman had a real gift for taking in poison-gas dealers.

B-B Eyes, February 4, 1942.

Old Mother Trueheart was a pretty game girl herself. "Tess and Tracy think I'm an old fogey!" she winked at Junior Tracy, enlisting him in a secret scheme to shadow the suspicious new roomer and get the goods on him. Prune Face saw through the plan and socked the old lady good. Then he set out to kill Junior. And on Christmas Eve 1942, two steps behind the kid, Boche slipped on the winter ice and broke his leg.

On Christmas Day, Chester Gould delivered his greeting of the season, by now an annual tradition, to his readers. "Good cheer this Christmas Day, folks," Gould wrote, in the thick of the blackest time the United States of America had ever known. "Everything's going to be ALL RIGHT."

IN A DRIVING SNOWSTORM IN EARLY FEBRU-

ary 1943, Dick Tracy and the law cornered the crippled Prune Face in a broken-down old mansion and froze him out of it, and that was the end of Boche. "Crime against nations always loses out in the end!" Tracy lectured the Axis agent's beaten, frostbitten form as the blizzard flew.

Thereafter, Nurse Frizzletop went to work for a wealthy patroness named Potter who had public-spiritedly decided to convert her estate into a day-care center for the small children of war workers, and Dick Tracy met Myrtle Wreath.

Ms. Wreath was a hardworking truck driver, a divorced mother scrambling to rear her son as best she could against the harassments of her ex-husband, the no-good gambler Nifty Wreath. "A free nursery!" she breathed when she heard of Mrs. Potter's project. "Just the place for Johnny." The ex-husband kept following her around, muttering blackly: "Court or no court, he's my kid! My own flesh and blood! What right has she to him?" Little Johnny, for his part, was pretty hilarious. "Are you going to drive a truck someday like your mother?" Frizzletop would ask, chucking his little chin. "No, me go downtown like Da Da an' bet horses!" little Johnny would reply. "Big bum! Some day when me grow up, me be big bum too, like Da Da!"

Late in February, the aggrieved fathers'-rights champion Nifty snatched his kid and took off into the wintry world, and a few weeks and several mishaps later, Dick Tracy and critically feverish little Johnny Wreath found themselves together on foot in the desolate midwestern countryside, lost in the worst snowstorm the world had ever seen, twenty-five miles from anything.

"I said I'd get you to a hospital and I'm going to do it even if we have to WALK," Tracy pledged.

A few miles into the deep freeze, even the

The terrible swift sword of Dramatic Irony smites tire-bootlegger B-B Eyes, April 16–17, 1942.

Prune Face's last stand, January 28–February 2, 1943.

invincible Tracy was sagging. "Fellow can't see very far in this stuff," he murmured to the comatose baby in his arms.

And a few miles later, Tracy was near death. "Just a farm shack or a barn," he was gasping. "Anything. We've got to get inside." Through the snowblind night he at last made out the form of a small structure. It was only a rural bus stop. It was all Tracy had. He fell face forward beneath the lean-to, sheltering the little boy's body with his own. He put out his hand. In front of him was a discarded, crumpled newspaper. Dimly he made out the bold headline, letter by letter.

"RICKENBACKER—LOST—IN THE PACIFIC—DYING OF THIRST—HUNGER—"

The detective shuddered, and became resolute. "He prayed," Dick Tracy murmured.

THE CELEBRATED AMERICAN AIR ACE EDDIE

Rickenbacker, his B-17 down in the Pacific in the fall of 1942, had bobbed on a raft for nearly four weeks with a couple of other men and little more than the Gospel of St. Matthew for sustenance, and the tale of Rickenbacker's single-mindedly devout survival was among the most inspirational yarns of the day. Dick Tracy prayed, humble, quaking, the immense unknown looming before him.

Chester Gould, simultaneously a Christian man who did not disregard miracles and a savvy entertainer who did not disregard the box office, made it his business many times thereafter to drop his characters to their knees to plead for salvation and deliverance. There were times that prayer didn't work, as occasionally prayer does not, but prostration before the Master more

Nifty Wreath disenrolls his son from Frizzletop's day-care center, February 20, 1943.

often than not signaled something joyously life affirming, and in this instance little Johnny Wreath came through. The dog Nifty Wreath, the saint Myrtle Wreath, and the cop Dick Tracy all embraced at the little boy's hospital bedside, the life energies coursing through them.

Thus did Nifty Wreath, just a footnote to a great global war, become one of the few rats who was given another lease on his own life. Dick Tracy let him go. "We're going to make a new start," Nifty said gratefully, holding his wife and son. "Call a cab," Tracy directed Pat Patton. "Three people are going home."

A YEAR LATER, IN MAY 1944, DICK TRACY WAS commissioned a lieutenant, senior grade, with United States Navy Intelligence, as all the liberty-loving forces of America went to war against the likes of such swine as the Axis agent called The Brow. "It won't interfere with his regular work," one Captain Bowline of the Navy assured Chief Brandon as the appointment was made. "He'll operate in plain clothes."

The Brow, June 17, 1944.

In the speech balloons:
WHAT'S THE IDEA?

I JUST WANTED TO SEE HOW YOU'D HANDLE 'EM ALL AT ONCE.

CHAPTER 15

DICK TRACY'S GREATEST HITS

Flattop and the Classic '40s Bad Guys

HE WAS ONE OF THE UGLIEST HUMAN beings imaginable: pug-nosed, fat-lipped, fish-faced, imbecilically flat-headed, the top of his dopey, truncated skull just a clean, straight, horizontal line. His name was Flattop and from the moment he first appeared, just before Christmas 1943, he was the single most celebrated rat of Dick Tracy's whole life, as popularly identified with the great detective as Moriarty is with Holmes and The Joker is with Batman. Through the spring of 1944, Flattop was a national sensation. When Chester Gould finally wiped him out, he was deluged with wreaths from Flattop fans who couldn't stand it that the crummy little killer was really gone.

Gould could barely stand it himself. The professional playwright Captain Joseph Medill

TOP LEFT: A gag drawing Chester Gould made for *Life* magazine in August, 1944 pitted Dick Tracy against "his most famous recent villains," and Gould's selections provide insights into his own critical assessment of his work. Seen here are (front, left to right) The Brow (1944), The Mole (1941), Prune Face (1942–43), Flattop (1943–44), Mrs. Pruneface (1943), Little Face (1941), and Jerome Trohs and Mamma (1940), and (rear, left to right) B-B Eyes (1942), The Blank (1937), and 88 Keyes (1943). Seen here accordingly is Gould's great pride in the seven-year-old Blank story and his complete dismissal of the 1938–39 material that followed, and seen here as well is his opinion that the absent Yogee Yamma (1940), Black Pearl (1940), Deafy (1940), Krome (1940–41), and Laffy (1943) were lesser creations. The *Life* caption explained that the Gould self-caricature was standing ready "to erase [the assembled villains] if they prove too much for Tracy," but the art gum also represented the cartoonist's good-natured concession that he was not really one of the more naturally gifted artists in the business. Indeed, had the art gum been put to more judicious use in this very drawing, Tracy might not have had hands ludicrously larger than his feet.

Jerome Trohs scrams, May 30–31, 1940.

Patterson had given him good sound dramatic advice about villains once upon a time—"Mr. Patterson always used to say," Gould told an interviewer in 1955, "kill them before they outlive their usefulness; leave your readers longing for another look at them"—and the cartoonist hewed to that dictum quite regularly, dropping his rats at the height of the game and then breathlessly crashing forward into the lives and times of other rats and then swiftly dropping them, too. But Flattop was another story. "I got so fond of that little moron I couldn't BEAR to bump him off," Gould sighed regretfully.

He always cited the war as one of his primary creative influences. The front page was a tough act to follow if you happened to be a famous cartoonist who liked to think that your strip was the principal reason people bought the paper, and Gould perceived that it was now incumbent upon him to be better than World War II. At once, DICK TRACY plunged into its inspired golden age, a period of extraordinary fertility that saw the arrivals not only of some of the strip's most important supporting players but of a classic, virtually unbroken string of TRACY villains whose names instantly became part of the national mythology.

Every element that would indelibly define DICK TRACY in the popular consciousness for years to come was now arriving in one great sustained wave of memorable storytelling as Chester Gould went face-to-face with World War II, the competition.

THE STRIP HAD BEEN METHODICALLY GATHER-

ing its energies for several years in any case, as formal Grotesquery increasingly superseded the gangbusters sensibility and a fascinatingly quirky crew of players began to develop. There had already been, in the spring and summer of 1940, the midget rackets boss Jerome Trohs, so tiny that his gang carried him around in a suitcase, so nimble that he rode about on dogback, so formidably in charge of things that he brooked no nonsense from the immense adoring wife who was at least four or five times bigger than he was ("Shut up! Where are my slippers? Get me a glass of beer!"). Trohs, one of the first villains to carry a name identifiable with his physicality—spell "Trohs" backward—was also among the first to meet that sort of bizarre, nongunshot death that DICK TRACY rats became famous for suffering: Abandoning his wife and fleeing town after a misstep, Jerome ended up running a Montana tourist camp, and his aggrieved helpmeet trailed him there, locked him in an extremely hot shower, and scalded him to death.

And there had been Yogee Yamma (July–

September 1940), apparently a Hindu swami of wisdom beyond understanding but in truth just an ex-con named Malor Moan who was successfully working the old phony-psychic scam on various daffy rich widows. Drawing most of its momentum from the weird-pulp tales of the day, the Yogee Yamma yarn posited a turbaned, goateed mystic who kept squirreling out of police dragnets because it seemed he had the power to cloud men's minds. "Let's sit down and talk this over," Yogee would smile whenever Tracy showed up, and then he would release secret fumes, and the detective would instantly agree to whatever Yogee suggested ("Yes! Sit down! Relax! Very tired!"). "You told us to let him go!" the uniformed cops would shrug. "What in—?" Tracy would gasp. The genre story inevitably led to an underground headquarters in an abandoned subway wherein Yogee Yamma kept shackled an old wretch of a scientist, and Dick Tracy freed him, and the old man now let on that Yogee's nerve gas was actually pretty volatile stuff and if Yogee didn't keep it refrigerated then it would quickly

Little Face, August 19, 1941.

turn incendiary. Even at that moment, a startled Yogee was going up in flames in his hotel room.

There had been the hard-of-hearing Deafy Sweetfellow (October–December 1940), who ran a penny-ante hot-bicycle racket that served largely to showcase young Junior Tracy in his own crimebusting adventure while Dick Tracy took a vacation with Tess Trueheart. There had been Krome (December 1940–March 1941), the efficient contract assassin whose Crime Inc. took on hit jobs for the underworld. There had been Little Face (July–September 1941), the hot-gems kingpin who finally lost his ears to frostbite.

Finally, in November and December of 1941, there had been The Mole, the earth-dweller thereafter celebrated for generations as one of the all-time essential DICK TRACY Grotesques.

ACTUALLY QUITE A SHORT-LIVED FIGURE IN

the strip, The Mole was a onetime mobsman, believed dead since 1926, who was now living beneath a junkyard in a subterranean chamber that he had apparently clawed out with his own hands and then equipped with bootleg electricity and closed-circuit 1941 television.

Yogee Yamma, July 31, 1940.

It's running in **ALL AROUND.** The warmth of my dugout is melting the piles of snow. I'll be flooded!

Reg. U. S. Pat. Off.
Copyright, 1941, by The Chicago Tribune

The Mole, December 5, 1941.

The Mole was quite patently and creepily insane, and Gould's bosses began to hear the old subscriber complaints again after the lunatic little digger strangled a hood who was hiding out with him ("Digging in the earth has made The Mole's hands very strong! VERY strong! Ha ha! Ha ha! VERY strong!") and then offhandedly dumped the corpse into a sewer. Responding personally to the horrified *Omaha World-Herald* in this instance, Captain Joseph Medill Patterson stated the DICK TRACY credo again on November 28, 1941:

> We . . . have had a number of kicks about Dick Tracy violence . . . But if you should ever go to the movies on a Saturday afternoon when they have a western serial, you will see what the kids want . . . They like primitive action, violence, gun-play, falling off cliffs, etc. It is the old dime novel in modern form . . . If they please grown-ups in all ways, I fear they might not please the children in many cases. It is when the boys are in the dirty-face, dirty-clothes, fighting, heedless age that they like such serials as Dick Tracy. I have made a long study of this subject and I think I know what I am talking about.

Patterson sent a carbon to Gould along with a cover note. "You see that I come to your defense to the best of my ability," The Captain wrote. "But nevertheless, Chester," the old patron sighed, "I think you do go a little bit too far sometimes."

"Mole dig his way out! Easy for Mole!" The Mole cackled crazedly as the law demolished his underground redoubt and he began to tunnel frantically through the earth. Tracy was waiting for him topside, and that was the end of The Mole. He was last seen in his cell on Christmas Eve. Dick Tracy had thoughtfully sent him cigarettes, fruit, and candy.

THERE HAD BEEN THE LEGENDARY WARTIME Grotesques B-B Eyes and Prune Face. There had been 88 Keyes (April–July 1943), a suave bandleader, no thug to speak of, merely a gold-digging heel who had conspired with a millionaire's wife to murder her husband for the insurance money. 88 Keyes—a relatively minor villain in a relatively minor story, his position in the rogues' gallery won solely on the strength of his imaginative name—spent most of his story on the lam, eventually settling in as a hired hand on a dairy farm in Chester Gould's great heartland midwest, and the story was largely notable for its introduction of the Foolish Farmgirl, a subspecies of Innocent who would go on to become an occasional Type, forever falling for fugitive crooks and helping them make their getaways. Sometimes the farmgirls paid dearly for their foolishness, and sometimes they merely learned a good lesson, as was the case with 88 Keyes's little friend Nellie ("You see, Nellie, when we're very young, and before our judgment has matured, we sometimes make mistakes." "Oh, mother.") It was the heartland itself that at last tripped up the city-slicker piano player; his speeding car crashed after it hit a pig. On foot, he was waiting to hop a freight to safety when Dick Tracy cornered him on the tracks and machine-gunned him.

And there had been Laffy (October–December 1943), the hyena dope dealer who chortled his way through several killings and who kept howling and slapping his knee until suddenly his wide-open jaws locked on him. "I can'd get my mou'h shud!" he glubbered. "Ow! I've got logjaw!" A good belt in the mouth later, Laffy's jaws were freed, and then just as suddenly they were locked shut. "Just like a vise!" he sweated. "Teeth are set. Oh-ohhh! I'll starve!" That's exactly what happened. In the spirit of things, the strip played it as high black comedy, and everyone had a good hoot as Laffy quickly wasted away to nothing and died, prisoner of his horrible rictus.

And now, on December 21, 1943, the repulsive Flattop Jones was arriving in town on the train. He seemed to be a businessman. "Five grand isn't bad for such a small job," he was muttering to himself.

"H'm," the cab driver noted when he dropped Flattop off at the hotel. "Funny looking egg."

"IT WON'T REALLY SEEM LIKE CHRISTMAS TILL

everyone's sons and brothers are back," Tess Trueheart reflected trueheartedly on Christmas Eve.

"May that day come sooner than any of us suspect," prayed Dick Tracy.

"What if it IS Christmas?" Flattop was shrugging on the other side of town. "I want to get this job done and over with."

Flattop—the character was supposedly inspired by the day's flattop aircraft carriers—was a hired killer from the Cookson Hills of Oklahoma, imported by the city's black marketeers to rub out Tracy for once and all, and within

88 Keyes, May 21, 1943.

Laffy achuckle after a good kill, October 18, 1943.

days he had snatched the detective off the street and was taking him for a ride into the country. "Some jobs only bring a grand," Flattop told his captive. "I'm one of the better corpses, eh?"

Flattop for Xmas, December 25, 1943.

Flattop definitively fails to rub out Dick Tracy, January 17–20, 1944.

Tracy mused. And Tracy was actually this close to being real dead, spread-eagled on the floor of Flattop's car, the gun to the back of his head, for once powerless to help himself. What was called for here was a good deus ex machina.

"No, wait, I just got an idea," Flattop said on the count of two and a half.

"Make up your mind, will you?" Tracy snapped.

The hired gun had suddenly decided to double-cross his employers. Now he wanted fifty grand, or he would turn the detective loose. "He's nothing but a crook!" ranted the black-market bosses. Zero hour finally came again for Tracy, but the few extra days he'd bought had given Pat Patton and an army of officers time to surround Flattop's apartment. This time, on the count of two and a half, there was a sensational shoot-out, and when it was over, Tracy was alive and kicking, Flattop's whole mob was annihilated, and Flattop himself was on the run in the City, his photograph all over the papers.

There weren't a lot of places anyone so instantly recognizable as Flattop could go. At one point he was reduced to hiding in a chimney full of honeybees. At another point he gasoline-torched a random Innocent to death in a vacant storefront just so he could plant his ID on the charred corpse. Finally he made a last stand in front of a crowded movie theater, and on March 19, 1944, Pat Patton shot him through the throat, and Flattop was finished.

Well, no, he wasn't. Things just didn't feel right with Flattop put away so soon. A month later he broke out of jail and ingeniously established quarters inside a decorative ship replica in the park lagoon (see Chapter 17). And as Dick Tracy and the U.S. Navy finally closed in on him, Flattop hit the water and tried to make a swim for it. Suddenly he was wedged fast between underwater pilings, his clothing snagged on a rusty spike. Suddenly, flailing and thrashing, Flattop had drowned.

He made his final appearance on a morgue slab on May 17. "Thus we take our last look at Flattop," Gould noted in an aside to the reader, ruefully.

Even so, the strip couldn't tear itself away from the immortal Flattop. On May 20, a couple of gravediggers were seen solemnly at their labors. "They all reach the same destination," one was saying. "Some of 'em take a little longer, but they always end up in our department."

The end of Flattop, May 16, 1944.

"Ain't it the truth?" agreed the other, shoveling clods of eternal black earth over the last of Flattop.

PONDERING MORTALITY, GOULD HAD BEEN

riding his tractor around his Illinois farm one sunny afternoon when, so the story goes, he suddenly had a vision of a body plummeting through the air and impaling itself on a flagpole. Now, working one of those few stories whose ending he already knew, he introduced another of his landmark grotesque classics.

The Brow (June–September 1944) was a ruthless Axis spy, an evil-looking figure whose forehead was deeply furrowed and whose ears were missing, and his nefarious operation came to the attention of Lieutenant Dick Tracy of Navy Intelligence after a pair of country-girl pickpockets Tracy had his eye on accidentally stumbled into it. The young Summer Sisters, May and June, paid with their lives for helping the Navy smash The Brow's spy ring, and after that The Brow was on the run through an exciting summer-long chase sequence (see Chapter 18) that climaxed on September 24 on the eighth floor of the city jail, when the wicked foreign agent crashed backward out a window in an abortive escape attempt.

Down through the air he plunged.

Below him was a small American shrine—a plaque bearing the names of the neighborhood's war dead, and a proud flag.

LIKE A MIGHTY SABER, wrote Gould, who had been waiting for this, THE FLAG POLE REACHES UP TO MEET THE EVIL FORM.

Old Glory spiked the plummeting Brow squarely between the shoulder blades. It took a derrick to spring him.

SHAKY (September 1944–January 1945) was a violently trembling figure, apparently the victim of a nervous condition. He did shakedowns. One of them was a cheap shotgun-wedding racket in which a bridal-gowned girl accomplice would fling herself at some wealthy target and make a public Mann Act stink that could be settled by a few bucks, and this was how Shaky came to police attention one night as Dick Tracy and Junior were returning to the City from a fishing holiday. "She stopped the wrong car!" Shaky's men groaned. "I NEVER did like that wedding dress gag," Shaky scowled. Most of the Shaky story ran parallel to that of the girl's, the tragic Snowflake Falls (see Chapter 17), and in the end it became a cruel cat-and-mouse yarn as Shaky dedicated himself to revenging himself on the young woman who had wrecked his operation.

On the run at the last, Shaky's men burned to death after they accidentally set their hideout afire and Shaky himself escaped in a Fire Department car and led Dick Tracy and Pat Patton on a thrilling chase through the icy winter streets. It climaxed at the stormy waterfront, where, just a half skip ahead of the law, Shaky

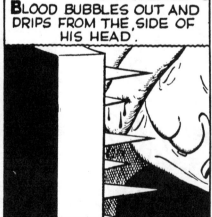

The Brow: Trapped in his fiendish machine by his former captives, the Summer Sisters, July 11–12, 1944.

Shaky entombed, January 15, 1945.

frantically took refuge in the only hiding place in sight, a hole in an old pier. He hadn't counted on the breakers, whipping in from the harbor and freezing as they landed. Momentarily he was sealed into a ghastly ice prison. In his last minutes, Shaky was shrieking and banging.

"That's odd," puzzled Patton, as the cops searched the blizzard-howling docks only feet away. "I imagined I heard a faint call for help."

THE SKIN-DISEASED YOUTH CALLED MEASLES (January–May 1945) showed up in the wake of an unusual Big House Confidential sequence in which it was seen that there was a flourishing dope traffic behind the walls of the state penitentiary, overseen by a diesel of a matron named Anna Enog. Measles was her nasty little thug of a son and he was the supplier, and between the racket and the attitude and the bright red splotches on his forehead, you always wanted to wash your hands whenever you saw Measles. "Catching Measles is poison!" he grinned evilly when Dick Tracy caught him for the first time. Indeed, he was responsible for one of Tracy's woollier Near-Deathtraps, when the detective's overcoat got snagged on the rear bumper of the car in which Measles was fleeing at sixty miles per hour. After the dope racket came apart, events settled into the sort of fast-action chase thriller that was always the signature of the strip's best stories. Measles hid out for a time in a rural railroad town, then stowed away aboard the westbound silver streak as Tracy closed in on him, then was caught up in a spring flash flood, and Tracy finally nailed him from a pursuing motorboat. "Looks like a permanent quarantine!" Tracy cracked as he brought the half-drowned rat back to dry land.

STILL ANOTHER GUY WITH A SKIN CONDITION, the vicious gang boss Itchy Oliver (September–December 1945) figured initially as a player in another story (see Chapter 18) and then assumed his place in the firmament of Dick Tracy's foremost torturers. Before he ever got to Tracy, the great rat Itchy, forever digging beneath his collar and scratching fiercely like some flea-stricken animal, had blowtorched the feet of a captive, slain a woman cohort, invaded a wedding party and shot up random Innocents, bludgeoned Junior Tracy, kidnapped and terrorized Tess Trueheart in a high-speed auto flight through the autumn cornfields, and murdered a motorcycle cop. Then he got to Tracy.

In a house in a quiet residential neighborhood, the detective was suddenly the trussed-up prisoner of Itchy and a woman named Kitty, who proved to be the revenge-bent widow of the late B-B Eyes. They had decided to starve

Itchy eats hot lead, December 21, 1945.

him to death for their amusement. Two boiled turnips a day was the ration, plus, twice a day, all the water that would cling to a fork. "Got a calorie table?" guffawed Itchy. "Let's see how long this will take."

Tracy endured it for several weeks, growing weaker and thinner by the day. He was skin and bones and close to dead by the time brave Junior Tracy, still his detective pal's dependable little lifesaver when the going got tough, tracked him down and brought in the cops for a blazing denouement just before Christmas. Tracy personally shot Itchy to death. "Oh, if only I'd been satisfied to let bygones be bygones," mourned Mrs. B-B Eyes, learning too late that Crime Doesn't Pay and You Can't Win.

THE BROAD-SHOULDERED SHOULDERS (June–July 1946), big and beefy and possessed of vaguely matinee-idol looks save for a disfigured ear, was a small-time fixer who happened to have enough petty political clout to let him run a modest piece of the City's rackets. He was, as it turned out, basically just a supporting player in his own story, which otherwise introduced and showcased a hard little street tyke named Themesong, who at this point joined the TRACY strip's regular cast of characters for a time. Themesong, six years old, her father a bush-league hood in Shoulders's employ, her mother a bedridden cripple, made her living by singing on street corners to the accompaniment of her battery radio. She had grown up in the life and she

hated cops on sight and she proved to be a plenty tough little customer whenever Tracy and Patton sought to quiz her on her old man's activities ("I'll stand on my constootional rights! I want a mouthpiece!"). Tracy had his work cut out for him as he kept shadowing Themesong and visiting her at home ("Don't open yer yap, Ma! Don't tell him nothin' till we get a mouthpiece! I don't like gumshoes follering me around!"). Even as with the analagous Junior Tracy of years earlier, though, Tracy finally began to win the little girl over with kindness and decency. Shoulders might still have been able to keep the kid on his team had he not one day elected to shoot her twice in the chest.

As Themesong fought for her life in surgery, the hunted Shoulders fled to a private airfield, commandeered a single-engine plane, tried to lift off with a cold engine, and took a dive straight into a huge gas tank. The fire burned for days.

RIGHT UP THERE WITH THE ROTTENEST RATS of them all, the obsessively mouth-flushing Gargles (September–November 1946) was a semi-comedic figure when he first appeared, a protection racketeer who had a silly business muscling small druggists into buying cheap cinnamon-water mouthwash of his own basement manufacture ("You'll take a hundred gallons or get your window smashed!"). Apparently it was possible to make a living like this in 1946, as Gargles appeared to be quite prosperous, to the degree that he fancied himself a man about town and was determined to win a date with a glamorous radio star named Christmas Early. Indeed, it was via his fan letter to the beauteous broadcaster that Tracy and Patton succeeded in tracking Gargles to his mouthwash factory, where, as the goofy story abruptly turned murderous, his whole mob died in a withering shoot-out. Gargles himself made a getaway.

Themesong and her feeble sickly old mother, at this point, were renting out rooms, and Gargles took one.

But the savvy little girl knew a crook when she saw one, and she started getting the goods on him for her friend Detective Tracy. Gargles wasn't in the mood for it. The old lady, one of the great touching Innocents, just got in the way. On October 26, 1946, Gargles shot her down in cold blood.

An entire outraged City was on the lookout for the lousy widow-killer as tear-stained little Themesong went on Christmas Early's radio program to broadcast his description. "You can't get away with it!" she promised, and she was right. For Gargles, there was nowhere to go. He ended up crouching in a glass company's storage loft, shooting it out with Dick Tracy as things shattered and crashed all around. On November 10, he backed through a railing and fell down a stairwell, and a dolly loaded with heavy glass panels tipped over after him, and great sharp shards rained down atop Gargles and sliced him into luncheon loaf. They took Gargles away in baggies. The first news report of his death was made on the Christmas Early show, by Themesong.

IN THE TRADITION OF THE MIND-CLOUDING Yogee Yamma, the wild-eyed mesmerist called Influence (December 1946–March 1947) could stare anyone into immediate total submission with the help of special optical lenses that gave him a truly unsettling appearance. Indeed, Influence was so dreadful that he kept looking out of the comics page straight into the eye of the reader and the reader would instantly turn away, and Gould at one point openly challenged the folks at home to try staring him down and see how long they could stand it.

He specialized in getting people to give him

Shoulders and Themesong, July 15, 1946.

Mouthwash racketeer Gargles and radio hepcat Christmas Early, September 20, 1946.

money, and he figured principally in a shakedown yarn that involved the old actor Vitamin Flintheart (see Chapter 17), but of course he was also good at persuading policemen not to arrest him. Pat Patton, for one, was straightaway stared out of the idea. "Hand me your gun, it might go off," Influence intoned. "Gun might go off," Patton nodded, turning his rod over. Tracy fared better when the final showdown came at an upstate ski lodge. Tracy had thought to wear special mesmero-repellent lenses for the occasion, so Influence had nothing on him, and Influence kept saying things like "You have never been up against anything like me, have you?" and "Your firearms are useless, aren't they?" and Tracy just kept grinning. Tracy had also thought to bring along a small chain, and he used it to whip Influence's eyeballs practically out of their sockets. The

Gargles under glass, November 11, 1946.

trick lenses shattered, his great power stolen, Influence was swiftly behind bars.

"EMUS BINA DOPTA TRYSILI STUNTLITHA," were his first words. Someone nearby was forever demanding: "WHAT DID he say?" and someone else would translate: "He said he must have been a dope to try a stunt like that." The sleepy-eyed little guy would look up from his guitar and say, "Hanme cigretsina ovct," and some-body would say, "He said to hand him his cigarettes in his overcoat." This was Mumbles (October–December 1947), who led a quartet of singers that played high-society bashes and then relieved the guests of their sparklers, and sometimes his utterances were even semidivinable, but most of the time he needed a translator. Flinging an auto seat cushion into the path of a pursuing motorcycle cop, he whooped, "Acar seatal waystps acob!" as the officer went somer-

Influence, February 1, 1947.

The Mumbles Quartette woodsheds, October 25, 1947.

saulting to his death. "What did he say?" one of the boys inquired. "He said a seat cushion always stops a cop," another explained. It never appeared that Mumbles had any physical defect in particular. He just mumbled.

Despite the cop killing and the society heists, there was no evidence on which Dick Tracy could hold the Mumbles Quartette, and for the moment he had to let them go, and they happily chartered a yacht and headed for the Car-

ibbean. Little did the boys realize that Mumbles, in the wake of a money quarrel, was now plotting to kill them all. Late one night, in a raging storm, as the boys popped champagne and sang drunken bawdy songs ("I called her my delicate flower till I saw her move the piano"), Mumbles lit a few sticks of dynamite and went over the side in a rubber raft.

Tracy, who had been following the party boat in a Coast Guard helicopter, swung himself

Mumbles at sea, December 1, 1947.

down just in the nick of time to stop the blast and Mumbles's boys finally all went to jail. Mumbles, for his part, was long disappeared into the dark. Days later, lost at sea, he broke his wooden paddle and then accidentally punctured his raft with one sharp end of it, and, hundreds of miles from anything, sat in pop-eyed disbelief as the tiny craft slowly started folding up.

"Thairs gonout ovit!" Mumbles cried. "Il-drown!" He didn't have a translator with him. The reader had to figure it out.

He was last seen on December 9, his arms wrapped forlornly around the raft's last remaining bubble of air, trying to wave at liners on the far-distant horizon, a bobbing speck on the great sea of life. "ELP ELP!" Mumbles bleated. "Mdone fr!"

WITH THE PASSING OF MUMBLES, THE GREAT

spurt of '40s intensity came to something of a discernible finish. While it was scarcely the case that Chester Gould would never again do a great villain, the strip's sensibilities were changing again in the modern postwar period—by the end of 1948 Dick Tracy would have a new partner (see Chapter 23) and he would be increasingly reliant on higher-tech crime fighting—and the brief return of Shoulders in early 1948 was notable in this light. It seemed that Shoulders had somehow managed to jump clear of his airplane an instant before it went into the gas tank, and now he was working a stolen-gems dodge, but it fell apart on him fast and he fled into the countryside and took refuge as a handyman at a rustic antique shop. When Tracy showed up to bust him, he wasn't even good for much of a fight. He accidentally shot himself in the head. Gould had brought back Shoulders purely to close the books on him.

More to the point, in the summer of 1948 the strip introduced a tiny man named Heels Beals, who had in his absolute thrall an enormous woman named Acres O'Riley ("Heels, honey, you're wonderful!" "Get inside! Shine my shoes! More ice!"). With the reprise of virtually the same midget-and-giantess characters who had opened the 1940s, a specific period of time pointedly concluded.

Acres O'Riley
and Heels Beals,
August 5, 1948.

I'VE DITCHED B.O. PLENTY AND DICK TRACY. I'VE GOT MY OWN QUARTERS AND I'M INDEPENDENT! BREATHLESS, DARLING, YOU'RE POSITIVELY BRILLIANT.

CHAPTER 16

DON'T MAKE ME FORGET YOU'RE A LADY

Breathless and the Classic '40s Broads

FINALLY IT CAME DOWN TO A CONTEST of endurance and will, the sharpie girl and her sharpie mother resolved to settle their catfight over the cash-stuffed basket by staying awake until one or the other of them dropped. "I'll give you a fourth of it," the old lady offered. "I want HALF," the girl insisted. "I have stay-awake tablets and you don't," Mom crowed, popping a half dozen. "What a mother you are," Daughter said disgustedly.

On the fourth day, Mom suddenly clutched her chest and fell out of bed. "Oh—OH!" she cried. "UH—I can't breathe—oh—"

The girl took a chair and sat and watched, smiling sweetly.

"Heart attack, Mother dear?" she inquired.

The old lady was flat on her back, clawing at the air, choking. "Call . . .doctor . . ." she pleaded.

"I win," said Breathless Mahoney.

SHE WASN'T PRECISELY THE FEMALE FLATTOP—
she was, for one thing, gorgeous, a trim young blonde in the fashion of Veronica Lake—but

Breathless Mahoney, during her homicidal romp through the strip in the summer of 1945, quickly rose to preeminence as the archetypal girl rat, as famous a period figure as Chester Gould ever created, heading up the gallery of fems who had come to be a distinct Rat Subset.

By the time Breathless came along, her sisters had long since established themselves, a remarkable collection of witches, black widows, and she-demons. As early as 1932, Larceny Lu had been a gang boss clearly to be reckoned with ("You yellow-livered school boys! All right, if you're gettin' the willies I'll pay you a grand for your share of the hot stuff and you can blow town.") The gangstress Zora Arson and the tommy-gun-packing Ma Barkeresque Maw Famon (1935) were both as trigger happy as anyone Tracy ever ran into. The 1935 women's-prison break in which Toby Townley lost her sight featured a couple of extremely tough cupcakes ("Come on, stupid, the fireworks are on! In through the laundry, girls! Into the washer with the guard!"). In 1936, the notably nononsense mob queen Mimi forced a doctor to amputate her gangrenous hand at gunpoint ("Or

Mimi, August 3–4, 1936. Following the grisly amputation of her left hand, Mimi always carried a towel over her wrist, doubtless by directive of Gould's syndicate bosses.

Waterfront racketeer Lily, June 6, 1939, with undercover-man Junior Tracy, resourcefully disguised as a crippled button girl.

your life won't be worth a plugged dime!"), and then, with her arm still in a sling, jumped into the harbor and swam out to a yacht to join forces with a racketeer pal; as things climaxed, Mimi first stabbed Pat Patton nearly to death and then swallowed poison rather than be taken alive. In 1939, a husky, rip-roaring, Calamity Jane–like lady named Lily tried to use Junior Tracy as a shield in a shoot-out with police.

And in April 1940, as the strip's burgeoning rogues' gallery introduced the classic midget Jerome Trohs, the fem force brought in his equally classic wife, the big, brawling babe called Mamma.

MAMMA WAS A HUGE, DIAMOND-GLITTERING,

chocolate-chomping amazon who happily waited on her little husband day and night despite all the abuse he flung at her ("Shut up with that sugar drivel!") but who was also quite capable of enforcing gang rule by energetically drop-kicking some errant thug in the teeth. It was Mamma who personally did the honors when Jerome decided to wreck the captured Dick Tracy's gun hand by crushing it in a vise. It was Mamma who gave the desperately outclassed Pat Patton one of the streetcorner scraps of his life, swinging him around and around like a sack of yams and finally throwing him through a plate-glass window. It was Mamma who sicked her great phantom St. Bernard on Junior Tracy's little terrier Oscar just for fun,

Jerome Trohs and Mamma, May 21, 1940.

Bathing Jerome, July 5–6, 1940.

the incident that finally led police to the Trohs mob's hideout, once Junior laid hands on the St. Bernard's dog tag. It took two cops and a flying tackle to bring Mamma down, and she was none too happy. "Wait till Jerome and the gang get their hands on you!" Mamma spat at Tracy. "Nobody will even know WHERE THE BONES ARE." "Gag her, boys," Tracy said.

Unfortunately for him, Jerome Trohs decided to duck out on the little woman when the shooting started, and he went west, and Mamma was left stewing in jail. "The little rat!" she fumed. "He DITCHED me. I could break his neck in the palm of my hand!"

She wasn't kidding. Consumed with fury, Mamma staged an appendicitis attack, overpowered the ambulance crew as they rushed her to a hospital, and then headed west herself,

commandeering a ten-ton transport truck and taking it all the way to Doggie City, Montana, where her hubby was now running a tourist camp.

Jerome was cheerily taking a shower when Mamma caught up with him. "Hey, let me out of here!" he squalled as she nailed the door shut, ran in a length of garden hose, and started firing up a nearby hot-water boiler. "Shrimp!" she seethed. "Double-crosser!"

"OW-W! OW!" Jerome Trohs shrieked as the scalding water cascaded in upon him. "OW-OHHHH!"

Hard on the heels of the fugitives, Dick Tracy roared into camp, freed Jerome from the deadly shower stall, and then, his right arm still in a sling, went into the main house to do hand-to-hand combat with the barricaded Mamma.

Tracy dukes out Mamma. July 9–10, 1940.

"Come and get me, one-arm!" she sneered, putting up her dukes. "I'll break your spine for you and ram that hook nose clear down through your collar!"

"Listen, don't make me forget you're a lady," Tracy said.

She belted him halfway across the room. She yanked out half his hair. She jumped up and down on him like he was a trampoline.

"All right, you asked for it," sighed the detective.

Outside, the local law was doing what it could for the brightly parboiled Jerome Trohs. The little man had just expired of third-degree burns when Tracy came out of the house with his bloodied, bruised, black-eyed, thoroughly whipped prisoner.

"I suppose you're satisfied now, fatty," Tracy

grunted. And Mamma went back to prison, for life.

THAT FALL, A TERRORIST-BOMB INCIDENT THAT

had international overtones led Dick Tracy to the doorstep of one Black Pearl, a thin, sharp-featured woman who was known to be some sort of foreign propagandist. "This is a very delicate situation," Tracy chuckled just like a man as he and Patton went calling. "Big brutes calling on one woman. Straighten your tie!" Black Pearl (September–October 1940) had the drop on them in about half a minute, and instantly she had slashed Tracy's face with a savage claw she called a ka-wag. "I hope my little Oriental weapon has taught you to respect a woman's will!" she hissed.

Things only got worse. "I shall prepare many more bombs before I am through!" Black Pearl gloated. "Fifteen years of scientific study! Long hours of research!" She had, she explained, successfully invented a flying submarine, powered by liquid air. "A military implement of unparalleled power," she said ecstatically. "Imagine what a warring country would give."

"You're stark mad," Tracy decided.

Whatever she was, she was in charge of this show, and before long Tracy and Patton had been spirited up to Black Pearl's proving grounds in the mountains, and it seemed they were being pressed into service as the guinea pigs who were going to test her fantastic machine in

Black Pearl, September 30 - October 1, 1940.

its first field trials. First they had to take the clanking beast sixty feet underwater. Then they were required to see how they could hold up against a flamethrower. Things would probably have gone quite badly for them had the foreign-government emissary witnessing the tests not turned out to be their old G-Man pal Jim Trailer in disguise, making his farewell appearance in the strip. They were very glad to see him.

Black Pearl and her gang went to jail. The flying submarine was turned over to the government. "Black Pearl has been doing Uncle Sam a good turn after all!" Tracy observed patriotically.

IN JULY 1943, DICK TRACY MET THE AWFULEST

woman of them all, the unbelievably ghastly Mrs. Pruneface, grieving muscle-bound widow of the late saboteur.

She was a huge, hooded, hollow-eyed thing, and she carried a whip and she had a pet rat named Toodles and one rainy night she overpowered Tracy as he walked home and when he woke up he was in chains. She had plans for her husband's killer. "We could seal him up in the brick wall of the basement," she mused. Finally she settled on something even more hair-raising. She took a long bolt filed to a very sharp point, and she drove it through a plank, and then she positioned the plank atop two large cakes of ice, bolt point down, and

Mrs. Pruneface eliminates a nuisance, September 16, 1943.

then set a refrigerator on top of that. Tracy, shackled to the floor between the ice cakes, the point straight over his heart, was going to be very slowly spiked as the ice melted and the heavy refrigerator descended floorward.

Fortunately, as was usually the case with these preposterously complicated Near-Deathtraps that crooks always insisted on using on Dick Tracy when they might just as easily have shot him, there was a way out of this one: The floor slanted slightly, and Tracy managed to slide the ice cakes just enough millimeters to save himself, but it was a close one. "I want to warn you, boys, this thing we're dealing with isn't human," Tracy said grimly back at headquarters.

Indeed, Mrs. Pruneface practically wasn't. Even disguised in a wig and dark glasses, Mrs. Pruneface was just horrible. Good help was pretty hard to get in 1943, though, and before long she landed a job as personal cook to His Honor the Mayor of the town, a fellow named Norris. He had a teenage daughter who one

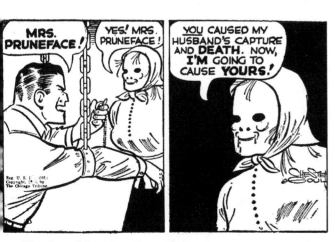

The horrible Mrs. Pruneface, August 2, 1943. Unlike her late husband, Prune Face's widow spelled the name as one word.

night happened to throw a pool party for all the kids. One of them, a fun-loving lad named Chuck, one of those Innocents, inadvertently took the cook's wig off during the festivities and recognized her on the spot. So she drowned him.

As things just got more and more grotesque, the mayor's wheelchair-bound wife rose to her feet, confronted Mrs. Pruneface in the kitchen, and on September 26, 1943, shot her to death.

"How is it you can walk?" Mayor Norris inquired.

"Stanley, I believe when emergencies arise we somehow find strength to meet them," the First Lady said.

"It's a miracle!" the Mayor cried.

LATER THE WIDOW B-B EYES WOULD PUT IN

an appearance, and she was none too lovely either, and thus, when a cuteheart like Breathless Mahoney showed up, on May 10, 1945, it naturally didn't occur to Dick Tracy to ask if she happened to be related to anyone. But she happened to be Shaky's stepdaughter.

Five months after Shaky's death, Breathless and her mother were finally laying hands on the contents of the strongbox the late great racketeer had left behind him. The two of them got along fine until the box was opened and was found to contain $50,000 cash money.

Whereupon both of them instantly turned into snakes, each refusing to let the other out of her sight, and they settled in for the long siege that ended when Mrs. Mahoney suddenly seized her chest.

"I win," said Breathless, and she snatched up the money and was almost out the door before her stricken mother gathered her wits sufficiently to pick up a gun and shoot her.

The flight of Breathless Mahoney, bleeding and increasingly panic-stricken as things closed in all around her and she tried only to preserve and protect the burdensome load of cash that she had to carry with her everywhere she went, continued into September 1945, and much of the story was intertwined with that of the newly introduced farmer B.O. Plenty (see Chapter 18). By the time she met him, she had killed a man and she was at large in a stolen truck, one of

Breathless Mahoney and her loving mother, June 2, 1945.

the strip's great viper desperadoes, and before things were over she would nearly succeed in bumping off Dick Tracy, too, and plainly Breathless was doomed to come to no decent end.

NILON HOZE (April–June 1946) also had doom written all over her, and it was even possible to feel sorry for Nilon, who wasn't a criminal schemer to speak of, just a rich girl who wanted to stay rich and who accordingly perpetrated a little family mischief that happened to turn ugly on her. Nilon had a dotty, love-struck old aunt who had struck up a mail-order romance with an Arizona con man named Mortimer, and Nilon and her cousin Rod were determined to save the old lady from herself and thus keep the family fortune intact. Their plan was merely to intercept Mortimer at the train station, put a little fear into him for a couple of days, and then dispatch him back west. Indeed, mischief was all it was. Unless Mortimer were going to

Nilon Hoze and Rod: Getting rid of Mortimer, May 1, 1946.

press kidnap charges—and he was a fraud in the first place, patently after the old aunt's money—there was no crime here. Except that, bound too tight into a chair, Mortimer keeled over dead of a heart attack, and that made Nilon and Rod manslaughterers at the very least.

And that meant the only thing to do was dump his corpse somewhere. With their chauffeur, the frightened cousins late one night buried Mortimer in the gravel roadbed of a new highway.

And it was still really only a tale of a game gone unpleasantly awry, until the moment when the chauffeur got himself sloshed and started loudly shooting off his mouth and demanding a payoff, and Nilon Hoze, drawn relentlessly into dark circle after dark circle, now found there was nothing for her to do but pour the chauffeur a glass of poison.

Of course, everything came apart. Dick Tracy was on the case, and the trail of justice soon led to Mortimer's body in the countryside. "It's no use," Nilon choked, staring dazed into her empty future. "This will kill Auntie," Rod muttered.

Handcuffed to his cousin at the side of the highway, the broken Rod Hoze availed himself of the only exit from shame, disgrace, and electrocution. A twenty-two-wheeler milk truck was coming down the road. "Rod!" Nilon shrieked as he gave a mighty yank and flung the two of them straight into its path.

The old lady took it pretty hard. All she'd done was dizzily fall in love with a guy who'd written her letters. "Rich, but alone," Dick Tracy clucked, on behalf of a stern and wrathful God.

AUTUMN HEWS (July–September 1947) had started out as just a minor associate of a crook named Coffyhead (see Chapter 21), but she was left on her own after the gang went to jail and the first thing she did was shoot a policeman who interrupted her as she was fetching cash that Coffyhead had left in a safe in the garage and body shop that had been his front operation.

In flight, almost nobody ever had the rotten luck Autumn Hews had. With the garage surrounded by cops, she had to hide beneath a pair of coveralls in a pan of crankcase drippings. Covered from head to foot with grease,

Autumn Hews in the garage, September 8, 1947.

she frantically took shelter in a doghouse and then discovered that the dogs that lived there were man-eaters. She got out of that one by torching the kennel, but then the smoke quickly brought Dick Tracy and several squads right down on her. Autumn Hews never even got close to a clean getaway. "She's going to be with you for a long time, I suspect," Tracy beamed at the jail matron, handing Autumn over.

THERE WOULD CONTINUE TO BE MEMORABLE

fems as time went on, but even as the Classic Bad Guy period had measurably come to a close after 1947, so, too, did the malevolent Mrs. Volts now conclude the run of great '40s fems. Mrs. Volts (March–May 1948) ran a gang of electrical-equipment thieves and she was a notably disagreeable person by reason of the fact that she was endlessly pulling on and poking at and generally tormenting her little lap Spaniel Flapsie, who plainly despised her. After Dick Tracy smashed the gang, Mrs. Volts went on the lam and hid out with her nephew Brier, a pipe-smoking fellow who had the idea to conceal her in the gas oven in his kitchen when cops came knocking. When Brier checked on her again, Mrs. Volts was dead as a doornail. Her racket had been busted in the first place for one reason only: A truck driver the gang had hijacked at one point had managed to palm the little Spaniel's dog tag, and Dick Tracy had only to follow the license to Mrs. Volts's address. It was exactly the same device that had led Tracy to Mamma, eight years earlier.

HE'S USELESS TO US, PAT
GET HIM TO THE HOSPITAL
AND INTO BED   HIS
NERVES ARE SHOT

12-23-'44

CHAPTER 17

PERCHANCE TO DREAM

The Ordeals Of Vitamin Flintheart

HE WAS ADMIRING HIMSELF IN THE MIRror of his fifty-cent-a-night hotel, an elegant, silver-haired squire perhaps fallen on momentarily hard times but still the owner of a cigarette holder and a fine silk smoking jacket, as befitting any gent who looked like John Barrymore. "Yes, Vitamin Flintheart," he was declaiming, "you still have your snap and dash in spite of your fifty years. Why SHOULDN'T you stage a Hollywood comeback?" His door was slowly opening. Flattop, who had moments earlier torched a man to death in a hallway downstairs, was prowling the floor, rattling doorknobs, looking for the first empty room.

"All right, my good fellow," the squire said as the intruder slipped in. "What's this all about?"

Flattop thought fast. "I thought this was the room of a friend of mine," he said. "I came in here by mistake." He had already spotted the makeup kit. A few minutes later, the hunted killer, now in wig and pancake and powder, passed successfully through the hotel lobby under the noses of Dick Tracy and Pat Patton.

Upstairs, the policemen followed a trail of moans and found the old actor bleeding on the floor.

"Who are you, old man?" Tracy inquired.

"Old man?" The old man sat up indignantly. "FAW! I AM VITAMIN FLINTHEART!"

Tracy and Patton looked at one another.

"The great actor," Vitamin Flintheart explained helpfully. "Idol of millions."

SUCH WAS THE FIRST APPEARANCE (MARCH 10–13, 1944) of the famous Shakespeare-quoting ham who would come to be popularly regarded for generations unto this day as one of DICK TRACY's most durable supporting players. The recognition owed more to his many subsequent appearances in the TRACY film, radio, television, and TV-cartoon oeuvres than to the strip itself. Indeed, the Vitamin Flintheart character showed up in the canonical newspaper strip just a handful of times, and in fact Chester Gould never used him after 1950.

In a strip brimming over with wonderful walk-on characters who had a turn or two and then vanished, this one seemed only another.

"Ah, the excitement has unstrung me!" moaned Vitamin Flintheart, who was brought along on the Flattop search because he would be the one to spot Flattop's disguise. "My NERVES. Ugh. Hand me my bismuth . . . Egad! I'm falling apart! As the great bard once said . . ." Pat Patton rolled his eyes. The manhunt ended in front of a movie theater not far away, and Flattop was shot down, and there was a scramble to save his life, and suddenly Flintheart was absently holding the fugitive's gun. "Unstrung! Nerves completely unstrung!" the old actor shivered, and he wandered away from the grisly scene, the gun in his overcoat pocket.

Later, befogged in a tavern, he accidentally shot a bartender with it, and presently Vitamin Flintheart ended up in jail, just a cell or two away from Flattop himself.

"This thing's getting funnier every day," Flattop reflected.

A FEW DAYS LATER, WHEN FLATTOP STAGED

his jailbreak, he decided to take Vitamin Flintheart along with him as a shield.

"My boy, do you realize this is the servants' entrance?" Flintheart said indignantly as the two of them crept into the alley.

"Shut up!" Flattop snapped. "Didn't you ever see the back of a jail?"

Through the park they slinked, looking for a rowboat. "My feet are killing me," Flintheart groused, popping vitamins. "Cut out the PILLS," Flattop hissed. And in the dark they rowed across the lagoon to the famous ship-replica hideout.

"What about food?" Flintheart demanded. "And bedding? And wine and good books?"

"Listen . . ." muttered Flattop.

Holed up, sharing blankets and matches, they got to be, after a fashion, friends. Late at night, Flattop would make rowboat grocery runs. "And while you're there, get me another bottle of stomach medicine and some vitamin pills," Flintheart would instruct. "WHAT?" Flattop would gape. Nightly the beleaguered killer rowed back to the ship in the dark, pharmaceutical packages under his arm. "You owe me three bucks," Flattop would say. "Charge it," Flintheart waved him off.

On the lam with Flattop, April 22, 1944.

The uproarious hideaway sequence rode out its plainly predictable course, Flattop daily made more and more berserk by his impossible prisoner. "Gargles! Pills! Nose drops! CUT OUT THE NOISE!" Flattop would plead. Vitamin would settle serenely against his pillow and light a cigar. "Yes, I remember once in Budapest . . ." he would begin. "SHUT UP!" Flattop would shriek. Dick Tracy and the law really couldn't have arrived soon enough to suit Flattop.

Cleared of the bar shooting in the wake of Flattop's demise, toward the strip's exit door now trudged Vitamin Flintheart, though en route he got a glimpse of the newly introduced girl characters called the Summer Sisters and decided that it was his mission to make their careers in show business. "MY DREAM GIRLS!" he roared. "The police may think they're crooks— but to me—ah, they're two delicate flowers! I must FIND them." And he did, jotting down the address of their rooming house. Tracy got there in minutes, but not soon enough to keep them from getting seized and borne away by The Brow, into whose fifth column nest the hapless cookies had stumbled. But that no longer had anything to do with Vitamin Flintheart, who in mid-June 1944 got the hook at last, and out he went.

BUT PLAINLY HE WAS TOO GOOD A CHARACTER

to lose, and he made the first of his several reappearances that fall, after Dick Tracy had snatched away the girl called Snowflake Falls from the thrall of the master extortionist Shaky.

Onstage with Snowflake Falls, November 25, 1944.

Frail, fragile, and visibly drugged, the lovely young actress-model Snowflake (first appearance, October 1) had been Shaky's dazed captive accomplice, and Dick Tracy compassionately gave her a second chance at life after he released her from her cruel bondage. "We're going to rehabilitate you, Snowflake," Tracy said. "I'm going to get you a job."

And he picked up the phone and called Vitamin Flintheart, who was now in the money again, having hit the jackpot with a successful stage play called *Love's Afire*, and who at this point had servants bringing him his jars of vitamin pills on silver trays. "Ah, the women—bless 'em!" Vitamin cried warmly. "If she's A FRIEND OF YOURS, my boy, I'll make her a STAR."

Tracy, a bit cynically, had really only envisioned a decoy operation via which Shaky might make a run at Snowflake, but as it turned out, the girl was sensational on stage and suddenly her name was really in lights. The original leading lady took a walk. "This is the end," she snapped at Vitamin. "Can I bank on that?" he inquired politely. It rapidly became apparent that the ham and the ingenue were becoming an item. "I love you—love you with all my heart!" he pledged. "Won't you say the word?" "Oh, Vitamin!" Snowflake trembled.

Otherwise never much of a busybody, Dick Tracy was considerably appalled by this situation he had inadvertently orchestrated. "Don't you think you're rushing things just a little?" he counseled Snowflake backstage. "Vitamin's nearly 30 years older than you. He's a great man, but . . ."

Alas, Vitamin overheard. He slapped the detective in his face. "YOU DOUBLE CROSSING CAD!" he boomed. Out of the show he walked, refusing to carry on, and it closed on the spot. "YOU'VE WRECKED MY LIFE!" Snowflake blubbered. Tracy could only shake his head helplessly at the consequences of his meddling.

The gin-soaked Vitamin found Snowflake's prostrate form in a snowbank in front of the theater that night, and immediately they rushed off to be married, stopping just long enough to call up Vitamin's new friend Shaky, who had recently passed himself off to the old actor as a distinguished United States senator, to invite him to the reception. On December 16, 1944, in a justice-of-the-peace ceremony, Vitamin Flintheart and Snowflake Falls were pronounced man and wife.

Thereafter, Shaky's mob stormed in, pounced on the girl, and carried her away to exact their final revenge. On the way to the waterfront, Shaky bludgeoned her half to death. Then, bound and gagged, the battered Snowflake Flintheart was pitched off a pier into the freezing bay.

"My bride! My darling bride!" the distraught old actor grieved as the police search began. It happened that Snowflake had miraculously landed on a derelict barge laden with Christmas trees, but by the time a harbor patrol boat came across her she was cold and blue and bleeding from her ears. It was one of the gloomier Christmases the strip ever saw.

And, as Dick Tracy and Pat Patton went into the night for the final roundup of Shaky and his mob in a burning apartment building as 1945 arrived, Vitamin Flintheart was on his knees at his stricken wife's bedside. "Can you hear me, beloved," he whispered. The doctors gave him ten minutes; he stayed twenty-four hours. "We won't take him away," the doctors whispered among themselves. "It might be fatal to both."

There was a recovery, but only of sorts; Snowflake, none too sturdy to begin with, would never really be the same again. She and her husband clasped hands as Dick Tracy trailed Shaky to his icebound end, and by the time the detective got back to headquarters the two of them were already gone from his life.

One–Two—Heave!

At last, little double-crosser, we're square with each other.

The angry waves splash upon the pier, freezing almost as they land! And the blizzard rages.

Snowflake Flintheart's wedding night, December 22, 1944.

THEY SHOWED UP AGAIN, FLEETINGLY, IN APRIL

1945, as passengers aboard a train that the fugitive dope racketeer Measles had boarded during one of his several getaways. The Flinthearts were on their way to California at this point, set to star together in a major film. Prowling the sleeper car, Measles turned a doorknob and backed into Vitamin's suite exactly as Flattop had done a year earlier. The actor was accustomed to the drill by now, and this time he matter-of-factly conked the intruder with a cognac bottle and put in a call to his old pal Tracy. Measles made another escape, but Vitamin's tip-off did lead directly to his ultimate capture. By the time that occurred, the train had gone on, and Vitamin and Snowflake were en route to Hollywood.

But suddenly Vitamin Flintheart vanished.

So did Christmas Early and Themesong, for that matter, Chester Gould by now having fully patented his specialty of throwing away good strong characters like they were paper towels. Vitamin, for his part, turned up again presently as the prisoner of a onetime casino boss to whom he owed a great deal of money. This was the mesmerist Influence (see Chapter 15), who had by now stared him down into a condition of abject slavery.

"You realize, of course, that from now on I'm taking full charge of your life," Influence announced. Vitamin cheerfully assented. "You are going to do exactly as I say," Influence said. "Yes, Influence," the old actor agreed. "You have no wife—no friends—no acquaintances. I

A YEAR AND A HALF LATER, THE RADIO STAR

Christmas Early stopped in for a bite at a crummy little diner and found Vitamin Flintheart behind the counter, humbly slinging hash.

The old ham, it was now explained in November 1946, had come back east after falling upon unfortunate times. He had lost a fortune at the gaming tables. His film career was over. The picture he and Snowflake had made together would not be released. And Snowflake, he sadly reported, was critically ill out on the coast. Goodhearted Christmas lined him up a job as speech coach to her protégée, the little orphan Themesong, who was now pursuing a radio career.

Can you hear me, beloved? It's your husband

We'll leave Vitamin with her for about 10 minutes it may be their last moments together

The deathwatch, December 29, 1944.

Prisoner of the mesmerist Influence,
December 19, 1946.

ALONE am your friend." "Yes, Influence," Vitamin said. Under Influence's sadistic training, Vitamin Flintheart gave up vitamins and started popping seed peas instead, and soon he was drinking nothing but lukewarm tea. "I detest lukewarm tea," he said. "Then you shall drink lukewarm tea," Influence directed. "It's delicious," the prisoner nodded.

Neither could the ancient stage queen Florence Lane bear up against Influence. In the early 1920s, Florence Lane had played opposite Vitamin Flintheart in a theatrical sensation called *Ice Floe*. Now she was a rich old widow, and Influence decided that she would invest her entire fortune in an *Ice Floe* remake produced by himself, and he dispatched the old ham to bring her back. "Be seated on the floor," Influence instructed when she showed up, and the old lady's mind was gone on the spot. She did everything she was told, chirping happily as Influence and his boys moved into her mansion and took it over. "Dismiss your servants," he told her. "Go to your bank and get $5000." "Yes, Influence!" she said. He let her sleep on a cot in her furnace room. "It will be nice and cozy," he said. "Oh, thank you, Influence!" she beamed.

Vitamin Flintheart and Florence Lane continued to live like dogs until Florence's cash reserves ran out. On February 5, 1947, in a scene brutal even by Chester Gould's standards, the killer hypnotist visited the sleeping old lady at her cot and strangled her with a length of clothesline.

Flintheart was luckier. Halfway to a ski resort in Florence Lane's car, Influence simply let him go. "You are to drive this car back to Florence Lane's home," Influence said. "You will forget that you ever saw me or knew me." "Yes, Influence," the old actor agreed. Indeed, when he came to his senses in a cell sometime later, he had no memory whatever of the previous several months. "What am I doing in this VILE HOLE?" he demanded. "I've got radio commitments, man!"

Snowflake Flintheart, briefly rallied from her sickbed, came east to take custody of her husband as Dick Tracy dispensed with any formal charges in the Florence Lane killing, and it was announced that in fact Vitamin had just landed a role on a popular radio soap opera called "John's Wife's Other Uncle."

"Don't forget to listen every day!" he waxed. "Radio's golden interlude."

Then, on March 16, 1947, he took his young wife's arm and strolled out of the strip again, jauntily swinging his cane.

IN MAY 1950, HE SHOWED UP ONE MORE time—unemployed again, and now a widower—and he remained a major figure in the strip for the rest of the year, instrumental in bringing to justice the fiends Blowtop (see Chapter 26) and T.V. Wiggles (see Chapter 25), both of whom abused the man every bit as much as had Flattop and Influence. And then, abruptly, he was gone again, this time for good.

Popular memory continues to celebrate Vitamin Flintheart as the comic Shakespearean thesp, goofily reciting from the Bard at every turn; he is still seen that way in the 1940s TRACY movies on late-night television and he shows up often in the current post-Gould newspaper feature in the service of gag relief. In truth, he was a terribly tragic figure, a doomed, fate-freighted man laboring under more burdens than could be known. He was a figure behind whom the sagacious old counsel of The Captain—KILL THEM OFF—tolled like the awfulest of bells. Gould never killed off Vitamin Flintheart. Gould reduced him to the most pitiable of crawling insects, but he could not bring himself—indeed, he was simply never kind enough—to actually kill him. And Chester Gould would have killed anybody.

YOU SEE, I WAS ONE OF 8 BOYS. MY PAPPY TOOK US WEST FROM OHIO IN '93—

CHAPTER 18

NO FLIES
Gravel Gertie and B.O. Plenty

CHESTER GOULD WAS, AFTER ALL, BY training and by temperament and by range of technical skills, a bigfoot gag cartoonist, and though he managed to get along with Dick Tracy well enough over the years, the grim policeman was essentially an odd match for such a genial and good-humored fellow as himself.

So it was that DICK TRACY, punitive and retributive and life-poisoning and cruel, was also quite often a screwball laff riot. Broad comedic sequences frequently leavened the unremitting horror; as often as not, the two sensibilities were even welded together. It was a little disturbing sometimes. The Grotesques were grotesque, for example, but they were also, by definition, pretty funny looking guys, and they were sometimes dealt with as such. The famous bullets through the skulls in the unceasing mad shoot-outs always left things swimming in blood and brain matter, but the cartoonishness of the proceedings established these things as cartoon bullets and cartoon corpses. Most of Gould's

characters were inarguably 'toons, and most of his mayhem and bloodshed was not unlike, for example, Tom and Jerry machine-gunning one another or blowtorching one another's feet. A mild difference, to be sure, is that 'toons do not die when pianos fall on them and dynamite sticks blow up in their faces, and DICK TRACY characters certainly died.

Comic "relief" had been a firm presence in the strip from the first, embodied by both the buffoon partner Pat Patton and the early Sunday sidebar feature CIGARETTE SADIE, but there had been many other characters brought in to stand as comic elements. For a short time in 1936, Dick Tracy picked up a standard period Banjo-Eyed-Negro valet whose feets were forever doing their stuff. The 1938 amateur-detective Brighton Spotts was a broadly drawn doofus, silly in every respect. Beyond that, the killers themselves were often kind of lovable. Jerome Trohs was really a pretty funny little man, galloping around on his vacant-eyed St. Bernard; Mamma's homicidal rages were hilarious; the sight of Dick Tracy and Pat Patton encased in B-B Eyes's wax cylinders like a couple of dopes was ludicrous in and of itself. It was possible to find something uneasily gut splitting about B-B Eyes's last drowning moments in a scow full of goopy garbage. It was the sort of thing that must have happened to Bugs Bunny once or twice.

There was a part of Gould that always needed to do the sort of funny stuff he'd been trying to sell before DICK TRACY accidentally became his destiny. As well as CIGARETTE SADIE, there had been a late '50s domestic sitcom called THE GRAVIES accompanying the TRACY Sunday page in the *Chicago Tribune*, and through the '60s and '70s several TRACY characters were gag cartoonists whose work was often seen. In the mid-1940s, meanwhile, Gould had already put into place inside DICK TRACY his perfect alter-strip, a feature he gave much of his energy and affection, all but another comic strip unto itself.

It starred a pair of uncouth hillbilly farmers who found one another and made a life together and loved one another sweetly all the rest of their days. Their names were B.O. and Gertie Plenty, and they became two of DICK TRACY's best-loved characters, brilliantly successful creations, and had there never been a DICK TRACY per se, and had Gould marketed this parallel strip entirely on its own merits, he would probably still be honored today as one of the immortal practitioners of his craft.

When Gould first dreamed them up, they were just another couple of TRACY walk-ons, and they were scum.

THE HAG GRAVEL GERTIE FIRST SHOWED UP

on August 30, 1944, during the final manhunt for the memorable wartime villain called The Brow. The Brow had not himself been a particularly funny fellow. He was a foreign spy, like Prune Face before him, and thus he was engaged in the enterprise of costing Our Boys in Uniform their lives, and all America was hissing and booing The Brow as, after a skirmish with Dick Tracy, he sped through the fugitive night in a stolen station wagon, bleeding, blinking, careening across the highway, clinging to consciousness. When he crashed the wagon into

an abandoned gravel pit, the sole witness was the occupant of a nearby shack, a hideous woman who was quite irritated by the intrusion.

"Trespassing!" she snapped. "Driving into my property without permission!" Investigating the car, she found the bloodied Brow. "Please—help me—" he gasped. And Gertie's eyes went radiantly alight. "Ah!" she said. "A MAN!"

She was thirty years a widow, and she was a lust-crazed old coot, and even somebody like The Brow looked good to her. "Companionship has come to Gravel Gertie," she burbled.

She took The Brow in and nursed him like Florence Nightingale. "I shall make my entire abode over," she crooned starrily. "For you and me, who are starting life anew—together. Sleep, my darling! Sleep and relax while Gravel Gertie watches over you. Just dream and rest." The Brow, whose entire head was swathed in bandages, fell hard for her, sight, as they say, unseen. The days went by, and they tenderly clasped hands, and she serenaded him with her mandolin, and the previously savage Brow yarn dissolved into rhapsodies. "If ONLY I could SEE you!" he cried. "Your voice is soft and low. And your hair is long and silky—"

"Don't you see I LOVE YOU?" she breathed.

"YES—my dearest!" cried The Brow. "I've GOT TO SEE YOU! OFF WITH THIS CURSED BANDAGE!"

At first glimpse, his jaw dropped. He turned and fled. Now she was indignant. She clung to him. "I WON'T LET YOU GO!" she bellowed, clinging to his neck. "Let me out of here!" he yelped. "Unhand me!" A lamp was overturned. The shack went up in flames.

Dick Tracy and Pat Patton were already arriving with carloads of cops, and that was it for The Brow and his benefactress. Back at police headquarters, it was Gravel Gertie herself who triggered the events that resulted in The Brow's famous death fall (September 24, 1944), by hooking Tracy's gun and tossing it to her knight for his last desperate escape bid. Fast-thinking Tracy flung an inkwell at the gunman, hit him in the head, and sent him reeling backward, straight out the window, and The Brow, enemy of all America, plunged straight into the Stars and Stripes below, impaled on the standard of the

The Brow beholds Gravel Gertie,
September 15, 1944.

liberty-loving peoples of the American heartland.

Gertie bought jail time for having harbored him, and off she went, just another passing creature the strip had apparently now used up.

BUT SIX MONTHS LATER SHE WAS BACK. FRESH

off the Shaky case, Tracy was summoned to the women's section of the county jail to quell a rumpus: Gravel Gertie, on January 19, 1945, was flatly refusing to leave, even though she had served her time. "I WON'T GO!" she bellowed. "You LIKE it here?" Tracy blinked.

The warden shrugged. This was an old lady. What could you do? Gertie, apparently quite serenely institutionalized, got a twelve-dollar-a-week county job mopping the floors and she was permitted to keep her cell, for twelve dollars a week board. "So we're even," the warden said. "At last I have security!" sang Gertie.

Something had to be going on here, Tracy figured, and he decided to keep an eye on her. Shortly he discovered that game Gertie had turned up a big-house dope ring run by the wicked prison matron and that she was re-

solved to stay behind bars long enough to get the goods on them all; her father, she explained, had died of the dope habit. The drugs-in-prison story line, quite startling for the funny papers of 1945, almost killed Gertie off, but in the end she single-handedly stamped the racket out and then decided to leave after all.

Out in the world, she found work at a rural greenhouse. Her employer, one George Decopolus, grasped that his new hire was not the sort of human who should be meeting the public, and he kept her repotting flowers in the back room. That's where she was when the late matron's son, the savage, zit-faced dope dealer called Measles (see Chapter 15) shortly showed up to put in an expensive floral order in memory of his late mother.

Law-and-order Gertie called Tracy on the spot. Then she helped save the detective's life by radioing the highway patrol after Measles briefly got the best of Tracy and drove away with him. Then she held Measles's confederates at bay with an ax until cops arrived.

"Our heroine!" Pat Patton jubilated after Tracy had been rescued. "Gorgeous Gertie!" cried a bystanding news photog, lensing her for the early edition.

On March 27, 1945, Gravel Gertie dropped out of the strip again. "If you ever want me," she beamed at Dick Tracy in his hospital bed, "you'll find me at the greenhouse."

Thus was the foolish crone of some months earlier rehabilitated into a woman of wit, intelligence, brave heart, moral verity, and abiding strength of character. She was still completely daffy, of course, but it was evident that God thought well of her in His heart. Maybe Dick Tracy would even have occasion to encounter Gravel Gertie again someday. He could find her at the greenhouse.

THAT SUMMER, THE CLASSIC GIRL VILLAIN

Breathless Mahoney (see Chapter 16), all her grand plans undone, found herself on the lam at last, seeking someplace, anyplace, to hide from the relentlessly pursuing Dick Tracy for five minutes. Plying the rural back roads in a stolen laundry truck, Breathless finally ran out of gas, and she climbed out and dolefully sur-

B.O. Plenty and the first woman on his place in twelve years, July 23, 1945. Initially introduced as a farmer who had worked his place for nigh onto fifty years, the beloved B.O. Plenty has subsequently remained with the strip for nigh onto another fifty, durn near.

Cross-country with B.O. Plenty and Breathless Mahoney, July 30, 1945.

veyed the great endless expanse of Calvinist midwestern farmfields.

Plowing which, on July 10, 1945, was first seen the disgusting figure of a ragged, bewhiskered, pith-helmeted, tobacco-spitting, egregiously malodorous farmer who was introduced as B.O. Plenty.

B.O. stood formally for Bob Oscar. Gould evidently regarded this entire set-up as quite the knee-slapper, and he labored to make things as broad as possible. "Phew!" Breathless would say, slapping her hand against the wind and scrunching up her nose. The fugitive vamp paid the dirtbag farmer a fast grand and holed up with him in his miserable shack for as long as she could stand it. Dick Tracy, meanwhile, having found the abandoned laundry truck, was already coming around to ask questions.

The detective and the hillbilly first met on July 17. "Detective, eh?" said B.O. Plenty, shaking hands. "Woman? There ain't been a woman on this place in twelve years. You won't find any woman on this place, Mr. Macy."

"The name is Tracy," Tracy said politely. In the beginning, Tracy always made a point of correcting the mistake as B.O. Plenty perpetually addressed him as Macy or Dacy or Bracy. Eventually he gave it up.

Tracy did find the woman on the place, and he put both fugitive and farmer under arrest and sat down to wait for backup. During the night, Breathless seized an opportunity to slip rat poison into the detective's coffee, and that left B.O. Plenty and Breathless alone with one another. She was ready to be on her way. And he, having discovered that she had $50,000 on her person, had other ideas.

It was Breathless Mahoney's lot in life. In an exact replay of what she'd already had to put up with from her mother, now she was saddled with B.O. Plenty, and the two of them were stuck like glue for weeks, lurching antically toward the City, both of them tugging at the cash prize. She won the game the first time around, grabbing the money and running as he dozed aboard the bus. Left stranded at a small-town stopover, the farmer was briefly arrested at one point by Dick Tracy, but he craftily managed to walk out of the one-horse jail when Tracy's back was turned and he grabbed the train. "Too quick for 'em!" B.O. Plenty nodded. "They ain't no flies on B.O. Plenty!"

The romp continued in the big City, as B.O. Plenty found a job as a nightclub doorman and was suddenly seen resplendent in medals and epaulets. Breathless, meanwhile, was still desperately on the run. In one of the thoroughly improbable coincidences that Chester Gould liked to lace his stuff with from time to time, the doorman was one day asked to park a car in whose backseat was hiding none but Breathless herself.

"I'll be galdarned," mused B.O. Plenty. "To think that fate should fetch us together like this."

They went together to the bank vault where Breathless had stashed her funds. B.O. wanted every dollar. "And if I don't get it, I'll take you by your wicked little wrists and turn you over to the first policeman," he promised.

"You stinking snake," she spat at him.

Out of nowhere, the pleasant little farce went suddenly into deep shock as the smelly, funny hick farmer settled matters by throttling Breathless Mahoney and leaving her in the vault in a puddle of gore.

BREATHLESS SURVIVED THE IMMEDIATE VIO-

lence, though she spent many months in a hospital bed and eventually expired. In any event, the incident took her off the list of Rats at Large and officially put B.O. Plenty on it. Meanwhile, $50,000 richer, B.O. took a good hotel room, clipped his hair and beard, decked himself out in fine clothes, bought a $4,200 diamond ring, and for a time, for the first and last occasions in his lengthy run in the strip, comported himself as something of a dude.

He was, however, only a country boy, and the city boys spotted him and sheared him like a sheep. Almost immediately he fell into the hands of the rat Itchy Oliver (see Chapter 15), who blowtorched his bare feet until he confessed where the remaining $42,000 could be found.

"YOU GOL-DURNED GANGSTERS!" B.O. Plenty raged helplessly.

The time had come for B.O.'s payoff. "We're not going to drill him!" Itchy winked at his boys. "We're going to let the sewer swallow him! Mr. B.O. Plenty will just disappear from circulation!"

In a sinister moment in a dead-end alley behind a shuttered factory in the dark of night, Itchy lashed B.O. Plenty to a plank, lowered him through a manhole, and cast him to the mercies of the subterranean tides far beneath the City.

And he sailed into the maw of a great black sewer tunnel, the last sight of him in early October 1945 his great terrified eyes as he silently disappeared into the belly of the underworld.

As dispatches went, this one was fairly nightmarish. "THUS ANOTHER MEMBER OF THAT LITTLE GROUP, WHO LET EASY MONEY CHANGE THEIR LIVES AND BECOME THEIR

The strangling of Breathless Mahoney, September 3–4, 1945.

B.O. Plenty in the big city, September 26, 1945.

GOD, PAYS FOR HIS FOLLY!" Chester Gould thundered, headline-style, and it could be surmised that Gould never really expected to see B.O. Plenty again.

On the other hand, he had also dumped Dick Tracy down a caisson once upon a time.

B.O. Plenty underneath the big city, October 7, 1945.

111

CHAPTER 19

HEY, THIS ISN'T A WRISTWATCH

The Most Remarkable Invention of the Age

S TILL RECOVERING FROM HIS RECENT STAR-vation at the hands of the evil Itchy Oliver, Dick Tracy in the first days of January 1946 was summoned to the estate of the portly industrialist Diet Smith, who provided a luncheon of something like half a cow for his guest and then popped open a jar of baby food for his own repast. "Ulcers," the great man groaned, clutching his immense growling belly. "I can't eat anything but strained vegetables and milk. Bah. It's my nerves. I'm a busy man."

"Often wondered what these billionaires eat," Tracy said to himself.

"Burph," grimaced Diet Smith.

Aides were running up all around, sticking telephones in Diet Smith's face. "Plant three calling on this radiophone, sir!" "Duluth calling on this line, sir!" In between bites of baby food, Diet Smith took care of business. "Yes, send Omaha 5,000 diesel motors and Chicago 8,000 car frames! Tell Bethlehem to buy 5,000,000 shares of the Detroit plant stock! Burp!" In between calls, he matter-of-factly explained why

he had called Tracy over. "I have," said Diet Smith, "murdered a man."

Apparently he had. His business partner was dead in the billiards room, wrists wired to the overhead lamp, electrocuted the instant Diet Smith had turned on the light switch.

"I'm ruined," the industrialist groaned.

And as luck would have it, even as Dick Tracy examined the stiff, Diet Smith's new yardman was shoveling the snow out by the servants' entrance.

B.O. Plenty had unexpectedly reappeared on December 27, 1945. It seemed he had gone through the entire sewer system all the way out to sea and been picked up by a tramp steamer. "Clean to China and back!" he'd stewed, walking the streets, pondering his future. He had a bit of money on him, but the YARDMAN WANTED sign on the iron gate outside the great mansion gave him pause. "I orta get a job," he'd mulled. "It ain't respectable to be idle." And now, Diet Smith's household staff had just taken on B.O. Plenty for twenty-five dollars a week, and the new hire was hard at work with his snow shovel.

He thought the little machine was a wristwatch when his shovel first uncovered it. "Watch, huh?" frowned his buddy the chauffeur. "Hey, this isn't a wristwatch."

"It ain't?" wondered B.O. Plenty.

AND SUCH WAS THE FIRST APPEARANCE, ON

January 13, 1946, of the immortal 2-Way Wrist Radio, DICK TRACY's primary emblem for a full generation.

By the prevailing standards of its day, the 2-Way Wrist Radio was a fantastic piece of science fiction. It is not recorded what Mollie Slott, the syndicate editor who routinely objected to any scientifica more sophisticated than basic fingerprinting, must have thought of this ugly tale of high industrial intrigue, but it is known that Chester Gould's own studio assistants pleaded with him to forget about the credulity-straining little instrument. Gould was undissuaded. "The most remarkable invention of the age!" marveled Dick Tracy. By now, Diet Smith was in jail, charged with the murder of his partner inasmuch as there were no other suspects, and B.O. Plenty was technically under arrest on all the old Breathless-related charges, though Tracy was letting him go free as a material witness in the Smith case. Tracy donned the 2-Way Wrist Radio, running its aerial up his sleeve. "It both sends and receives! Tiny tubes, battery, microphone! It's miraculous! Yes, Chief," Tracy told Brandon, "this 2-Way Wrist Radio is undoubtedly the prize at stake in this murder."

Indeed, it began to appear that some third party had set up the electrical kill of the business partner and then dropped the radio in the snow as he or she fled. Tracy went to free the industrialist, who was meanwhile running his empire via the bank of telephones he'd had installed in his cell. "Ship Hartford 2,000 motors and Pittsburgh 10,000 car bodies!" he cried. "Tacoma on this line, sir!" a clerk announced. Tracy came around and held up his wrist. "WHERE DID YOU GET THAT?" Diet Smith blanched.

"It was taken from the wrist of your dead partner by the murderer," Dick Tracy said.

"Our top secret," Diet Smith said gravely.

THE CRIME OF THE CENTURY BEGAN TO UN-

ravel when Dick Tracy visited the Diet Smith laboratories to question the secret radio research team that had developed the phenomenal 2-Way. At once he began to suspect the device's actual inventor of record, a stout, white-haired woman named Irma. "That's impossible," considered Diet Smith. "Why, Irma has worked with us for twenty years." Diet Smith was, of course, your archetypal American robber baron when you came down to it. "She's been legally compensated for all discoveries while in our employ," he declared. "She's quite happy."

Considering that Tracy had now found a four-fingered handprint in another sweep of the snow outside Diet Smith's mansion, the four-fingered Irma interested him regardless of the top man's protestations. Irma saw it coming down. "They're trying to close in on us," she was suddenly

Diet Smith in his bath, January 5, 1946. Despite the various secret atomic research divisions, the tycoon seemed in the beginning to be principally a carmaker.

Establishing what the 2-Way can do,
January 23, 1946.

radioing her confederate husband. And as Dick
Tracy and Diet Smith called in Irma for another round of questioning, suddenly an intruder burst into the room, carrying some kind
of lamp.

"SUDDENLY, A BLINDING FLASH FILLS
THE ROOM!" Gould headlined. "AN IM-
MEASURABLY WHITE, BRILLIANT LIGHT—
BLINDING LIGHT!"

"That's another one of my inventions," Irma
said as her boss and the nosy cop clawed at
their eyes. "The Atom Light. You will not be
able to see for at least eight minutes."

"Ye gods!" Tracy shouted. "I'm blind!"

Diet Smith groped at the tables. Every extant
Wrist Radio model and blueprint was now
stolen.

"We can get a grand apiece for these things!"
the husband yelled happily at Irma as the two
of them sped away.

WHATEVER SYMPATHIES THERE MIGHT HAVE

been for the oppressed wage earner Irma were
speedily diminished when it was learned that
she herself had swiped the 2-Way Wrist Radio
and the other wonderful inventions from her
own teenage-wizard son. His name was Brilliant and he was a nobleman, forgiving of his
mother despite the fact that she had accidentally blinded him in a laboratory mishap some
years earlier. "What matters the loss of eye-
sight if one's inventions benefit all mankind!"
Brilliant would cry, joyously mixing chemi-
cals. "Brilliant thinks his Atom Light is going
to be used as a paralysis cure!" Irma would
meanwhile snicker behind his back. "Ha!"

They lived on a boat in the harbor, Brilliant
and Irma and the husband. "I visited the children's hospital, son!" Irma would tell the lad.
"We treated several little victims!" Even the
old man couldn't stand such smarm. "Why soft-
soap the kid?" he demanded. Irma just pushed
him aside. "Brilliant, my son, do you think we
can build a thousand Wrist Radios?" she breathed.

"One thing we're very low on is lithium,"
Brilliant considered. "That's a highly critical
material, Mother. I doubt that you can obtain it
in quantities."

Ah, but Diet Smith Industries had just received a lithium shipment. Irma sent the husband to fetch a load of it.

Dick Tracy, perhaps remembering Yogee
Yamma and the enslaved professor in the old
abandoned subway, was already concluding that
there was some locked-up genius behind the
2-Way Wrist Radio when the news came in
that a lithium thief had just been shot to death
by a Diet Smith Industries security guard.

Irma heard the news on the radio, too.

"The last straw!" she raged. "Diet Smith has
worked his devilment on me and mine!"

She invaded the industrialist's house, locked
his servants in a refrigerator, galloped upstairs,
and faced down Diet Smith as he sat in his
bath.

"My best years were given to YOU," she
shrieked, "while you GREW RICH. . . ."

She shot him twice. Then she put a bullet
into her own head.

Outside, the yardman B.O. Plenty heard the
gunshots, and he rushed upstairs and held Diet
Smith's head above the bathwater until further
help arrived.

"WHERE ARE MY PARENTS?" BRILLIANT ASKED,

tapping his cane.

Tracy had bad news for him. "You look like
a kid that's got lots of guts and a good heart,"
Tracy said. He gave it to Brilliant straight. "They
were using you for many purposes. They're
both dead."

Diet Smith, critically wounded in the hospital, was calling for Brilliant. He wanted to offer
his condolences. "He can't understand why he
doesn't come," the nurses were whispering. A

Diet Smith in his bath, March 3, 1946.

few minutes later, Dick Tracy arrived with the boy, entered Diet Smith's room, and then excused himself. "I'll be back in a few minutes," Tracy said.

Left by himself, the blind boy approached the foot of the bed, pulled out his pistol, and fired four times. "At last, Diet Smith, my parents are avenged!" he cried. "Now we are SQUARE!"

The detective was back in the room now. "Finally got it out of your system, eh?" he asked quietly.

"I am ready to face the consequences." Brilliant shook. "I have just KILLED Diet Smith."

"No, you haven't," said Tracy, motioning toward what the reader, although not Brilliant, could now see plainly was an empty bed. Tracy explained that he had called ahead to have Diet Smith moved into another room. Brilliant fell to his knees and sobbed. "Thank God, Mr. Tracy!" he said.

"I knew you had to blow your top," Tracy said softly. "But you're too fine a boy to let something happen that you'd regret."

He held the weeping young genius. "Have it out, kid," he said. "Let those tears wash everything clean. This is going to be your and my secret forever."

A few moments later, Brilliant was at Diet Smith's bedside. "Tell me that we're going to be good friends," the tycoon begged. "Let me offer you a home with me . . . let me make amends . . . there's a place in my organization for you, if you'll accept. . . ."

"Sometimes entire lives are changed by a handshake," said Dick Tracy. "Sometimes out of chaos a great career is launched."

And thus did brilliant young Brilliant, inventor of the 2-Way Wrist Radio, go to work for

Diet Smith Industries as its chief of research.

Diet Smith was seen a last time in his bed, showing his appreciation for all that Dick Tracy had done for him. "I'm turning the 2-Way Wrist Radio over to you exclusively," he said. "It will be kept OFF the market! Your Police Department will be the FIRST IN THE WORLD to be equipped with the 2-Way Wrist Radio."

Tracy studied the little contraption that was about to become famously and irrevocably associated with his life and times. "Thank you,

Sightless Brilliant and the empty bed,
March 16, 1946.

115

The 2-Way Wrist Radio saves Pat Patton from incinerating, January 28–29, 1947.

Mr. Smith," he said politely. "It will be invaluable, I'm sure."

LITTLE DID HE KNOW, THOUGH, FOR A WHILE

the 2-Way was just a headquarters toy that Tracy and the boys enjoyed playing with sometimes. "It's a great step forward in scientific crime fighting," Chief Brandon would say as they all stood around fiddling with the knobs and the air filled with squawks. "What an age!" exulted Pat Patton. The thing was finally put into official field service on June 19, 1946, when Dick Tracy, sitting in a squad car, put out a street call to Pat Patton (the Historic First Broadcast: "Where are you? You're coming in very weak"). It was used again a week after that, when Tracy sat down with a lying gun moll and had her tell her phony story straight into it as Patton recorded the transmission in the next room. The recording was never put to any investigative or evidentiary use, but the point was now clear that crooks had just better watch what they said around the wonder radio.

By fall, Tracy and Patton were using the 2-Way routinely. It took the underworld a little while to become aware of the thing. In January 1947, the killer hypnotist Influence didn't bother to remove the radio from Patton's wrist when he dumped Pat into an old refrigerator and set him afire, and Tracy used loop equipment to trace his trapped partner's signals. "Close call!" Tracy mused as the semiroasted Patton panted for air. "Influence undoubtedly thought it was

just an ordinary wristwatch!" Indeed, time and again the 2-Way got the boys out of various tight squeezes as a growing collection of crooks kept wondering why the policemen seemed to be talking into their ordinary wristwatches. "Here we are minding our own business, and a beautiful model pulls a gun on us," Tracy intoned, wrist to his mouth, when a gun moll named Dahlia Dell got the drop on him in April 1947. "He's trying to tell me something!" Patton deduced miles away, mobilizing a rescue squad as Tracy kept up a running line of trackable chatter. "Don't think for a minute we'd CALL FOR HELP AT 2011 MURRY STREET," Tracy said. The gun girl had no idea where all the cops suddenly came from.

Even years later, there were still thugs who would bludgeon Tracy, carry his limp form off someplace, stare at his wrist, scratch their heads, and mumble things like, "Say! What's that?" As word got out through gangdom, though, sometimes the radio backfired on him: More than one crook unmasked an ostensibly disguised Tracy over the years specifically because the 2-Way identified him as a cop. By and large, though, it was a handy thing to have around.

Diet Smith reappeared in July 1947 to present Tracy with another one of young Brilliant's inventions, the Ring Camera, although this one didn't particularly capture the Police Department's imagination and was never used very much. In late '48, he showed up again to unveil Brilliant's Teleguard Camera, which introduced sophisticated closed-circuit television technology to the strip (see Chapter 22) and presaged many developments in real-life police work. There were other inventions over the years from Diet Smith Industries, but the tycoon himself was just an occasionally seen figure until 1962, when he single-handedly propelled DICK TRACY into the Space Age (see Chapter 34).

AS FOR THE ORIGINAL 2-WAY WRIST RADIO

itself: Despite the criticisms that it was naught but the wildest of comic strip fantasies, in real life such a thing was quite realistically inventable in the postwar period. Scientists in both government and the private sector, by now blessed with such modern developments as subminiature tubes and printed circuits, were already on the job. By late 1947 a Dr. Cledo Brunetti of the National Bureau of Standards had devised a working three-ounce model with a reliable range of about a mile, and he created a sensation when he demonstrated a prototype before a conference of the Institute of Radio Engineers in New York in March 1948. Standards patented the unit and licensed several companies to produce it, and the Federal Communications Commission set aside a band range (460–470 megacycles) against its eventual adoption by law-enforcement agencies. Meanwhile, by late 1947 the Dick Tracy 2-Way Wrist Radio manufactured by Da-Myco was an enormously popular piece of toy-store merchandise, and regular fellers everywhere were keen to have one. Basically just a cheap radio ("Connect to any bedspring!" the ads urged young shoppers), it did feature as well a "telephonic transmitter with built-in earphone" and the thing was more or less able to transmit a kid's voice ("over short distances!") via the miracle of a "war-developed crystal rectifier!" Many thousands of them were sold at $3.98 apiece.

For all the hoopla, the Brunetti radio wasn't destined for much of a future, as Bell Laboratories was already developing the revolutionary new transistor, thus instantly sending most existing communications technology to the scrap heap. The landmark breakthrough came in April 1952, when the Radio Development and Re-

Life imitates art: Chester Gould accepts a kind of 2-Way Wrist Radio thing from Western Electric Company, Allentown, Pennsylvania, June 13, 1952. (New York *Daily News* photo.)

search Corporation figured out how to mass-produce transistors, and just two months later Chester Gould traveled to the Western Electric Company's plant in Allentown, Pennsylvania, to proudly accept his own working 2-Way Wrist Radio. It was mostly a ceremonial keepsake, as the FCC never assigned Gould an actual transmitting frequency, but he was able to tune in his favorite radio programs on it, and it was a popular novelty in his studio for some time.

None of these true-life experimental models was ever commercially produced, but the 2-Way Wrist Radio of the DICK TRACY strip became a household word in America, a device as familiar as Tracy's hat and overcoat, and it continued to perform faithfully and well until April 1964, when Diet Smith Industries came up with the successor 2-Way Wrist Television, and the famous old workhorse was phased out of service.

CHAPTER 20

A HAPPIER LIFE AMONG THE BIRDS AND BEES

Sweet Dreams and Sunny Dell Acres

GRATEFULLY RECOVERING IN THE HOS-pital, and having mended relations with the boy Brilliant, industrialist Diet Smith now turned his beatitude upon B.O. Plenty, the simple yardman who had saved his life.

"I'm just learning that true character and greatness hide only in the breast of the common man," the big shot said humbly.

"Never knowed that myself," B.O. Plenty said.

"You saved my life," Smith said. "I want to compensate you. I want to reimburse you."

"What?" B.O. spluttered. "After all I've done for you?"

And so began the patron Diet Smith's abiding friendship with B.O. Plenty, an affection that has spanned the generations. B.O. was still technically in trouble with the law over the old Breathless Mahoney business, and Smith stood for his bond and insisted upon arranging for his counsel. But he wanted to do more. Wasn't there anything . . . ?

B.O. thought it over. Well, maybe a little plot of land near the City? A little truck farm? Where he could raise vegetables?

Diet Smith couldn't believe his ears. As luck would have it, he just happened to own a little plot of land near the City, and he was overjoyed at the prospect of getting rid of it. "An old subdivison that never developed!" he proclaimed. "You can have the entire parcel of land free! It's even got an old real estate office on it that you can make over into a house. It's called Sunny Dell Acres."

He sat back in bed. "The house may need a little fixing," he reflected.

SUNNY DELL ACRES (FIRST APPEARANCE, MARCH

24, 1946) was nothing less than the postwar American suburban nightmare. Chester Gould's midwest was full of such once-ambitious boom developments whose planners had laid out fine little streets with names like Paradise Lane and Rainbow Drive during the good times (Tracy, indeed, while briefly a beat cop back in February 1932, had trudged past a sign advertising "choice 50×125 lots" at a development called "Sunny Dells") and had then bailed out during the bust, leaving their projects to the pit and the abyss and the Illinois weeds. The real estate office—the property's lone structure, a ludicrous shanty stuck behind a grandiose portico and planted in a hilarious sea of street signs with ever-changing names inscribed upon them—was a wreck, sunken on its foundations, walls crumbling, floors buckled. "Say, it's plumb purty," said B.O. Plenty on his first visit. "And sech a civilized neighborhood. Factory on one side and railroad on t'other."

Also there was a greenhouse next door. B.O. noticed it on his first full night in his new home as he sat happily beneath a full moon. Music was coming from the place, rather insistently. "Sounds like a banjo or a mandolin!" he said. "I hear a woman singin', too. Voice is a little squeaky, but it's purty. Yep, it's shore nice to live in a good neighborhood."

"ONLY A BIRD IN A GILDED CAGE," came the voice across the night.

"Yes, sir!" nodded B.O Plenty. "I'm being serenaded."

"DON'T SWEETHEART ME," came the yowl from the greenhouse.

B.O. Plenty went inside and slammed his door. "Hm!" he grunted. "She shore sings loud!"

Genuine inspiration had illumed Chester Gould.

AS B.O. PLENTY AND HIS NEIGHBOR ACROSS

the way began to get the occasional glimpse of one another, he realized her to be a noisy,

The courtship of B.O. Plenty and Gravel Gertie, May 6, 1946.

Welcome to Sunny Dell Acres, March 25, 1946.

evil-tempered harridan with a face that could scare a cat off a fish wagon and she realized him to be a smelly hillbilly who spat tobacco on the floor and never took off his pith helmet, and they despised one another at once. She was, of course, the same Gravel Gertie of yore, making an honest living at the greenhouse, sleeping there nights as well, and the neighbors would go on to court and spark and spoon and then to marry and then to parent a gloriously beautiful daughter who would utterly seize the public's affections and sell three million dollars' worth of dolly merchandise to little girls all over the land and finally to become beloved fixtures forevermore—occupying a position in the comic strip firmament approximately akin to LI'L ABNER's Mammy and Pappy Yokum—the embodiments of the Christian American family in the warmhearted, decent place called Sunny Dell Acres.

This was all down the road yet. In the spring of 1946, B.O. Plenty and Gravel Gertie couldn't bear the sight of one another.

A pair of eyes would be peering at him

The official proposal, July 27, 1946.

through the trees as he chopped up stumps. "Without a doubt that's the UGLIEST ONE HUMAN I ever saw," Gravel Gertie muttered. And he would be gaping at her as well as she pushed around her wheelbarrow. "Without question that is the ugliest one human I ever laid eyes on," B.O. Plenty ruminated from his side of the property line.

"What are you gawking at—you—you—WALKING CONVULSION?" Gravel Gertie demanded.

He tendered an apology. They found themselves going for a walk on a country road. "My name's B.O. Plenty," he introduced himself. "I was one of eight boys. My pappy took us west in—"

"Ugh! He's repulsive!" Gertie snorted.

"Neighbors orta be friendly," he ventured.

"Double dipped idiot," she shook her head.

It was a beautiful thing to watch.

IT TOOK A FEW MONTHS YET. BY JULY, B.O.

Plenty and Gravel Gertie were tittering like birds.

In their fashion. "I could never marry you," she snapped at him. "Your etiquette—it's terri-ble." "I'll have it laundered," he offered. But she was playing romantic mandolin tunes in the greenhouse window ("Coax me a little bit! Coax me a little bit!") and on July 28 she deliriously accepted his proposal ("I surrender! This is D-day! Take all of me!"). "She won me!" B.O. Plenty proudly informed Dick Tracy. Formalizing his noble intentions, he bought the little lady a plow. "I'm going to give her them three back acres to put into an onion crop! She can make five or six hunnert dollars a year!"

He was still under indictment, and he was looking at a possible prison term, but nightly did the swain and his lady bill and coo 'neath the summer moon and together plan their lives at Sunny Dell Acres, 808 Joy Terrace, at the corner of Hope Street.

"You'll give up chewing tobacco for me, won't you, honey?" she fluttered.

"Now, looky here, woman," he scowled.

"Did you read the etiquette book like I asked you?" she inquired. "Why—huh? What are these brown stains on it?"

Inside the strip, Hollywood columnist Hedda Opper did an item about the pending nuptials and they became a national event. Outside the strip, the wire services picked the story up and the wedding got headlines out there as well. Breathless Mahoney, now dying of a mysterious illness in the prison hospital, ranted and railed in fury and sent her lawyers to court to seek the revocation of her attacker's bond. It happened that the judge was a hanging judge, and even as B.O. Plenty was being fitted for his cummerbund ("No, you don't let that stick out. You fasten your vest over it." "Dat-dratted new inventions"), the forces of justice were mobilizing to bring the prisoner in.

On the sunny summer Sunday morning of August 18, 1946, bride and groom and preacher and guests assembled at Sunny Dell Acres, mobile radio units broadcast live, and the entire nation tuned in. B.O. Plenty and Gravel Gertie exchanged their solemn vows ("Do you, B.O. Plenty, promise to—" "Why, shore!" "Darn you! Take off that hat!") and were then pronounced man and wife, and suddenly peace officers with official court papers stormed the wedding and arrested the groom and jailed him in his wedding suit.

Members of the wedding, August 17, 1946. The cartoonist was genuinely enchanted with the developments. He almost never signed himself "Chet."

"I'll be back!" B.O. Plenty cried. "Love will find a way!"

To think that something like this could happen. It was the talk of all America, within and without the strip. The public outrage finally even got to Breathless Mahoney, feverish in her bed and momentarily facing the Great Beyond. She had listened to the wedding broadcast, too. "They're trying to gain happiness. . . ." she mumbled. "I'm dying. . . ." On August 25, she called for Dick Tracy and laboriously scrawled out a document absolving B.O. Plenty of everything, and then smiled faintly and expired. "Give him another chance," she wrote. "I forgive. Breathlesssssssss" and her final signature trailed off the bottom of the page as the pencil dropped from her hand.

"Well, Breathless," Dick Tracy said softly. "You had a little kindness in your heart after all."

She was last seen in her prison bed, the soul flown from her ravaged body. "A misspent life!" Tracy declared. "Crime, disease, and death— finis!"

The chief complainant having withdrawn her grievances, there was no longer a case against the prisoner, and the hanging judge was none too happy about matters as he called his court to order for the purpose of freeing B.O. Plenty. Did the defendant, he snarled, wish to make a final statement?

"Well, you see, I was one of eight boys. . . ." the defendant said.

On September 1, the loving B.O. and Gertie

Plenty faced the setting sun, arms entwined, all their ordeals behind them.

"WE LEAVE THEM," the strip captioned the farewell appearance, "TO WHAT WE HOPE IS A HAPPIER LIFE AMONG THE BIRDS AND BEES OF B.O. PLENTY'S TRUCK FARM."

The end of Breathless Mahoney, August 25, 1946.

The world's first look at Sparkle Plenty, in the pages of *Glance* magazine, June 6, 1947.

And they were gone, though the business with the birds and bees did seem to signal something or other.

INDEED, JUST ABOUT PRECISELY NINE MONTHS

later, B.O. Plenty abruptly reappeared in the strip, whispering something excitedly into Dick Tracy's ear.

"No kidding!" Tracy said.

Intimations were dropped for several weeks. "What in the dickens does B.O. Plenty keep dropping in here to see Tracy about?" Chief Brandon demanded. "Tracy won't tell me," Patton shrugged. B.O. Plenty was seen buying cigars. B.O. Plenty was seen rushing into the night to make a frantic phone call. The reader began to get the drift.

On Friday, May 30, 1947, Gravel Gertie issued.

"Oh, brother, what an offspring!" Tracy howled. The world had to wait for a full week to get a look at what kind of horror such a crew as B.O. Plenty and Gravel Gertie could have possibly produced. "Was it born with a long neck?" Tess Trueheart wondered. "Does the baby have a beard?" guessed Chief Brandon. "It has two heads?"

Finally, on June 6, the strip showed the little girl's face.

She was just beautiful, a radiant little thing with silken blond hair, flowing to her waist.

Her name was Sparkle.

She was a sensation. She showed up in *Life* magazine. The Ideal Toy Company rushed into production with Sparkle dollies that were on store shelves just weeks later. Readers swamped Chester Gould's studio with baby presents. Gertie rocked the tyke and crooned baby songs

("Oh, Little Sparkle, weep no more/Your little face ain't dirty/Brave B.O. Plenty is your pop/And your ma is Gravel Gertie"). The roll continued until July 14, when the three Plentys were seen on their Sunny Dell Acres doorstep, saying farewell again.

"I guess that's the finish," B.O. said.

And man and wife looked at one another in the midwestern summer evening, comic strip characters patently finished with.

"And now, to just live a quiet life and bring up our little baby Sparkle," Gertie said.

"Yes, Gertrude," said B.O. "What we want is solitude."

Showering Baby Sparkle, June 10, 1947. The clutter at Sunny Dell Acres was reflective of Chester Gould's studio, which was also full of goodwill offerings from the public.

The most famous Near-Deathtrap of them all, August 15, 1943: Mrs. Pruneface's kitchen, scene of the horrible rig that would slowly spike Dick Tracy through the heart. It almost never occurred to villains just to shoot Tracy and be done with it.

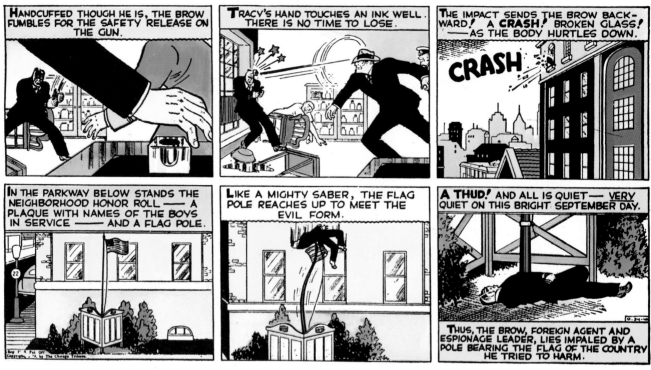

Crime must pay the penalty: The Brow and the mighty saber, September 24, 1944.

Crime must pay the penalty: Nilon Hoze and Rod beat the chair, June 2, 1946.

Crime must pay the penalty: Shoulders crashes an airplane, July 28, 1946.

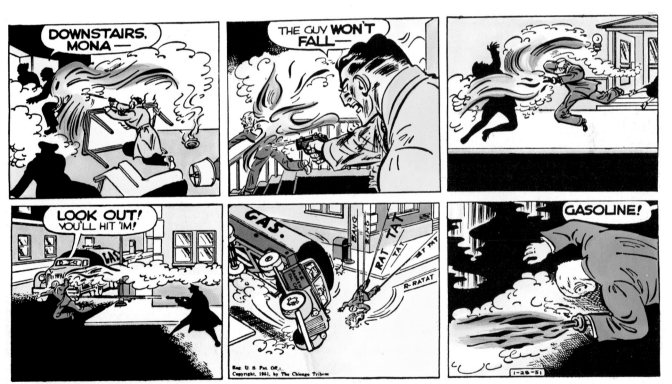

Crime must pay the penalty: The soon-to-be-cinders Doctor Plain, January 28, 1951.
Doctor Plain was a crazed surgeon who packed a flamethrower in his artificial hand.

1

2

3

4

SUPPORTING PLAYERS:

1. Frizzletop, July 26, 1942. The amputee ex-Army nurse was a Tracy companion through several adventures; here she finds work at mobsman Tiger Lilly's gangland country club.

2. Misty Waters, March 16, 1947. Tracy was not a gent who routinely set the ladies aflame, but young Misty Waters fell out of her shoes at first sight and resolved to win him. "My sleuth-heart!" she was forever cooing. "Screwball," Tracy kept grunting. Misty finally got the message and took a walk.

3. Photographer Eddie Johnson, April 13, 1947. Johnson helped Tracy get a line on killer photographer Hypo, later became affiliated with *Glance* magazine, and made the first pictures of Baby Sparkle Plenty.

5

4. Spike Dyke, August 14, 1949. Zany bandleader Dyke was modeled after zany bandleader Spike Jones. He showed up again in 1957 when the fugitive Kitten Sisters hid out with his road show.

5. Al the Police Pilot, June 27, 1954. Helicopters joined the strip virtually as full cast members in the mid-'50s, and Al was invariably the man at the stick whenever Tracy went aloft.

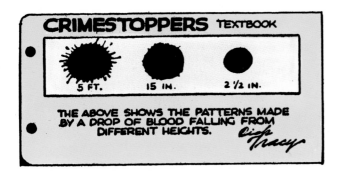

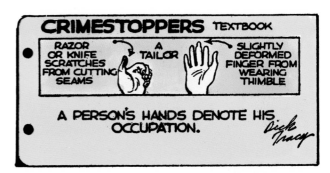

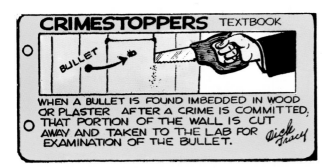

Crimestopper's Textbook: a selection. The famous scrapbook feature was launched
in September 1949 and continues to this day.

Comic book ad for Genuine Dick Tracy Wrist Radio, October 1947. Get on the road to popularity.

Easter Sunday, April 16, 1950. Chester Gould celebrated by blowing up Dick Tracy's house.

COMIC BOOKS:

DICK TRACY crossed over to comic books in February 1936, in the first issue of the Dell Publishing Company's POPULAR COMICS. For the next twenty-five years, over hundreds of issues of one book series or another, there was almost never a time when the great detective's reprinted newspaper strip adventures were not prominent at the nation's newsstalls.

At left, DICK TRACY MONTHLY No. 1 (Dell, January 1948). This issue contains 1934 strips: the (non-Gould) cover depicts Larceny Lu's whip-snapping confederate Mortimer. In 1950, TRACY moved to Harvey Publications—at right, DICK TRACY COMICS MONTHLY No. 118 (December 1957, featuring the 1949 Sleet story)—and finally expired in April 1961. TRACY was not seen in comics again until 1986, when Blackthorne Publications launched an ambitious reprinting program. Following Blackthorn's demise three years later, Gladstone Publications in 1990 launched another.

THIS IS A COMPARISON MICROSCOPE FOR EXAMINING BULLETS. TODAY, I'LL SHOW YOU HOW IT OPERATES.

CHAPTER 21

WORK AND WIN
Junior Tracy and the Crime Stoppers

NOTWITHSTANDING ALL THE BLOODCUR-dling mayhem that the garden clubs were forever bawling about, Chester Gould knew in his heart that his jut-jawed policeman was absolutely a role model for the youngsters of the day and he knew that his comic strip was performing social good works. Crime didn't pay. Criminals couldn't win. Any boy could see that with his own two eyes. No less a public hero than J. Edgar Hoover himself agreed that DICK TRACY was something a right-thinking young fellow should read and respect and learn a thing or two from. Gould always took very seriously indeed the responsibilities of the mantle of moral leadership.

In April 1947—his strip very successful and very much talked about in the popular prints, his straight-shooting cop a regular feature on radio and in the movies and on the brightly colored ten-cent comic book racks—he went straight to the youth of every hamlet and valley of America. Junior Tracy—the little freckle-faced fellow's unceasing law-and-order pieties by now frankly close to unbearable—formed a boys' club of his fiercely conscientious band of manly little law-abiding friends. The notion was not

without its antecedents: indeed, Gould probably lifted it directly from his friend and fellow *Chicago Tribune*man Harold Gray's patriotic Little Orphan Annie Junior Commando organization of several years earlier. Elsewhere in comics, the war had produced the Newsboy Legion and the Boy Commandos and their numerous liberty-loving variants. Outside of comics, to be sure, Lt. Gen. Sir Robert S.S. Baden-Powell had long ago formed the Boy Scouts. Outside of comics, so far as that went, der Führer had once created the Hitler Youth.

"We're going to call ourselves the CRIME STOPPERS," Junior earnestly explained. "We feel we can do a lot of good among kids. We'll help kids that need help. We'll find odd jobs for 'em to do after school. We'll be friends with 'em."

"Sort of a detective club of helping hands," one of his pals added.

"We figure we could do a lot of good helping kids who MIGHT go wrong BEFORE they get started," Junior summed it up.

Had you been one sort of lad in the American school yards of 1947, you would have wanted in a minute to throw in with an outfit

Crime Stoppers at muster: Let's be careful out there, May 14, 1947.

like the Crime Stoppers and you would have been proud to mail in your twenty-five cents for the Crime Stoppers badge-and-ID-card kit that presently began to announce itself on cereal boxes everywhere. You would have resolutely been a participant in the club's first rehab project, a would-be bicycle thief named Zip Smith. "You can't STEAL BIKES around here and get AWAY with it!" quailed Junior, gamely lacing into his somewhat larger quarry. "One thing Crime Stoppers won't stand for is pilfering!" Moral rectitude prevailed, and the whipped Zip hung his head. "I never had a bike," he blubbered. "Did you ever think of earning some money and BUYING a bike?" Junior retorted. "We Crime Stoppers have a club to HELP kids like you." And Zip signed up on the spot and he was straightaway taken to meet Dick Tracy himself. "Glad to know you!" Tracy boomed as he pumped mitts with the bruised albeit cheerfully grinning Zip, clearly a boy who had just resolved to be as honest as the day is long for the rest of his entire life.

Had you been another sort of lad in the American school yards of 1947, on the other hand, Junior Tracy's little gang of goose-steppers could probably have handed you a good laugh. A bully named Bronko was of this persuasion. Bronko liked to break into candy machines and pay phones, and he didn't much appreciate these little buttinsky Crime Stoppers. "SISSIES!

STOOL PIGEONS!" he would bellow whenever he saw them. Sometimes he tried to run them down with his car. "Dirty guy!" Junior would yelp, leaping from his bicycle, spilling the groceries. Bronko kept all his stolen coinboxes hidden in his pigeon loft. After much dark-of-night surveillance, the Crime Stoppers found the stash. "For crumb's sake!" they whistled.

For some few months in 1947, the strip had been featuring a soon-to-appear *Life*-like national picture weekly called *Glance*, and early in the Crime Stoppers' career Dick Tracy made a large point of persuading *Glance* editor Amon Clark to feature the club in the magazine's forthcoming June 6 premiere issue. "I think it would make a great layout!" Tracy affirmed. "Good picture story!" Clark nodded at his photographer. "Good influence on juveniles!" the photographer agreed. Introduced to Editor Clark, Junior threw out his chest and explicated his personal code: "We feel that too much idleness is not good. We believe in having odd jobs after school and our motto is Work and Win." Editor Clark rubbed his jaw, no doubt astounded that such a young sprout as Junior would think of

Code of the Crime Stopper: A Crime Stopper's gotta do what a Crime Stopper's gotta do, May 20, 1947.

Badge and everything, June 19, 1947.

referencing a cheap popular novel that Horatio Alger Jr. had published sixty years earlier. "WORK AND WIN!" Editor Clark reflected thoughtfully. "It could very well become a national slogan!"

The Crime Stoppers did get into *Glance*'s first issue when June 6 rolled around, and so, too, did the Exclusive First Photographs of little Sparkle Plenty, who had been born a few days earlier (see Chapter 20). In the wake of all the attention, a number of real-life Crime Stoppers chapters popped up around the country and proceeded to become involved to one degree or another in the greater good of their respective communities, no doubt directing a lad or two onto the right road and inculcating them with the values and verities that would serve them in good stead all their days. And no doubt they launched many a dedicated career in law enforcement; indeed, it is recorded that in January 1949 one particularly hotshot Crime Stoppers unit in Arkansas tracked down an escaped convict to his lair in the hills and held him down squealing till the very impressed local constables showed up.

Even the likes of Bronko came around, finally, after he crashed his jalopy into the river and Junior Tracy personally pulled him out of the rushing waters, and thereafter he was proud to join the Crime Stoppers, too ("You're my

REAL friends! I see it now! I'm a heel!" "You mean you WERE a heel, Bronk. Those days are over, eh? Shake"). And thereafter Bronko even made something of himself, demonstrating once again that every good boy does fine, once you save him from drowning.

But after that there was only one more Crime Stoppers yarn to speak of—this was later in 1947, when a crook named Coffyhead attempted first to discredit Junior and his pals by pinning a shoplifting rap on them and tried next to gas them to death—and then the club quickly receded from the story line, bobbing up only infrequently as the time went by; before long, it disappeared altogether.

On September 11, 1949, the DICK TRACY Sunday page carried on the short-lived organization's earnest legacy by launching the famous scrapbook feature entitled CRIMESTOPPER'S TEXTBOOK, which for another twenty-eight years—unto the very day of Chester Gould's retirement—would offer useful public-service tips to rookie policemen and concerned citizens alike. "While shopping, never leave your purse lying on the counter. Thieves await such opportunities." "Altered documents can be detected under ultraviolet light." "Courteous driving prevents accidents."

Solicited by Coffyhead, August 6, 1947.

I'M GOING TO THE MAYOR AND TENDER MY RESIGNATION AS CHIEF OF POLICE, EFFECTIVE IMMEDIATELY.

I CAUSED THAT BOY'S DEATH.

CHAPTER 22

NOT FIT TO CARRY ON

Chief Brandon Goes Down

CAPTAIN JOSEPH MEDILL PATTERSON DIED at sixty-seven in May 1946, and his memory was suitably revered for the usual decent interval, and suddenly in the fall of 1948 there were interesting developments. In September 1948, his *New York Daily News* at last added to its comic strip stable BRENDA STARR, a soaper that had been running successfully for eight years in the sister *Chicago Tribune* but which Patterson loathed so much that he had by personal fiat forbade it from running in his own paper. There may be no more telling indicator of his immense power than that he managed to keep BRENDA out of the *News* until after he'd been two full years in his grave. Meanwhile, inside The Captain's protégé DICK TRACY strip, Chester Gould was suddenly killing off one major character, dropping a second, introducing a third, and repositioning a fourth, and he was also bringing in a strong new villain, a brusque, impatient, minion-mistreating ogre of man who looked just like Joseph Medill Patterson.

Big Frost (first appearance, September 25, 1948) was a racketeer who was trying to get his hands on the industrialist Diet Smith's still-under-wraps and quite astonishing Teleguard Camera. "To think it can telecast over 1,000 miles on its own batteries!" observers marveled. "The greatest crook-stopping device in the world!" belched Diet Smith enthusiastically. "We have overcome the obstacle set up by the curvature of the earth's surface!" explained the boy inventor Brilliant. "A modern miracle!" Diet Smith boasted. "Truly a product of a NEW age," said Chief Brandon. "It sounds impossible," Tracy hesitated. "Nothing is impossible," said Brilliant.

Tracy was sold. "It could be bigger than the 2-Way Wrist Radio," he agreed. Actually, the Teleguard never seriously threatened the 2-Way's popular primacy, but it was big enough that Diet Smith got shot up pretty good when Big Frost's mob marauded his penthouse in search of the blueprints. Diet Smith always kept them strapped to his own body, though.

Heedless of the gangland plot against him, Diet Smith insisted on demonstrating the Teleguard before a national conference of two hundred police chiefs. "The most important meeting in police history!" he declared. "A symbol of science's victory in the field of criminology!" barked Chief Brandon, glaring straight into the reader's eyes.

Big Frost got wind of the gathering. It just happened that he had a large collection of phony police badges. Passing himself off as a small-town chief from Oklahoma, he presented himself to Chief Brandon, standing guard at the confo's door.

Having done many less than bright things throughout his career, Brandon now made his final colossal boneheaded blunder, failing to make a sufficiently careful inspection of the gangster Frost before admitting him. "Odd," the chief mused, looking over the guest list. "Doesn't list an Ilton, Oklahoma. Well, the man looked all right. Credentials seem okay."

Inside, Frost quickly learned that Brilliant alone possessed the secrets of the Teleguard, its design committed to his memory. And that night, announcing himself to be Diet Smith's chauffeur, he called at Brilliant's apartment.

Big Frost, October 5, 1948. The Captain Patterson look-alike, two years after The Captain's death.

Blowing away Brilliant, October 16, 1948.

Back at headquarters, Chief Brandon had become fretful. "But there must be an Ilton!" he gasped, thumbing through book after book. "Isn't listed," worried Tracy.

It was late. Brilliant had just been retiring for the night. In his final seconds, he grasped that something was wrong. "Chauffeur?" he puzzled. "What do you want?"

Big Frost didn't know it, but there was a Teleguard Camera recording everything as, on October 16, 1948, he pulled the gun from his pocket—"You're the blind genius, are you?" he chuckled—and shot young Brilliant to death.

"He was like a son to me," Diet Smith grieved at the graveside. That was true. A few days later, Diet Smith confided to Tracy that he and the late Irma had once been man and wife, and Brilliant was, in fact, his natural son.

Diet Smith Industries went on. So, for a time, did the severe Big Frost. What had been a minor comedic substory, meanwhile, now came to the forefront of the narrative.

BIG FROST HAD A HOMELY DO-GOODER DAUGH-

ter named Flossie, a girl who was determined to reclaim her father from the jaws of crime and who was forever showing up at his doorstep carrying books with titles like "Crime and Its Price" and "You Pay for Your Deeds." "Please, Papa, I want to save you from yourself," she would waggle her finger. "Let me read from page three." Flossie was exactly the sort of reform-bent little dweeb who could drive anybody to a life of lawlessness, and Frost was always aghast when she came knocking. "Tell her I've left town! Tell her anything!" he would gulp at some confederate as he ducked into a

Flossie Frost and Papa, October 25, 1948.

closet. "That's too bad," Flossie would frown. "I wanted to leave him with these pamphlets."

The hilariousness of Flossie (first appearance, October 2) is notable in that not only did Chester Gould seem to be enjoying a good joke on himself—Flossie was, after all, parroting what had been the strip's own social message for years—but that he was now, two years after the great editor's death, gleefully flinging into the Patterson-like visage of Frost the same Crime Can't Win sentiments that had been The Captain's mandate in the first place. (Patterson, not incidentally, also had an impossible daughter; the socialite Alicia Patterson Guggenheim, a onetime *Daily News* reporter who had since founded the Long Island paper *Newsday*, had for years exasperated the old man to the point that her whinings were a standing *Daily News*

joke, though one that wasn't necessarily brought up when The Captain was in the room. Flossie Frost, as it happened, looked a bit like Alicia Patterson.)

As comedy, it didn't go on for very long. Big Frost, not much in the father department, finally ordered his men to kill the nuisance girl. Flossie was snatched off the street, beaten into a bloody pulp, and dumped into a roadside snowbank somewhere outside the city. "I feel a lot better with that goofy daughter of mine out of the way," Big Frost toasted the occasion.

There was a happy ending here, as the snowbank turned out to be Sunny Dell Acres' front yard, and the comatose Flossie was saved after little Sparkle Plenty stumbled across her. Little Sparkle was talking by now. "Me find woman in thnow!" she chirped. And so Big Frost's daughter survived, though all memory had been bludgeoned out of her. "My name?" she blinked, rubbing her brow like Mary X. "She's got magnesia," B.O. Plenty clucked. "Tch-tch! Magnesia is shore a terrible thing!"

As for Big Frost, he was tracked down soon enough by Dick Tracy, who installed the Teleguard Camera behind the grille of the gangster's car and orchestrated the First Time in History Television Was Used to Catch a Criminal. His auto's location constantly known to the police, Frost was presently running into roadblocks wherever he turned. "Now I'll cut

Demolishing Flossie, November 2–3, 1948. Chester Gould gave it to the girl pretty hard.

Television nails Big Frost, November 16, 1948.

down to the waterfront," Frost was deciding. "He's going west," Tracy was messaging Car 10 from his TV monitor. "Where are all these squad cars coming from?" the bewildered gang boss cried. Finally hemmed in by what looked to be every policeman in the city, he surrendered meekly and was led away in cuffs as Dick Tracy gravely announced to the reader that television had proved itself as an effective crime-fighting tool. "The very device that Big Frost set out to destroy has had him for its first victim!" the detective declared. "The television burglar alarm has justified its existence!"

BUT THAT WASN'T THE ENTIRE STORY.

Chief Brandon had considered himself directly responsible for the murder of Brilliant. Overcome with guilt and remorse, he had thrown down his star and left the strip. "I'm not fit to be police chief," he said. "I'm a murderer." The mayor accepted his resignation. A final scene on October 24, 1948, found Brandon at his home, sunk into an armchair, his ashen face buried in his hands. "I'm not fit to carry on," he mourned.

And Pat Patton, once the funny little buffoon of a sidekick, was appointed chief of police to succeed him. Gould regularly made a point of telling his interviewers that Tracy had been offered the job first and had declined it. The two policemen formally redefined their relationship on the spot and thereafter Tracy always respectfully addressed Patton as Chief. Patton,

for his part, evolved into a patriarchal senior officer in a matter of weeks and his seventeen years of service as Dick Tracy's partner were almost never mentioned again.

AND THESE CIRCUMSTANCES LEFT TRACY NEED-
ing another sidekick.

The new guy showed up over Christmas, an exuberantly wisecracking character with a knobby nose and a face full of freckles. His name was Sam Catchem.

Chief Pat Patton in charge, December 11, 1948.

HE'S COMING DOWN HERE, TRACY.

2-WAY WRIST RADIO

CHAPTER 23

OI YI!

Sam Catchem

FROM AN INITIAL FLAT SALARY OF VIRTU-
ally nickels and dimes, Chester Gould became monied by his strip very early on,
and by 1936 he could move his family to
a sprawling farm in Woodstock, Illinois, where
he lived comfortably and well for the rest of
his life. The mounting strip revenues themselves, which he split with the Chicago Tribune–
New York News Syndicate Inc.—$1,555 a week
in April 1937, $1,825 in April 1938, $2,250 in
July 1944—were the least of things. There were
bijou serials, feature films, a long-running radio program, an endless stream of comic books
and Big Little Books and related ephemera, piles
of popguns and wind-up squad cars and secret
code books on department-store toy shelves.

Throughout these enterprises, Gould's trusted
agent and negotiator through the increasingly
handsome series of contracts with both the syndicate and the licensee merchandisers had been
one Al Loewenthal, who had a knobby nose
and a face full of freckles and who was, in the
late 1940s, nudging his client to incorporate "a
Jewish character" into the strip. As Dick Tracy
now needed a partner anyway, Gould obliged
the old friend who had made him rich, and the
character Sam Catchem arrived as more or less
the spitting image of Al Loewenthal. Sam's os-
tensible Jewishness was never formally explicated, but he did cry "Oi yi!" a lot, and he was
known to carry salami sandwiches in his coat
pockets.

Sam Catchem had a fully constructed history, unlike, for example, Dick Tracy, about
whom precious little personal information was
ever recorded. Sam had once been a dentist,
apparently he had once briefly been a lawyer,
he had been a schoolmate of Pat Patton's, and
he'd been an army fingerprint man during the
war. He'd been a policeman for twenty-five
years in a number of cities (Brooklyn, Syra-
cuse, most recently Boston). His arrival (on December 24, 1948) brought another temperament
to the strip, as, in the late '40s, it was changing
its appearance in any case, moving toward
sleeker, more modern graphics even as philosophically it was shedding such a pterodactyl
as the gruff old Irisher Brandon.

Tracy and Catchem made a tough professional
crimebusting unit, the both of them forward-
looking guys, changing with the times. "When
I think of the progress that's been made since I
entered police work!" Sam marveled, admiring
the banks of closed-circuit television monitors
at police headquarters. "I was a young guy
then," he reflected on New Year's Day 1949. "I
thought a billy club, a star, and a six-shooter
was as scientific as you could get." "Yes, Sam,
this is 1949!" Dick Tracy said proudly.

Touring the jail, the new guy recognized practically everybody as somebody he'd popped once
upon a time. "Yes, the name SAM CATCHEM
has struck fear into the heart of many a crook!"
the partner grinned. "I don't doubt it a bit,

Sam," said Tracy, clapping him on the back, and a lifelong friendship was forged on the spot.

The partner was pretty useful from the first. Right away, for example, he knew Sleet.

SLEET WAS ONE OF THE MEANEST OF THE STRIP'S

'40s broads, a chilly blonde with her nose high in the air, a racketeer's stylish widow, the daughter of an old woman who'd been nailed as she mirror-flashed messages to Big Frost in his cell. Sam Catchem had been a pal of Sleet's from the old days, and now he was muscling her into setting up the last remaining members of Big Frost's mob for a bust. "I've got enough on her to send her up for 20 years," he winked at Tracy. "I thought I was rid of you when I left Boston," sniffed Sleet (first appearance, December 30, 1948). "Fate just won't keep us apart," Sam shrugged. "I hope you drop dead," she said, icily.

She made a mistake. She tried to have him killed. She almost succeeded, a couple of times. Sam Catchem finally woke up black and blue in a hospital bed after she'd dumped him off a bridge. "Is THIS embarrassing," he sighed to Tracy. "Yi! How would you like to give me a swift kick as soon as I can stand up?" "Easy," Tracy assured his pal.

The episode left Sleet on the run. With millions in a strongbox she couldn't go near, the proud Sleet was reduced to washing dishes in a restaurant kitchen and borrowing small change from a grubby second cook who decided he was God's gift to her. "Richest moll in the country hiding out a dishwasher!" the cook snickered. "Now, baby, you're gonna play ball with me!" They went for a late-night stroll on an elevated platform. He wanted ten grand. "You're kinda cute," she nuzzled him, and then she pushed him over the rail.

The ID in the stiff's pockets only brought Tracy and Catchem in closer. The vicious Sleet was cornered at last hiding out in the home of Mrs. George India, widow of a world-famous adventurer who had spent his life filling his house with stuffed zoological specimens of every persuasion. "Yi!" yelped Sam, suddenly face-to-face with a python, his hat flying off his head. "Easy," Tracy assured him.

Sleet, having belted Mrs. India with an ax, was already on the roof, leaping to a water tank next door. Exactly repeating an old March 1932 situation involving the crook Three Finger Haffy, Sleet now crashed through the tank's frail wooden lid and became immutably lodged. "What do you know," Tracy smirked. "Must have stopped to wash her feet."

It was April 1949 and Sam Catchem had wrapped up his introductory story, live and well.

"April in Paris," Sam hummed, cuffed firmly to Sleet in the backseat of the squad car. "April in solitary."

And that was the end of Sleet. Back on the train, she went to Boston to pay up on old accounts. "Kind of hate to see that dame go," Sam yawned, inspecting his nails.

Right behind Sleet, January 16, 1949.

Baptizing Catchem, February 11–12, 1949. Junior Tracy and his Crime Stoppers found the new guy after he'd been bopped, chloroformed, and thrown into the city's underbelly.

A FEW MONTHS LATER, THE NEW SIDEKICK almost bought it again when, investigating the murder of the baby-diaper czar Talcum Freely (see Chapter 25), Tracy and Catchem collided with the mad clothing designer Sketch Paree. Otherwise only a pathetic loon, Sketch Paree became one of the great horrible Grotesques whenever he donned his mask, a shapeless blob of a water-sloshing sponge with which he drowned his victims, pressing his face fast to theirs as he bear-hugged them. "Oi, yi!" Sam Catchem choked, having just barely fought the monster off. "A face of water!" And together Dick Tracy and Sam Catchem nearly perished in their first mutual Near-Deathtrap, an awful hydraulically sinking room that had them mouth-deep in the river and going under fast before arriving officers finally pulled them out.

Sketch Paree was already at large in the land, and he would successfully drown a few other people before Tracy and Catchem ran him in. Before the story was done with, Chester Gould would write into the action his zany loud-suited novelty bandleader buddy Spike Jones, who showed up in the strip in the summer of 1949 as a zany loud-suited novelty bandleader called Spike Dyke. On stage, the sponge-masked Sketch Paree attacked Spike Dyke in live performance, and it appeared to be just another Spike Dyke gag, and how everyone howled and hooted until the instant Dick Tracy leaped from the wings and drilled the madman. "Glub!" Spike Dyke coughed.

"Well," said Sam Catchem to Spike Dyke, "I hope lovers of good music everywhere will forgive us for saving your life."

SAM WENT ON TO ENDURE PLENTY MORE AS

Dick Tracy's number two, and arguably there has never been a more definitive second banana than Sam Catchem, a man whose middle name was sidekick from the first minute and who forevermore remained a rock of utter reliability, always there when Dick Tracy needed him, always putting his life on the line, always standing unobtrusively two or three steps behind the star of the show despite his never-questioned professional status. Throughout, he has always been purely one-dimensional, almost never figuring more than indirectly in the strip's narrative action, almost never stepping out of his place, almost never representing any-

Trapped in the sinking room, August 28, 1949.

thing other than Usefulness. He's the partner anybody would want in a pinch. He always understood that the comic strip wasn't called DICK TRACY AND SAM CATCHEM.

Craftily disguised as a matron in the crackdown on weight-loss racketeer Pear-Shape, May 22, 1949.

CHAPTER 24

FOLLOW THAT CAR WITH THE DOG ON TOP

The Boxer

FOR A TIME, DICK TRACY HAD A DOG SIDE-kick, too, a huge and ebullient boxer who liked to ride atop squad cars. His proper name was Barbel Von Nikelslit Dauber of Purple Woods, though he was never called anything but Mugg, and when he was first seen on April 6, 1949, he was vigilantly guarding his old master's corpse inside a small house on the outskirts of town. He hadn't eaten for days, and Dick Tracy and Sam Catchem befriended him on the spot with a salami sandwich. "We'd better take the dog," Tracy said as medics removed the old man's body. "Take 'im?" Sam grunted, at this point fighting off the joyful animal's affections. "Hah! We'll never get RID of him."

Mugg's arrival in the strip brought a racketeer named Pear-Shape to Tracy's attention. Pear-Shape was an uncommonly corpulent crook who operated a phony weight-loss clinic and who happened to look exactly like Chester Gould, a stout man not unwilling to enjoy a chuckle at his own expense. Pear-Shape (first appearance, April 14) also dabbled in jewel theft, and it developed that he was attempting to retrieve a half-million dollars' worth of hot stones that Mugg's late master, an accomplice, had stashed somewhere in his house. Tracy and Catchem, staked out in the shadows as Pear-Shape and his men showed up to ransack the place, couldn't have had a bolder backup than Mugg, who charged headlong into tear gas and gunfire and started bowling over gangsters like so many tenpins ("The dog's back!" "Drill him!" "Ow!"). Mugg single-handedly put the whole mob out of business, save only for Pear-Shape, who got away, barely. "I'm contending with a MAD DOG!" the fugitive grumbled, nursing the ripped-out seat of his pants.

Mugg also found the hidden gems all by himself—"This dog is smarter than both of us, Tracy," Sam posited at one point, and it was probably true—and he was subsequently on hand when his cop buddies tracked Pear-Shape to the reducing salon and the obese crook made a frantic, clumsy bid for freedom, squeezing through hallways, rolling down staircases, Mugg never more than feet behind him. Mugg even turned doorknobs with his teeth. "He'll kill me!" Pear-Shape groaned. The crook made it to his getaway car, but one good jump and the dog was on the car's roof, doggedly on the case as Pear-Shape sped through the City. The circumstance enabled Dick Tracy to get off one of the best lines you could ever utter when you jump into a taxicab: "Follow that car with the dog on top!"

Pear-Shape got rid of Mugg by swerving into the park, brushing a low-sitting tree limb, and clubbing the rooftop rider unconscious. "We'll find him!" Dick Tracy promised Mugg at the hospital. "We'll find Pear-Shape!" "Woof!" the dog agreed.

Still recuperating, Mugg didn't happen to be around at Pear-Shape's finish, which occurred in June 1949, when the fat little man fell into the lion pit at the zoo and was more or less had for lunch, but thereafter he was a familiar strip mascot, regularly riding aloft as Tracy and Catchem drove to crime scenes, regularly sniffing out holed-up underworlders, regularly coming through like a champ. Ultimately a number of characters owed their lives to Mugg. He was a pretty good dog to have around the house, actually.

Pear-Shape, April 24, 1949.

In October 1950, Dick Tracy assigned Mugg to protect Sparkle Plenty and Vitamin Flintheart from the homicidal T.V. Wiggles (see Chapter 25)—and inside the television studio where Wiggles had trapped the old man and the child, he faithfully did his job, making a flying leap across the room and knocking aside Wiggles's rifle even as the gunman was drawing a bead on the little girl. It ended the dog's career. The enraged

Mugg mops up, April 28, 1949.

Noble dog rescues child lost in maze
of subterranean utility tunnels,
October 2, 1949.

Wiggles put a bullet point-blank into his chest.

In a hospital scene on December 3, the wan, heavily bandaged Mugg gravely shook hands with Dick and Junior Tracy.

"He's recovered," Junior breathed.

"We could NEVER forget Mugg," Tracy pledged.

And maybe they never did, but this was the last time Mugg was ever seen. It is nice to think that the brave police dog, desperately wounded in the line of duty, surely must have been retired from service, with full honors.

Wounded in action, October 24, 1950.

CHAPTER 25

AND TO THINK WHEN SHE WAS BORN SHE COULDN'T PLAY A NOTE

Sparkle Plenty Goes to Market

CHESTER GOULD, A CANNY BUSINESSMAN always attentive to the licensing and merchandising possibilities of his commercial product, knew he had a knockout in little Sparkle Plenty from the first minute she came into this life. So, too, did many another entrepreneur who was entirely willing to collect a fortune on the adorable and quite patently sellable tot, both within the strip and without. The first of them was a gladhander named Lurch, who made a single appearance on June 15, 1947, when Sparkle was barely two weeks old. "I'm in the investment business," Lurch introduced himself at the door of Sunny Dell Acres. "Congratulations on your beautiful baby. You're a lucky man, Mr. Plenty."

B.O. Plenty eyed the interloper warily. "T'warn't all luck, sir," he said.

"Heard you came into considerable money through the sale of your baby's picture to *Glance*," Lurch continued. "Have you thought of putting that money in a safe place?"

B.O. Plenty squinted hard. "I'll thank you to leave my property at once," he said.

That pretty much set the tone for anyone who wanted to do business with Sparkle Plenty. It is undocumented what Chester Gould's terms had been with the Ideal Toy Company, which rushed its storied Sparkle dollies into production overnight and had them in the nation's department stores before the end of July and ultimately sold a good half million of them at $5.98 apiece, but the onetime Northwestern night commerce major is believed to have done well enough. The wild success of the Sparkle doll, the single most sensational piece of DICK TRACY merchandising ever, was all the more remarkable given the fact that by the time Sparkle hit the shelves Gould had already dropped the Plenty family from the strip, and it was going to be many months before any of them were seen again.

Then, when they finally did reappear in the spring of 1948, the first thing Gould did was blow up their house and kill them.

THE LITTLE COCKER SPANIEL HAD COME OUT of nowhere. Her name had been Flapsie and she had been the pet of the gang boss Mrs.

137

THE **CRASH!** A BURSTING GASOLINE TANK! **FLAMES!**

WHEN I STEPPED OUT OF THE TRUCK, I FORGOT TO TAKE IT OUT OF GEAR.

IT WENT RIGHT **THROUGH THE WALL OF THE HOUSE.**

I DIDN'T EXPECT THIS. I'VE GOT TO GET AWAY FROM HERE.

FED FROM THE INSIDE, THE FLAMES **COMPLETELY** ENGULF SUNNY DELL ACRES!

The tragedy at Sunny Dell Acres, April 17, 1948. Revenge-bent Mrs. Volts had planned merely to shoot the Plentys as they slept, but things went awry.

Volts, and one night she had seized an opportunity to flee her hateful mistress. On April 1, she had appeared on the doorstep of Sunny Dell Acres, tail wagging. The Plentys named her Heyyou—Chester Gould himself had a dog called Hey—and little Sparkle loved her to pieces. "Daw! Daw!" little Sparkle kept shrieking happily, her official first words. Mrs. Volts, meanwhile, determined to have the animal back, was already casing the Plenty household in a pickup truck. Mrs. Volts didn't drive real great. The truck went careening headlong into the place, there was a terrific explosion, and suddenly Sunny Dell Acres was burning to the ground.

There was not so much as a charred evidence of B.O. Plenty and his family. "This is one of the great tragedies of my life," mourned Dick Tracy, poking through the embers. "What is to be will be," a uniformed cop mused fatefully. Citizens stopped on the street to gawp at the headlines and to exchange stunned condolences with one another. "Aren't there enough things WRONG in this world already?" they lamented.

Gould kept up the cliffhanger for a few days in late April 1948. Finally the Plentys turned out to have been merely spending the night elsewhere, dog and all. "What happened?" B.O. Plenty said, gazing upon his ruined home.

"Tell me everything that led up to this," Tracy said.

B.O. scratched his head. "I was one of eight boys. . . ." he said.

"Our dream house!" wept Gravel Gertie. "Our honeymoon cottage!" The patron Diet Smith, his heart melted, built the Plentys an exact replica of the original Sunny Dell Acres, down to every crack in the plaster, down to the twin of the ancient wood-burning stove. "I could have bought a battleship easier than I bought that stove," he grunted. "Everything's just like it was before!" Gertie wept inside the brand-new hovel as Sparkle celebrated her first birthday. "These are shore happy days for the B.O. Plentys," B.O. jubilated thankfully.

And so it was in mid-1948 that the Plentys, their lives first smashed and now courageously rebuilt, were somehow even more celebrated in the firmament than they had been a year earlier.

Unhappy headlines, April 21, 1948.

Pop celebrity being what it is, suddenly one day in late August there appeared a billboard high above the streets of the City, advertising delicious Sparkle Plenty Cola.

HOW MUCH OF THIS COLA STORY MAY HAVE

had its basis in real events is no longer immediately clear these years later, but there were in fact one or two not fully licensed Sparkle Plenty enterprises in the wake of Ideal Toy's tremendously successful Sparkle doll, and a couple of sharpies had run headlong into the extreme disapproval of Chester Gould and Al Loewenthal and their lawyers.

"Huh?" B.O. Plenty blinked at the huge DRINK SPARKLE PLENTY billboard. "Why, I didn't give nobody permission to use Sparkle's name on a sody bottle!"

Straightaway he went to Dick Tracy and an attorney. "Dad-blamed thieves, that's what they are," he snorted. The cola-company president kept wiping his brow. "I—I HAD planned to give you SOMETHING," he sweated. "Perhaps a little royalty? An eighth of a cent on every bottle sold?" B.O. Plenty scribbled out a few figures. "One-eighth of a million—H'm? No, one million times five—no—"

He finally settled for a deal that included a territorial sales franchise and he took custody of a twenty-foot promotional papier-mâché soft-drink bottle that he planted on the roadside at

Sparkle Plenty Cola, unauthorized, September 2, 1948.

Sunny Dell Acres. "Yes, Gertrude, we're exclusive distributors of Sparkle Plenty Cola!" he boasted to his wife. "Soon as they sell eight hundred million bottles, I'll be a millionaire!" And through the fall of 1948, B.O. peddled Sparkle Plenty Cola by the bottle from his front yard.

In early November, Gravel Gertie finally dragged him indoors. "Looks like snow tonight," she said. "Soft drink season is over, if you ask me."

"I've got four bottles left over," B.O. inventoried. "Reckon I'll drink 'em myself and close up for the winter."

"Good," she snapped. "Sparkle and me can't hold any more."

Sparkle Plenty Cola, authorized, July 3, 1949. B.O. Plenty operated his roadside soda stand for several seasons.

Now we are two, May 30, 1949. Marking Sparkle's birthday was an annual custom in the strip into the '50s.

THE FOLLOWING SUMMER, THE MARKETPLACE seriously discovered the kid and started going to town.

Two years old, tiny Sparkle Plenty was now doing strenuous yard chores under her pop's supervision. "Plague take it," she grumbled. "Rake's too dad-burned BIG. Dad-burned axe is too big." B.O. Plenty clapped his head. "Kids don't want to work these days," he sighed. Meanwhile, Tess Trueheart had recently opened a commercial photography studio and she was landing one of the country's largest accounts, the famous baby-clothes manufacturer Talcum Freely. "I want some REAL baby pictures!" Talcum Freely was blowharding. "I want pictures of a 2-year-old child with character! Charm! Background! I want an UNUSUAL child!" "Come to think of it . . ." Tess realized.

Tess Trueheart and Talcum Freely met with the beauteous little diamond in the rough at Sunny Dell Acres in July 1949. "Been helping pappy cut the dad-gum underbrush," the little scutter reported. Talcum Freely fell head over heels at first sight. "Gad!" he cried. "Just what I've been looking for!"

The first shoot didn't go all that well. Talcum Freely wanted to cut the kid's hair. "The back of the dress must show," he decided.

"WHAT?" exploded B.O. Plenty. "My child's charms can't be bartered for PALTRY GOLD!" Talcum Freely immediately put on his hat and took a walk. Gravel Gertie immediately hit B.O. Plenty over his head with a chair.

"Remember, Sparkle, as long as Pappy lives, he'll always watch over you," B.O. assured the little tyke.

"Dad-blamed right," she scowled.

EVENTS TOOK A TURN WHEN TALCUM FREELY was thereafter shot to death and B.O. Plenty, fearing he was the likely suspect, became a fugitive for many months. In fact, Freely's murder was the work of the revenge-bent clothing designer Sketch Paree (see Chapter 23) and B.O. Plenty was finally cleared and he came home again and Gravel Gertie whacked him over the head with a washboard and life at Sunny Dell Acres thus continued blissfully and harmoniously.

And later, in the summer of 1950, when the strip's attention again returned to the Plenty household, it developed that Gertie had been teaching little Sparkle to play the mandolin just like mammy. "TWO SONS FROM TUCSON," little Sparkle was whanging away.

"SHUT UP!" B.O. bellowed, trying to watch TV. Sunny Dell Acres at this point had a wonderful new television and the biggest aerial in the county. It seemed that Gravel Gertie had gone on a quiz show and won all these consumer goods by delivering the correct answer to some phenomenally obscure question ("President Garfield!"). B.O. was now absorbed in the Friday-night "Kid Talent" program, hosted by the popular TV personality Ted Tellum.

"If you have a child WITH TALENT," Ted Tellum was saying, "write me and tell us all about it."

"Plague take it," said Sparkle Plenty. "I can do that."

Lights went on over B.O. Plenty's brow.

And just a few nights later, Sparkle was on her way to becoming a national hit on network television.

"NOBODY'S DARLIN' BUT YOURN," the little thrush belted. "BURY ME NOT ON THE LONE PRAY-REE. OH, YOU MAILED MY HEART TO THE DEAD-LETTER OFFICE."

"Phone calls!" cried the stunned network execs. "Letters! Thousands of 'em!"

Diaper tycoon Talcum Freely seeks a two-year-old, July 5, 1949. Tess Trueheart by now was a successful commercial photographer. Freely was presently slain by clothing designer Sketch Paree.

Sketch Paree and his little friend Babee, August 10, 1949. The bonkers clothing designer drowned several persons with his ghastly water-dripping sponge mask.

Sparkle Plenty on the air, August 13, 1950.

Dick Tracy read the newspaper like everybody else. "Says she's destined to become the country's top child prodigy," he marveled. "Reckon it won't hurt 'er none effen she keeps healthy," B.O. Plenty shrugged.

"I'm as good as Arthur Goshfry!" the kid gloried.

"And to think when she was born she couldn't play a note," B.O. Plenty said proudly.

Sparkle Plenty, suddenly a star worth a couple grand a week in 1950 dollars, suddenly needed an agent. The summons went out to the old ham actor Vitamin Flintheart. "I might be able to help that moppet," he decided wearily. On July 27, Dick Tracy formally introduced Vitamin Flintheart to the B.O. Plentys.

"He'll make the right connections for her," Tracy offered.

B.O. gave Flintheart the same look he'd given Lurch three years earlier. "Agent?" he scowled. "Last agent we seen sold us six bottles of liniment."

Tracy set everything right. B.O. Plenty and Vitamin Flintheart cut a deal and shook hands. Little Sparkle was on her way to the big time. "I'm made!" Vitamin cried gleefully. "I again will be able to live as befits one of my reputation."

He climbed into a cab, and the next thing Vitamin Flintheart knew he was getting blackjacked.

T.V. WIGGLES WAS A SMALL-TIME PROTEC-
tion guy approximately on the order of the late great Gargles. As taverns across the land began to install television sets over their bars in golden 1950, T.V. Wiggles, a jittery crook who looked like somebody slightly out of horizontal hold, was just the man who was going to make sure nothing ever happened to all those TVs. He had a hundred-dollar-a-month service fee. Otherwise his boys were apt to squirt corn syrup into the expensive sets and wreck them. In retrospect, it is really quite astonishing how dopey much of the early- and mid-century's petty protection racketeering really was, exactly analagous to some schoolyard bully's demanding a fee for safe passage to the water fountain. Mobs of the day really did make whole livings at moronic dodges like this.

"We already have a lucrative business," Wiggles explained to Vitamin Flintheart. "But we want to expand." What Wiggles wanted was every dime of Flintheart's agent commission.

A bad moment with T.V. Wiggles, October 24, 1950.

The broken Flintheart assented for a time, particularly once Wiggles, a onetime professional wrestler, had demonstrated his proficiency at blacking out the child with a secret neck grab, but finally it occurred to him to go to Dick Tracy.

Whereupon Tracy, in a wonderful instance of art's imitation of life's imitation of art, set up T.V. Wiggles by replacing Sparkle Plenty with a Sparkle Plenty doll. Thereafter the gangster was plunged into desperate and thrilling flight sequence—in which he shot and gravely wounded B.O. Plenty—and T.V. Wiggles finally died, very much like Gargles, when he holed up in a county-highway maintenance garage and a load of sharp sheet steel fell over on him and stapled him to the floor.

That left the bewhiskered old hillbilly dying in the hospital, and Dick Tracy again fell to his knees in prayer, in the most egregiously Christian moment the strip had seen since God and Tracy and Eddie Rickenbacker had preserved the life of little Johnny Wreath in a snowstorm nearly eight years earlier.

"The world needs this old fellow, Lord," Tracy whispered at the bedside, hands clasped, eyes shut fast.

"His simple faith and homely, direct way stand out like a beacon in these confused days," he continued.

The B.O. Plenty Deathbed Vigil,
November 19, 1950.

"Won't You save him?" Dick Tracy pleaded. "You're our only hope. Amen."

Tracy stared out the window into the snowstorm.

And then little Sparkle came around with her ukelele and started singing.

"DADDY'S LITTLE GIRL," she twanged. "COME AND SIT BY MY SIDE LITTLE DARLIN'. THERE'S A LONG LONG TRAIL A-WINDIN.'"

B.O. Plenty awakened and recovered. "Shock treatment!" the attending surgeon exulted. "Thought I'd passed through the pearly gates and gone to my reward." B.O. nodded weakly.

At Christmas 1950, this was now suddenly the end of the public career of Sparkle Plenty, age three, who hereafter would never be more than just another little hick girl like every other little hick girl and who would almost never again over the rest of her life have occasion to remember that once upon a time she had been the grandest little darlin' of all America.

The evil Wiggles pays the price,
November 12, 1950.

CHAPTER 26

THE HOPES AND FEARS OF ALL THE YEARS

Mr. and Mrs. Dick Tracy at Home Before the Hearth

IT WAS CHRISTMAS AGAIN, AND DICK TRACY had celebrated by trapping the fugitive fur thief Mousey in a streetcorner pile of Christmas trees and threatening to set it aflame if she didn't come out right now.

"Good night for a bonfire!" Tracy bantered at Sam Catchem. "You light that side and I'll light this!"

"Sure thing!" Sam agreed.

"No! No!" Mousey screeched, scrambling out of her nest and going gladly to prison.

It was a fine, festive season, and there was peace on earth again, and love was in the air. During this Christmas Week of 1949, Clark Kent married Lois Lane, and Clark Gable married Lady Sylvia, and New York City Mayor William O'Dwyer married Sloan Simpson, and on December 20, the day after Mousey had been bagged, plainclothes detective Dick Tracy showed up at work with a goofy grin on his face.

"What's the matter with that guy?" Patton scowled.

"Just a holiday daze," Sam suggested.

Well, no. Over the next couple of days, Dick Tracy and Tess Trueheart were seen huddling and conferring and embracing and forking over dollars to the county clerk. "Tess Trueheart, I know you're dreaming!" Tess cried starrily into her mirror. Tracy started handing out invitations to some notably special Christmas dinner at an address nobody recognized.

"Don't ask questions!" Tracy winked. "Just come. We'll have the biggest Christmas party you ever saw!"

Chief Pat Patton looked straight out at the reader. "Something fishy here!" he confided.

Nah. It couldn't be happening.

DICK TRACY'S ALTOGETHER UNTELEGRAPHED

marriage to the long-patient Tess Trueheart surprised everyone on earth, chiefly the *Saturday Evening Post*, whose December 17 issue was still sitting on coffee tables all across the land with a substantial Chester Gould profile containing Gould's personal assurances that of course a guy like Tracy could never possibly think of settling down because after all he spent all his time crouching in ditches and shooting people and how could he possibly expect to deal a lady into a life like that? The entire point of the *Post* piece was that basically Tess Trueheart could forget about it. The *Post*'s interview, of course, had been done some months earlier, and essentially what had happened here is that Gould had just changed his mind. Ideas just came to him sometimes. "No fanfare, no buildup!" Chief Pat Patton pounded the table at the wedding supper in the fine new home Dick Tracy had built for his bride. "They just went out and got married! It isn't fair!"

In an editorial some weeks later, the embarrassed *Saturday Evening Post* characterized Gould as "bewildered" by the sudden union, and for a cartoonist who worked on the fly, that was probably true. The magazine griped that Gould might at least have invited the profile's author to have been the best man. As the story hit the national newswires, Gould just kept shrugging that he didn't have the remotest idea what his detective was going to do from one minute to the next anyway and that he was personally as stunned by the marriage as anybody else. "I couldn't help it," he sighed. "Tracy never tells me anything."

There was even more than that. Suddenly Tess Trueheart Tracy was a thoroughly changed woman. "Newlyweds are supposed to go on a honeymoon, darling, but I understand," she smooched the big guy when the guests were gone. "It's all right with me. You're busy. I don't mind." Astounding as this change of tune was from the woman who had been badgering him for decades to get out of police work and open a shoestore or something, Dick Tracy's own behavior was even more remarkable. On the spot, he ripped the antenna out of his 2-Way Wrist Radio, rendering himself unsummonable by all the world. "We're leaving in ONE HOUR!" he said. "We're going to forget there's anyone else in this world but US."

Presently they were on their way to a North Woods honeymoon lodge, driving through a midnight snowstorm. The blizzard was too much, and the car stalled in a drift. Neither one of the happy newlies cared a jot about such a trivial thing. They found shelter in a nearby farmhouse, where another stranded couple had also been taken in, and they spent their honeymoon night huddled together in a rocking chair. By morning the storm had cleared,

Mr. and Mrs. Tracy, December 25–26, 1949; they had been married Christmas Eve. The house was the detective's surprise present for his wife. "Marge" is the infrequently seen Mrs. Sam Catchem.

and Mr. and Mrs. Tracy were on their way again, along with their fellow strandees.

It is one of the most tired old plot devices in all literature, and it always works fine. As Dick Tracy and the other fellow made their polite good-byes, they accidentally picked up one another's suitcase.

WORMY MARRONS WAS ONE OF THE TRULY

unlovelier of the great Grotesques, a man of such hideous complexion that it was not regularly possible to distinguish his mouth from his eyeballs. He was an ex-con, currently wanted for murder in three states, and he was traveling with his meek, battered wife in a station wagon mounted with machine guns disguised as air

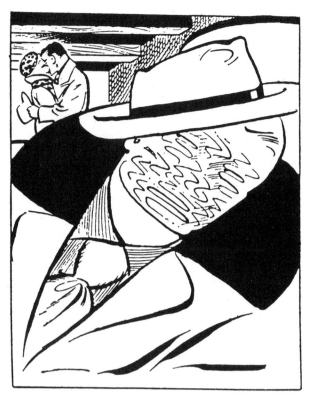

Wormy, December 30, 1949.

horns. Inside Wormy's suitcase, Tracy discovered, was a small rug with large red stains.

Wormy had overheard the Tracys' destination, and suddenly he was calling at their hotel room, and it developed now that Plainclothes Tracy, notwithstanding his having made a large show of dismantling the 2-Way, had thought to pack his wedding-night bag with a chemical kit. "Stall him a minute," Tracy told his wife as he tested the stains and the banging on the door got louder. "Ye gads!" the little woman screeched, instantly reverting to form now that she finally had a ring on her finger. "This is our HONEYMOON!"

A check with headquarters established that Wormy Marrons was a desperate known killer. Dick Tracy leaped into his car and gave pursuit. "I know I shouldn't!" he mused. "Tess and I are on our honeymoon! But what else CAN I do? That bird Wormy is a KILLER!"

Well, what else could he do? Tess, meanwhile, stood watching from the window, tapping her foot, steam billowing from her ears. "I might have known!" she fumed. "There goes the GREAT LOVER! I should have known being married to Dick Tracy would be like this!"

After eighteen years of keeping company with the man, that was certainly true enough. And

Tracy, for his part, probably should have guessed that the speeding car he was at this moment forcing off the road would have machine guns in the air horns. Right away he was on his back, disabled, disarmed, being dragged to his death on the bumper of Wormy's flying wagon.

"He's off on ANOTHER CASE!" Tess wailed back in the room. "I might as well NEVER HAVE EXISTED." Married to Tracy for practically only minutes, she was already packing her bags.

"HELP!" Tracy was yelling over his 2-Way Wrist Radio, whose wire he had fortunately reinstalled at some point. "I can't take it much longer! He's trying to finish me off!"

State cops found him slammed into a bridge abutment, soaked in blood, half-dead. "It's a miracle," Tess bawled, forgetting about going home. "Oh, Dick darling, WHY do you take such chances?" The cops also found the telltale rug, evidence of a recent killing that Wormy had tried to burn, and the healing Tracy examined it for clues and instantly went alight. "Cliff Hotel?" he said. "How far is that from here?"

Oh, that man. "Dick!" Tess frowned somewhat less than approvingly. But now there was a hint of pride in her, and after that there wasn't another peep out of the woman as the bandaged Tracy put on his clothes, dashed out the door, abandoned his honeymoon, and indeed did not set eyes on Mrs. Dick Tracy again for another couple of months.

ONCE THAT DUST SETTLED, THOUGH—AND IT ended in one of the most explosive shoot-'em-ups the strip had ever seen, the artillery flying for days, the unstoppable Wormy still on his feet and trying to escape across a frozen lake despite dozens of bullet holes through him— Dick Tracy officially began his new life as a suburban burgher.

"Tracy, don't forget you're due home at six for dinner," Junior suddenly said one day.

"Yeah, you're a family man now, remember?" said Sam Catchem.

Back at his fine new house, Tracy proudly showed off what he described as "my latest invention." This was a remote door control for the family dog, the big boxer called Mugg (See

Dick Tracy's honeymoon, January 11–13, 1950.

Chapter 24), and he had cleverly patched it into the master bedroom's clock radio, a device that at the time was quite the hot new consumer item. "You know," Tracy explained to his family, "on cool mornings it's nice to be able to let the dog out without going downstairs. Then by the time you're shaved and bathed and get down to breakfast, the dog will be ready to come in." Tracy continued to explain the wonderful clock radio to his little brood at some length. "You see, you set the clock for the time you want to get up," he went on and on.

"Gosh, a clock radio," Junior Tracy marveled.

"Then, when the alarm goes off, the radio starts," Tracy said. "At the same time, current is turned on in this extension cord plug in the back. Downstairs the door to Mugg's quarters is pulled up by a contrivance I put together myself."

Chester Gould here drew a panel that cross-sectioned the entire electrical hookup. "A trip turns off the current and locks the door in the up position," Tracy finished. "And, zip, OUT goes Mugg!"

"Tracy, you're a GENIUS," said Junior. "I can't get over it."

Gould was so awed by the clock radio and electric dog-door opener that he continued to describe it for days and days. "I can let the dog out without coming downstairs!" Tracy kept boasting. The milkman stopped to admire the apparatus. The newspaper sent over a reporter to write up a human-interest feature. The Society of Amateur Inventors named Dick Tracy an honorary member.

In another part of town, a fellow called Blowtop read about Dick Tracy's dog door in the morning paper.

Blowtop, so named because he was forever blowing his top—"How many times have I told you not to TWIDDLE YOUR CIGARETTE?" he would rage at one of his confederates. "You know I can't stand that!"—was the kingpin of a two-million-dollar Boston express robbery. He was also the grieving brother of Flattop, dead these six years, and he was sworn to make Dick Tracy pay for that. Blowtop's mob thought this

Blowing away Wormy, March 23, 1950.

The holocaust, April 17, 1950.

was needlessly dumb. "Please don't tangle with Dick Tracy," pleaded Blowtop's moll Toots. "Better men than you have tried it!" But there was no reasoning with the irascible Blowtop. "DON'T TAP YOUR FINGERS THAT WAY!" he quaked. "How many times have I told you—" The dog door interested him. The electrical diagrams interested him a lot. It appeared that Blowtop knew a little something about explosives.

Life was ever more serenely pleasant and rewarding at Dick Tracy's home. "Will we have a lot of fun here this summer!" Junior cried, surveying the huge backyard and the patio and the grill. "I want to put in several big beds of flowers back of the barbecue," Tracy decided.

"Dick, I hope nothing ever happens to our home," Tess breathed happily, telegraphing the forthcoming developments just as blatantly as she possibly could.

"Tess," Dick Tracy promised in the golden spring afternoon, "we'll live here for the rest of our lives."

In the dead of night a pair of shadowy figures, having previously tossed the dog Mugg a pound of doped meat over the wall, marauded the premises, scurried to the storied automatic door raiser, and wired twenty sticks of dynamite to its workings.

And at 6:50 A.M., on Sunday, April 16, 1950, the clock radio clicked in and Dick Tracy's house exploded.

IT BURNED TO THE GROUND IN MINUTES.

Tracy and Tess were lucky to escape with their lives. As the heartrending missing-Plentys gag had worked so successfully following the Sunny Dell Acres holocaust of just two years earlier, for a time Junior Tracy was believed lost to the flames. It turned out, however, that he had merely been kidnapped by Blowtop, and once he was saved from rolling over the side of a cliff inside a steel drum, Junior drew a picture of his abductor and it went to the papers—on May 7, 1950; this occasion more or less officially launched Junior Tracy's career as the Police Department's staff artist—and that was the downfall of Flattop's brother.

"SHUT UP!" bellowed Blowtop in the gang's hotel-room hideout. "I want to think. DON'T BREATHE IN MY FACE! I can't stand that! Woo! Gosh!"

"We're fed up with you, Blowtop!" the moll Toots snarled. Whereupon she and mobsman Joe Lead pumped the boss full of holes and scrammed.

And as Dick Tracy and his family sought

now to rebuild their devastated lives, a once-familiar figure, gone from the strip for more than three years, abruptly returned.

"And so this is farewell!" the silver-haired old fellow announced to a group of actresses. "Lunching with you ladies of the radio has been most charming. And although VITAMIN FLINTHEART has been fired, he holds his head high! You will hear more of him, anon! Adieu."

AND THIS TIME, MAINTAINING THE SYMMETRY

of things, it was Vitamin Flintheart who blundered into someone else's quarters.

Vitamin Flintheart's sad life had hit new depths. His wife had recently died. And he had just been sacked from the "John's Wife's Other Uncle" radio series. Still, with a couple of belts in him, he was feeling pretty buoyant as he took a hotel for the night. "Ah!" he cried, letting himself into the wrong room, oblivious to the bleeding Blowtop on the floor beside the bed. "To sleep! Perchance to dream!"

In the light of day, he was puzzled. "Zounds!" he reflected. "To awake and find a scoundrel prostrate at my bedside! My very being REVOLTS!" Vitamin shook himself awake and popped a handful of vitamins. "Undoubtedly a LOW ROGUE," he decided. "A hanger-on! Phaw! Begone, knave, ere I call the innkeeper."

Blowtop, not badly wounded as it turned out, was stirring now, and instantly he recognized in Vitamin Flintheart precisely the same stooge that several other strip villains, including his own late brother, had discerned. This was, after all, why Vitamin Flintheart had been put here.

He passed himself off as a rich man assaulted by thieves. "Oil wells! Uranium mines!" Blowtop said, showing off a suitcaseful of hot express-job cash. "Adventure is in my soul!" He took Flintheart into his confidence. "I want to own and produce a Broadway show!"

"Ah, fate hath surely brought us together!" the old actor said mistily.

"DON'T SPRAY MY FACE WHEN YOU TALK TO ME!" Blowtop erupted. "That's one thing I can't stand! Woo, gosh!"

They were together for some few weeks as Blowtop used the old ham to fence the hot

Vitamin Flintheart and Blowtop, June 5–7, 1950.

money for him, a dribble at a time to a laundry that was packing Blowtop's freshly pressed shirts with greenbacks. It was on one of these errands, one day in the early summer of 1950, that Flintheart met another of the TRACY strip's great parade of walk-on characters who might have served some other feature for years. This was the Little Borneo Man, a visiting lecturer in the United States, caretaker of a grisly collection of Bornean anthropological artifacts. He'd just been nicked by a car on a street corner, and the goodhearted Flintheart was pulling him to his feet and helping him collect the contents of his spilled bags.

"One set of nose rings, two human-bone hair ornaments, and one shrunken head," the Little Borneo Man was calculating. "Yes, everything is here."

Vitamin Flintheart took one look at the shrunken head and realized it was patently destined to play Yorick in the great production that his new friend Blowtop was about to bankroll.

But he had no money to offer for the shrunken

Waiting for the house to be rebuilt, July 17, 1950. The Tracys had been living in a tar-paper shack for a few months. Consulting with Tess is interior designer "Jean Ellen," modeled after Gould's daughter. On television is the starlet Sparkle Plenty.

head. All he had was one of Blowtop's freshly laundered shirts. And the struck-down Little Borneo Man needed a clean shirt. Surely his friend Blowtop wouldn't object if . . .

Blowtop listened to the story and he looked at the shrunken head and he puffed on his cigar. "Where be your gibes now?" Vitamin declaimed. "Your gambols? Your songs? Alas, poor Yorick." Blowtop started to twitch. "Flintheart," he said, "I'm going to kill you."

It got worse. Years earlier, the old vaudevillian Flintheart had once been a stage ventriloquist. "There's a divinity that shapes our ends!" the shrunken head cried. "Rough-hew them how we will."

"WHAT?" Blowtop roared.

Even as his late brother before him, Blowtop now concluded he had had absolutely enough of Vitamin Flintheart. "Anything to get away," he moaned, beating it down the stairs. "I'll take my chances and fence the rest of this dough myself." The indignant Flintheart, who had been promised a show, trailed him to a riverbank far out in the countryside. There, Blowtop put a bullet into him. And then, as the law closed in from all sides, the man who had blown up Dick Tracy's house tripped over the

shrunken head, took a pratfall, and conked himself unconscious.

"SHACKLES, SHAME AND DISGRACE," the strip trumpeted as Blowtop was taken steaming to prison, never to be seen again.

In the hospital, Tracy paid his respects to Vitamin.

"Me the hero?" Vitamin shrugged modestly. "Perish the thought! Me shrunken friend there is the real hero."

"Righto! I just saw me duty and I did it," the shrunken head agreed.

"Say," said Vitamin Flintheart to Dick Tracy. "What's this I hear about your building a new house?"

THE TRACY HOUSE HAD GONE UNMENTIONED since the April blast, and readers had been inquiring. In the Sunday page of July 16, 1950, the strip returned its attentions to the place, printing a semidetailed set of plans for a rebuilt successor home as designed by a pert young woman named Jean Ellen, who was introduced by Tess Tracy as "my friend from art school." This was Gould's twenty-three-year-old daughter Jean Ellen Gould. Like many other cartoonists, Gould occasionally drew various friends and family members into his strip, and this page was his affectionate nod toward a daughter who had made it her business to present him with detailed floor plans for the new house.

"I've added sliding doors off the dining room area," Jean Ellen said earnestly.

"I sure like Tracy's gun room, Tess!" Junior noted.

"Jean," Dick Tracy sighed happily, speaking for both cartoonist and cop, "you and your ideas are going to ruin me."

Actually, Mr. and Mrs. Tracy didn't have their house ready for them until the end of 1950, young Jean Ellen having apparently dawdled somewhat in her duties. "But, Jean, you promised we'd be in our new house by CHRIST-MAS!" Tess wailed at her in the first week of December. The painters were sore at her, too. "Interior designers are all alike," they grumbled. Jean had changed the color scheme several times. At this point the walls were paprika, but she was still fussing with swatches of fabric.

THE WARM FESTIVITIES—SIMULTANEOUSLY THE

holidays, a housewarming, a celebration of Mr. and Mrs. Tracy's first wedding anniversary, and a thanksgiving for B.O. Plenty's recent recovery from gunshot wounds (see Chapter 25)—occurred over much of the week before Christmas. The little television star Sparkle Plenty and her mammy and pappy went on national hookup to serenade America with Christmas carols from Sunny Dell Acres.

"Above Thy deep and dreamless sleep, the silent stars go by," the Plentys sang as Dick and Tess and Junior Tracy watched from their own living room.

"This is kind of a Fred Warin' arrangement," Sparkle noted.

The television camera moved in close on all three of them. "The hopes and fears of all the years," they choired, "are met in Thee tonight."

Tears were rolling down Tess Tracy's face. "It's the most beautiful music I ever heard," she whispered.

On Sunday, December 24, in the middle of it all—"God bless us every one!" somebody was saying—the phone rang and Tracy got called out to look into still another couple of killings.

"Thanksgiving Day, Christmas Day, Labor Day," he sighed as he whipped his prowl car into the Christmas Eve snow. "They're all alike in this business!"

That was just weary cop talk. He didn't have a clue yet that Jean Ellen and her ideas really were going to ruin him.

Season's greetings, December 23, 1950.

CHAPTER 27

SHE-DEVIL
The Woman Who Stole Dick Tracy's Daughter

DICK TRACY HAD SEEN SOME PRETTY despicable characters in his time— saboteurs, widow-killers, dog poisoners, just the worst class of people—but very few of them ever violated the order of things quite so much as did a mug named Empty Williams, who, in February 1951, hijacked a truckload of diapers.

It was even an accident. Empty Williams (first appearance, February 6) thought he was hijacking a truckload of furs. Empty had some real dumb boys working for him, though. "It's just a mistake," the boys explained in their garage after the bungled job. "Everybody makes a mistake once in a while. We nabbed the WRONG truck, Empty, that's all." Empty shook his head as he rooted through his ridiculous stolen trailerful of 120,000 cotton didies. "Disgusting," he muttered.

It happened that the baby-booming nation was suffering a grave diaper shortage this particular season, and Chester Gould and his syndicate were instantly swamped with letters from furious mommies everywhere. "That load of diapers was to be delivered to me," railed a

new mother of twins in Elizabeth, New Jersey. "This brazen theft has curtailed the supply in this community," fumed a woman in Fayetteville, North Carolina. The situation made headlines coast to coast (initiated, as TRACY news usually was, by simultaneous feature stories in the flagships *Chicago Tribune* and *New York Daily News*), and Gould now started to hear from commercial diaper suppliers as well. "Please contact if there is any possible chance of purchasing the 120,000 diapers you have available," wired the Tiny Tots Laundry in Uniontown, Pennsylvania. A Chicago service offered a nickel apiece for the didies. Sun Ray Diapers of Poughkeepsie, New York, offered fourteen cents.

Empty and his goons should only have gone with Sun Ray. Instead they sat around contriving more and more preposterous schemes to somehow make a buck out of their jugheaded operation. "Maybe we could muscle some of the leading hospitals into taking diapers off us," one gang member suggested. "Maybe we could sell 'em to night clubs for dish towels!" brainstormed another. Finally, Empty decided to sell the entire haul for five grand to one Karl the Carwash King, who used three hundred polishing cloths a week in his chain of carwash parlors and who couldn't believe his good luck. "Four cents apiece!" he gaped. "This is a steal!" "As a matter a' fact, yes," Empty agreed.

(In Ottawa, the Wilcox Manufacturing Company, inventor of the Wash King automatic car washer, told inquiring reporters still working the Dick Tracy Diaper Beat that actually it was a terrible deal. "We do not think it would be logical to use diapers instead of turkish towels," the company stated, "due to the fact that six turkish towels will complete approximately 1,500 complete car washes, which is as economical as you can hope to get.") Karl the Carwash King felt the same way. He took a hard look at the stuff he'd bought, saw it was merely cotton cloth, and realized he was in the middle of a shakedown. "I'm calling the cops!" Karl bellowed.

So Empty and the boys shot him to death and scrammed, leaving the truck behind them. That was the last time the diapers were seen, and it can only be hoped they somehow eventually found their way to America's sopping infants.

BUT IT SEEMS THAT THIS EPISODE GOT GOULD

to thinking about babies and the nature of things in the forward-flowing tide of time, and later that spring Tess Trueheart Tracy abruptly began to look, as they say, radiant.

"What's the MATTER?" Junior Tracy inquired.

"I'm not sure!" Tess said, apparently puzzled.

"Gosh!" the kid said. "Tracy ought to be here at a time like THIS!"

Oh, that man. Even at this watershed domestic moment, wouldn't you know, Dick Tracy was climbing into a treetop to fetch down the fugitive Empty Williams. Empty—so named because he was missing a chunk of his skull, thanks to a badly done brain operation once upon a time—had been running for months; now, finally, he was holed up in a kid's wooden treehouse in the City's factory district. "It's all over!" Tracy cried, gun trained. "Fool!" Empty spat, brandishing a broken bottle.

Back home, Junior had flagged down a pass-

ing squad car, and now he and Tess and two cops were speeding to the hospital, crashing red lights, siren screaming. "Easy, Mrs. Tracy, we'll do the best we can," one cop said. "Sergeant, I need HELP back here," gulped the second. Junior took the car and floored it as the officers bent to their heroic task. They ran out of time minutes before they got to the hospital. Dick Tracy's daughter was born in the backseat of a police car on May 4, 1951.

And now the fierce playhouse fistfight was proving too much for the rotting, cracked old tree in the industrial flats, and suddenly down it came, pinning the detective and his quarry beneath the weight of its splinters and shards in the great final payoff. Tracy, dazed and bloodied, was pulled free. Empty Williams, meanwhile, in the immortal tradition of Gargles and T.V. Wiggles, had been speared through most of his vital organs, stuck like a butterfly to felt.

In her hospital bed, Tess Tracy clutched her baby, a little blonde who sported long eyelashes and ribboned braids. "Her father!" Tess frowned. "WHERE IS THAT MAN?" Sam Catchem stood by, preparing to give the 2-Way Wrist Radio still another Classic Moment. "THE NEXT VOICE

Empty Williams, March 8, 1951.

The birth of Bonny Braids Tracy, May 4–5, 1951.

YOU HEAR," he broadcast as the bandaged Tracy walked into Chief Patton's office at headquarters, "WILL BE that of—your DAUGHTER!"

"Waw!" the kid went, obligingly.

"I'll be doggoned," mused Tracy, apparently also having had zero clue to this impending development.

GIVEN ITS FIRST PREMIUM-GRADE CHILDBIRTH

since that of Sparkle Plenty four years earlier, and looking straight in the face of the same sort of department-store dolly merchandising, the strip spent several weeks milking reader interest in what the little Tracy was going to be named. Her father leaned toward Alice, Faye, Mabel, or Edna. "Sensible names," he explained. Junior liked Lana. Sparkle liked Jacqueline. B.O. liked Ecinue, until it was pointed out to him that he was misreading Eunice. The Police Department voted for Glory, after Sergeant Glory, the officer who had delivered the babe.

It was the attending nurse who came up with Bonny Braids, over Dick Tracy's protests. "Ixnay! Phooey!" Tracy groused. The nurse kept waving aside his objections. "Come, Bonny Braids, it's time for your feeding!" she would chirp. "Nervy nurse!" Tracy would growl. Reader mail was overwhelmingly on her side, and Tracy finally gave up. "You win," he sighed. And Bonny Braids the child stayed, though after a while the strip started to spell it Bonnie.

Tracy was precisely the kind of twitchy new father you'd expect the World's Greatest Detective to be. He mounted a Diet Smith Teleguard Camera at the little girl's cribside and strung up microphones across the room to monitor every burble and coo. Chester Gould had listened for years to his friend Harold Gray's dour predictions that honest citizens would one day have to put up walls and barbed wire against

Bonny Braids, May 9, 1951.

the predators that would surely overrun the body politic. Now, in fact, that's what Dick Tracy was doing.

And when, one day, Tracy spotted a young blonde loitering on the sidewalk outside his home, he was on her in a flash with a backup squad. "What's this all about?" he demanded.

She was just a struggling baby photographer, she introduced herself. The name was Louise Brown. Crewy Lou, people called her, as she wore her hair trimmed quite short. She was hoping she might have the opportunity to photograph the celebrated little Bonny Braids Tracy.

Tracy didn't think so. His own wife, he pointed out, was a baby portraitist. Crewy Lou knew that, too, but still she just thought that maybe . . .

"Goodbye," Tracy said, and the next thing he knew the girl had introduced herself to Tess and impressed her considerably with her very professional portfolio.

"These are beautiful!" Tess insisted.

"But she looks screwy to me," Tracy grunted.

Tess Tracy shook her head. "Don't you trust anybody?" she wondered. "ANYBODY AT ALL?"

BEFORE THINGS WERE DONE WITH, THE PHOTO-

graphess Crewy Lou (first appearance, May 22, 1951) was going to rank up there with the most monstrous of the strip's mad collection of witches, and she and Bonny Braids Tracy were destined to meet again.

For now, she was merely an ambitious little small-timer. Crewy Lou had a grandiose jewel heist in mind, and her interest in Dick Tracy's daughter was purely tactical: Such a credential in her portfolio, she reasoned, correctly, would certainly get her into the home of millionaire businessman Fortson B. Knox, also the father of a newborn. With her business associate, the eerie mute known as The Sphinx, Crewy Lou staged a phony photo shoot in the Knox manse in an elaborate scheme to make away with a half-million dollars' worth of diamonds.

The otherwise quite straightforward program was now ingeniously complicated by a couple of factors. One, Fortson B. Knox's indolent young trophy wife despised him, and during a bou-

Baby photographer Crewy Lou, June 4, 1951.

doir quarrel that occurred even as the photographers were setting up their lights downstairs, she shot him to death. "What a break!" whooped Crewy Lou, proceeding to bop Mrs. Knox over the head and rifle every drawer in sight. Two, it shortly developed that Fortson B. Knox had been, in a secret life he lived beyond his boardrooms and his country clubs, a top boss in what had lately become known as Organized Crime—the first real taste of which had just come to DICK TRACY.

The televised hearings of Senator Estes Kefauver's Special Committee to Investigate Crime in Interstate Commerce had transfixed modern America from May 1950 until May 1951, and the public was grasping that apparently there really was a national crime syndicate that really did parcel out the country into rackets territories. Chester Gould had already flirted from time to time with the recognition of some kind of formal criminal organization: His Crime Inc. story of early 1941, for example, had certainly derived from the sensational revelations of Albert Anastasia's Murder Inc. outfit in New

York, and occasionally there were passing indications that somewhere out there dwelt unseen overlords. Generally, though, Gould had kept his strip populated with local independents—petty racketeers, little-league torpedoes, triple-A gangs, entirely inconsequential operators in the larger firmament, whatever their celebrated capers. In the wake of Kefauver, DICK TRACY now addressed itself to the matter of the Syndicate.

It was embodied in the person of a sleek, ruthless man known only as The King, who appeared just briefly in the summer of 1951 but who was quite evidently the single most powerful criminal figure the strip had seen since Big Boy had been put away twenty years earlier, and who began to set the stage for the series of national crime bosses who would follow him. The King was concerned that the late Fortson B. Knox's widow, now charged with the killing of her husband, would sing to the cops, and he was quite right. "You've heard of the CRIME SYNDICATE?" Carol Knox sang. "Keep talking, Mrs. Knox!" Tracy said heartily.

As if that weren't enough, now here was this little amateur Crewy Lou trying to fence mob sparklers. He intercepted her one day in mid-transaction and, a reasonable businessman, attempted reasonable dealings. "By the time you'd have 'em recut and then peddled, your take would be very small," he explained patiently, offering another arrangement.

"So you're willing to take a half million dollars' worth of ice off our hands for 5 grand, eh?" Crewy Lou sneered.

"Cute, isn't she?" The King winked at his boys. "Well, maybe ten grand," he reconsidered, smiling benevolently. "You're smart, I got to admit that!"

Not only was she smart, she was armed. Crewy Lou shot the nation's number-one crime kingpin point-blank in the chest. Then she cleaned twenty grand out of his pockets. Then she beat it. "The Crime Syndicate, eh?" she snickered over her shoulder. "What a bunch of sissies!"

The caper did nothing to put Crewy Lou's star into ascendancy so far as the Syndicate was concerned. She was seriously on the run now. The pursuing mob didn't get her, but they did get her pal The Sphinx, and they stretched him out at the bottom of an elevator shaft and then went up, sending down the two-ton counterweight down atop him—this brilliant dispatch, on August 5, 1951, resulting in the one and only utterance that ever passed The Sphinx's lips throughout his appearance ("OHOO! WA!")

Meanwhile, The King's shooting did bring down intense public scrutiny of the Syndicate's activities, and all summer long Dick Tracy and Sam Catchem had nothing on their hands but blistering gunfights, rooftop chases, high-speed auto pursuits, blood feuds, mob wars, one thrilling thing after another, and by September the Syndicate had been pretty effectively dismantled.

None of this had very much to do with little Bonny Braids Tracy, but it was about to.

AT THE END OF THINGS, CREWY LOU WAS AT

large in the North Woods, fording streams, climbing boulders, heading relentlessly for a High Sierra-like desperate last stand in the rugged wild. Upstate lawmen were circling all around. And Dick Tracy, who had driven up from the City to fetch home his wife and daughter from a month's summer vacation, realized he was just a few miles away from the action.

Arriving on the scene, Tracy momentarily left Tess and Bonny Braids alone in the car to go scope things out. A minute was all the time Crewy Lou needed. Leaping from the underbrush, she clubbed Tess Tracy with a rock, threw her from the car, and took the wheel of Tracy's Cadillac convertible. "This thing'll do a hundred and it's full of gas," she puffed as she screeched the car out of the vortex. "It'll be at least 30 minutes before they can get roadblocks organized. . . ."

She was miles down the highway before she ever noticed the baby in the backseat.

"WHAT?" she gaped.

She careened off the highway onto a gravel side road and pulled over to think about it. "This is BAD!" she muttered. "What can I do with the brat?"

Hunted, fear-stricken, Crewy Lou suddenly realized that now she had a hostage.

CREWY LOU WAS THE WORLD'S WORST NANNY.

Straight up the mountainsides she drove, the

Crewy Lou afield, September 26–27, 1951.

car bouncing off rock shelves, losing fenders and headlights every minute, radiator wheezing, tires smoking, and she kept punching the kid in the seat beside her whenever she had a minute ("Don't go bawling for food!" "Bawwww!" "Shut up!"). They were days in the wilderness, climbing higher and higher, the crazed Lou flooring the wreck of a car through creeks and ravines as the tiny starved girl thrashed at the air with her little hands and cried out more

and more feebly. A police helicopter circled overhead. Night fell again. And at last the hunted Crewy Lou gave up the car and continued through the brambles on foot, leaving Bonny Braids Tracy to the dark and the cold and the wolves.

In a mad last stand from a ranger lookout tower she had commandeered, Crewy Lou shot it out with the helicopter. Dick Tracy pitched in tear gas at her. Blinded, berserk, choking,

Bonny Braids misses a few feedings, October 5, 1951.

157

Bonnie Braids and the beasts,
October 15, 1951.

she crashed over the rail and fell to her death on the jagged rocks sixty-five feet below.

Momentarily the search party found Tracy's car—empty, the upholstery clawed, the convertible roof torn to shreds. "Forest animals," a uniformed cop gulped. "No." Tracy stared.

Gould even kept it up for a while longer. The tragic search for Bonny Braids Tracy continued as Tess moaned in her home and gulped sedatives and the detective plunged on sleepless and haggard to the brink of exhaustion. The little girl finally turned up in the home of a remote mountaineer couple, who had found her and taken her in as their own and kept her alive with goat's milk.

On November 4, in an entirely wordless Sunday page, Bonny was airlifted home and returned to the breast of her weeping mother. A final panel left the Tracy family embracing in the dark rear ground as Chester Gould focused in on, and silently illuminated, the family Bible.

THE FOLLOWING SUMMER, ONCE MORE VACA- tioning in the great North Woods, Bonny Braids Tracy was lost yet again (see Chapter 30), and there was still another sleepless, haggard, tear-jerking manhunt for the kid, and after that Gould decided he had no further use for her. Through the rest of '50s, she would show up from time to time whenever Dick Tracy happened to be seen at home, and she usually figured in the annual Christmas-card celebrations along with the Sam Catchems and the B.O. Plentys, but there was never another story in which she particularly figured. After Christmas 1960 she was gone. A decade later there was a passing explanation that she was living on the West Coast and working as a schoolteacher. Like Junior Tracy's mother before her, Dick Tracy's own daughter was ultimately just one of those dear relatives nobody really had any reason to pay much attention to.

The end of Crewy Lou, October 20, 1951.

CHAPTER 28

PLAINCLOTHESMEN DON'T MAKE THAT KIND OF DOUGH

The Scandal

IT WAS, TRUE ENOUGH, A PRETTY SPECTAC-ular home that Dick Tracy had moved his family into, and never mind even the automatic dog door and the fancy new clock radio; this was a huge and well-appointed residence, located in an obviously good neighborhood, on a leafy street near a park, and it was full of ferns and strikingly modern furniture. The family automobile, meanwhile, the one in which Tracy had recently fetched Tess and Bonny Braids from their North Woods vacation and which the desperate Crewy Lou had stolen in her flight into the mountains, was identifiably a late-model Cadillac convertible. In the fall of 1951, a considerable number of readers all at once began to wonder how Tracy was able to live like this. Wait a minute. On a cop's salary?

Law-enforcement officials had also been wondering about their brother officer's unseemly extravagances. *Editor and Publisher* magazine reported that "police organizations in many states" had complained to the Cook County Sheriff's Office, "demanding an explanation";

columnists around the country had a gleeful field day with the news; things, to Gould's drop-jawed disbelief, got rowdier and rowdier. Finally, Cook County State's Attorney John S. Boyle actually wrote an official letter to the *Chicago Tribune*, the strip's flagship paper in the Great Plains. "I have received many complaints from police officers concerning the manner in which Richard Tracy lives," Boyle wrote. "They refer to his $100,000 home, his 1951 Cadillac convertible . . . They are sort of hinting that a grand jury investigation might be a very helpful thing for the community." Thirty-five years later, the public could shrug off as show business the fact that television's "Miami Vice" featured a cop who drove a Ferrari and owned a closetful of Armani suits, but in 1951 it was a different story. This was a serious matter, and Gould was obliged to address it.

And so it was that in early November, even as the Tracys knelt in prayer at the safe return of their long-missing infant daughter, Chief of Police Pat Patton was visited by a grim Sheriff John Jugg, who presented him with a file of

Solidarity, November 21, 1951.

documents. "Sheriff, this must be a joke!" Patton gasped. "Those are the facts!" Jugg barked. "Get him down here!"

Tracy was called on the carpet. "What's the gag?" he wondered. "I hope you won't get sore," Patton said uneasily. "It's been kicking around and it's so ridiculous WE'VE been laughing at it, but we can't laugh at it any more—the pressure is TOO great."

Patton stood and looked his old friend and partner in the eye. "They've forced me to ask you!" he said. "WHERE DID YOU GET THE MONEY TO BUILD YOUR HOUSE?"

"Are you guys SERIOUS?" Tracy blinked.

"Yeah!" said Sheriff Jugg "WHERE DID YOU GET THE DOUGH?"

Stunned but manful, Dick Tracy proceeded to make a remarkable full disclosure of his personal finances in the nation's funny papers. "I've had a steady job here in the Police Department for 20 years," he said. "I was a bachelor for almost 19 of those 20 years, and a penny pincher! A Scotchman!" This wasn't news, of course, to anyone who remembered his tight-wad courtship of Tess Trueheart. "I SAVED my dough!" he said angrily. "I bought that old corner property during the real estate depression of the thirties. It was a WRECK! I paid $3600 for it. That's all there is to it. I built my home with money I SAVED! And, I might add, there's a nice little plaster on the house—a small mortgage, gentlemen! Now tell me, Sheriff, just who—"

Jugg wasn't finished. "WHAT ABOUT YOUR CAR?" he demanded. "You've been driving an expensive automobile, a rich man's car! People aren't so dumb, Tracy. They know plainclothesmen don't make THAT kind of dough."

The car, actually, was a bit of a problem. Cadillacs weren't parked in everybody's driveway in 1951. Chester Gould was simply a Cadillac man himself, ever since Colonel Robert McCormick of the *Chicago Tribune* had appreciatively presented him with a shiny new one in 1949, and Tracy had started driving one later that year. It may have only been that Cadillacs were easy to draw, since Gould happened to have one right outside the window. Tracy's Cadillac had been in the strip for a while without undue public uproar—he had driven his bride to their honeymoon lodge in a Caddy at Christmas 1949—but lately the Kefauver hearings had been sensitizing the public to cops who lived well, and maybe Tracy's current heap really was a new '51 model. Maybe Tracy was in the habit of getting an identical new Cadillac convertible every year. Even so, Tracy assured everyone, there was a perfectly reasonable explanation: "The people who build that expensive car want to get into the police field with a car for specialized work! They sold that buggy to me for about ONE-THIRD ITS COST, fitted with special equipment that I'm TESTING for them." He just happened to have the corroborating contract in his jacket pocket. "It's supposed to be secret," he said.

"Humph," said Jugg.

Other critics weren't much impressed either. "Even from Dick Tracy, it sounded thin," grunted *Time* magazine. "The fuller explanation of Cartoonist Gould was no more convincing," *Time* added, quoting the exasperated Gould: "I don't *know* Dick's salary." And *New*

York Daily News columnist Bob Sylvester noted that there had never been any previous exhibition of the Cadillac's supposed special scientific equipment. "Also," Sylvester sniffed, "if the car is such a special job and so full of scientific gadgets, how come Crewy Lou could steal it and run off with Tracy's own baby?"

Meanwhile, John Jugg got to the point. "Is that your signature?" he asked, producing an access slip to the vault of the police custodian. Tracy considered this. "Yes," he admitted.

"We have six of those slips with your signature on them," Jugg said. "And in each case the CONTENTS OF THE BOXES ARE MISSING! Over HALF A MILLION DOLLARS taken from the police custodian's vault. WHERE IS IT?"

"Why, I ought to . . ." Tracy growled.

So that was it. Dick Tracy stood accused of stealing trial evidence from police custody—specifically, the Knox Jewels, stolen by Crewy Lou a few months earlier, and the proceeds of a "Boston robbery" that was apparently Blowtop's 1950 express job. "Of course my name is there!" Tracy protested, waving at the empty strongboxes in the property vault. "The custodian and I photographed those jewels, as we have in many cases." Mrs. Knox's patently shifty lawyer arrived on the scene and made unpleasant insinuations. "Everybody's been asking WHERE DID DICK TRACY GET THE MONEY TO BUILD THAT HOUSE? I think I'M beginning to see." Tracy socked him good, sending teeth flying; in those days you could still do that to lawyers. The police custodian, meanwhile, a fidgety fel-low named Charlie, was rather noisier about things than seemed quite necessary. "I demand an investigation!" Charlie blustered. "I demand an end to these monkeyshines in my office! I want my good name and reputation cleared and the GUILTY parties PUNISHED!" Tracy shot him a hard, knowing look. The sharp reader grasped right away it might be a good idea to keep an eye on Charlie.

Indeed, after a supportive D.A. agreed to postpone taking the ugly matter before the grand jury, Tracy went straight back to the vault, where he and Sam Catchem took comparative paint scrapings from both pilfered and unpilfered strongboxes, and this made Charlie very nervous. "Hm? Paint scrapings?" he muttered. And the sharp reader knew at this point that Scientific Crime Detection was once again about to do its job.

Spectrograms, of course, found the two paint samples to be different, proving that the strongboxes hadn't been rifled but replaced entirely with ringers. This finding had little or nothing to do with establishing Tracy's own guilt or innocence, if Charlie had thought about it for a minute, but the custodian was next seen, panic-stricken and going to pieces, in the office of an elegantly silver-haired record-shop owner named Spinner ReCord (first appearance, November 26, 1951), who listened to him whine for a while and then shot him to death.

As this new and relatively brief story unfolded —it consisted mostly of Spinner's frantic effort to recover an incriminating recording—it was

Spinner ReCord and the custodian, December 3, 1951.

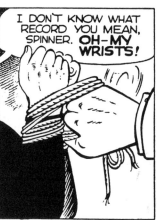

Spinner and an Innocent, January 3-5, 1952. The plucky girl, a record shop customer, had accidentally been sold Spinner's private recording of his dealings with the late custodian, realized its significance, hidden it away, and now elected to endure a drubbing while she waited for police to arrive. This was Rough Stuff in the grand old tradition; had he had more time, Spinner might even have blow-torched the kid's feet.

explained that Spinner and Charlie had been partners in a vault-looting enterprise of long duration and then in a scheme to pin the shortfalls on some hotshot like Tracy. "The bigger they are, the quicker the public is to accuse 'em!" the late custodian was heard to say on the telltale recording as Gould began to get in his licks at the critics who had forced this story to begin with. Spinner ReCord (last seen January 20, 1952) went to jail. So did the smarmy Knox lawyer Tracy had punched out, after he was found to be a third co-conspirator.

Gould exacted his full measure of retribution. "So that clears up the thefts from the police custodian's vault," Tracy politely told Sheriff John Jugg. "I hope you're satisfied."

"We owe you an apology," Jugg gabbled, pumping the detective's hand. "Audits show your financial records are perfect. We're even happier than you are." "Save it," Tracy murmured.

"We're glad it's all over, Tracy!" said Chief Patton. "That charge against you backfired, and we caught some rats."

"I'm glad it happened!" Tracy replied. "It gave me a chance to smash the idea that suspicion should fall on any policeman frugal enough to have a nice home."

And that was that, and Chester Gould saw to it that it stayed that way: Nothing more of Dick Tracy's house than its living room was ever seen again, and if Tracy kept driving new Cadillac convertibles, he didn't do it on strip time.

Revelations, January 17, 1952.

CHAPTER 29

LIFE DEALS 'EM THAT WAY ONCE IN A WHILE

The Kid Grows Up

JUNIOR TRACY TOOK HIS SWEET TIME GET-
ting out of childhood. The Great Depression dragged on and on, all of World War
II came and went, Harry Truman won his
second presidential term, and in September 1949
Junior made it to the seventh grade. Dick Tracy
had continued to instruct him in the mysteries
of spectroscopy and bloodstain analysis and
whatnot, and by now he was practically a professional para-policeman, but he was still a
funny-looking little freckled kid all the same,
and crooks still targeted him for regular unpleasantness, as it was no complicated deal to
run down his bicycle with a dump truck or
whatever. A lesser boy might have been plenty
fed up by now with all the calamity and woe

he'd had to endure since 1932, but Junior hung
in there, cheerily taking everything crime could
dish out. In April 1950, Blowtop had chloroformed him and sealed him into a fifty-gallon
drum and attempted to roll him over a cliff. In
July, the suicide-bent thug named Joe Lead almost took Junior with him in a jump from a
sixth-story window. Really, it was still just one
thing after another for the kid.

The time had, in fact, come for Junior Tracy
to become a man, and to think as a man, and to
walk as a man, and to put aside childish things.
Dick Tracy had a wife and baby daughter now.
What did he want with a Boy Sidekick who
was forever getting kidnapped and tortured?
Thus, in early 1952, there were two develop-

Junior in love, January 26, 1952.

ments in Junior Tracy's life that significantly repositioned him. One, he formally went to work as the Police Department's staff artist, and for years to come he was regularly seen sketching suspects at a drawing board and sculpting likenesses out of clay, and ultimately he came to be defined as Junior the Police Artist by a full generation of new TRACY readers who had never known the Boy Sidekick.

Two, he met Model Jones.

She was Junior's first girl, she was the love of his life, she was a vision of everything joyful, she was doomed. He met her nights at the roller rink, and together the two of them waltzed through the rituals of adolescent courtship. "Can I walk with you?" he gulped. "If you want to," she smiled. "Gee, Model, you skate swell," he managed, holding up his end. Suddenly Junior was wearing ties, brushing his jacket, shining his shoes. It didn't go unnoticed at home. "What's HAPPENED?" Tess Tracy clucked. "The kid's got a girl somewhere," Dick Tracy concluded. "Junior has changed. Combing his hair,

washing his neck . . . Only a GIRL could make him do all that." The standard teen comedies occurred as the young swain bumped starry-eyed through the motions of everyday affairs ("Junior! You're pouring the syrup in the SUGAR BOWL!").

But it wasn't a sitcom, and it never truly felt like it. It was a dark and awful and heartbreaking story, the tale of Junior Tracy's terrible passage from youth to tentative manhood, and it was one of the strip's great crucial transitions.

The lovely, laughing Model (first appearance: January 23, 1952) had two unspeakable secrets. One of them was a worthless bum of a brother who broke open parking meters for petty change, and the other was a revolting couple of parents she couldn't dream of taking her boyfriend home to meet because they were lying in alcoholic stupors on the floor. The circumstances were redolent of both the JD/hot-rod/reefer-fiend cinema of some years earlier and, somewhat self-referentially, of the burgeoning new community anxieties across the land over reprehensible crime-comic features such as, for example, DICK TRACY, from which punks like Larry Jones might easily learn how to break into parking meters. Model and Junior were Good Kids of the day—in Chester Gould's America, in any case—and family was vital to the both of them. "How can I ever tell him?" Model would sob, once she ditched Junior for the night. "Funny she never invites me in," Junior would muse. The contemptible punk brother Larry Jones, at least, dealt with the drunken folks fairly efficiently whenever he came in with his sacksful of coins ("Nickels? A whole BAG of nickels?" "Keep your mitts off 'em, Pop, before I break your wrists!"). "He's really a good brother," Model faithfully professed to the appalled Junior after Larry threatened to smash her face if she didn't cough up a couple of dollars.

For an instant, they both agreed to gamble against the fates. They eloped, happy youngsters on an overnight bus to the next state, squeezing hands. At a midnight hamburger stopover, Model overheard a snatch of a radio report that the parking-meter goons had finally killed a cop back in the City, and she fled devastated into the night. "No, this is silly," she laughed wildly. "Me? Marry a little crime-

Couple guys standing around talking guy talk, February 3, 1952. Responsible role model Dick Tracy demonstrates proper parental interest in activities of our young people (Right).

stopper like you?" "But—" Junior blinked in disbelief. "SO LONG, SQUIRT!" she yelled back. Alone aboard the homebound bus, looking out the back window, Model fell apart: "I had to do it—I had to do it—I just COULDN'T get you mixed up with that awful family of mine! I-I love you too much! My brother a murderer! My parents drunkards! Perhaps some day, you'll know—perhaps—"

It was one of those dramatic banalities that in good hands could still tear you to pieces. Junior walked long miles home through the desolate snowfall. And as the grim soap opera ground toward its wretched resolution, Model went to see her brother in his hideout flat.

"I want you to give yourself up before it's too late!" she shrieked, beating on his chest. "For Dad and Mother's sake—for my sake—before police bullets end your life!"

"Why, you little JERK!" he laughed.

Tipped off to Larry's address, Dick Tracy and Sam Catchem were arriving downstairs and sirens were wailing, and brother and sister wrestled over the gun.

Model took the bullet straight through the neck.

"It was an accident," she gasped as Sam Catchem called for medics. "He didn't mean to—"

Pale and cold in her hospital bed, Model came out of deep shock just long enough to murmur a single word. "Junior," she said. He was there, and she died, weeping and smiling

and reaching for him, in the classic Sunday page of March 23, 1952.

Tracy and the kid sat together in the dark. "That's the way it is," Tracy offered. "Life deals 'em that way once in a while."

Model at home, February 2, 1952. Evidence of inappropriate parenting (Wrong).

The long road home, February 21, 1952.

The bullet, March 9, 1952.

Intensive care, March 18, 1952.

"Model, I'll always love you," Junior said quietly in the stark last cemetery scene, all stone and wreaths and veils and the thud of absolute finality.

"I'll never have another girl," he sobbed. "Never."

HE ALMOST WASN'T KIDDING. JUNIOR TRACY

didn't look at another girl for another eleven years. In the interim, he retreated from the strip's active story line. Junior was often seen at his drawing board, a somber and hardworking civilian employee of the Police Department, and he remained an identifiable member of the Tracy household and the Christmas get-togethers at the B.O. Plentys. But he seldom figured directly in the narrative. He appeared to hit Official Responsible Adulthood on September 1, 1957, when he showed up at headquarters with a couple of buddies, the three of them sharp in jackets and ties, and engaged Sam Catchem in a discussion of Proper Male Attire in this day of the Chester Gould heartland's anti–Elvis/ Dean/Brando backlash. "You mean no more monkey suits of tight pants, sweat shirts and motorcycle boots?" Sam chuckled. "No, sir!" Junior replied. "They're a laugh—infant stuff. The regular guys are dressing up. We figure if you're going to be a jerk, you dress like a jerk. As for us—we're men—and we want to dress like men." "Fellows, you've got something there!" Sam nodded avuncularly. "I notice in many of our criminal cases the boys involved

are sloppily dressed." Gould delivered all this quite unblushingly. The sequence possibly owed something to the fact that a few months earlier he had won an award from a menswear trade group that liked the fact that Dick Tracy always wore a hat and tie.

JUNIOR REJOINED THE STRIP AS A PRIMARY

player in late 1961, when remarkable things occurred at Marybelle Manor, a ruined estate outside the city, and he crossed paths with someone from his distant past (see Chapter 33). Then, in January 1963, the long-monastic police artist—by now a college student who was admirably bettering himself by taking night courses, even as Chester Gould had done forty years earlier—finally met another girl.

Thistle Dew was a curious choice for a man of Junior's white-bread instincts, a tall, feline, faintly cadaverous, black-turtlenecked redhead who smoked cigarettes and started many of her sentences with the word "like"—the "beatnik type," as they said—but there is a school of male that could agree with the smitten Junior that Thistle was pretty interesting, despite the fact that she really did have No Good written all over her. Unfortunately for him, she was a decoy job, daughter of a hood who had been sent to the chair by the police artist's sketch of him, and before long Junior was her prisoner. It took Dick Tracy to save Junior's bacon, and Tracy was personally pretty disgusted when he finally got a look at Thistle. "What did you

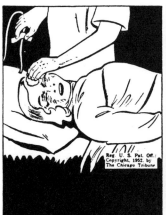

Systems disconnected, March 24-25, 1952.

Next stop, mob temptress Thistle Dew,
January 22, 1963.

ever see in a bum like this?'' Tracy sneered.
''When it comes to women, kid, you sure can
pick 'em.'' While character building, the crack
might have been just a little insensitive, considering that Junior hadn't talked to a girl for
eleven years and the last one had died in his
arms.

The kid sure could pick 'em, though. Two
years later he eloped to the moon with Earth's
First Visitor from Outer Space (see Chapter 34),
a woman who had horns on her head and a
built-in electrical force field that jammed radar
stations. ''Life on a new planet with the girl I
love!'' Junior Tracy cried. ''Yes, the universe is
mine!'' Back home at headquarters, Dick Tracy
could only shake his head at such a development. ''Gosh, this all seems unreal,'' he marveled. He could say *that* again.

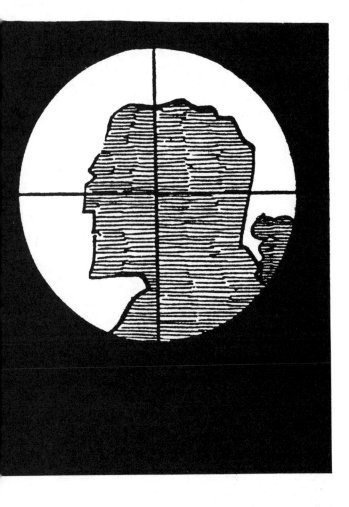

CHAPTER 30

WHEN DID YOU FEED THE FISH LAST?

Incident on the Lake

AN EARLY-MORNING SPEEDBOAT RIDE. Summer vacation, the Dick Tracys and the B.O. Plentys together, two weeks at a North Woods resort. The little girls, Sparkle Plenty and Dick Tracy's daughter, who was by now spelling her name Bonnie, just loved the speedboat. "Faster!" they cried. "You kids are all speed demons," Tracy laughed, opening the throttle.

From a rocky ledge in the wilderness high above, the cross hairs of a 30-30 rifle's telescopic sight tracked a point an inch behind Tracy's left ear.

The cross hairs had been there for several mornings, as the rifleman tried to marshal his nerve to pull the trigger. "I can't," he moaned. "Uh—I—I gotta. It's him or me—this time I won't fail—" And this time he didn't.

"All right, girls," said Tracy, "we'll go around one more time. Then we'll go in."

The slug got him in the base of his skull. For a single split second Tracy shot straight up from his seat, hands clawing at the sky, and then he crashed backward into the water.

"MR. TRACY!" shrieked Sparkle Plenty.

From the hillside, the shooter watched as the boat began to career crazily out of control. Then he threw down the 30-30. "Tonsils, you're a free man," he breathed in relief.

And this, in early August 1952, is where the strip froze the detective and the little girls, the one thrashing in the water, the two screaming in terror as the speedboat hurtled toward shore, already beating itself apart on the rocks.

Crooks had tried many times to kill Dick Tracy. They had shot him, stabbed him, gassed him, torched him, encased him in wax, dropped him into pits, tried to drive spikes into his heart. Nobody ever came closer to actually doing the job than the young man called Tonsils.

And Tonsils wasn't even an especially bad guy. Tonsils was just a frightened would-be pop singer on the fringes of the underworld, and with another set of breaks there might have been a way out for him. It was always clear that he had been cornered into this thing by forces well beyond his control, that he would never have done it by himself, that all he wanted to do was go on living. He was as tragic a victim as anyone, and this was the man who really, finally, almost killed Dick Tracy.

TONSILS HAD BEEN AROUND FOR A WHILE

already. He'd first been seen on March 28, 1952, a broad-shouldered young zoot-suiter with a funny cowlick and an odd popeye, and his agent, one Dude the Dapper, had brought him to a night spot called Club Blue, whose manager was trying to explain that he got his talent from booking agencies. "I said this guy is going to do an audition," Dude said, pulling a rod. Tonsils took the mike and kicked into a dreadful Tin Pan Alley confection called "The Rainbow Turned Muddy When You Turned Me Down." "That's Tonsils, the new American sensation!" Dude boasted. The manager covered his ears. "Shoot me," he pleaded. So Dude did.

Tonsils himself harbored no great illusions. "Aw, I can't sing," he kept muttering. "I can't remember the darn words. Why don't you let me go back to hiking cars in the parking lot,

The new American sensation, March 28, 1952.

like I useta?" "REHEARSE!" Dude bellowed at him. "MUDDY RAINBOW, WHERE'S MY LOVE?" Tonsils sang dutifully. Dude was sort of semitouching in his own goon way, a torpedo who had persuaded himself that Tonsils was his ticket out of the rackets. "No more hijacking!" Dude would say wistfully. "No more horse meat! No more shakedowns! I can turn respectable! I'll be known as agent for America's greatest singer!" And at gunpoint they kept crashing club after club and at gunpoint the audiences were always applauding enthusiastically ("Yowee! Clap clap clap! Ha ha!") and then the singer and his agent would be gone in the night as Dude kept laying grander and grander plans ("I'm gonna take over a record company and make and distribute my own platters! I'm gonna muscle into the juke boxes!").

Chester Gould had presumably modeled Tonsils after Johnnie Ray, a twenty-six-year-old sensation who had exploded across the music charts in 1951 with a weepily florid singing style many listeners of Gould's generation could agree was

Cop shot, August 1, 1952. Sparkle Plenty and Bonnie Braids Tracy rode the runaway speedboat into oblivion.

ridiculous. (Ray's early hit "The Little White Cloud That Cried" did seem meteorologically akin to "Muddy Rainbow.") Tonsils had an effulgent personal signature, too—he jerked his thumbs up and down while he sang—and it turned out that Dude had been right about his boy's star quality all along. One night they crashed a radio station and Tonsils sang his terrible trademark tune as Dude held a gun to the engineer's head and happily tapped his foot ("Now sing "I've Got Youse Under My Skin"!"). Later the station tried to apologize to its listeners, but the phones were already ringing off the hook, and the next day Tonsils was all over the radio columns. "The first smash hit we ever had!" station jock Joe Noe cried. "We've got to find Tonsils!"

But gangdom wanted to find Tonsils, too. Dude's old pals didn't much appreciate that the star-struck little man was seriously jeopardizing their horsemeat racket with all his big ideas, so they killed him, and then they figured they should probably also silence Dude's boy while they were at it. Clean, out of the life, having already spilled everything he knew to Dick Tracy, Tonsils was now a hot ticket on local TV. After a show one night, the gang snatched him out of a cab, beat him half to death, and sewed him up inside a huge tractor casing in a tire yard.

And he would have gone to the mercies of the reclaiming mill, save for a tiny dog who belonged to the nice old couple next door and

Tonsils' agent Dude gets him a booking, April 2, 1952.

who sniffed him out. The old lady insisted upon taking in and nourishing the bloody, dirt-encrusted figure. "We found him! He will be our son!" she gabbled to her husband. "What you're doing is foolish!" the old man warned her. "This man has had evil companions!" The terrified Tonsils went berserk. He slugged the old man with a bottle of gasoline. The stove was a foot away. The house went up like a tinderbox. The old man died. The old lady was critically burned.

And Tonsils having just taken things over the line, was now seriously on the run.

THE MARKED MAN TONSILS FRANTICALLY

walked the streets, at his wit's end. "Yes, Tracy, it's a race between us and the underworld,"

The taking of Tonsils, May 6–7, 1952. Out of the rackets at last, he had become a regular on TV star Dot View's variety show, but the rackets weren't finished with him.

Summoned by Mr. Crime, July 7–8, 1952.

Sam Catchem observed back at headquarters. "WHO WILL GET TONSILS FIRST?"

The underworld won. In the tradition of Gravel Gertie, Tonsils was working in a greenhouse when the mob showed up—how they found him was unexplained, but the mob has its way—and the next thing Tonsils knew he was being presented to the powerful underworld boss called Mr. Crime (first appearance, June 24, 1952), who lived in opulent secret quarters beneath a swimming pool.

"We like you, Tonsils," Mr. Crime said affably. "We see a great future for you."

"You mean singing?" Tonsils grinned despite the blindfold. "You know I'm a hot singer."

Mr. Crime thought this was pretty funny. "Forget singing," he counseled Tonsils. "Believe me, VERY bad voice. We want you to kill a man."

Tonsils said thanks, he really couldn't. "I'm not a gunman," he explained. "I can't—"

Mr. Crime smiled and turned to his lieuten-

Tonsils tartare, August 20, 1952.

ants. "When did you feed the fish last?" he inquired.

"What fish?" Tonsils said.

The boys took him upstairs to poolside, removed his blindfold, and showed him the fish. Chester Gould, nearly operatic in his awfulness at this point, had given Mr. Crime one of the great Criminal Pets. "That's a ninety-pound barracuda," Tonsils's captors explained, tossing the horrible thing a side of meat. "Can you swim?"

Gould lingered over immense close-ups of the beast as it gobbled up great chunks of flesh. Downstairs, Mr. Crime watched his wristwatch. Tonsils was back about a minute later, close to a dead faint and quite agreeable to anything. "Sure, I can shoot ANY gun," he gulped. "But where will I—how—"

"Our friend Tracy has made it all very easy for you," Mr. Crime said. "He's on vacation in the North Woods."

THIS IS WHAT HAD BROUGHT TONSILS, WHO
wanted only to go back to hiking cars in the parking lot, to the lake.

Search parties pulled up a boat cushion, bits of wreckage. In the hills they found evidence of the sniper. "It doesn't seem possible all are lost," Tess Tracy sobbed. It was the sixth wedding anniversary of B.O. and Gertie Plenty. "Little Sparkle," Gertie mourned. "Things look bad," Pat Patton said softly.

Not so bad as they looked for Tonsils, who had, like a dummy, actually reported back to Mr. Crime. "Yes, I did my assignment!" he said. "Now, can I go free?" Mr. Crime was amused. "Oh, not yet," he said. "I want to hear another song." "Oh, the rainbow turned muddy," Tonsils complied, jerking his thumbs. "Ah, ha, ha!" Mr. Crime roared, falling off his chair. "Take him away," he waved.

"Well, I'll be seeing you," Tonsils told the boys back upstairs, turning for the door. "So long, fellows."

The boys were having a good chuckle themselves. "This is as far as you go," they informed him. "But—" he said.

Tonsils had time for just the faintest glimmer of understanding before he went into the pool.

Rifle Ruby, August 22, 1952. Not only did she save Dick Tracy's life, the extraordinary Samaritan Ruby saved Bonnie Braids Tracy and Sparkle Plenty as well.

The big fish flashed across the last panel of the August 20, 1952, strip as he hit the water. Tonsils was never going to sing again.

WEEKS OF HEARTBREAK LATER, THE NEAR-
dead Tracy turned up in the cabin of a burly, sharpshooting mountain woman named Rifle Ruby, who had pulled him from the lake and was nursing him. Once she heard there were kids still missing, Ruby put herself in charge of the police search. "I know this lake like a book," she said. "If airplanes couldn't find a boat with two kids in it, there's only one place to look."

And she took the law straight to a wall of glacial stones that created an illusory shoreline. "We were back there at least twice," Sam Catchem said. "You THOUGHT you were back there," Ruby said. Wedged in the crevices were the boat and the tots, nearly gone by now, but not quite.

"Aw, forget it," grinned Rifle Ruby, waving good-bye and turning back into the mountains.

Summer vacation. Happy ending. Back in the city, Mr. Crime read the papers and tapped his fingers darkly.

MR. CRIME, BY DAY A CIVIC PILLAR NAMED

George Alpha and by night the current number-one national gang boss, had a couple of other Criminal Pets even creepier than his barracuda. These were the ghastly man-eating muerte plants from the Amazon Valley, which he kept in a refrigerated mushroom house far outside the city. One of them was regularly seen gnawing away at a heap of human bones in its clutches, and they turned out to be those of one Judge Lava, a disappeared jurist in the Judge Crater tradition. Throughout the TRACY strip there were a number of memorable characters who were seen only as decedents, often for protracted periods of time, and Judge Lava was certainly

one of the finest of them. At first, Judge Lava was an intact skeleton. As time went by there got to be less and less of him.

In December 1952, having smashed most of Mr. Crime's city operations, Dick Tracy raided the gloomy mushroom house and was instantly pounced upon by a hungry muerte. Outside in the snow, meanwhile, Sam Catchem was getting flung over a cliff. These were impressive Near-Deathtraps, but Tracy and Catchem survived them and went on to corner Mr. Crime even as he and his crooked pal Judge Courtney Rulings were minutes away from making a safe dash to the airport, and on January 11, 1953, there was at last the blistering showdown with the man who had sent the ruined Tonsils to put a bullet into Tracy's head.

The judge elected suicide on the spot. Mr. Crime thought for an instant he could shoot it out. Both their corpses at his feet, Dick Tracy took the occasion to make a speech. "Two wasted lives!" he cried. "Amidst their own blood, and money that was never theirs. A symbol of crime and its reward!"

Once more, they couldn't get away with it. Once more, justice trapped the guilty. Once more, crime had to pay the penalty. The rats just never learned.

A few days after that, Tracy gently escorted the black-veiled Widow Lava to the morgue. She had insisted upon personally inspecting what was left of the late Judge Lava, and she made the definitive ID as she held his skull to her loving breast. "My husband's teeth," she said. "I remember them well."

Mr. Crime, citizen, November 13, 1952. In which we see again that our crime-boss slugs are so often leading taxpayers and after-dinner speakers.

At the mushroom house with the muerte plant and the nourishing Judge Lava, December 12, 1952.

A KARATE BLOW TO THE WRIST—

CRACK

CHAPTER 31

NOTE THE CLENCHED HANDS TO THE SOLAR PLEXUS
The Policewoman

LATER SHE WOULD BECOME THE TOUGH, glamorous lady cop who was forever judo-tossing some pop-eyed mug or another over her shoulder and coolly snapping on the cuffs before he knew what hit him, but when she made her early appearances in late 1955, Lizz—she never had a last name—was a young nightclub photographer and she was getting herself beat up pretty good.

She was a spirited little pony, though, and presently she got it into her head that she wanted to make a career in police work. For a few years Lizz was cast as the strip Rookie, an understudy and apprentice to Dick Tracy somewhat as the younger Junior Tracy had been once upon a time. Her immediate forebear was Chick Smithly, a society dish who had bravely dealt herself into a dangerous police investigation two years earlier to avenge a murdered sister, and this was exactly Lizz's reason as well. Probably more to the point, though, is that Lizz was officially taking over the Female Interest role that had heretofore belonged to

Tess Trueheart, who by the mid-1950s wasn't being seen very much anymore now that she was a respectable married lady with a baby to feed and beds to make and kitchen counters to wipe and really very little time for getting herself tied up in burning warehouses.

Lizz came along in a story that involved a contract killer named Oodles (first appearance, August 20, 1955), an immense 467-pound blob of a man usually seen weighing himself and carefully counting out calories even as he plowed through enormous meals and then called out for more ("And five gallons of chop suey, and 25 pounds of barbecued ribs, and nine roast chickens!") He was a huge slab of ghastly jolliness, the sort of guy who would chuckle pleasantly even as he gassed a crippled old lady to death in her car, and the girl photog was first seen on October 25 as the jovial Oodles visited his pal Nothing Yonson's nightclub in search of a missing calorie counter that would turn out to be a damaging piece of evidence against him. "Picture, sir?" she inquired.

Lizz, with Oodles and Nothing Yonson, October 25–26, 1955.

She had close-cropped blonde hair and strikingly distinctive eye makeup, a real cupcake, plainly a great character from the first minute.

She was the fiancée of a newspaper reporter named Jimmy, and it was through the boyfriend that she met Dick Tracy, who had already linked the hunted Oodles to Nothing Yonson's club and was hoping that Lizz might have a photo of the fat man. Nothing Yonson didn't appeciate his employees talking to cops. On November 23, Lizz was accosted in a dark alley by a prettyboy in a black leather jacket, a cigarette dangling insouciantly from his lips. "Joe Period, they call me, baby, just Joe Period," he introduced himself. "What do you—" she began, and that's as far as she got.

Joe Period did a job on her, smashing her cameras and breaking her face. The show of gang muscle steamed Jimmy the Reporter plenty. He took the bandaged Lizz, now his bride, to see Tracy, who was at this minute discovering that Oodles and his mob were holed up in a North Woods cabin. "Go on a nice honeymoon," Tracy ordered the newlyweds. "Leave this business to the police." Nuts to that, Jimmy decided. "Back of this mess is the biggest news story of the year, and I'm going after it!" he decided, for if he could only win the $2,500 best-reporting award, he could make a down payment on a house. Jimmy dug up the hide-away's location on his own, and then he and Lizz drove north through another grand Chester Gould midnight snowfall to get Oodles by themselves.

"You're with me, are you, kitten?" Jimmy asked. "You know spying on hoodlums can be pretty dangerous."

"I'm with you, baby," Lizz breathed. "All the way."

There were immediate echoes here of more than a few of the Innocents who had gotten themselves mayhemmed in the course of their meddlings with the lawful administration of criminal justice. "You by-line crazy darling!" Lizz winked at her husband as they left their car and set off cross-country on skis. "What a story!" he exulted. "Cub Reporter and Wife Trail Killer to Lair!" He looked around. "Where are you, Lizz?" he said.

She was already tumbling downhill and crashing into the side of Oodles's cabin is where she was, and both Jimmy and Lizz were instantly prisoners, and it could have gone quite badly for them. But in the end, Dick Tracy and Sam Catchem and a small army of cops saved the newsies in the nick of time, and Oodles went to his reward, and then shortly after Christmas Jimmy and Lizz were seen arguing in their home.

"I WANT TO BE A POLICEWOMAN!" she was saying. "My mind's made up." The hubby couldn't believe his ears. "But Lizz," he said, "you're not the type."

What did he know? Jimmy the Reporter passed from the strip very soon thereafter and at some point later he apparently died. As for Lizz, she passed her civil service exam and went into intensive training, and for a time in early 1956 the entire strip turned into something akin to an enlarged version of the Crimestopper's Textbook as the rookie took endless judo instruction ("The short cut method of breaking a choke hold! Note the clenched hands to the solar plexus") and started learning about fingerprinting and spectroscopy.

Meanwhile, the punk Joe Period had reappeared.

JOE PERIOD WAS A SOCIOPOLITICALLY VITAL

turning point in the DICK TRACY worldview, the strip's first real acknowledgment of a specific youth culture emerging from the rebel energies of primordial rock and roll. In January 1956 there was not yet even an Elvis Presley in the popular ken; Joe Period, motorcycle-jacketed, poutish, greasy locks of hair tumbling over his forehead, had come out of Brando, Dean, Mineo,

and Bill Haley and the Comets, and it was fairly prescient of Gould to recognize the Type at this early point. As Types, to be sure, there had long been Young Bums populating DICK TRACY; indeed, just four years earlier the teenage parking-meter bandit Larry Jones had illustrated the kind of problem that responsible society was having with wayward juvenile delinquents. Still, you had to know that Larry Jones's idea of a real hot hepcat platter would have been the latest Eddie Fisher.

Joe Period ran considerably deeper. It wasn't even that he was a nasty little hood; he was *disrespectful,* and he was *good* at it. He swaggered, he wore tight jeans, he talked smooth at the fillies, and he had the hottest car in the world. Joe Period was rock and roll. Joe Period was *cool.*

Not one of the pathological little misfits Gould had ever previously dreamed up had been cool, and there were evidences throughout the story that he somehow understood this fundamentally different thing about Joe. At age fifty-five, a stout Illinois farmer watching the world as he knew it approaching the brink of thunderous societal disruption, he could only have resented how cool this kid Joe Period so obvi-

Muscled by Joe Period, November 23, 1955.

Rookie cop, January 4, 1956.

ously was. Years later, as the elderly, cranky cartoonist became increasingly obsessed with his Nixon-era parade of longhairs and folkies and protest marchers and rock-and-rolling disrespecters, it was always possible to see the archetypal Joe Period in their moves. Chester Gould must have hated Joe Period just about more than he ever hated anybody.

The two of them—the newly arrived Lizz the Policewoman and the sneering little punk Joe Period, both riding the incoming tidal wave of massive social change—collided like trains. He killed her sister. She went after him. Period.

JOE PERIOD, JUST A SMALL-TIME HOOD WHO

worked as a wheelman and general errand boy, had been called on by a portly, middle-aged, lovelorn ex-lawyer named Paul Pocketclip to carry his foolish importunings to a nightclub thrush named Julie Marrlin "You're just the type she'd listen to!" the gross Pocketclip pleaded. "You've got a way with you! Get me a date, Joe?" "A big shot like you can't get introduced to a girl singer?" Joe wondered, combing his hair. Pocketclip had once represented the singer's gangster husband. "Unfortunately, they sent him to the chair," he sighed. "No WONDER she doesn't want to see you," Joe said. "I love her," Pocketclip moaned.

Julie Marrlin was a swell blonde who, like several popular ladies of 1950s show business, had known a few wiseguys in her time. Joe did the best he could, but there wasn't much Miles Standishing he could manage for the likes of Pocketclip. The two men finally had a falling-out in the hallway outside Julie's apartment, and suddenly Pocketclip was dead on the carpet. More than one jury might have called it self-defense, actually, but Joe panicked hard and he crashed Julie's place, and as Tracy and Catchem made routine floor knocks to inquire about the body, he put a bullet through the girl and went out the window.

Lizz the Policewoman arrived at the hospital and clutched the dying singer's hand. "We were separated at the orphanage fourteen years ago!" Lizz wept. "Only in recent months did I learn her identity. THIS GIRL IS MY SISTER!"

By rattler to South Platt, South Dakota, March 15, 1956. The bum was one Doc Forbes, an ancient sawbones who had saved Joe Period's life. Joe paid off the Samaritan by flinging him from the train.

The tank car Near-Deathtrap, April 10, 1956. Policewoman Lizz survived her first ordeal by the numbers.

Mob girl Julie Marrlin expired on February 7, 1956. "My sister chose the wrong road," Lizz mourned at the deathbed. "It's up to me to make amends for her." In the sad hospital corridor, she made a vow: "As a policewoman, I shall dedicate myself to finding Joe Period, her murderer."

SHE FOUND HIM. JOE PERIOD HAD CRACKED

up his car in his wild flight from Julie's place and, critically injured, had gone to see Nothing Yonson, who had shrugged and let Joe fall into a coma and then dumped him in a westbound boxcar. The punk's trail led into the Great Prairie's rail yards, and Lizz the Policewoman was called upon to join Dick Tracy and Sam Catchem in a South Dakota dragnet. Joe was hiding in a tank car, and Lizz found him, and she pulled some fast judo on him, and that would have been the end of him right there except that at this point a neighborhood thug who'd been watching things joined the fracas and gave Joe a hand, and together they got the best of Lizz and scrammed. "I never did like policewomen," said Joe's new pal.

"Lizz, you dizz!" the rookie lamented. "Oh, brother, they really outsmarted me. Took my gun, my ammo, my star! Oh, Mr. Tracy, I've been such a stupid dope—boo hoo hoo hoo—"

More than a little chastened, Lizz the Policewoman went back to the City to hit the books

some more as, meanwhile, Joe Period and his buddy teamed up for a marathon cross-country auto flight back to the big City, with police of several states in hot pursuit by car and by helicopter.

Joe Period's partner (first appearance, April 4, 1956) had a distinctly recognizable countenance—freckled, fish-faced, pug-nosed, pucker-lipped, flat-headed.

In the middle 1950s there had suddenly re-emerged the sort of classic Grotesques who had characterized the 1940s. The great fat Oodles was one of the best of the bunch. And Nothing Yonson, a severely pinch-faced, almost entirely featureless man, was nothing if not reminiscent of Little Face Finney. Indeed, in early 1955 the memorable Mumbles himself came back. Mumbles, it turned out, had been plucked from the ocean by a yachtsman named George Ozone, an elderly bodybuilder who swam miles every day and did handstands and gulped vegetable-essence potions and who was patently modeled after the robustly bizarre health-nut magazine publisher Bernarr MacFadden ("Soft living! That's what's ruining mankind! Gad! You wouldn't think I was 84 years old, would you?"). Now Mumbles was tutoring Ozone's noble-savage young sons, a pair of wild boys who had become every bit as incomprehensible as himself ("Neki hokey! Wa-ak! Ya Ya!"). Forced to drink one healthy spinach juice too many ("Ono! Not that!"), the tutor finally bumped the old boy off, and after that the formerly hilarious story turned into Evil Incarnate as Mumbles fled to a fog-blighted seaside, beat his girlfriend to death with a shovel, and then drowned, again.

So Gould happened to be thinking of bygone sensibilities and bygone characters. Now, in the spring of 1956, Joe Period's new buddy was nothing less than the Son of Flattop.

FLATTOP JONES JR. HAD, IT WAS EXPLAINED, been six years old when his old man had died in 1944, and he'd been reared in the South Dakota sticks by his aunt, a preposterously ugly woman who looked just like her brother and nephew. The kid was a mechanical genius, and he'd custom-equipped his automobile with a refrigerator, stove, running water, TV, and short-wave radio, and it was in this wonder car that Joe Period and Flattop Jr. led Dick Tracy on a two-month chase to the city, where Joe wanted to settle a score with Nothing Yonson before the two-teen crime wave continued.

Lizz the Policewoman was meanwhile busy learning more judo and Scientific Crime Detection ("HOW you men can find readable finger-

Joe Period's last stand, June 9–10, 1956. Joe's erstwhile companion Flattop Jr. went his own way in his wonder car after the shootout at Nothing Yonson's nightclub.

Flattop Jr. eats death, November 26–27, 1956.

prints on windows, milk bottles, dresser tops, and such, is beyond me!"), and she finally had very little to do with events when her sister's killer shotgunned Nothing Yonson to death on June 6, 1956, and was immediately busted by Dick Tracy and packed off to prison.

Flattop Jr., meanwhile, remained at large for months. He had thrown a girl Innocent off a rooftop at one point, and her translucent ghost had thereafter clung to his neck, strangling him, driving him increasingly bonkers, and he was white-haired and completely mad when Lizz, working another case at the time, happened to run across him. On November 27, 1956, she shot young Flattop in the face and scored her official first kill.

After that, like Junior Tracy at his drawing board, Lizz dropped into the background—answering telephones, sifting through files, occasionally showing up at a crime scene to take fingerprints or a spectroscopic sample or something—until July 1959, when, in the course of an undercover job, she made another kill by matter-of-factly judo-tossing a hired killer out a window. That single incident caused an uproar that would galvanize DICK TRACY forever, throwing the strip headlong into the damn-the-rights-of-criminals political stance that came to characterize it through its subsequent years of decline in a newer world it had never bargained for.

CHAPTER 32

THE MOST IMPORTANT WORDS US GUILTY CRIMINALS EVER USED

Flyface and the Fifth

CAMELOT HAD NOT COME TO THE UNITED States of America in 1959, and nobody was talking about Miranda and Escobedo and nobody was talking about Supreme Court Chief Justice Earl Warren's nine old men. There were, however, TV talk shows.

On August 2, in the course of a witness-protection operation that required her to go undercover as a cow-milking farmgirl, Lizz the Policewoman had run up against a cheap contract killer named Halffa Millyun, and she had summarily stomach-tossed him out a window, and he had gone head-down into the concrete footing of the farm windmill with a satisfying crunch. "Your weekly judo practice paid off!" Sam Catchem told the lady. "And how!" she agreed. "A third-rate hoodlum who would kill for as little as fifty dollars!" Dick Tracy epi-

taphed the dirtball corpse, making things quite plain. A few weeks later, the popular TV program "What's Your Job" called Lizz up and invited her to be a guest.

"Really, I'm not a judo authority," Lizz said modestly.

Host Matty Munkie insisted. "I'm sure my audience would love to meet you!" he said. Reluctantly, she agreed. "Is she crazy?" Sam Catchem blinked. Indeed, Matty Munkie was a notorious ambusher, and he had already decided to show up the lady cop on live TV. "Am I going to have fun with that policewoman!" he giggled to his staff. "Judo expert? I'm going to throw her clear across the stage!"

On the air, he attacked like a pit bull. "Isn't it true that you couldn't toss a fly?" he shouted. "Isn't it true there were TWO STRONG-ARM

COPS in the room that night and THEY PUSHED Millyun to his death? I think the use of jujitsu by policewomen is an overrated joke! I think our TV audience is entitled to know the truth!'' He jumped up and threw himself at her, leering. ''Suppose I came into your room—''

Lizz the Policewoman flung Matty Munkie about thirty feet. The whole nation cheered, and Matty lost his sponsors and then his show, and a network official personally thanked Lizz for getting the distasteful noisy boob thrown off the air at last.

Watching all this with great interest was a burly, cigar-chomping crime boss named Willie the Fifth, a.k.a. Fifth (first appearance, September 22, 1959). ''Uh, I refuse to answer,'' Fifth would murmur automatically whenever anyone even asked him what time it was. He happened to be the late Halffa Millyun's brother, and he wanted revenge upon the policewoman who had killed him, and he Near-Deathtrapped her by sticking her beneath a huge rooftop magnifying glass. The sun's rays had her clothing in flames by the time Tracy and Catchem crashed in. ''Close one!'' Tracy pondered. After that, Fifth and his lawyer sat down in their hideaway to hash things out.

''According to Chapter 38, Paragraph 6, Crim-inal Code, you could be charged with attempted murder,'' the lawyer said.

''What else?'' Fifth inquired.

''Ummm—'' counsel considered flipping through his books. ''They can revoke your liquor license.''

In the immortal tradition of the Hy Habeases and J. Peter Twillbrains of nearly thirty years earlier, there had now arrived another lawyer in DICK TRACY's modern America—a land in which the lowest forms of life could post bail in a minute and could walk on writs of habeas corpus before the bodies got cold, well before Miranda, in the innocent pre-Camelot United States of 1959.

HIS NAME WAS FELIXWEATHER LIMPP, BUT HE

was called Flyface, as he was one of the most disgusting Grotesques the strip ever saw, a repulsively unwashed dirtbag of a creature so malodorous that everywhere he went he had swarms of flies buzzing around him. He was a self-taught legal expert, forever reading books with titles like *Criminal Law and the Parole System*, and Willie the Fifth hugged him gratefully. ''He taught me to say I REFUSE TO ANSWER!'' Fifth would cry. ''The most important

Lizz the Policewoman on the air with Mattie Munkie, September 23, 1959.

Flyface, Fifth, and Fifth's fastidious moll Olive, December 5, 1959.

words us guilty criminals ever used!'' Chester Gould might as well have put up a neon sign on Flyface. From this point forward, DICK TRACY would be fixated upon namby-pamby courts and bleeding-heart parole boards and career criminals who never stopped whining about their civil liberties and their constitutional rights.

And Gould was dumbfounded when an enormous hue and cry went up all over America.

It wasn't fully apparent just yet, but the continued-story strip was already beginning to die as a form, even as once-vital radio drama had already died, even as cliffhanger film serials had died, victims of the swift new entertainment delivery system called television. In any case, there was by now another generation of newspaper editors assuming their places in the information process, and beyond that there was another generation of newspaper readers falling into their positions as well, and what had once been Gould's personal franchise was

not intuitively familiar to either of them. Flyface revolted everybody. It wasn't even Flyface alone. Suddenly Flyface also had a sweet old mother, who was just as loathsome as she could possibly be, bugs flitting all around herself as well. Worse yet, Flyface had a nephew. Little Doc was his name and he was just stomach-turning, crawling with even more vermin than his uncle and his granny. The kid was the breaker. Outraged fumings hit the wire services and newsmagazines, and papers started dropping DICK TRACY in droves.

By 1959 standards, Gould really had gone too far at last. It was only fourteen years earlier that his strip had contributed to the folklore an unbearably offensive creature named B.O. Plenty, and Gould was bewildered and deeply saddened by the violent national reaction against the not dissimilar Flyface. Flies hadn't even been the point. The point had been the Fifth Amendment.

Flyface and family, December 11–12, 1959. Period America could just only barely stand Flyface and his repulsive mother. The little kid was too much.

CHAPTER 33

MAMMA RABBIT'S DAY

The End of Mary Steele

LATE IN 1961, THERE WAS A REMARKABLE occurrence at Marybelle Manor, a ruined estate outside the City. Decades earlier, it was learned, the place had belonged to a crime boss named Etah, and he was rumored to have left a buried fortune somewhere on the grounds; a crook named Spready Spensive was after the stash; Dick Tracy was after Spready Spensive. After the inevitable climactic shoot-out, Dick Tracy discovered that this once-glittering underworld retreat was now occupied by a ghostly old woman (first appearance, October 18) and two small orphans, who were, she explained, her wards.

Satisfied that the crone was an apparently law-abiding pensioner who was renting the crumbling old pile legitimately, the detective tipped his hat and went on his way. But the spectral figure watched him from a window as he departed. "H'm?" she murmured. "He didn't remember me. There wasn't the remotest shadow of recognition in his eyes. Has he forgotten?"

And outside, Tracy was scratching his head. "I had a feeling I'd seen that face before—somewhere," he told Sam Catchem.

Then he shrugged. "Oh, well."

The gun battle at the old-time crime club was a big news story in Dick Tracy's town, and reporters swarmed for days. A national magazine commissioned police artist Junior Tracy to make sketches of Marybelle Manor. When the old lady espied Junior from her window, she burst into bittersweet tears.

"What a fine young man he's grown into," she reflected. "A handsome, clean-looking lad."

"Gee, Granny," the two tykes puzzled as she buried her face in her hands.

She secretly followed him around the grounds, clutching at her wrap in the cold. "To hold him in my arms again and tell him the truth—" she mourned. "No, he'd have forgotten me. It wouldn't be right. It would only confuse him—"

And she doddered forlornly back to her rocking chair.

On Sunday, November 5, 1961, she sat the little boy and girl in her lap and began to read from *Mamma Rabbit's Day.*

"And then," the old lady twinkled, "when the mamma rabbit returned to her warren, what do you suppose she saw?"

ABOVE: Dick Tracy presents peace on earth and a public service announcement: Holiday greetings from the national police cable TV net, Christmas Sunday 1955. Television-conscious since tycoon Diet Smith had introduced the closed-circuit Teleguard in 1948, Tracy's department had inaugurated the net in January 1953 to allow intercity showups. As usual, the strip was a few years ahead of the real world. Children, left to right: Sparkle Plenty, Bonnie Braids Tracy, Sparkle's adoptive sister Wingy, and the Neki Hokey Kids, wild boys who had been featured earlier in 1955; the parrot at left is their pet.

BELOW: Junior Tracy and the fellows get the straight dope on a young man's future in law enforcement, December 15, 1957.

A PLENITUDE OF STORIES FROM SUNNY DELL ACRES:

Sparkle Plenty acquired a little sister in 1953 after gangster Odds Zonn abandoned his three-year-old daughter, Susie; the Plentys rechristened her Little Wings. For a while she glowed in the dark (1. March 29, 1953), since she had radiation poisoning. Sparkle and Wingy had an adventure or two together—notably, they got swept away in a damburst (2. August 8, 1954) and were missing for months—but in 1960 Wingy disappeared. It was explained that she'd moved to Australia.

Meanwhile, B.O. Plenty was, of course, one of eight boys. The first of many Plenty relatives to arrive in the strip was B.O.'s oil-millionaire brother Kincaid, better known as Uncle Canhead, who provided Sunny Dell Acres with modern indoor plumbing (3. October 25, 1953). Later, B.O.'s spry eighty-eight-year-old father, Morin Plenty, showed up with his child-bride Blossom (4. June 9, 1957), the two of them making a coast-to-coast walkathon. After mobsters murdered Blossom, the frisky old fellow took up with her twin sister, Carduey.

Plenty more relatives have been turning up ever since. Even Little Boy Beard, a mutant tyke found abandoned in a park, proved to be kin (5. December 11, 1960; Sparkle Plenty is here seen in her Fat Period). Notable to the family was B.O.'s goofy artist nephew Vera Alldid, who showed up in the late '60s, instantly became concupiscent with his by now quite nubile cousin Sparkle, and, on July 5, 1969, married her. Vera and his bride were a pair for some years (6. October 6, 1974); later Sparkle divorced the dope and married Junior Tracy.

ROGUES GALLERY, ADDENDA:

1. Deluded Tracy assassin Open-Mind Monty, May 23, 1954. The broken knife blade in his forehead gave Open-Mind his name, but—like The Blank's fearsome mask and Influence's terrifying eyeballs—it wasn't real, just a plastic prop the crook had devised the better to encourage his mob's respect.

2. Fur thief Rughead and his boy Happy move in for a kill, December 5, 1954. Tracy survived it. Happy didn't.

3. Bonkers Elsa Crystal chats gaily with her deep-frozen husband Claude in the basement refrigerator, September 8, 1957.

4. Pantsy and his moll on the convoluted trail of buried treasure, February 23, 1958. The longtime apparent Chicago setting of Tracy's city came into some question in this story when the Atlantic seacoast proved to be only thirty-two miles away.

5. Headache and Popsie, December 28, 1958. In an America recently scandalized by Vladimir Nabokov's *Lolita*, the pubescent nymphet Popsie ignited a national furor as she forever slurped on both her lollipop and the middle-aged mob boss.

6. Fugitive kidnapper Spots and his verse-quoting pal Ogden, hiding out in a war-tank park monument, October 2, 1960.

1

3

4

5

6

MEANWHILE—

YES, MY NAME IS CHICORY AND I RAISE GAMECOCKS, BUT WHEN IT COMES TO BEING A STOOL PIGEON, I NO SPICK THE LANGUAGE.

NO SPICK THE LANGUAGE, EH?

THE GRAPEVINE TELLS ME THIS WOMAN VISITED YOU NOT MORE THAN AN HOUR AGO—OH—

OH—THIS LANGUAGE YOU SPICK —EH? WELL, LET'S TALK.

1

I SAW THE PLANE THAT BROUGHT YOU, AND I SAW THEM KICK YOU OUT—JUST LIKE THEY DID ME.

YOU?

I'VE BEEN RATIONING IT TO MYSELF, BUT YOU NEED FOOD.

DICK TRACY ABROAD:

1. In Havana, July 27, 1958.

2. Somewhere in the South Atlantic, August 31, 1958. Dumped by the Cuban gangsters on a remote granite island, Tracy spent many Robinson Crusoe-esque weeks fighting for survival. His fellow strandee was a long-missing Scotland Yard inspector named Whitehall.

3. Deus ex machina, September 28, 1958. Tracy and Whitehall made it off their otherwise inescapable rock when an American nose cone dropped atop them, the entire military tracking its path.

4. In Hawaii, May 1, 1960. Tracy was on the trail of the fugitives Fifth and Flyface, who failed to outrun a tidal wave.

5. Mysteries of the volcano, June 12, 1960. Tracy with Honolulu Police Chief Dan Liu.

2

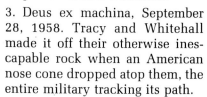

3

IF THEY SURVIVE DROWNING, THEY STILL CAN'T SURVIVE THE CRUSHING WAVES.

FIFTH, WAIT, WAIT!

4

HUH?

IN THE FLICKERING LIGHT—THERE ON A LEDGE.

YES, I SEE.

TWO OF THEM.

5

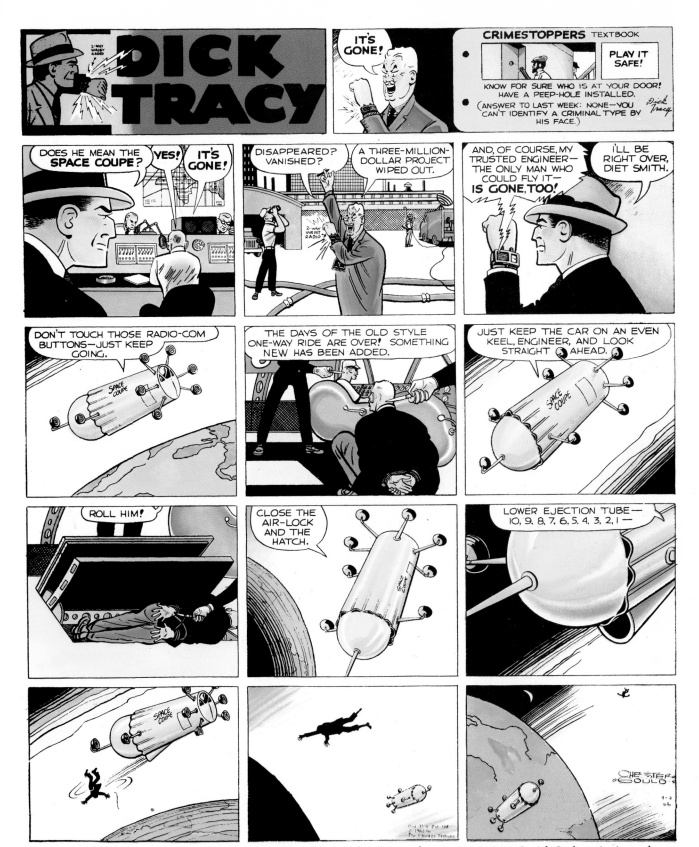

A new day: The world's first Outer Space One-Way Ride, September 9, 1962. Diet Smith Industries' newly introduced magnetic Space Coupe had been hijacked by a world crime league for the elimination of a foe.

ABOVE: Dick Tracy on the moon, June 4, 1967. With Diet Smith and the Moon Governor in a typical scene from the Space Period, as a new generation of readers came to know Tracy as a space cop.

CRIMEBUSTING IN THE SPACE AGE:

1. In pursuit of Space Coupe thieves Mr. and Mrs. Chin Chillar, July 9, 1967. Like Wrist Radio inventor Irma before them, the Chillars were disgruntled Diet Smith employees.

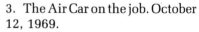

2. Purdy Fallar on ice, May 5, 1968. Gold thief Fallar froze solid when he stepped out of a lunar airlock and was turned over to medical researchers for creepy cryogenic experimentation.

3. The Air Car on the job. October 12, 1969.

ABOVE: Latter-day Chester Gould, August 11, 1974. The old cartoonist, much helped by studio assistant Rick Fletcher, could still turn out a pretty stylish tornado page when he felt like it, but Tracy wasn't kidding about the ended-before-it-got-started part; by the mid-'70s, the now creaking strip was regularly noodling with semi-stories that sometimes went on for no more than a few days.

BELOW: Gould's last DICK TRACY strip, December 25, 1977. The model Perfume Plenty, yet another Plenty relative, had been showcased through much of '77 as the elderly Gould amused himself with TV-commercial gags.

ABOVE: DICK TRACY, by Rick Fletcher (art), Max Allan Collins (script), and Chester Gould (emeritus), August 13, 1978. Services for Junior Tracy's wife, Moon Maid, who had been killed by a car bomb, closed the book on the strip's Space Period.

BELOW: DICK TRACY, by Dick Locher (art) and Max Allan Collins (script), March 25, 1990. Tracy in the Florida Everglades, in a representative contemporary Sunday page featuring a bit of droll old-time mayhem. It developed that the missing third man was eaten by an alligator; cleaving to modern funny-papers standards of taste, the specifics of the luncheon occurred off-screen, though at one point the beast was seen chewing happily on a shoe.

Granny and the babies, October 26, 1961.

Whereupon a stray golf ball from the country club next door sailed through the window, struck her in the temple, and killed her on the spot.

Kids and book spilled to the floor as she pitched forward and landed on her face. "Grandma?" blinked the children.

Rummaging through her effects, Dick Tracy and Sam Catchem found a little knitted bootie and a musty old photo album filled with faded pictures of the Colorado mountains and a small boy who very much resembled young Junior Tracy.

"This is the most startling thing I've run into in all my detective work," Tracy said. "To think the dead woman is—"

He shook his head. "Not one word to Junior."

SUCH WAS THE FLEETING FINAL APPEARANCE OF

Mary Steele. Junior Tracy had apparently never stayed in touch with his natural mother after

The keepsake, October 30, 1961.

The children's hour, November 5, 1961.

her disappearance from the strip in 1938. It was now explained that long ago she had gone back to California and had lived out her life as a housekeeper to the family whose children these orphans were. As public record, the story was also useful for establishing that Dick Tracy had indeed adopted Junior at some earlier point—formal adoption proceedings had not pre-

The scrapbook, December 5, 1961.

viously been documented—and for citing the death (in 1953, of a heart attack) of Steve the Tramp.

The golfer whose ball had dispatched Mary Steele from this earth was found to be a respected philanthropist named George Pardy, but Pardy had a big secret, and even in death the good Mary did her part to assist the law in its unflagging War on Crime. Investigation quickly unmasked the old fellow as a long-hunted cop killer named Tommy McConny, who forty years earlier had cheated the gallows by successfully breaking jail.

"The MOST WANTED ESCAPEE in police history!" Sam Catchem cried.

"As a patrolman, I carried your picture for 10 years!" said Chief Patton, pointing Pardy in the face. "That gallows is still waiting for you!"

"Yes—" the treed old man admitted, lowering his head.

The former Tommy McConny had spent years knowing that this was going to happen to him someday, and he had his getaway carefully planned. Out a window he bolted, down a rooftop he scrambled, and down a stepping-stoned, ivy-trellised wall he began a hand-over-hand climb to freedom. "I made an escape forty years ago—and I can do it again," he snarled.

He was wrong. The footing gave way. There was a grab for the ivy. And into the thick of the plant fell Tommy McConny, a single sturdy vine locking fast around his throat as he struggled and gurgled and, finally, swung.

The dramatic irony of the moment was fairly hard to miss, but Chester Gould had long since learned to spell things out.

"Thus he carries out his own execution single-handed," Dick Tracy noted grimly.

"He tended to that himself," barked Chief Patton.

"Fate does funny things," a uniformed cop mused thoughtfully.

TRACY REMAINED ADAMANT THAT JUNIOR would never learn that the dead woman was his mother. "Junior doesn't know?" wondered Lizz the Policewoman. "No, and we'll never tell him," Tracy said somberly. "There's no need to drag him into this. He wouldn't remember. Why clutter his life?"

And Junior, accordingly, was never told.

Nor did Junior ever say out loud to anyone that he had maybe figured things out for himself. Mary Steele went to the earth in a cemetery called Rest Hill, and one day shortly after she was buried, Tracy and Catchem found an inexplicable wreath at her headstone.

"I'll be darned," Tracy said.

"Who would have known?" Sam wondered.

"Yes," Tracy nodded, evidently baffled forever. "Who could have put a wreath on Mary Steele's grave?"

CHAPTER 34

YOUR WICKED EARTH

The Nation That Controls Magnetism Will Control the Universe

ON DECEMBER 31, 1963, THE DICK TRACY strip as anyone had known it effectively ceased to exist.

Thirty-two years old, still vigorously in its prime, appearing in hundreds of newspapers and followed daily by millions of readers, the famous feature suddenly careened into another plane. All at once, Dick Tracy threw himself into the Space Age and became interplanetary in his concerns. Suddenly he was flying through the void in a cockamamie machine called the Space Coupe, fighting crime on the moon. It was an extremely controversial move, and Chester Gould took heavy criticism for it, and—even as another generation of funnies readers grew up knowing Dick Tracy only as a space cop—Gould spent years testily defending the decision.

It was even possible to follow the logic. It was possible to see the Space Coupe as nothing more than a fantastic extrapolation of the equally science-fictitious 2-Way Wrist Radio of 1946, or for that matter the marvelous clock-radio of 1950. Several nations had space-exploration programs in place in the early 1960s, and the global stakes were manifold and high, and it was readily possible to suppose, even in this last season of sweetness before John F. Kennedy traveled to Dallas, that there were a few secret agendas in the world and that someone like the great industrialist Diet Smith, with all his resources, might have an edge on things.

The Space Coupe had first been seen on August 26, 1962, just another of Diet Smith Industries' many forward-looking developments. It was an engineless cigar-shaped machine that could either hover silently for extended periods or zip to the Andes and back in twelve minutes merely by pointing its weird extruding ears in various directions. "Our staff has discovered the secret of planetary attraction," Diet Smith said gravely. The secret was magnetic pull from the planets. "No blastoff, no launch pad, no flames!" Diet Smith cried. "Sixteen atom-powered energizers multiply the magnetic attraction millions of times! Space travel is just as simple now as getting into your car!" Diet Smith gave Tracy a quick joyride to Egypt, and Planet Earth was nothing but a tiny rubber ball outside the window. Dick Tracy wiped his brow. "I've seen everything," he said.

And immediately the Space Coupe fell into the evil hands of the world crime syndicate, fifty-two hooded men and women who bore the names of playing cards and who had targeted for assassination one Orner Jamison, director of the World Organization of Crime Fighters. Having commandeered the Coupe at gunpoint, they now snatched Jamison, took him up, and—on September 9, 1962, in the world's first space murder—dumped him alive into earth orbit. "One who went to Washington with a loose tongue!" his abductors hissed. "Roll him! Close the air hatch!" For months thereafter the fast-frozen Jamison was a familiar figure in the strip, slowly circling the planet, limbs akimbo. "One by one our enemies will disappear!" screeched the 52s' chief, the Ace of Spades, at the gang's hideaway on a South Dakota mesa. "With our new Space Coupe it is obvious we are invincible!" They were tough enough, actually, that Dick Tracy finally had to use napalm to incinerate virtually all fifty-two of them.

In December, back in the hands of the just, the Space Coupe retrieved Orner Jamison's body for a decent burial, and after that it stayed on as the strip's star attraction, all its systems forever being explained at great length. "The secret combination of asbestos, magnesium and pure carbon dust makes the hull immune to heat!" Diet Smith would point out earnestly, flying Tracy somewhere or another in just instants. "The 16 atomic energerizers also furnish heat, power and cooling."

Gould, a man to keep up with scientific possibilities, seems to have brought himself to believe genuinely and emphatically in the magnetic frontier. "The nation that controls magnetism," Diet Smith announced, easily hundreds of times over the years, "will control the universe." Indeed, in June 1965 a senior official of the Bendix Corporation predicted that by 1971 there would be a sensational breakthrough in the field of space propulsion, probably involving magnetism, and Gould had a good crow over this in the public prints, proudly noting that he'd come in with it already. That there was no such breakthrough only affirmed the scent of paranoia that slowly began to pervade the strip. "Why do they keep fooling with all that rocket and blastoff business when you have this?" Tracy inquired. "Diversionary in my judgment," Diet Smith confided. "The rocket system is as obsolete as the raccoon coat! Politics!" In private conversations late in his life, in his eighties, Gould would sometimes hint darkly that he was sure NASA regarded him as a meddling whistleblower.

Whatever else the Space Coupe was for Gould, it was one of the best toys an old man ever had, just as much fun as the little wrist radio that twenty years earlier everyone had tried to tell

Around the world with Orner Jamison, September 17, 1962. World crimelords figured space for the perfect dumping site. The moon looked good too. "Nice place to leave an enemy," the 52s Gang agreed.

Christmas in space, December 24–25, 1962.

him was quite insane and in his mind every bit as visionary. He always contended that the Space Coupe was nothing more baffling than Charles Lindbergh's *Spirit of St. Louis* surely must have been in 1927 to those louts who were convinced that man was never meant to fly. And, philosophically, he was absolutely right.

But on December 31, 1963, a seminal new character arrived in the strip, and she changed things forever.

The Space Coupe had recently made a trip to the moon to dig for minerological samples, and it had come back with a stowaway. She was a cuteheart little blonde in a spectacularly form-fitting black bodysuit, and she had horns on her head that absorbed solar energy, and she had a built-in electrical forcefield that could knock out commercial television transmissions and government radar, and she could change her own body temperature from freezing to metaboiling at will. She was, in short, an extraterrestrial. Her name was Moon Maid.

PULP SCIENCE FICTION HAS ALWAYS BRIMMED

with such stock figures as Moon Maid. But what was she doing in DICK TRACY? Only Chester Gould knew. Camelot was suddenly dead, and it would be more than five years yet before man would take his small step on the face of the moon, and Gould was looking eastward at the morning sun, and he was boldly flying the Atlantic.

The historic first visitor to Earth, as the strip kept billing her, could turn water to ice with her bare hands and she could detonate mines just by pointing at them. Naturally the Department of Defense was more than a little interested. So, it turned out, was police artist Junior Tracy, who started taking her to the candy store to sip sodas. The little teen angel's first English word was "neat." The second was "home." The third was "love." Junior, who had frankly been with not so many girls in his time, was blown away in a minute. "We're getting married and nobody can stop us," he was suddenly shouting, and the next thing anybody knew, the two crazy kids had grabbed the Space Coupe and eloped to the moon to build a life together.

Late in April, 1964, Junior Tracy made landfall in the mother country of his intended. Moon Valley was a vast, verdant, mile-deep canyon, a place of hot steaming springs and great ice cliffs, where the days were twenty-seven Earth days long, where the weather was almost never anything but perfectly clement, where precious jewels spilled out of the soil. The advanced race of moon people feasted endlessly on giant escargots and watched Earth baseball games and comedy shows on immense television screens in the public plazas and flew around in

Air Cars that looked like airborne trash cans. Mostly it was straight out of "The Jetsons," a popular futuristic TV cartoon series of the previous season. Gould had loved the show.

Reigning over this Utopian higher life was the Governor of Moon Valley (first appearance, June 3), a man of commanding presence who happened to be Moon Maid's father. Junior Tracy, onetime grubby thieving little boxcar brat, had come to be the prospective son-in-law of the ruler of the moon.

In dogged pursuit of the fool for love Junior, Diet Smith speedily built a second Space Coupe and then he and Dick Tracy went to the moon themselves. "You have nothing to fear, gentlemen!" the moon police assured them, showing every hospitality. The Earthmen were both quite surprised that everyone spoke English so well. "The answer is television!" said the Governor, gesturing at Casey Stengel and Jack Benny on the various big screens embedded in the cliffsides. "We pick up your Earth programs!" "Television!" meditated Tracy. "Is that to be the universal vehicle for interplanetary understanding?"

Even as he pondered the brotherhood of the spheres, suddenly he and Junior and Diet Smith were all getting tossed into jail, and now it developed that Moon Maid had been only a shill in a great scheme. "We are seizing your ships!" the Governor cried. "We are far ahead of you Earth people in everything except heat-resistant metals! Consequently we could not explore space as you have done! But now we have your ships! Now our lack of titanium will no longer hold us back! Take them away!"

"Me too?" protested Junior Tracy, not believing this.

And how Moon Maid laughed and laughed at the good one she'd put over on the dumb Earth boy with the funny head, even as he wept again at his unbelievably rotten luck with women.

"Kid, if only someday you could meet just a nice plain farm girl from Kansas ..." Dick Tracy sighed as they all sat in the clink, 238,700 miles from home.

BUT, WELL, MOON MAID TRULY LOVED JUN-ior Tracy after all, and a couple of nights later in the course of this ludicrous interplanetary soap opera that had nothing even remotely to do with the feature that DICK TRACY had been once upon a time, she freed the captives, swiped back one of the Space Coupes, and flew with them back to Earth, where she announced she wished to to stay with Junior forevermore, if he would have her, and he would, and they embraced.

Meanwhile in 1964, there had been introduced into DICK TRACY a boffo gag cartoonist named Chet Jade, who, along with four grinning assistants named Rick, Al, Ray, and Jack (the very names of good old Chet Gould's own studio staffers on the DICK TRACY production line at the Woodstock farm), produced a famous newspaper comic strip called SAWDUST, which consisted of dialogue balloons emanating from nothing but little dots. Gould was having a little fun here with the increasingly minimalist nature of the modern comic strip racket. "Isn't this about as close to no work as

Diet Smith puts Moon Maid through her paces, February 2, 1964. A stunned government official (with Tracy at right, greatly resembling Secretary of Defense Robert McNamara) decided at once that the powerful visitor from afar had to be sent home. The real McNamara, of course, would have shipped her to Southeast Asia in minutes.

you can get?'' Tracy had puzzled. ''Each of these dots has personality!'' Chet Jade had insisted. SAWDUST was just terrible, full of the worst gags anybody had ever heard, one little dot saying something like, ''Tell us about the time you were a wheat farmer in Kansas, Grandpa!'' and the other little dot going, ''I can't! It goes against my grain!'' and it was the most popular comic strip in the whole universe and DICK TRACY characters were forever reading it aloud and socking their knees and falling backward out of their chairs. Upon returning to Earth in the summer of 1964, Moon Maid went to work as SAWDUST's chief gag writer. So it was that science met bigfoot.

And thereafter, as Moon Maid walked back and forth to her job—nobody on the street seemed unduly startled by the sight of a bodysuited blonde with horns on her head—she began to see Modern Earth Crime for herself. Instantly there appeared a series of muggers, molesters, and hit-run drivers entirely unconcerned with the consequences of anything they did, as they were now beginning to have the Fifth Amendment and Miranda and the whole rest of the criminal-mollycoddling justice system on their side. Moon Maid couldn't believe her eyes. ''Won't someone help her?'' Moon Maid would plead at a crowd of gawkers as she came across some savage streetcorner beating. And the marauder would look up and sneer, ''Them cowards aren't going to involve themselves and maybe get arrested for violating my constitutional rights!'' and would then blithely continue with his stabbings and pillagings. This was just shortly after New York's celebrated Kitty Genovese murder—which had literally occurred before the eyes of dozens of bystanders who couldn't be bothered to lift a finger to call a cop—had shocked the entire nation and thrust the phrase ''I don't want to get involved'' into the language.

And the electric Moon Maid—suddenly a precursor of the folk-hero urban vigilante who would come to dominate a good many of the popular entertainments a decade and more later—would point her finger and fire an angry lightning bolt and set the goon aflame, and then disappear into the night.

A few instances of this and there were a lot

of headlines. MYSTERIOUS FORCE STRIKES AGAIN! the papers screamed. ''Hm?'' Dick Tracy scratched his head. ''Thank goodness they're on the side of the law!'' Sam Catchem observed.

And what had begun somewhere between a good-natured 'toon yarn and black paranoia—Chester Gould had not only been an ardent fan of ''The Jetsons,'' he had been a lifelong friend of LITTLE ORPHAN ANNIE's Harold Gray, who had always warned that someday decent citizens would have to bunker themselves against the marauders—now began to reach a terrible fruition, as DICK TRACY collided headlong with the tumult of the middle '60s.

''Cutthroats! Stabbers! Murderers!'' Dick Tracy spat. ''And all cry constitutional rights! What a laugh! In my opinion, whoever is using this flamethrower certainly deserves our vote of thanks.'' Granted it was a stacked deck. Granted the mysterious flamethrowing vigilante was taking out nothing but plainly identifiable scum as opposed to Stray Innocents, or even Presumed Stray Innocents who had managed to dump their screwdrivers before they got popped. Two decades later the issues of crime and punishment would be murkier, and the nation would writhe and anguish over the social implications of, for example, the New York ''Subway Vigilante'' Bernhard Goetz, a mild-mannered citizen who elected to defend himself against a gang of goons who were patently attempting to harm him. In 1964, it could still be readily agreed that Moon Maid was just, as Chester Gould presciently began to project a time when the dirtballs would walk and the law-abiding American would only pay and pay. Indeed, only a few years later the courts were all but routinely awarding compensatory damages to housebreakers who got shot by their victims.

Gould was turning most of his fury at this point on the modern parole system that was arising in the season of Miranda and Escobedo. At once, nearly every casual thug who showed up in DICK TRACY was seen to be some hardcase career criminal who had been disimprisoned just weeks earlier after the parole board had cried its eyes out over him. Gould even came up with a criminal character named Paroll Lea. Many of these guys, in early 1965, were seen to be working for a gang boss named Matty Square,

Matty Square and Ugly Christine, October 7, 1965. Matty's corpulent, cigar-smoking cat was one of the period's memorable Criminal Pets. Recent others in the same vein had included a cigarette-puffing crow and a martini-swilling chihuahua.

who was very annoyed about the vigilante Moon Maid. He sat at his desk, his square eyeballs gazing squarely into the distance, puffing at his cigar and contemplatively blowing square smoke rings. "There must be a way to neutralize this wicked woman who violates our constitutional rights," Matty Square mused.

Matty tried several times to have Moon Maid wasted as a public service to all gangdom, and he always failed, for one thing because he kept accidentally wiping out his own boys and for another thing because Moon Maid was basically indestructible. Finally, his whole gang gone, he threw in with the big fix, one Mr. Bribery, a grinning, bespectacled, rose-sniffing man who was regularly seen pressing wads of cash into the the palms of legions of petty councilmen and commissioners and who for some reason looked exactly like Franklin Delano Roosevelt.

Mr. Bribery (first appearance, July 2, 1965) was one of the best characters Gould ever did, and so was Mr. Bribery's sister Ugly Christine, apparently so horrifying that she wore her hair down to her chin and never showed her face, and they were both around for more than a year, the longest-sustained villains the strip had done since the likes of Steve the Tramp. They were his last truly memorable characters, as the grand old cartoonist began to slip into his dotage.

The evil Mr. Bribery kept a wall-case collection of his enemies' shrunken heads. He kept a cocaine-snorting Ecuadorian Indian called Nah

Tay to shrink heads for him in ghastly boiling kettles. He had branded his own sister in the forehead with a hot iron. The three of them accidentally killed the hapless Matty Square by dropping him into a vat of scalding water. It was spectacular material, Gould's last great burst of grisly energy, and it was the characters' misfortune that they came along in a period when Gould had already locked himself into his space stories.

THERE HAD BEEN PARALLEL DEVELOPMENTS,
increasingly unsettling to DICK TRACY traditionalists. The Moon Governor had proven to be contrite in the wake of his daughter's defection, and in the summer of 1964 he had come to Earth bearing peace offerings. One of them was the Air Car, a fleet of which he donated to Dick Tracy's Police Department and which then became strip staples, flitting through the skies, running policemen out to crime scenes, buzzing after fleeing cars. And then the Governor had gone into business with Diet Smith, trading moon gems for earth titanium, and Diet Smith had built a huge industrial complex on the moon and Space Coupes started to make regular commercial runs back and forth.

And on October 4, 1964, Junior Tracy and

Mr. Bribery.

Mr. and Mrs. Dick Tracy Jr. and the in-laws, October 4, 1964.

Moon Maid had been married, at Diet Smith's Earth Complex, and the earth and the moon joined hands of festivity and goodwill. (Actually it was just the United States and the moon. Diet Smith, by now a bombastic jingo, regarded the moon as an exclusively American colony, and he was laying plans for its statehood.)

By early 1965 it was known that a momentous baby was due in June, essentially a product not unlike Sparkle Plenty, and indeed the nation's toymakers were already lining up.

In the meantime, the Governor had been taking a dim view of his daughter's vigilante adventures among the constitutionally protected predators and marauders and suddenly he had kidnapped her and borne her back to the moon where she belonged. "I can't leave my husband!" Moon Maid had pleaded. "Never again will you return to Earth!" boomed her stern father, firm in resolve at the wheel of a Space Coupe. "No daughter of mine is going to live on a planet where her life is in constant danger. Hypocrites and barbarians! I've had enough of them!"

Junior Tracy pursued his bride back to the moon and had it out with the old man. "There are no treaties between Earth and Moon that legally force you to return my wife, but I'll find a way!" the kid cried. "You try Earth violence in Moon Valley and you'll end up as elements of gas floating around the universe," pop warned him. Moon Maid was meanwhile knitting little booties. "He is one of us exactly as our flesh and blood," Moon Maid's mother pleaded. "This is our daughter's mate." The Governor melted and gave up. It turned out that Moon Maid was wrong about June anyway. She'd been confused by Earth's calendar and actually the baby wouldn't be coming until autumn. "Moon women are terrible at arithmetic," the Governor shrugged.

Honey Moon Tracy was born aboard the Space Coupe, midway between the earth and the moon, on September 12, 1965. Dick Tracy's granddaughter had horns. "Let this child be a symbol of the new millennium!" prayed Diet Smith over the stateless little issue.

Thrust into this extraordinary set of circumstances were the great strip characters Mr. Bribery and Ugly Christine, who in 1947 would have been evilly plotting to kidnap Sparkle Plenty but who in 1965 were stuck with a story line that required them to kidnap a semi-extraterrestrial. It was getting harder for TRACY villains to keep straight faces as they went about their nefarious activities.

The point of the snatch was that Honey Moon would lure Dick Tracy into a Near-Deathtrap wherein the necklaced, headdressed, chanting Nah Tay would chop off the detective's head and shrink it for Mr. Bribery's shelf. Moon Maid busted up the kidnap scheme herself with a well-placed lightning bolt, and now, with a child to think about, she was suddenly agreeing with her father that this was no planet to live on. Even as Tess Trueheart Tracy of yore, changing her mind every four minutes, Moon Maid was now packing her bags. "I do not belong on your wicked earth!" she screamed at her glubbering husband as she headed for the door.

The Moon Governor had a private prophetic word with Dick Tracy. "We moon people," he said, "could rid your earth of all criminals with our laser beams." Tracy sort of liked the sound of it, but, just as with Stud Bronzen in 1938, he was responsibly obliged to think about the fact that there was probably some kind of interplanetary twelve-mile limit. "It's not that simple," Tracy cautioned. These days he had the Bill of Rights to gnarl over. Otherwise there really might have been moon cops all over DICK TRACY minutes later, vaporizing everybody in a flash. It certainly could have settled the hash of a lot of previous customers, all of World War II included.

EVER PLOTTING HIS FEATURE FROM PANEL TO

panel, Gould had probably never planned it this way, but suddenly it was no longer possible for any one of his story lines to proceed without the intervention somewhere of either Diet Smith Industries or the Governor of the moon. In February 1966, for example, Mr. Bribery's primitive colleague Nah Tay realized in one of his exotic ritual trances that it was not good to kill Dick Tracy after all ("Moon gods not want head shrunk! Bribery bad man!"), and Mr. Bribery, who years earlier might have sim-

Chester Gould with Ideal Toy's Honey Moon dolly, October 1965.

ply taken his troublesome employee for a ride in a Chevy and shot him in the head and dumped him in a sewer, was now obliged by the newly emerged strip conventions to steal a Space Coupe and eject Nah Tay into orbit just like Orner Jamison. In October, Ugly Christine plunged eight hundred feet to a sensationally fiery death in the maw of a blazing factory smokestack, but she didn't fall out of a small airplane, she fell out of an Air Car for the helm of which she had been wrestling Lizz the Policewoman.

This was, finally, the formulative problem that beset the period's DICK TRACY:

Space cops on the job, September 18, 1966.

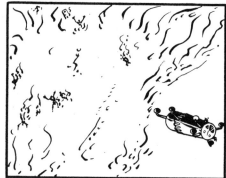

Mr. Intro departs in a flash, June 9, 1968.

Since there was no longer any point in being a crime boss unless you had the Space Coupe in your possession, story after story revolved around one Space Coupe hijack after another, and a certain sameness set in. Meanwhile, since conventional police units couldn't begin to deal with the new super-criminals and their stolen Space Coupes, it was necessary to devise more and more fantastic weapons with which to battle them. (In December 1967, for example, DICK TRACY acquired atomic laser guns, fiendish machines that could vaporize entire cities. "They could maintain law and order throughout the world, in the hands of a moral and strong people!" nodded Tracy, speaking up once more for bullets and prayer.)

But once there were atomic laser guns, immediately the super-criminals had to become even more super yet, or there would be no one to shoot at. You couldn't use atomic laser guns on car thieves. Finally, in the spring of 1968, it became necessary for Gould to invent Mr. Intro, who was bent on nothing less than total global domination. Like some SPECTRE kingpin in the popular James Bond series of novels and films, which DICK TRACY by this point resembled more than considerably, Mr. Intro was a sinister, never-seen figure who surrounded himself with tattooed beauties and who lived in the Caribbean aboard an opulent yacht with a companion submarine affixed underneath. He was orchestrating the theft of moon gold from Diet Smith's lunar mines, scheming to dump it willy-nilly into the earth market. "One by one the economy of nations I select will be wrecked!" Mr. Intro shrieked happily. Far out at sea, Dick Tracy closed in on him at last, for a contemporary version of a climactic TRACY shoot-out, this one between submarine and Space Coupe. In a blinding orange flash on June 9, 1968, the atomic laser gun blasted Mr. Intro and his entire floating empire into fumes.

Another Space Coupe came around to give Tracy's ship backup support. "Where's Mr. Intro?" someone asked.

"You're breathing him," Dick Tracy said.

AFTER THAT, WHERE COULD THE STRIP GO?

In April 1969, Dick Tracy was named Chief of Moon Security. It was, he explained, a consulting position. "You might say I'll be moonlighting," he chuckled.

Newspapers started dropping TRACY from their comics pages in droves. The strip was still called DICK TRACY, but who knew why? DICK TRACY had obviously gone mad.

CHAPTER 35

MERRY CHRISTMAS
The End

MAN WALKED AT LAST UPON THE STORIED moon in July 1969, and man now saw that not only was the place uninhabitable, it wasn't even very interesting. With the empirical evidence before the eyes of every reader in the world, the ostensibly reality-based DICK TRACY became commercially obliged to retreat back to Planet Earth and to delete all memory of the past five years.

Chester Gould, who had spent the last half of the 1960s imagining himself to be a modern Jules Verne—"It's a good bet that by the 21st Century there will be a police force on the moon!" he had promised the press as late as January 1968—at last gave the game up. In November 1969, four months after the American moon landing, Dick Tracy flew again to Moon Valley and made a proud farewell speech to the moon people. "I sense a new day for civilization," he said. "A clean slate! A chance to start anew!" He gazed magisterially out at his readers. "Can civilization measure up to it?" he implored.

On Christmas Day, the great detective was back on Earth, bowing his head at his dinner table with his family.

"As the universe gets smaller, let men's minds get bigger," he prayed.

Thus did DICK TRACY's forward-reaching moon period come to an end.

Unlike the transistor, unlike the closed-circuit television, unlike all the rest of the Diet Smith wonderments over the years, the Space Age prophecies were now publicly invalidated. DICK TRACY had been deceived.

GOULD WOULD CONTINUE TO PRODUCE HIS
strip until December 25, 1977, but already the life was visibly bleeding out of the thing.

The moon stories and their corollary chest-thumping polemics had been done at great cost; between 1960 and 1974, TRACY's circulation dropped from about 550 newspapers to about 375. Particularly unkind to the strip's fortunes was the atomic wipeout of Mr. Intro, which

Groovy Grove and policewoman, February 6, 1975. The strip's longhair rookie cop, introduced presumably to appeal to youthful readers, fast won the heart of Lizz, who became increasingly torrid with the years. He declined her marital stipulation. A few years later he was killed in action.

occurred the same week that presidential candidate Robert F. Kennedy was assassinated and which touched off a firestorm in a land all at once prone to self-flagellation. Newspaper editorials were again seething that brutal DICK TRACY itself was surely a principal contributor to this violence in America. "What deep solace to the family of the deceased," Gould wrote testily to one of the papers that had dropped him, the *Greensboro* (North Carolina) *Daily News*. He noted that modern crime fighting "has assumed the aspect of war" and announced that Dick Tracy would therefore "continue to use violence when necessary." He inquired if the Greensboro editors also disapproved of the violence with which the nation had answered Hitler and Pearl Harbor, and he seemed certain that the question itself would give them sleepless nights. "God give you strength to bear up under these horrendous stresses," he sneered. "I hope you do more to avenge the tragic death of our public figures than kick a comic strip in the slats."

And so he went into the twilight, a cranky old man who had generations earlier created the Great American Crime Stopper, had shepherded him through a celebrated career in the nation's popular entertainments, and had proudly watched him triumph again and again, and who was now lamentably living to see his life's work the subject of jeers in an awful time when geometrically increasing numbers of citizens were learning to equate domestic law and order with the storm troopers of 1968 Chicago and international supremacy with My Lai. It wasn't quite the same as taking out Baby Face Nelson. It didn't really play like Pappy Boyington charging bravely into fighter squadrons.

Chester Gould was a professional showman, and he worked the room as best he could. Attempting to infuse his strip with what was now regarded as "relevance," he tried adding a new Rookie Cop to the cadre, a long-haired, mustachioed, "youth-oriented" figure whose name was Groovy Grove (first appearance, May 6, 1970). The new guy was one of those "mod" young fellows, and Lizz the Policewoman, who became his partner and subsequently his lady friend, kept referring to him as "the new breed." Indeed, Dick Tracy himself grew a mustache and started to wear his hair longer. The smart young rookie quickly turned into a robo-cop precursor, and he spent a good bit of time designing futuristic scenarios wherein riot cops would be armored like tanks in imperviously high-tech uniforms against the depredations of those who would rant and rail and natter and overthrow in these fearsomely polarized days of the First Nixon Republic. Groovy was a terrible character in the first place, and it didn't help at all that he appeared in the funny papers the same week that the Ohio National Guard fatally mowed down four young anti-Vietnam demonstrators at Kent State University.

And meanwhile the whining little rats of the world were forever spitting at Dick Tracy as he roared in to bust them. "Don't lay a finger on me!" they would yelp, caught red-handed in some self-evidently criminal act. "I've got constitutional rights!" In 1971, The Mole of yore returned—a doddering old grandfather by now, still living underground, and in cahoots with a stolen-sparklers mob—and despite clear and present evidence that should have sent anybody to the slammer for years, legal technicalities required Dick Tracy not only to let the whole gang walk but also to politely return all their hot jewels to them. "This has to be a musical comedy!" snarled Police Chief Pat Patton. Dick Tracy gazed once again into the eye

The litany. A 1970s medley.

Representative latter-day villains: (1) Phony fitness guru Big Brass tapes a New Age TV spot, April 21, 1974. At right, his star-gazing confederate Crystal. (2) The dope dealer Hairy plucks himself, August 22, 1975. (3) Feminist armored-car bandit Lispy and her girlth, January 17, 1976. (4) And the late Harris (Diamond-Tooth) Rinkles, December 21, 1973. A memorable Decedent in the fashion of Judge Lava and Orner Jamison, Diamond-Tooth was purely a skull, lately recovered by police divers from the river bottom and now turned over to his deranged half-sister Florabelle, who mounted him in his favorite chair, gave him a cigar, and watched television with him. Thereafter the skull was a bizarre strip fixture for months, played mostly for black laughs. A sideshow knife thrower used it for target practice. A teenage hotrodder turned it into a hood ornament. At one point wrens built a nest in it. (The sound effect is from the old lady's guillotine in the next room, with which she subsequently almost beheaded Lizz the Policewoman.)

of the reader and spoke: "Yes, under today's interpretation of the law, it seems it's the police who are handcuffed. What crud!"

They were ambivalent days. The United States was never, for example, Albania, but neither were fears of an emerging police state entirely unrealistic at a certain point in the early '70s. At the same time, the country was full of idealistic young Vietnam-vet cops who slaved their hearts out for a decent public order and who buried their faces in their hands and wept as one murdering louse after another walked out

of the courtroom, free to murder again. The frustrations on all sides were palpable.

In fact, there were echoes here of the same state of affairs that had birthed DICK TRACY in the first place, forty years earlier. The difference was that then the storyteller Chester Gould had been forty years younger and burning with ideas. Forty years later, his politics really hadn't changed at all, but now he was less interested in the storytelling. Increasingly, DICK TRACY became only a formulaic philippic, wherein the cops would catch some crook and then have to let him go and would then sit around grumbling about the Supreme Court. Tracy formed a national organization called Law and Order First and he did much public speaking before conservative civic groups. In a not-at-all-atypical passage such as the Sunday page of February 29, 1976, dialogue became nothing but a string of platitudes. "Court decisions and sociological beliefs won't help you when you're being mugged!" "Law-abiding citizens have rights, too!" "Perverting words of the English language doesn't change the dictionary!" "No war was ever won by kissing the enemy to death!"

Gould's own progressive creative enfeeblement aside, there were other factors working against him. By the middle '70s, the story-strip form of which he had been one of several acclaimed masters was an anachronism. Most of the great serials of yore were by now either dead or comatose, and there was a great shrinkage of available space in any event when through 1973 and 1974 all the comics-supplying feature syndicates agreed to their client papers' demands that strips start running quite smaller than they had ever run before—fewer words, fewer panels, considerably less space for running dialogue. In October 1974, the TRACY Sunday page was cut back from its familiar twelve-panel format to a new configuration that usually left Gould with a maximum of eight panels. He never successfully adjusted to the reduction, and his pacing fell off badly.

Space junk, May 13, 1974. Though the moon stories passed away, the accoutrements did not: the Air Car remained in active police service and sometimes even the Space Coupe still turned up on surveillance jobs. This was one of the Coupe's last appearances.

The great man who had been Chester Gould at last found all the cards dealt against him. He ran out of friends, he ran out of stories, he ran out of room, and he ran out of time.

"There's a revulsion against the aggressive, destructive hero," a pop-psychiatry professor from Northwestern, Gould's own alma mater, assured the *Wall Street Journal* in March 1974. In that same forum, the Chicago Tribune–New York News Syndicate's new president Robert S. Reed defined the nature of the contemporary comic strip business. "Most editors are looking

Former Police Chief Brandon, the cameo, April 28, 1975. Not seen since late 1948, the old chief, now in landscaping, had some information about a current case. In the spirit of the period strip, Brandon called his business Lawn Order.

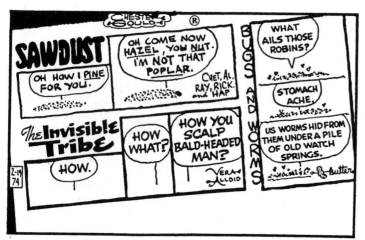

The funny papers, February 19, 1974. The original SAWDUST (featuring dots that took five men to ink) had been joined by BUGS AND WORMS (featuring squiggles drawn by a precocious nine-year-old boy) and THE INVISIBLE TRIBE (featuring blank panels doggedly produced by Sparkle Plenty's husband Vera Alldid). Oft-seen within TRACY, the minimalist features were Chester Gould's commentary on the state of the modern comic-strip business. He apparently also thought the groaners were pretty uproarious.

for good topical contemporary strips in the mode of B.C. or WIZARD OF ID,'' Reed said. By which he meant, not incorrectly, that most editors weren't looking for some wheezing old pterodactyl of a feature that, however classic, had outlived itself.

In 1977, Gould decided to retire and turn the strip over to successors. He was an old man. His back was hurting him. He couldn't sit at the drawing board anymore.

Arrangements were made for the feature's continuation. Rick Fletcher, Gould's chief assistant for the previous sixteen years, was retained by the syndicate to draw the strip, and a young mystery novelist named Max Allan Collins was commissioned to write it, and an orderly transition was crafted.

There was, at the end, some sad miscommunication over the precise terms of the departure date. Chester Gould made his final appearance in print on Christmas Sunday 1977, and when he had drawn the page sixteen weeks earlier he hadn't known that it was going to be his last strip. It was a trivial gag page, and there was nothing at all in the way of farewells. Old Chester Gould went out not knowing he was going out.

THEREAFTER HE STAYED ON FOR A TIME AS A

"consultant" to the post-Gould DICK TRACY and his name appeared daily on the new strip along with Collins's and Fletcher's, but he had little to do with its production. For a few years he enjoyed considerable hallowed status as an elder statesman of the comic strip industry. In April 1978, the National Cartoonists' Society honored him as Cartoonist of the Year and presented him with its Reuben award, the comics' equivalent of the movies' Oscar. He had won it already, in 1959, and this conferral was purely honorific. In April 1980, the Mystery Writers of America presented him with a special edition of its prestigious Edgar trophy— it was the first time the Edgar had ever gone to a cartoonist— and the group feted Gould as the father of "the American police procedural detective story."

Also in April 1980, the editorial page of the New York Times ran a short meditation on the subject of how Dick Tracy had been the James Bond of his day, and made a reference to the great detective's creator as "the late" Chester Gould.

A special retirement drawing for The American Cartoonist magazine (No. 4, September 1978), on the occasion of Gould's having won his second Reuben.

In October 1982, during one of the periods when the nation's art critics were conceding that the classic funny papers of the American press had perhaps contributed something faintly worthy of discussion to the permanent record after all, the *Times* reconsidered its view that Gould was deceased and dispatched *Times*man John Russell to the Graham Gallery, where there was now mounted an important showing of original DICK TRACY art. Chester Gould, Russell wrote, had been a "workman of a very high order," a man who had given "weird coherence" to the lives of his millions of readers over several generations. The exhibited pieces, he concluded, were "tokens of a time when issues were clear cut, when law was law, order was order, and the best man won in the end." Of the cumulative body of Chester Gould's work, Russell said generously: "Rare is the novelist who could not learn something from the conciseness, the pace and the unfailing momentum."

New York Daily News columnist Lars-Erik Nelson had a look at the Graham show as well, and it was he who wrote Chester Gould's definitive elegy:

The artistic handicap that burdened Chester Gould and [POGO creator] Walt Kelly and [Disney DONALD DUCKman] Carl Barks all these years is that they were enormously popular. And if popular, therefore somehow not serious, not worthy of intellectual appreciation, just as *Huckleberry Finn* was regarded for years as nothing more than a children's book. . . . If the vast public out there really enjoys something, goes the unspoken rule, it must be trash— for forty years or so. And then it becomes a cult. Eventually it becomes academically respectable. By which time, hopefully, its creator is dead and so cannot cash in on the proceeds.

"Chester Gould is still alive," Nelson whooped. "Make 'em pay, Chester."

YOU LOOK TRIM FOR A MAN YOUR AGE, DETECTIVE TRACY—

I WORK OUT WHEN I CAN—

DICK LOCHER MAX COLLINS

3·22 Ⓡ

CHAPTER 36

MODERN DETECTIVE
After the End

IT IS JUST A FACT OF LIFE IN THE COMIC strip business that a popular and money-making property is not necessarily going to vanish merely because its creator dies or retires or moves along to something else. This has been the case at least since a famous court ruling permitted the survival of THE KATZENJAMMER KIDS before World War I, and thereafter there has always been a successor who could be found when one was wanted—when Sidney Smith died in a 1935 auto crackup, for example, and of course there was no question that his massively successful THE GUMPS would go on regardless; when THIMBLE THEATRE's E.C. Segar took ill and expired in 1938; when FLASH GORDON's Alex Raymond went off to war in 1944; when Milton Caniff walked out on TERRY AND THE PIRATES in 1946; when LITTLE ORPHAN ANNIE's Harold Gray went to his reward in 1968. Sometimes the inheritors are distinctly inferior to those who came before them, and there has been more than one prosperous feature run swiftly into the ground by some bullpen-hack appointee who just didn't get it. Sometimes they brilliantly show themselves to be their predecessors' betters. Most often they are professional workmen who simply carry on quietly and creditably and well.

But almost all the time, successors are doomed from the first minute to suffer everlasting comparisons to those whose work they have taken over, worse yet when the work is an acknowledged national treasure. Notwithstanding the clear and present flimsinesses of his latter years, Chester Gould went out a revered titan when he left DICK TRACY after Christmas Day 1977. And Max Allan Collins, a twenty-nine-year-old Iowa writer who on the strength of a burgeoning renown in the mystery field was hired to write the scripts for new TRACY artist Rick Fletcher to turn into daily comic strip adventures, realistically understood that in this time of smaller panels and fewer words there was scarcely a chance his material could ever stand up alongside the rip-roaring best of Gould's classic '40s and '50s stuff. Modestly, he made this point again and again in the press coverage that attended the passage of the old lion Chester Gould's strip into fresh hands. On the other hand, Collins—a devoted TRACY fan who knew the conventions and knew the drill—also grasped that whatever he did was going to be miles better than the dreary stuff Gould had been doing lately.

On Monday, December 26, 1977, Max Allan Collins came charging out of the box with a sensational new story that instantly introduced a fish-faced, freckled, pucker-lipped, flat-headed young woman called Angeltop. She was the late Flattop's daughter, and her companion was a creased young fellow who was the son of The Brow, and the two of them were sworn to slay

Angeltop, February 19, 1978. The first post-Gould story found Flattop's daughter, in concert with The Brow's son, seeking to dispatch Tracy in the same underwater pilings where Flattop had died thirty-four years earlier. Cartoonist Emeritus Gould continued to share the byline with writer Max Allan Collins and artist Rick Fletcher for several years.

Dick Tracy for the devilments he had worked on their respective families. They almost drowned him, in the same underwater pilings in which Flattop had caught himself thirty-four years earlier, beneath the famous ship replica in the park lagoon, and then everything went up in flames in a fiery orange denouement and Angeltop apparently burned to death. Meanwhile, the old ham actor Vitamin Flintheart had been resurrected and The Brow's boy had shot him. Young Brow proceeded to walk scot-free on a technicality. "Had his constitutional rights violated, D.A. says," Dick Tracy grunted.

It was hands down the best DICK TRACY story anyone had seen in ten years at least, arguably fifteen, and the strip was immediately reenergized. Collins's bosses at the syndicate had confided to him when he signed that frankly they weren't sure that the creaking old strip had

more than two years left in it. That was in 1977.

THERE WERE FEW PEOPLE MORE RESPECTFUL

of the great TRACY traditions that the syndicate could have brought in to take the reins than Max Allan Collins. Under his stewardship, there have been solemn devotionals to the memory of the grand old days and attentiveness to those matters that required repair. Solemnly the new strip resurrected not only Vitamin Flintheart but also Dick Tracy's old-time G-Man pal Jim Trailer, Tracy's daughter Bonnie Braids, and a whole mob of the great old bad guys—Big Boy, Mumbles, The Mole, many others. Attentively the new strip cleaned up various messy leftovers: In August 1978, Mrs. Junior Tracy climbed behind the wheel of Dick Tracy's car, turned

the key, and was blown to bits by a bomb meant for the detective. Bumping off Moon Maid was the single most loving and reverential action any TRACY devotee could have taken, and if Collins had never written another line, he would still be living in memory for having done the strip this affectionate good turn. The Moon Governor sent word that he was severing relations with Planet Earth forever. Honey Moon Tracy, the horned little remnant from the discontinued Moon Period, receded considerably from the story line, and that was that. Later, the new DICK TRACY made a point of dumping Rookie Cop Groovy Grove, the hipster who had been the strip's idea of a with-it character during Chester Gould's '70s. Collins killed him in action.

Beyond that, Collins also moved to establish his own view of what DICK TRACY should be. His new villains have included computer pirates, Wall Street bandits, rock-and-roll-business crooks, environmental terrorists, rogue cops, and other lifeforms lifted straight out of the headlines of the '80s. He added to the headquarters cadre a new Tracy sidekick called Johnny Adonis and a black policewoman named Lee Ebony. At one point he had Dick Tracy resign from the department for a time to go into business as a private eye. At another point he killed off Police Chief Pat Patton, though the death

Haf-and-Haf, with Lizz, May 28, 1978. Equal parts handsome rascal and horribly disfigured monster, Haf-and-Haf had been a 1967 Gould character; resurrected by Collins, he has since made several appearances.

Blowing up Moon Maid, August 7, 1978. The blast, meant for Dick Tracy, put a formal end to the Moon Period; indeed, writer Collins effectively deleted fifteen years of strip history. Daughter Honey Moon stuck around, but she got a new hairdo that covered up her horns. Widower Junior Tracy later married Sparkle Plenty.

Dick Tracy's ROGUES' GALLERY

BIG BOY—
CRIME CZAR
JAILED BY
DICK TRACY
(ON HIS FIRST
CASE); SOUGHT
REVENGE,
UNSUCCESSFULLY.
DIED OF HEART
ATTACK.

Dick Tracy's ROGUES' GALLERY

NILON HOZE
—HEIRESS WHOSE
SCHEME TO
PREVENT HER
RICH AUNT FROM
MARRYING LED
TO MURDER.
HER ACCOMPLICE,
ROD, TOOK HIS
OWN LIFE.
AND HERS.

Dick Tracy's Rogues' Gallery. Terminating the old Crimestoppers Textbook, the new TRACY team launched this remember-when scrapbook feature in its stead. The Textbook was resumed in the mid-'80s.

Lee Ebony and Johnny Adonis, September 25, 1982. The new troops joined Sam Catchem and Lizz on Tracy's Major Crime Squad.

Sparkle Plenty married the widower Junior Tracy, and the two of them had a daughter.

In recent years Max Allan Collins has had to endure criticism of the blandness that after a time began to overtake the modern DICK TRACY strip. It has not been entirely Collins' fault; he has been increasingly subject to the same external forces that beleaguered Chester Gould throughout his lifetime. Violence? Mayhem? The contemporary DICK TRACY has been forbidden anything akin to the old corrosive shoot-outs ever since Collins did one 1981 gunfight that unfortunately happened to run in the nation's newspapers the same week that Pope John Paul

was quickly rescinded by protesting syndicate bosses. Angeltop returned, a recurring leitmotif. A barracuda newspaper reporter named Wendy Wichel became a major figure, forever attacking Dick Tracy in print. Dick and Tess Tracy bore another child, a son named Joe.

Deputy Chief Climer, October 14, 1982. The character, no admirer of Dick Tracy's frontier justice, enabled Collins to address criticisms that the old strip was over the hill; after Climer succeeded Pat Patton as chief, Tracy threw down his badge and went into private-eye work (returning to the force after Climer proved to be crooked and was shot to death by an honest rookie).

Some modern bad guys. (1) Itchy's brother Twitchy, April 2, 1983. With B.D. Eyes, apparently a relative of B-B Eyes. (2) Nice old fences Ma and Pa Rockwell, July 3, 1983. In the '30s they'd been a Bonnie-and-Clydelike stickup team who called themselves Flo and Eddie. (3) The designer-clothing counterfeiter Murky, May 26, 1984. Even Mumbles was silver-tongued compared to Murky. When he was fatally injured in an auto crash, nobody could understand his last words. (4) Insecticide killer Bugsy Bugoff, October 18, 1984. Bugsy was, of course, finally brought in by the SWAT team. (5) Yuppie swindlers Uppward Lee-Mobile and wife Trendy, February 16, 1986.

II was shot, and suddenly were there shriek-ings all over again that TRACY was the world's leading cause of anti-social behavior. In recent years, the strip has enforcedly been relatively tame, the Calvinist severities of its point and purpose largely abandoned.

Crisp narrative drive? From the writerly stand-point, the strip's sheer physical reductions, the limitations on the number of words it is possi-ble to put into dialogue balloons from one day to the next, mean that it takes Collins a week or more to develop action that Chester Gould would have done in a day or two. In his last years, the great Milton Caniff himself could barely sustain a STEVE CANYON story under the constraints of modern syndicate-business realities.

Complicating matters was the strip's physi-cal appearance. Gould assistant Rick Fletcher had put in sixteen faithful years as a wonderful background man, and it was Fletcher who had been largely responsible for the stark, sharp-edged compositions that defined DICK TRACY through the '60s and '70s. But through that entire time, Gould had never once permitted Fletcher to touch Dick Tracy himself, and at last on his own, Fletcher simply couldn't draw the man particularly well. His Tracy was never right, and the increasing inauthenticity of his horsey detective lampoon diminished the strip's persuasiveness. Moreover, the artist

Fletcher's relations with the writer Collins were considerably strained: Fletcher had felt himself to be Gould's natural heir and he resented sharing the byline with the younger interloper. He died at sixty-six in 1983. Since then the modern DICK TRACY has been drawn by the *Chicago Tribune*'s Pulitzer Prize–winning editorial cartoonist Dick Locher, with whom Collins has enjoyed a more agreeable collaboration.

All those factors aside, there is a degree to which Max Allan Collins does bear personal accountability for the strip that DICK TRACY has finally turned into, and it has nothing to do with his intentions or his abilities, only his fire and fury.

"I came from Oklahoma," Chester Gould told interviewer Shel Dorf in September 1978. "Justice was quick and severe when they caught a red-handed culprit." The old man was remembering the Chicago days, when Al Capone ran the town and all the courts were bought and sold, and smarmy little lawyers kept coming in with writs of this and that and nothing would ever stick, nothing, and one night in the spring of 1931 he had angrily sat before a blank Bristol board and started to draw a relentless, unforgiving, square-jawed, crime-stopping in-strument of God's own wrath named Plainclothes Tracy.

"I would read in the paper about a continuance and another continuance," frontiersman Gould remembered for Dorf. "And then the judge finds a flaw in the indictment or something. I used to say to myself, '*They know this fellow's a crook. They know that he did this. They know that he is dangerous. Why don't they take him out and shoot him?*'"

"Dick Tracy and I," another generation's Max Allan Collins explained to one of his own interviewers in 1982, "don't share personal convictions."

That is the single fundamental difference between the two DICK TRACYs.

THROUGH THE SPRING AND SUMMER OF 1990,

the first TRACY film since 1947 drew popular attention, and there was much fanfare once more for a famous property that had many times already known celebration. Many of the classic newspaper-strip adventures were being reprinted. Tribune Media Services Inc., the current corporate title for the old Chicago Tribune Syndicate whose stable of features Captain Jo-

Diet Smith, having already replaced the original 2-Way Wrist Radio with the 2-Way Wrist TV (in 1964), now introduces the new 2-Way Wrist Computer, June 20, 1986.

Christmas 1986. In Memoriam. Dick Moores, a Gould assistant in the 1930s, had been the longtime producer of GASOLINE ALLEY at the time of his death. Young John Locher, assisting his father Dick Locher, had drawn much of the mid-'80s TRACY.

seph Medill Patterson had shaped with his own hands, began to find that the renascent DICK TRACY was actively selling in new markets. Merchandising opportunities were arising, toys were being licensed, Dick Tracy's official biography was being published. The world turned, and the world moved on, and another generation began to know the Great American Detective, and his permanence in the literature became assured, again, and life deals 'em that way once in a while.

CHESTER GOULD DIED AT HIS HOME IN WOOD-

stock, Illinois, on May 11, 1985, of congestive heart failure. He was eighty-four.

Over the many years when there had been the respectful interviewers who came and went,

he had always liked to quote the telegram of August 13, 1931, from Captain Joseph Medill Patterson of the *New York Daily News*, the battered, faded, prized old wire that was forever since framed and hung on his studio wall, the single document that had created an American legend. Toward the end of his life, taken to his bed, he fell into the habit of stopping whatever member of his loving family happened to be near him and proudly reciting it once again.

YOUR PLAINCLOTHES TRACY HAS POSSIBILITIES STOP

At the very last, the family remembers quietly, the old man could never get more than a few words into it before the tears started to well up and he would be crying.

ACKNOWLEDGMENTS

In the larger sense, of course: To the Fort Myers (Fla.) News-Press, the hometown paper in which I discovered DICK TRACY at age eight; and to my mother Catherine, who could always squeeze a dime out of a meager household budget whenever the new TRACY monthly hit the drugstore rack; and to the University of Tennessee librarian who in the summer of 1957 was nice enough to show a bothersome small visitor how to work a microfilm machine and then fetch him reel after reel of old Knoxville Journals for weeks; and to my wife Jo, who has never seemed to mind living amid flaking mountains of old newspaper comic sections, which is kind of baffling.

More specifically: To a community of friends and fellow scholars—Bill Blackbeard, Max Allan Collins, Bill Crouch, Jr., Shel Dorf, Ron Goulart, Maurice Horn, Richard Marschall, Greg Theakston, Dennis Wepman, and others—who have long shared information and resources in the pleasant spirit of collegial enthusiasm and who practically never regard themselves as in competition with one another.

To the library staffs of the New York Daily News and the Chicago Tribune, and to the curators of the Joseph M. Patterson Collection at Lake Forest College in Illinois.

To Jean Gould O'Connell.

To my colleagues at the New York Daily News Magazine, who uncomplainingly took on many of my duties while I ducked out to finish this sucker.

To New American Library's Arnold Dolin, who is a patient man; to my editor Rachel Klayman, who kept the trains running; and to the accommodating Elyce Small Goldstein of Tribune Media Services' licensing office.

And to my agent Ivy Fischer Stone, of Fifi Oscard Associates, New York, without whose sagacity this book would never have been more than the small and arcane fan project I had supposed it was.

INDEX

All entries in italic refer to real people or events.

About the Author

Jay Maeder is a New York City newspaperman who has written often on American newspaper comic strip history and lore for both specialty journals and the mainstream press. Most recently he has contributed material to *The Encyclopedia of American Comics*. He is currently a columnist for *The New York Daily News* and editor of the newspaper's *Daily News Magazine*.